THE
EMERALD
FRAME

THE
EMERALD FRAME

A Michael Garrett Mystery

Richard Blaine

First published by Level Best Books/Historia 2024

This novel is entirely a work of fiction. The names, characters and incidents portrayed in it are the work of the author's imagination. Any resemblance to actual persons, living or dead, events or localities is entirely coincidental.

Richard Blaine asserts the moral right to be identified as the author of this work.

Author Photo Credit: Ilsa Lund

First edition

ISBN: 978-1-68512-745-9

Cover art by Level Best Designs

This book was professionally typeset on Reedsy.
Find out more at reedsy.com

To DJ and of course to Ilsa Lund

Chapter One

It was one of those late-September days, the kind you only get in Los Angeles. A quilt of yellow-gray haze had settled over the city, the still air hanging listless among the buildings. The traffic noise along Wilshire Boulevard seemed muted, and the people in the street eyed each other, looking vaguely uneasy. It was the kind of day that cops hate. The ones on the beat get cramped fingers from writing traffic tickets, and the downtown boys don't get to stop for their usual noontime snort. Things are always happening in this town, but they seem to happen more when the smog settles. More fights start in more bars. More drunks get rolled in more alleys. And every little domestic quarrel seems to end in a shooting. It was the kind of day when some people even think about hiring a detective.

So far, 1948 hadn't been much of a year, but I was ready to tackle what was left of it. I had come into the office early that morning, so I could get a head start on my toe tapping and listen to my bills coming due. Business had been slow since my trip to El Paso, and that was all right with me. My Buick had turned asthmatic, and I'd had to leave it at a garage across the street.

The morning mail had brought a greeting from the phone company. "Dear Mr. Garrett: You are now seriously in arrears on your current service charges. Unless the enclosed bill is paid in full by the end of this month, your service will be discontinued."

I sat there behind the desk, feeling seriously in arrears and wondering what the office might be like without a phone. No more loud noises. No more interruptions to my toe-tapping. No more strained voices torn between hate and confusion. I stared at the arrogant, impersonal instrument on my desk. What service had the thing ever given me? I stared at it, and it rang.

"Michael, this is Fran...Fran Brekhammer. Are you busy?"

"Busy as hell," I said. "I'm hopping around the office with Eleanor Powell and the Rockettes."

A dry impertinence crackled in her voice. "I need to see you. I can be there in fifteen minutes."

"What for?"

"Not on the phone," she said and hung up.

I took a long time cradling the receiver. I lit a Lucky and went over to the window and opened it and blew some more smog into the street. We weren't exactly friends, although I had known Fran for almost five years. It wasn't unusual for her to call me about a case, but as long as I'd known her, she had never come to my office.

Mrs. Fran Brekhammer ran the second-largest bail bond company in Los Angeles. She had inherited the business some eight years earlier when her husband dropped dead. He was a former cop, with no head for business, a yen for the ponies, and unpaid bar tabs all over town. He died halfway through a pint of bourbon. Fran finished the bourbon, took over the business, and never looked back. With her husband's insurance money, she paid off all his debts and then began posting bail on high-risk-high-yield cases, ones the other companies wouldn't touch. She used off-duty cops and private detectives like me to chase after the jumpers. Since she paid top dollar, the runaways always seemed to get brought back...sometimes a little dented, but always able to stand trial. Fran made no apologies, and after a while, they stopped running. By the end of the first year, her business showed a profit. By the end of the third year, she was rich.

I waited at the window until I saw the car pull up across the street. There was no mistaking it, or the driver. I watched her get out and glide across Wilshire toward the Patterson building as easily as mercury falling in a thermometer.

Fran wasn't like other women. She wore tailored suits, drove a luxuriously long Packard Clipper, and smoked cigarillos. In two-inch heels, she stood just a whisker under five feet tall, and holding a brick, she might have weighed a hundred pounds. Her acorn-brown hair, demurely trimmed and arranged in bangs, was laced with snowy white strands, but her thin, reserved features showed no signs of middle-aged loosening. She wore almost no makeup, and her dark, attentive eyes were as clear as an October morning. She could have stepped out of a Victorian novel: Her movements were deliberate, her manner composed, her voice as smooth as maple syrup. And she was one of the toughest women I ever knew.

I stepped away from the window, crushed out the Lucky in an ashtray I keep on the desk, and then strolled through the outer office. I got to the door and opened it just as Fran was coming up the hall. She paused at the door and looked at me with quiet, careworn eyes.

"Thank you for seeing me."

I nodded and motioned her inside.

She went into the office and immediately sat in the client chair. I followed her, closing the inner door behind me, and settled behind the desk. She looked at me for a long moment, then reached inside her suit jacket and brought out a cigarillo. I got an ashtray out of one of the drawers and slid it across the desk in front of her. She struck a match, puffed quickly, then began dabbing at the ashtray. Fran wasn't one to fidget, but the cigarillo was too young to have much ash.

Finally, she leaned back in the chair and looked at me evenly. "Michael, I'm worried."

I didn't say anything.

"You remember Danny Nugent? He's a local private dick who does some skip chasing for me sometimes."

I knew the name. I wished I didn't. "I've run into him once or twice. Last time was on a tail job. He lost the mark in an empty hotel lobby. I don't think he could tail a fat man to lunch."

Her jaw muscles tightened a notch, but she let it go. "Well, I have a case for him, only he hasn't checked in. I don't know where he is."

I shrugged. "Probably resting up on a park bench somewhere, if he's not in the clink."

She shook her head emphatically. "No. He wouldn't do that. He knows I've got something for him. He said he was wrapping up an important case and that he'd call me when it was done. That was two days ago, and I still haven't heard from him. I tried his apartment early this morning. He wasn't there, and the landlady hasn't seen him in almost a week." She put the cigarillo down on the edge of the ashtray and folded her hands together with anxious precision. "I'm afraid he's in trouble."

"And you want me to find him?"

She nodded.

I slowly reached for another Lucky, lit it, and let the smoke drift out over the desk. I watched her watching me with a quiet, unruffled look of concern, eyeing me like an older sister who had been waiting up all night. We looked at each other while the traffic noise from the street slowly rose and intruded on the silence.

"Does this guy owe you money?" I asked her.

She shook her head again. "I just want to know that he's all right."

I took another steep drag and leaned back in my chair. "I don't get it. Danny Nugent's just a penny-ante gumshoe who can't even find his head with his hat. The cops run him in for vagrancy every month just for practice. He even got canned as the house dick in that fleabag over on Seventh Avenue. If you need somebody to chase a bail jumper, there are lots of guys in this town with strong legs and long guns who need the work. Why Nugent?"

She bit her lip and looked away. Her eyes became as cloudy as the smog in the street. "It's personal."

"How personal?

Fran set herself firmly in the chair and turned slowly back toward me, a defiant curl growing on the edges of her mouth.

"I know what you think of Danny," she said tartly. "I know what everyone thinks of him. But you don't know him the way I do. I've known Danny Nugent since high school, and except for Sam, I've never met anyone who was more decent. Sure, Danny's no world-beater. But he's never hurt anyone, and even if he only had two nickels to rub together, he'd give them away to anyone he thought was worse off than he was."

She reached for the cigarillo and methodically poked it in the ashtray enough to cripple it. I watched the memories drifting behind her eyes.

"When Sam died," she went on, "everybody turned out. He was a good-natured lug out for a good time, and everybody liked him. Only they didn't like him enough to help me clean up the mess he left or turn his business around. After the funeral, I got a lot of flowers and sympathy but no help. Sam owed a lot of people money, and they all came around with their hands out. I asked them to wait, to help me out…in Sam's memory. And all I got was the cold shoulder."

She set her jaw and leaned forward in the chair. "I wasn't asking for charity. I told them I just needed time…time to get organized and square accounts. But nobody listened. That is, nobody except Danny. He showed up every day. Helped me at home and in the office. Helped me sort through Sam's things. He even kept the shysters off me until Sam's insurance money came through."

She paused and picked up the dead cigarillo and examined it the way a pathologist looks at a specimen. Then she put it down and folded her hands again.

"Danny Nugent has never meant much to many people, but he was there for me. I was alone, and Danny gave me a helping hand. And he never asked for anything. Not then, not now."

I waited, then took another drag and flicked a long ash off the end of the Lucky. "Are you soft on him?"

Fran didn't move more than an inch, but on her, it seemed as if she had jumped a foot out of the chair. She put her hands on the arms of the chair and squeezed until her knuckles were white, almost up to the wrist. She glared at me, and then her expression gradually eased, and she let the chair breathe again.

"Michael, I'll admit this to you because I know it won't go outside this room. A lot of people wouldn't understand." She made a long sigh. "Years ago, I might have been interested in Danny…except for Sam, except for me, and except for a lot of things that get in the way when you're young. And I've never regretted the life I had with Sam."

She turned and stared toward the window without really looking through it. "Besides, ever since high school, Danny's been stuck on someone else. He damn near fell apart when she went back east and got married. He never was the same afterwards." She sat for a moment, then shrugged and turned back toward me. "So, the way it is now, Danny and I are friends, and I care what happens to him." She folded her hands again and gave me a stare that jabbed me like a pitchfork. "I think he's in trouble, and I want him found."

"Last I heard, the L.A. cops still had a missing persons division," I said.

She snorted and shook her head. "Uh-uh. No cops. You're right about them. They don't think any more of Danny than you do. Maybe even less. If I filed a missing-persons report on him, they'd take the next three election days getting around to it."

I took a last pull at the dying Lucky and put the rest of it out in the ashtray. "All right. Why me?"

Fran tilted her head and looked at me. "Because I trust you, because I can afford you, and because I know you'll take the case."

I shrugged. "What makes you so sure?"

The corners of her mouth began a wry dance up the sides of her face. "I know your story, Michael. I've watched you for a long time, even back when you and Sam were on the force together. They bounced you out for having a smart mouth. They called it insubordination, but you and I know what it really was. You were smart enough to be offered a lot of money and too honest to take it. You could have been lining your pockets at City Hall like so many others, but you wouldn't take a crooked buck. Instead, you became a private detective and settled in here," she made a sweeping gesture around the office, "so you could go on rubbing shoulders with the grifters and deadbeats."

I leaned back in my chair. "You left out that I manage to feed myself and tie my own shoes and stay out of jail most of the time."

She chuckled. "I know you do enough uptown work to stay in business, and you earn enough for someone who lives alone to be a little less than comfortable. But you still take too many cases from people who can't pay." She leaned forward, put her hands on the edge of the desk, and showed

6

me the first real smile I'd seen on her face in five years. "You go for the underdog...the same way I do."

"And now the underdog is Danny Nugent?"

She kept smiling. "I'll pay the regular skip fee."

I took in some air and let it out heavily. I glanced at the phone bill. "All right. When did you last talk to him?"

"Two days ago...Monday. I called his apartment and told him I had a job for him. Nothing big, just a small-time forger who skipped to Reno. Danny said he was working on a big case and that he was going to meet with his client that evening to wrap it up. He said he'd call me when he was finished." The corners of her mouth curled down into a grim smirk. "But he never called."

"Did he say anything about the case or the client?"

She shook her head and stared at me through a pensive frown. "Nothing. In fact, when I asked him about the case, he was evasive. He sounded strange. Not worried exactly, but...sad somehow. Almost wistful."

I reached for another Lucky, but the pack was empty. I crumpled it and tossed it at the wastebasket beyond the corner of the desk. I missed.

"Does Nugent have an office?" I asked.

"I don't think so. He's been saying for months that he was going to rent one, but somehow, he's never gotten around to it."

"Where does he conduct business?"

She snorted again. "Wherever they'll keep his glass full. Lacy's mostly, I think."

I shrugged. "Maybe you should look behind the bar."

She started to say something, but I held up my hand.

"Never mind," I said. "I'll see what I can find out. What's his address?"

"But I already checked..."

I held up my hand again. "Maybe someone in the neighborhood has seen him."

Fran reached inside her jacket and took out a small white business card and a mechanical pencil. She wrote something on the back of the card and then handed it to me. "He lives in a walkup at the corner of Eighteenth and

Descanso. Not much of a place." She motioned toward the card. "I wrote my home number on the bottom. Call me as soon as you have something."

I stood up, took the card, and tapped it against my thumbnail. "You know, Fran, there's always the chance that Nugent doesn't want to be found. Maybe he just got tired of dragging tail around town. Maybe he decided to try something on the sly, where the easy money is. He wouldn't be the first dick to go sour."

Fran looked at me as if I'd just moved my mouth without saying anything. She stood up and gave me the same businesslike smile she used on judges and prosecutors.

"Thank you for your help, Michael. I'm sure Danny will be grateful, too."

"Uh-huh." I shoved my hands in my pockets. "The same way I'm growing four thumbs."

She turned and started out of the office. Just as she stepped through the first doorway, she turned and looked back. She was wearing that big sister look again.

"Do you know what it's like, Michael...being alone?"

I shrugged. "How would I? I've got a dozen bartenders all depending on me."

She shook her head and smiled faintly. "So does Danny."

Chapter Two

I got a fresh pack of Luckies and a handful of business cards out of the desk and dropped them into my pocket. Then I went downstairs and across the street to Lester Mack's garage to see about the Buick.

Lester Mack was a retired Army sergeant who earned his stripes in the motor pool, patching up jeeps and dressing down non-coms. He was a thickset man, almost hairless, with a belly that even overalls couldn't hide and a florid face bloated from too many years of living on gas fumes and cheap whiskey. He had pale, dissipated eyes that jutted past loose, puffy lids, and he had the warming, good humor of a skin rash. His voice was still in top form. On a clear day, you could hear his cursing as far away as Encino.

As I entered the garage, Mack was pulling his head out of the Buick's innards. He lowered the hood, looked over, and saw me. "Goddamn piece o' junk is what ya got here," he hollered.

He pulled an oily rag out of his back pocket and washed it over his face, leaving a dark smear that went halfway up his bare skull. Then he blew his nose in the rag, stuffed it back in his pocket, and sauntered over in front of me. He wasn't quite my height, but his stuffed overalls and his shiny bald head made him seem taller.

"Why the Christ don't ya get somethin' good?" he rasped. "A Chrysler maybe, or one o' them new DeSotos."

I shrugged. "I might be mistaken for someone with money and taste."

He wheezed out something like a snicker, then pulled out the rag and assaulted his nose again. As he rubbed the thing around his face, he eyed me from behind it with a sudden air of cunning.

9

"I got the carburetor unclogged," he said, "but…it needs a brake job."

I shook my head.

"Listen," he went on, "I oughta know. I been at this stuff a long time. Goddamn cars are no different than jeeps."

"There's a difference with this one," I said. "Uncle Sam isn't paying for it."

"Look," he bellowed. "I'm tellin' ya, the damn brakes are no good. The parking brake's so worn if it gets even a little wet, the lousy car'd roll out of a manhole."

I shrugged again. "I'll remember that the next time I park in one."

He sucked in some air and thrust his chin out at me. "Smart stuff, huh? Maybe I oughta take ya down a peg."

I stepped as close to him as I could and poked a finger into his intervening belly. "Listen. It's not a day to be getting all heated up and bruised. You don't have the wind to last two minutes, and you might miss your morning belt. Now, behave yourself and tell me how much."

He shook his head, gave his mouth a rueful twist, and grumbled. "Some guys got no appreciation for a fella tryin' to make a living."

"How much?"

"Ten bucks."

I thought about telling him to get it from the phone company. Instead, I paid him, got into the Buick, and let him watch his easy-money brake job slowly back out of the garage. I could hear him yelling at me as I headed out onto Wilshire and turned east.

"No Goddamn class, that's what you got," he hollered.

I heard the yelling all the way to the first intersection until I put on the brakes. The car stopped, and so did the yelling.

I sat there and watched the traffic light and thought about Fran and Danny Nugent. I tried to picture the two of them together, but I couldn't make it fit. She was a woman of quiet determination who could go face to face with a leg breaker or the D.A. and not even blink, and he was a luckless character who went through life as aimlessly as a pinball. They had about as much in common as a preacher and a showgirl. But if Fran thought he was in trouble, then it was a good bet that he was. Danny Nugent could get in trouble just getting out of bed in the morning.

Still, it all sounded routine to me. Nugent would show up in some flophouse, broke and trying to figure out what he'd done on his two-day binge. Fran would look at him sternly, shake her head, and be quietly relieved. And good-hearted Garrett, friend to the downtrodden, would get his thirty bucks a day.

When the light changed, I kept going down Wilshire. It was almost noon, so I swung north on Alvarado, went past Beverly Boulevard, and stopped across the street from Lacy's. The lunchtime crowd was starting to fill the place, but I managed to find a table in the corner out of the way. I had a chicken sandwich and coffee and watched the over-dressed businessmen preening and gloating and lying to each other.

When I finished, I asked around about Nugent. No one had seen him in over a week, but the bartender a stringy young guy with Gable ears suggested I come back later and talk to the night crew. He said that Nugent never came around until after dark. Lacy's in the evening sounded like a good idea to me. I gave him a buck and thanked him for his trouble.

Outside, the sun was working its way through the smog, leaving scattered remnants of haze around the tops of the taller buildings. I got back into the Buick and drove down to Wilshire again, and headed east as far as Central Avenue. Then I went south to Eighteenth Street and turned east once more. I drove for a couple of miles past clusters of stores and markets and shabby office buildings until I reached Descanso.

The apartment building was four stories of faded brick and washed-out mortar, with windows that hadn't been cleaned or maybe even opened since V-J Day. A sign over the door said, "Hobart Arms." The building sat on the southeast corner, looking directly out into one of those mixed neighborhoods that were still trying to hold onto their memories. After the war, a lot of people and businesses had moved uptown out of neighborhoods like this, taking a lot of money with them. The ones who stayed fought against the creeping decay of the lower city. They fought hard and lost slowly.

I swung around and parked on the north side of the street in front of a small, prim-looking delicatessen. A wizened white-haired old man in an apron was sweeping the steps in front of it. He moved the broom back and forth with careful strokes and seemed to be mumbling to himself. As I got out of the car, he stopped and offered me a toothless grin. I described Nugent and asked if the old man had seen him.

He scratched his chin for a minute and studied the air about a foot above my head. He folded both hands over the end of the broom, propping it upright in front of him. He rested his chin on his hands. Then he looked at me. "Nope."

I motioned over my shoulder. "How about over in the apartment building? Think anyone there would know him?"

A sudden mirth showed in his tired eyes. "Can't say." He smacked his rubbery chops together, making an empty slurping sound. "But if I was you, I'd be askin' Beatrice."

"Who's Beatrice?"

The old man stared at me for the better part of a minute without moving… staring as if he'd just died and hadn't bothered to tell me. I was about to ask him again when he burst into a cackle.

"Who's Beatrice?" he howled. "That's a hot one."

He stood and laughed for a minute. Then, without waiting, he turned and started up the steps to the door of the delicatessen. He shook his head and chortled to himself as he climbed.

"Who's Beatrice, he says. Yessir. That's a hot one." He opened the door and disappeared.

I stood in the street looking after him and laughing to myself without knowing why. Sometimes, laughing is better when there's no reason for it. I was still laughing as I crossed the street and went through the front door of the Hobart Arms.

The doorway led to a narrow corridor that still had a little paint and the remains of a badly pummeled maroon carpet running toward the back and up a flight of stairs. Just inside the door was a row of numbered mailboxes with no names. I glanced at the first few doors. No names on them either. A home for the anonymous. It seemed like a good place for Danny Nugent.

I walked down the corridor toward the back of the building. As I passed the stairs, I heard music blaring from a phonograph. Someone wanted the world to hear Harry James. I followed the music all the way to the back of the building to a door at the end of the corridor. There was a sign on the door. It said "Manager." I knocked.

A woman opened the door and peered at me over four inches of chain lock. The music flooded into the hall from behind her, followed by the pungent mingling of gin and anisette. I couldn't see much of her, but what I could see I didn't like. A bare leg, heavy and pale, with too much vein showing, ran up out of a fuzzy blue slipper and hid under the hem of a pale green bathrobe. The robe was gathered and creased as if she were clutching it to her in desperate defense of her virtue. Just above the chain, a single bloodshot eye, almost glued together with mascara, squinted out from between several weedy tendrils of hair that was about the color and texture of shredded carrot.

"Whatcha want?" she blurted.

"Where can I find Mr. Nugent?"

"Who's askin'?"

I took out one of my business cards and poked it through the opening over the chain. She took it and made a long sniffling noise. There was a rustling of the bathrobe as she stepped away from the door. I could see her put on a pair of over-large horn-rimmed glasses. She held the card up in front of her and read it silently, mouthing the words with wide scarlet lips. Then she read it out loud.

"Michael Garrett, Private Investigator." She took off the glasses and put an angry eye back to the door. "Private dick, huh? Whatcha want with Danny?"

"It's a private matter."

She snorted. "Yeah, I'll bet. Another creep out ta roust him for a coupla bucks. Why don't you guys just leave him alone? Danny's a square guy. You got no business pushin' him around. Just beat it."

She slammed the door in my face. I heard her slippers shuffling across the floor. I heard the phonograph turned up louder. I knocked again.

More shuffling. She yanked the door open.

"I said beat it," she hissed over the blaring music. "Get the hell outta here before I call the cops."

It's always a pleasure dealing with the public in my trade. You meet such charming people. I took off my hat, gave her a warm, friendly smile, and put honey in my voice.

"I think you have the wrong idea," I said. "I just want to see if he's the right Mr. Nugent."

"Whatcha mean?"

I shuffled my feet, looked down, and put on an even sillier grin. If you could be six-one and middle-aged and look like an embarrassed school kid, I was doing it.

"Well," I drawled. "I'm not supposed to give out the details, but under the circumstances…You see, it has to do with an elderly gent in Des Moines named Horace Nugent who passed away recently. The old boy had a policy with Century Mutual Insurance naming a Daniel Nugent of Los Angeles as sole beneficiary. If the Mr. Nugent who lives in this building is the right party, the insurance people would like to contact him."

She hesitated. "I don't know…"

"There could be some money in it."

The lone eye in the door squinted on the outskirts of what must have been a hungry smile. She brought the door to, unhooked the chain, and opened the door wide. She stepped back and made an elaborate sweeping motion, inviting me inside.

"Well, now you're talkin', honey," she said. "C'mon in."

I walked in and stood in the middle of a living room that would have made a junk dealer's mouth water. It was small and crowded with cheaply ornate furnishings, all resting under an undisturbed blanket of dust. Around the room were piles of movie magazines and several half-empty bottles. The walls were lined with pictures of movie stars torn from the magazines—a sort of gallery of loneliness, the kind you often find in places like this. I felt like going off and having a good cry.

The woman backed into the center of the room and eyed me up and down like a lumberjack sizing up a tall, ripe pine. She had a broad, discontented

14

face, with several layers of rouge and face makeup having no success covering the dark circles under her eyes. She had what might have been a good figure once, but the hourglass now had enough sand in it for a week. And there was no point in guessing her age. She'd been past her prime for longer than her prime would have taken.

The phonograph in the corner was just saying goodbye to Harry James, the needle running down and scratching on the record label. The woman went over and shut it off, then swished her bathrobe over to a low rose-print sofa. She stood behind a coffee table that held a copy of *True Confessions*, a gin bottle, an ashtray with a carton's worth of butts, and a glass full of something with a dangerous smell.

She held the glass up and took a long swig, then looked at me. "Want some?"

Before I could say no, she grabbed a smudged glass off the floor and filled it half full out of the gin bottle. She pushed the glass toward me. I took it and brought it up slowly under my nose. Embalming fluid smelled better.

"Gin and anisette," she bragged. "My own invention. Drink up."

I put the glass down on the coffee table apologetically. "Actually, I'm not supposed to drink on the job, Mrs...?"

"Almore," she said. "Beatrice Almore. And it isn't Mrs., dearie. It's *Miss*."

"Imagine that." I thought about the old man across the street. This time I didn't feel like laughing. "Well, Miss Almore..."

"Call me Bee," she said. "They all call me that on account of I'm always buzzin' around here like one."

"With lots of men buzzing after you, I'll bet."

She tittered, took another drink, and measured me over the rim of her glass. "You know, you ain't so bad lookin' for a dick. Got a pretty good build."

I shrugged. "It gets me around."

"I'll bet it does, honey." She bent over slowly, making sure I'd notice she was wearing nothing under the robe and lowered herself onto the sofa. She crossed her legs and patted a dusty cushion next to her. "C'mon. Take a load off."

I went around and sat on the end of the sofa, just out of reach, and balanced my hat on my knee. "Can you tell me how to find Mr. Nugent?"

She flapped her gooey eyelashes and tried to look coy. "What did you say the name of that insurance company was?"

"Century Mutual."

"And how much're they shellin' out?"

"They didn't tell me."

She grinned. "But they wouldn't hire no detective for some pint-sized policy." Her smile turned cagey, and she looked away. "Course, I don't suppose there'd be a finder's fee."

"Only if I find Nugent." I pulled a buck out of my pocket and put it on the table under the gin bottle. "But I guess an advance wouldn't hurt."

She licked her lips,poured some more from the bottle, and put the bill in the pocket of her robe. "He lives upstairs in 405. Ain't seen him in a week, though." She yawned, draped an arm over the back of the sofa, and leered at me. "He sure must be comin' into somethin' big, with all the people been askin' for him."

"What people?"

She shrugged. "Some woman came around just this morning. Well-dressed little broad drivin' a big Packard. Then there was that guy last week."

"A cop?" I asked.

She shook her head. "Uh-uh. Said he was a lawyer. Didn't gimme no name."

"Uh-huh. How about letting me have a look at Nugent's room? Maybe I can get a line on him."

She drank some more of her drink and spoke into the glass without looking at me. "That's against the rules."

I put another buck down on the table. "Century Mutual doesn't have to know everything."

She scooped up the second bill in a greedy hand and stood up. "Lemme get my passkey."

We went up to 405, and Beatrice Almore stood in the doorway while I looked around. The room was small and neat, nothing like what I'd seen downstairs. It contained a maple-colored chest of drawers with a small mirror on the wall above it, a couple of wooden chairs, and a metal frame bed without a headboard. The bed was neatly made up, with all the wrinkles carefully smoothed out. A washbasin sat on a stand in the corner, with several towels folded and stacked next to it. In the closet, I found a couple of suits, some shirts, a pair of shoes, and a suitcase. It seemed pretty plain that Nugent hadn't moved out.

I went over and looked through the chest of drawers. I found the usual underwear, socks, and handkerchiefs. And tucked in the back of the top drawer, I found a high school yearbook, a photograph, and a rent receipt. The photograph was old and faded. It showed a blonde girl in a cheerleader's uniform, and it said "To Danny from Jeanie, 1927" across the bottom. The rent receipt was new and not faded. It was dated the first, and it showed one month's rent paid for suite 316 in the Hurley Building at 1723 Paloma Place. I closed up the drawer and went out in the hall.

Beatrice Almore locked up the door and then leaned against it. "Any luck?"

"Not much. I guess I'll have to come back later."

She leaned forward, took hold of my lapels, and exhaled in my face. "Good idea," she said sloppily. "Only why not come back when you ain't workin'? Maybe we can have some fun."

I excused myself, put my hat on, and legged it down the stairs and out the door before she could exhale again. I walked across the street and sat in the Buick, and thought about punching the old man in the nose.

* * *

You could spend your whole life in L.A. and never see Paloma Place. It was dark and dusty and narrow, and it worked its way through part of the Lower East Side the way a pickpocket slips through a crowd without being noticed. Number 1723 was in the middle of the block, a warehouse on one side and a pawnshop on the other. It was a weary brick and stucco building with a torn awning over the front and doleful-looking windows that faced the street. I pulled up in front behind a brown Nash sedan that was parked beside a fire hydrant. In this part of town, people just didn't care.

I went up a handful of cement steps and into the dimly lit lobby of the Hurley Building. It was like a boneyard for dying businesses. The tile floor was stained with several shades of brown from spills that had never been wiped up. In one corner, a majolica urn full of sand almost overflowed with cigarette butts and cigar stubs, little piles of ash covering the floor around it. On the near wall, a building directory, mounted behind a broken pane of glass, listed half a dozen tenants. These included a couple of shyster lawyers, a wholesaler, a painless dentist, a barber college, and a palm reader. Penciled in under the list was "D. Nugent, Investigations, 316."

Next to the directory was an open-grille elevator with the gate pulled back and a man asleep on a wooden stool. He was a shriveled gray-looking man in rumpled khakis and a brown work shirt. He had papery skin with veins standing out at the temples, and he hadn't gotten along with a razor in at least a week. As I stepped into the elevator, he stirred and looked at me. He had the same tired look as the front of the building. I asked for the third floor. He shut the gate and turned the crank.

The elevator squealed up two stories and stopped. I stepped out into the rancid, musty smell of closed-in air and listened to the elevator whine back down to the lobby while I looked up the dark hall. There were half a dozen doors with transoms over them and just one light, a single overhead bulb at the far end. I walked slowly past the first three doors, listening and looking at the numbers. I heard nothing. The transoms were closed. The offices dark. But the transom over the fourth door was open, and the number on the door was 316. I tried it. It was locked.

I looked quickly up and down the hall, then took my investigator's I.D. out of my wallet. I used the plastic casing to slip the lock, eased the door open, and stepped inside. A squadron of black flies buzzed around in the semi-darkness. They circled me with the impatient air of someone whose meal was just interrupted. I stood there for a minute, letting my eyes adjust to the dark. Then it came to me. Another, too familiar smell.

The office was a single room lit only by the afternoon sun coming through the cracks and tears in a window shade in the back. There wasn't much light, but there was enough to see a filing cabinet, two straight wooden chairs, and a desk. And there was enough light to see a man in his shirtsleeves behind the desk. He was slumped over in that spilled-milk position that always says the same thing.

I walked over to the desk and had a good look just to be sure. I needn't have bothered. Danny Nugent wasn't in trouble. He was past trouble. He was dead.

Chapter Three

He was pitched forward, his arms and face flat on the desk. His head was turned to the side, and his sandy hair was matted, as if it had been soaked in sweat and then slowly dried. The position of his cheek and jaw against the hard surface had twisted his mottled features into a kind of leer, his vacant eyes seemingly trained on a small caliber revolver in his right hand. I leaned forward and lifted his head. The eyes kept staring, but they didn't see me.

Something dark and sticky was spread over the top of the desk. It was what the flies had been after, and it had come from a small, neat hole in the front of Nugent's shirt, a hole surrounded by an ugly brown stain that covered most of his chest. I stepped around behind the desk and put a hand on the back of his neck. It felt as cold and limp as uncooked fish. I guessed that he'd been dead for more than a day.

I lifted the hand with the gun enough to get a whiff of the barrel, then popped the cylinder. It was a snub-nosed Colt .38. One bullet had been fired, but not recently. I placed the hand back down on the desk next to a telephone and an ashtray full of cigarette butts, and a crumpled pack of Camels. There was nothing else on the desk but a pen and a bell-shade lamp. I tried the lamp, but it didn't work.

I lifted the shade on the back window to let in some light. It helped, but not enough, so I went back to the front of the office and snapped on the overhead lamp. From there, I could see several dark spots on the carpet in front of the desk and a set of keys lying on the floor almost between my feet. I picked up the keys and tried several in the door. The third one worked.

I shut the door again, walked back to the desk, and inspected the spots on the carpet. They were dark brown, and they were part of a trail that went from the front of the desk over to the filing cabinet and then around behind the desk again. I opened the first drawer of the cabinet and found a small leather holster, empty, about the right size to hold a small revolver. The rest of the drawers were empty.

Next to the filing cabinet was a small potted fern, with more brown spots on the leaves attracting the flies and holes in the soil where someone had poked a finger to see if it needed water. It was sitting beside a spindly-looking coat rack, holding a hat and a suit jacket. I looked through the pockets. They were empty, too. I went back and checked Nugent's shirt and trousers. All I found were a wallet holding twelve dollars and an expired driver's license.

I turned and dropped the keys on the desk next to a lonely-looking telephone and noticed something brown and flaky on my fingers. I rubbed it around in my hand, then sniffed it carefully. A soft whistling noise ran out through my teeth, and I shook my head. Even days old, the stuff still had the tart smell of blood.

The desk seemed like the next place to look, so I used my fountain pen and went through the drawers. In the middle one, I found a detective license and an appointment book. I thumbed carefully through the book and found mostly pages with brown smudges and nondescript entries showing how little Nugent had worked. They went as far as Monday, September 19. The last entry was for eight p.m. It showed the name "Sterling Clavin" in bold letters. After that, nothing.

I returned the book and noticed an envelope with Fran Brekhammer's name written on the front and another brown smudge on the lower right corner. I put the envelope in my pocket and shut the drawer. In the deep drawer on the right, I found a half-empty bottle of Old Forester. I tried it out. At least Nugent knew how to equip the office.

I went over to the window and lit a Lucky, and used the street for an ashtray. I sat there on the windowsill for a long time while I ate up the Lucky and thought about things. I tried to imagine what I might say to Fran.

Nothing came to mind.

You probably couldn't find a dozen people in this town with a kind word for Danny Nugent and not one of them at the police station. To them, he was just something to sweep off the front steps. But he'd finally rented an office, one with a couple of chairs, a filing cabinet, and a desk. It also had a bottle of Old Forester and a lot of blood. He'd rented the office for a month. Now somebody owed him a refund.

I picked up the phone and dialed LAPD.

* * *

Detective Ed Rawls stood in the doorway of Nugent's office, watching the boys from downtown poke and measure and dust and take pictures. He stood with his hands thrust into the pockets of his squad-room tweed suit, and his hat pushed back on his head. He was one of the better men in the department that year, and there was enough of him to stand up to most of the punks that cops run into, both on and off the force.

To look at him, you wouldn't guess that Rawls had been a cop for almost nineteen years. His soft features had the unmoving expression of a druggist or of someone selling women's shoes. He was almost my height and a few pounds heavier, most of that starting to show around his middle. His light brown hair had gone white at the temples, and the crow's feet had gotten a little deeper. But the line of his jaw was still firm under his smooth, rounded face, and the corners of his mouth hadn't quite started to droop. It was in the eyes where you could just begin to see that beaten-down look that cops get after years of being lied to, shot at, and underpaid. Still, Rawls wore his age better than most. He had his own hair and his own teeth and something between his ears that wasn't just gruel.

After a few minutes of looking vaguely put upon, Rawls ambled slowly around the room, finally stopping at the desk. He nudged the ashtray, then picked up the keys and studied them for almost another minute. Finally, he dropped them back on the desk and spoke quietly to a young waspish man with close-cropped black hair, thick glasses, and a dark suit.

The man was just placing Nugent's pistol in a paper bag. He stopped and glanced at me, then nodded and picked up another bag. He gingerly lifted Nugent's appointment book and held it open while Rawls carefully flipped the pages. When Rawls was finished, the man put the book back in the bag, then leaned forward and mumbled something I wasn't meant to hear.

Rawls turned without responding and walked over next to me. He stood looking away from me toward the desk, as if I were a piece of furniture. Then he reached into his coat, took out a cigar, and stuck it in his mouth without lighting it. A long, slow sigh slipped out around the cigar.

"All right," he grumbled. "Tell it."

"There isn't much to tell," I said. "Nugent turned up missing, and I agreed to look for him. I traced him here from his apartment and found just what you see. I figure he's been like that for maybe a couple of days."

"How long you been here?"

I shrugged and looked at my watch. "A little over an hour."

Rawls snorted. He chewed on the cigar, folded his arms, and still didn't look at me. "And you found everything just like this, huh?"

"Almost." I pointed toward the desk. "Those keys were over here on the floor under the transom. One of them fits the door."

He made an elaborate bowing motion and spread his arms. "Oh, just like that. One of them fits the door. My God, I'm glad you said so. We mighta been weeks workin' that one out. While you were at it, did you straighten the furniture too?"

I pulled out a Lucky and lit it and didn't say anything.

The young man with the paper bags came over and waved them nonchalantly in front of Rawls. "I'll need a closer look at these. The gun's a .38, one slug fired. From the look, I'd say the dead guy did the shooting. I'll know that later, too. Maybe the dusting'll give us something." He glanced furtively at me again. "Maybe not."

For the first time, Rawls turned and looked at me. "I suppose we're gonna find your prints all over the joint."

I shrugged again. "Some. After all, I didn't come up here expecting to find a stiff."

Rawls turned back to the young man. "Lemme know what you find out. Make sure you gimmie everything, and make sure you get it to me quick."

The man wrinkled his eyebrows behind his glasses and looked puzzled. "What's the rush? Could be the guy just comes in here, shuts the door, and croaks himself."

Rawls chomped down hard on the cigar. "Yeah. And Eleanor Roosevelt is my sister."

Before the man could answer, Rawls took the cigar and poked it at the man's chest. "Look, Brice. First off, the guy was wiffed. Not one suicide in a hundred shoots himself in the chest. And nobody would do that and then get up and walk around the office just so he could bleed on everything before he died. Second, the guy wasn't exactly a nobody. The sign in the lobby says he was a dick. Not a good one maybe, and not in a good place. But a guy in that business makes enemies." He gave the cigar an extra prod. "Now you take the stuff in those bags and go over it with the lab boys like you were looking for gold. I want all you can get on it in the morning, and I don't want one damn thing left out."

Brice swallowed hard and nodded. Then he spun on his heel, headed for the door, and disappeared faster than a downtown parking space.

Rawls grunted after him. "Ya see what I get for help these days? Kids. Right away, they gotta act like big shots. Don't wanna work on anything if it isn't headlines. They get assigned to me, and I gotta wipe their noses for 'em."

I smiled at him. "You're just the fatherly type."

"Listen," he said sourly. "Like, I don't have enough to do tryin' to fit a collar on Joey Paris for the D.A? Now you gotta call and gimmie this?"

Rawls motioned toward the desk where two uniformed morgue attendants were methodically putting Nugent's body on a stretcher. "Right now, I'm fed up to the tonsils. So lay off crackin' wise."

I took an easy drag on the Lucky and looked at him offhandedly. "Are you that close to Paris?"

He snorted. "Are you kiddin'? Ever since he muscled in on Lefty Stark, Paris has had a string on every bookmaker from here to Tijuana. He couldn't operate that way without havin' some kinda clout with the downtown boys. I could be chasin' after him from here to the other side of my pension."

"You must have something, or else the D.A. wouldn't be involved," I said.

He nodded slowly. "One of the D.A.'s investigators put the arm on a couple of local bookies. Thinks maybe he can get 'em to turn state's evidence. Then maybe we get the goods on Paris for organized gambling and bribing public officials. You can guess what kind of cheers that brings from downtown."

He rolled the cigar around in his mouth, grunted, and went on. "Right now, the D.A.'s issuing a subpoena for Paris's records. He thinks he'll get some kinda proof. Only, I figure he has about as much chance of that as he has of finding feathers on a frog. Paris is no dummy. He's got his bookkeepers fudging every bit of paper he touches, and he's got some expensive mouthpiece runnin' interference with the D.A. And this guy's got most of the city's legal staff tied up in court on show-cause orders, while Paris moves his parlors around town faster than a one-man medicine show so the D.A. can't pin him down."

Rawls took the cigar out of his mouth and looked at it intently, as if he were talking to it instead of me. "Anyhow, the D.A. figures if he can turn the key on Paris, he'll be up for the job of State's Attorney. From there, he can run for governor." He stuck the cigar back in his face and gave a final grunt. "What the hell? It's all politics."

Something he had said rang a vague bell. "Who's the mouthpiece?"

"Some big shot from out in Bel Air. Never see him anywhere but in court defending crooks and politicians." He snorted disdainfully. "Like there's a difference."

I took another puff, walked over to the window, and threw the rest of the Lucky into the street. The attendants hoisted the stretcher and moved slowly into the hall, heading toward the elevator. Rawls and I were alone in the office.

"I can see how the D.A. would be keeping you busy," I said. I gave him a casual look. I wanted him to think the next question meant as much to me as the way he filed his nails. "Why so much interest in Nugent?"

A dark squall blew across his face. "What is this, Twenty Questions?" he snarled. "Look, buster. Don't try to con me. I don't like it when you hold back any better than I do when that weasel Brice does. You haven't come clean on this thing yet, so keep your goddamn questions to yourself."

I grinned at him. "You're not as slow as you look, Eddie."

He chewed on the cigar enough to turn it to pulp. "Yeah? Well, you weren't in any hurry—playin' with the keys and pokin' around in here for almost an hour before you called Homicide. You can dope this thing out as well as I can. And all bets are off when there's a killing. So, what's the stall?" His eyes narrowed. "Just who the hell thought enough about Nugent to notice he was missing?"

I took in a breath, let it out, and looked at him. "All right. It doesn't really matter now, and I guess I owe you that much. It's Fran."

He almost jumped at me. "Don't gimmie that. I said I wanna know who..."

I put my hand up and stopped him. "It's Fran, Eddie. She was interested in him."

His face went blank. He took the cigar out of his mouth and went over to the window. He leaned against the frame and spoke quietly in the direction of the street.

"I might've guessed," he grumbled. "For years now, she's been lookin' after that creep just like he was a stray pup. We'd run him in for some kinda screw-up, and she'd come around and bail him out. I was afraid she might be getting a little soft on the guy." He shook his head. "She probably figures nobody noticed."

"That's just what she figures," I said.

He turned and looked at me. "So why the mystery? Why would you need to protect her?"

Maybe it was just instinct, but something made me hesitate. Something he still hadn't told me. "I couldn't be sure of that. After all, she was one of the last people to see Nugent alive."

"Nuts," he said. "Not even Brice would try to lay this one on Fran Brekhammer."

Rawls walked around to the front of the desk and went on as if he were talking to a jury.

"Look at all this blood," he observed. "I figure Nugent gets caught in here with some joker who decides not to pay his fee. Maybe some guy who finds his wife's been steppin' out. He's upset. He decides to take it out on the dick who gave him the bad news. They argue. Nugent gets scared. He goes for his gun in the filing cabinet; the two of them wrestle for it, and the gun goes off. Nugent gets plugged, but he doesn't die right away—not until the guy's thrown him around enough to bleed on his potted plant. When Nugent finally croaks, the guy comes to and realizes what he's done. He's kinda rattled, but he figures maybe he can make it look like suicide. So, he props Nugent up in the chair and sticks the gun in his mitt. Then he straightens the furniture, takes the keys, goes out and locks the door, and tosses the keys back through the transom. A day or so later, you show up, find the door locked, the keys inside, and Nugent holding the gun."

I folded my arms. "Impressive, Eddie."

He held the cigar out and looked at it, this time with a hint of satisfaction. "I figure it had to be an amateur 'cause it's such a lousy setup. And it had to be a big guy, some kinda palooka. Nobody else coulda thrown Nugent around that way and then put him in the chair. No frail could do that, not once he was dead." He smiled grimly. "We may never get the guy, but Fran's off the hook."

"Thanks, Eddie," I said. "I'll tell her."

"Yeah." He shoved his hands in his pockets and looked down at his shoes. "Listen, Garrett. Sam Brekhammer and I were pals. Tell Fran…Tell her…" He looked up and then frowned and waved a hand at me. "Aw nuts. Just get the hell outta here."

I didn't move. The bell was still ringing in the back of my mind.

Rawls took out a small notebook and pencil, then went over next to the desk and began scribbling. It took him almost a minute to realize I hadn't left. He looked around, saw me, and glared. "You forget something?"

"Who's the mouthpiece?"

He slowly put the cigar back into his coat pocket. His eyes were slits. "As if you didn't know."

I shrugged. "I don't get around that much."

"The hell you don't," he growled. "You know the name as well as I do." He jerked his thumb toward the desk. "It's in the goddamn appointment book."

Chapter Four

A glaze of late-afternoon sun was spread over the street in front of the Hurley Building. Detective Brice was trying to interrogate the sleepy geezer who ran the elevator, and the attendants were just closing up the wagon after putting Nugent's body inside. After they shut the doors, they stopped for a smoke and a laugh as they needled each other about a couple of babes they'd met in a beer parlor the night before. There was no rush for them. Their next move would be to take Nugent to a cold locker downtown, a stopover on his way to oblivion. But there was no hurry. They had lots of time. So did Nugent.

It wouldn't have taken a Quiz Kid to figure out that Rawls had something crawling around under his collar. His theory about the killing was plausible enough, but so had been the idea that Hitler would never invade Poland. And there was no telling about an ambitious D.A. Cop's widow or not; even Fran Brekhammer could be put on the grill if it meant somebody's picture in the late edition.

I got into the Buick and drove west toward the sun. A warm wind was stirring now, mingling the dust from the street with the dry, corrosive air. It hurt my eyes, so I rolled up the window. This made the inside of the car feel like a slow oven. I took off my hat, loosened my tie, and tried to see if my brain was at home.

The name in Nugent's appointment book did mean something. Sterling Clavin was an uptown attorney who had made a name and a fortune defending some of the best-known racketeers on the coast. I had never actually seen him, but I had read enough about him: a Harvard-educated lawyer who was covered as much in the society pages as on the crime beat. Not all of it was good: he had a temper and a flair for beating up reporters. At a party in Beverly Hills last year, Clavin had punched a photographer and thrown his camera into a swimming pool. He never touched a case for under five figures, and when he wasn't in court defending some back-alley leg breaker, he was clinking glasses at poolside with the ritzy set in Hollywood.

The last I had heard of Clavin was over a year ago. He had been defending Lefty Stark, a two-time loser that the D.A. had dead to rights on a white slavery rap. The trial had been a circus, and somehow, Clavin had gotten him off. The papers gave it more ink than they gave MacArthur when he waded ashore in the Philippines, calling Clavin "the darling of the underworld."

Now Clavin was representing Joey "The Stick" Paris, another tough bird from back east. Paris had only been in town a couple of years, but in that time, he'd managed to muscle in and take over almost every horse parlor and numbers room south of Oxnard. This had brought him toe to toe with Lefty Stark. The papers had even speculated that it was Paris who tipped off the D.A. and helped set up Stark. One way or another, most of the L.A. cops were interested in what Paris was doing. That meant they also had plenty of reasons to be interested in Sterling Clavin. And not one of those reasons had anything to do with Danny Nugent.

I let the Buick cruise for a handful of blocks and then stopped in front of a flossy-looking drug store with a window display showing a family of beavers and a few hundred cans of tooth powder. I pulled out the smudged envelope I'd found in Nugent's desk drawer and studied Fran's name on the front of it. I tried to think of what Nugent might've had to say to her or to anyone else that he couldn't say over the phone. I rolled down the window, held the envelope up to the light, and looked at it for several minutes. A really clever detective would take it home, steam it open, and read it. Instead, I stuffed it back in my pocket and went into the drugstore.

I walked to the back and found a phone booth with a city book on a chain. As big as the L.A. directory is, it listed only one Sterling Clavin. But it was one worth noticing. The book listed an office number at an address on Laurel Avenue in West Hollywood and a residence at 1302 Dreams Landing in Bel Air. I dropped in a nickel and dialed the office.

A prim young voice told me that Clavin had left for the day and wouldn't be back until late the next morning. She asked if there was any way she could help. I told her I was alone and looking for company on the road to happiness and had nothing to do for the evening but go home and nurse a dying bottle of Scotch. She suggested I do it with the radio on. I hung up.

I tried Clavin's home number and got no answer, so I went back outside. The sun had turned a deep orange and was well along its descent toward the western hills, and the sound of something poured over ice at Lacy's was playing in my ears. But I knew that Rawls would be moving. He was a solid cop, not flashy, not brilliant, just relentless. I started the Buick again and kept going west.

With the late afternoon traffic, it took me almost an hour to drive the twenty miles out to Bel Air. I went all the way out Wilshire and then up Beverly Glen Boulevard through town and into the hills. It was like crossing into another time zone or another country or another planet just what southern California means to someone who has never been west of Pittsburgh.

This is where the beautiful people live with their convertibles and their sunglasses and their French poodles and their attitudes. This is where fortunes are made and spent and where a movie star lives on every block. And this is where the southern end of the Sierra Nevadas meets the Pacific. There's nothing quite like driving through the hills and canyons west of Los Angeles. The road bends like ribbon candy through a tide of wooded ridges and turns and sheer drop-offs rolling inevitably toward the ocean. And it takes you through about sixty square miles of the most expensive real estate in the world.

Dreams Landing ran off the main drag into one of the canyons just north of town. The narrow road snaked up the side of the canyon past dozens of homes of the kind you would never see in a Norman Rockwell painting. There were estates fronted by enough acreage for a national park and around them swank bungalows with two- and three-car garages nestled comfortably into the surrounding hillsides. Each driveway was outfitted with expensive machinery, Cadillacs, Lincoln Continentals, and even an occasional Jaguar roadster while all the landscaping looked as if it might have apoplexy if a weed so much as came across the county line.

Number 1302 was at the top of the canyon. It was a modest villa, with russet stucco walls and white brick trim and enough rooms for quartering a regiment. It looked out indifferently over a sward of impeccably trimmed grass that pitched sharply down a steep hill toward the street, almost like a wave cresting. A concrete driveway climbed up the right side of the hill past a line of acacias and cobalt blue hydrangeas that were something to see. Then it crossed in front of the house, passed a terraced front porch lined with spikes of blue and white delphiniums, and finally stopped in front of a garage the size of a fire station. I turned the Buick up the driveway and felt the strain on the gears as the car inched up toward the house.

I stopped just short of the crest of the hill, set the brake, and opened the door. As I started to get out, the Buick made a deep sigh and began rolling back down the driveway. I shut the door and let the car coast down to the street, as I swore to myself. Lester Mack's greedy smirk popped into my head. Maybe he was right about the brake job.

I parked the Buick on the side of the road and got out just in time to hear a door slamming somewhere up the hill. The sound rolled around the canyon and then gradually drifted off. It left a penetrating silence, broken only by the chirping of tree frogs and, somewhere behind that, the lulling sound of wind chimes. I put on my hat, straightened my tie, and started up the driveway.

By the time I made it to the front porch, my shoes felt like cement slabs. I tramped up the steps and pressed a button to the right of the door. A leisurely tolling of chimes sounded inside the house. They were still tolling when the door was yanked open.

The woman in the doorway wore a maid's uniform. She was of medium height and medium age, and she had a face like a bruised kidney. She looked me over quickly, then gave me a rock-hard glare and seemed to speak without moving her mouth.

"Yes?"

"Is this the Clavin residence?"

She ignored the question. "Was that your car in the driveway?"

"No," I said. "It was such a nice day. I walked here from downtown."

Her eyes beaded into tiny black points. "Just who are you, and what do you want?"

"The name's Garrett, and I want to see Sterling Clavin."

She folded her arms and opened her mouth, but the voice that came out wasn't hers.

"What is it, Amanda?"

The maid turned and spoke to someone behind the door. "Someone who says he wants to see Mr. Clavin."

"Who is he?" the voice asked.

The maid turned and gave me another glare. "Says his name's Garrett. Looks like another deadbeat to me."

"Good guess," I said. "I'm a detective."

A face peered around the door a soft face, not too old, with a tender, lightly rouged mouth and framed by silky brown hair that might have been blonde once. There wasn't much to tell about the face. Most of it was hidden behind a pair of Hollywood sunglasses almost a foot wide.

Nothing happened for a moment. The face drew in the lower lip and chewed on it softly, as if a lot of thinking might be going on behind the glasses. Finally, the face said, "Have you some identification?"

I slipped the investigator's I.D. out of my wallet and let her look at it. She held it up very close to her nose and studied it through the sunglasses. I waited and sorted out the lint on my suit.

After a few minutes of reading and lip chewing, the woman turned to the maid and said, "That will be all, Amanda. I'll take care of it."

Amanda fixed her glare on me again. "I don't think Mr. Clavin would want…"

"I said I'll take care of it," the woman said sharply.

Amanda's dark eyes flashed, and she let out the "humph" of an officious bullfrog. She turned and sauntered off into the interior of the house while the woman handed back my I.D.

"You may come in, Mr. Garrett," she said.

I took off my hat and stepped inside.

The interior hallway wasn't much. It was about the size of Lester Mack's garage, and it had an aquamarine marble floor around which were placed several tall potted palms, a dark walnut armoire, and a long table holding a miniature schooner in a bottle and a polished brass ship's clock. The pale turquoise walls, stretching up to a twelve-foot ceiling, were covered with a year's wages in oil paintings, mostly seascapes. And beyond the stairs on the left, a pair of double doors that could have let in a herd of cattle were set off like the entrance to a forecastle. I stood there looking around and thought about asking for a sailor's ration of rum.

The woman took my hat and put it in the armoire. Then she stood stiffly and gave me a half smile. "I'm sorry about Amanda's abruptness, Mr. Garrett. I...that is, we were expecting someone else."

"It's all right," I said. "I wasn't going to invite her to the prom anyway."

She hesitated for a moment, then smiled. Dimples deep enough to be coin slots appeared in her cheeks. It was a nice smile, what I could see of it. Her stance softened, and she held out her hand.

"I'm Barbara Clavin. Sterling Clavin is my husband."

I took her hand and shook it. She had a good handshake for a woman, delicate but firm. A lot of women approach, shaking hands as if they were taking out the garbage. They pinch your hand in the ends of their fingers and hold it as far away as they can, dangling it like something foul-smelling they plan to drop in the nearest receptacle. But Barbara Clavin gave me her whole hand, and she didn't seem to mind my holding it while I looked at her.

She was a couple of inches over five feet tall, with about a hundred and ten pounds neatly arranged in a black skirt and a blouse the color of beach sand. The blouse was open at the throat, revealing the usual Bel Air tan and a thin gold chain holding an emerald pendant. Above the chain, the few lines in her face and neck made me guess that she was about thirty-five. But it wasn't much of a guess. I'm not that good with necks.

She withdrew her hand and struck a business-like pose. "How may I help you?"

"I'd like to see your husband."

Her tone cooled just a few degrees. "Is he expecting you?"

"I tried his office and had no luck, so I thought he might be here."

"He's out on business," she said. "I don't expect him until quite late. Are you sure I can't help?"

"Not unless you know something about a man named Nugent."

She studied me through the cheaters and chewed on her lip again. "The name is familiar, but I'm afraid I can't place it. Why? Is he someone I should know?"

"Not anymore," I said. "He's dead."

She barely moved, but the muscles along her jaw rippled tight. "I'm sorry, but what does that have to do with my husband?"

"Maybe nothing," I said. "But the police are going to be asking him some questions. It might be better if I ask them first."

She pursed her lips and then motioned to her left. "Perhaps you'd better come in and sit down."

She led me into a living room that made the hallway seem small. It was filled with expensive furniture, more paintings, and more potted palms, and it was accented with more nautical oddments. On one side of the room, a long sofa sat quietly behind a coffee table made from driftwood. It faced several tall plush chairs and another table, with a ship's bell mounted on a wooden stand and a small display case showing a handful of Spanish doubloons. There was an anchor, cleaned up and polished, standing in a corner by the door. And at the far end of the room, an unused fireplace was partially hidden behind a large antique sea chest.

The room was enough to make Long John Silver drop his crutch. But what took my eye was the four-foot-high oil painting above the mantel. It showed a man in a yachtsman's outfit and a jaunty sailing cap perched in a captain's chair. He was a handsome man, with a tanned face and sharply chiseled features. He was neither old nor young, neither heavy nor thin. He had thick black hair, a cruel mouth, and eyes the color of gunpowder, and he stared out over the room like an undertaker inspecting a cadaver.

Barbara Clavin saw me studying the picture. "That's my husband, Sterling. He's very proud of that portrait."

"Uh-huh."

She turned abruptly and gave me what might have been a sharp look. "Just what do you mean by that?" she asked tartly.

"I mean, uh-huh."

She hovered uncertainly for a moment, like a hummingbird just before it darts off. Then she turned and walked curtly over to the sea chest and opened it up. A raised stand on telescoping legs slid smoothly up out of the chest. It held more than a dozen bottles and decanters, several tumblers, and a row of glasses enough for a good long voyage.

Barbara Clavin lifted a decanter off the stand and held it in my direction. "Would you like a brandy, Mr. Garrett?"

I nodded. "It might take the edge off the salt air."

She chuckled in spite of herself. "I'm sorry. I guess I am a little sensitive about Sterling. A lot of people resent him because of the work he does."

"Only because he's good at it," I said.

She let out a soft sigh. "Yes. He is very good…at everything."

She poured a slug of brandy into a good-sized snifter and handed it to me. Then she poured a larger dose for herself, drank half of it, and moved over by the sofa.

"Please sit down, Mr. Garrett."

I sat in one of the tall chairs facing the sofa and watched the last patch of sunlight edging its way down the leg of the coffee table toward the floor. Barbara Clavin settled down into the sofa, which was now mostly in shadows. She adjusted her sunglasses, but she kept them on. She took another drink and crossed her legs, letting her skirt ride up almost to the knee. From where I was sitting, she had a good pair of wheels.

"Now then," she said. "If this is a police matter, why aren't they here instead of you?"

I sampled the brandy and felt a smooth warmth in the back of my throat. "They're probably on their way. I'm here because a client asked me to locate someone who might be connected with your husband."

36

"May I ask the client's name?"

I took another sip of the brandy. It almost tasted like a real drink. "Why not?"

She laid out a fourteen-carat smile, the dimples deeper than before. "I see. You won't tell me. I guess that's part of a client's privilege?"

I didn't say anything.

"Tell me, Mr. Garrett. Don't the police object to your interfering with their investigations?"

"The police object to a lot of things, Mrs. Clavin. Sometimes they object just because I drive in their streets or put my hat on in their town."

She chuckled quietly. "It must be frightfully difficult, being a detective."

I shrugged. "It's a living."

"And what kind of living do you make? That is to say, how much do you charge?"

I felt impatience edging into my stomach. "Thirty bucks a day plus expenses, when I can get it. But I didn't come here looking for business."

"Of course." The smile faded. "I'm sorry. You came about my husband. Perhaps if you tell me what it's about."

"It's about a shooting," I said. "Two days ago, a man named Nugent was murdered, shot to death in his office downtown. The police think your husband might give them a lead to the killer."

She made a quick sucking noise. She uncrossed her legs, drank the rest of the brandy, and put down the glass. "How awful. But, Mr. Garrett, what could Sterling possibly know about a murder?"

I drained the brandy and put the glass on the floor. "A hard-nosed cop might point out that he makes his living defending killers. Where was your husband two nights ago, Mrs. Clavin?"

She wrung her hands together like a doctor scrubbing for surgery. "Why, he was here. At least, I think...That is,...." She shook her head. "I'm afraid I simply don't remember. But surely you can't think that Sterling..."

"Let's just stick to what the police might think," I said. "Is the name Nugent at all familiar?"

She swallowed hard and kept wringing her hands. "Yes. There was a man here about ten days ago. I'm not sure, but I think his name was Nugent."

"What did he want?"

"He wanted to see Sterling. He wouldn't say what for. I told him he'd have to go to the office, and he left."

I leaned in her direction. "Was that the only time you saw him?"

"Yes."

"Did your husband say anything about him?"

She shook her head. "No. Why?"

"Because Nugent was a detective and because your husband's name was in his appointment book. The name was written in for Monday evening at eight, about the time Nugent was killed."

She stood up. Her hands were balled into fists at her sides. "You...You must be mistaken."

I stood up. "Sure. I make mistakes all the time. I felt one coming on as soon as I pulled into your driveway. But just for fun, let's talk about a couple of mistakes the cops might make. First, they might figure your husband hired Nugent to dig up a little dirt for one of his clients. Nugent could have held out and decided to use something he'd uncovered to put the bite on your husband. On the other hand, the cops might decide that somebody hired Nugent to get something on your husband instead. Then maybe Nugent decided to up the ante and go to your husband first to try a little squeeze play. Either way, it amounts to a shakedown, one of the oldest motives for murder."

Her mouth fell open, and her hands flew up to her face just in time to rescue the sunglasses before they did a swan dive to the floor. "But...but that's ridiculous."

"What's ridiculous, Mrs. Clavin, is this little soft shoe number you've been doing. What was I supposed to do, roll over on my back, stick my paws in the air, and purr?"

She gathered what little poise she had left. "Now see here. You can't talk to me that way."

"You're right," I said. "Maybe you should have Amanda wash my mouth out with soap. Only spare me the righteous indignation. Most wives would have stopped a guy like me dead in his tracks at the door. One whiff of a gumshoe in a neighborhood like this, and every door gets slammed, every window locked, and every shade pulled down. But instead, you invite me in, sit me down, give me a smile and a drink, and try to dazzle me with your legs. They're pretty nice legs, and I'll bet they'd be good company. But don't waste your time trying to string me along by asking how much I charge and whether I can keep a secret. Just tell me what's on your mind. Or did you just want to see how a real grown-up detective works?"

She folded her arms tightly in front of her and set her jaw. Her voice was low and as thick as porridge. "I think you'd better leave."

"Fine," I said. "As soon as I take care of one more thing."

I stepped past her quickly and flicked on a small lamp on a table next to the sofa. She made a startled motion with her arms and half turned away, but not before I was able to reach out and pluck off the sunglasses. She gaped at me for a moment with a look of pale horror, then turned her back and hid her face in her hands.

The face she was hiding was a nice face; it was even better than nice. It had a graceful, slightly up-turned nose set between smooth cheekbones, and it had long, tender lashes surrounding almond-shaped eyes as blue as the delphiniums by the front porch. The eyes were limpid and deep, and they seemed to have a story to tell that was all their own, like the eyes in old paintings. It would have been a story told with some difficulty. The left eye was darkened and puffy, a bruise along the outer edge showing the outline of knuckles. It was one of the best shiners I'd ever seen.

She stood trembling with her back to me, her voice a low mewling noise. "Why did you do that?"

"I knew a guy once," I said. "He was a pug...a prizefighter. He spent a lot of time on the canvas. And after every bout, he'd be wearing sunglasses all day and all night for a week."

She didn't say anything. Her shoulders shook, and she began sobbing, wrenching sobs with tears trickling down her cheeks and staining her blouse. I felt like chewing off the end of the coffee table. I took her by the arm and sat her on the sofa. In a minute, the sobs settled down to a whimper.

"Please, Mr. Garrett," she said between sniffles. "Please don't tell my husband about this."

"Let me guess," I said. "He's been roughing you up, and you thought you might hire me to get something you could use against him in a divorce action."

She sniffed some more. "He's...he's intensely jealous if anyone so much as looks at me. And he has such a violent temper. I...I just..."

"I'm sorry, Mrs. Clavin. I don't do divorce work. Try a good lawyer."

"I don't know what to do," she said. "He's really a good man. He's just..."

"Sure," I said. "He's a swell guy. All he does is defend crooks and beat up women. I like him already."

She started another fit of sobbing. Her hands were wet with tears, and the front of her blouse was spotted like a leopard.

"Oh, hell," I said.

I reached into my pocket and took out one of my business cards. I pried one of her hands off her face and stuck the card in it. She brought the hand back up to her face and cried all over the card. I half hoped the tears would wash away my number.

The sobs were just starting to subside again when Amanda stomped into the room. She looked at Barbara Clavin, then at me, then proudly announced to no one in particular, "I told you he was a deadbeat."

Barbara Clavin pulled herself up off the sofa and took several deep breaths. By now, she must have been fully dehydrated. "What is it, Amanda?"

The maid threw her shoulders back and ignored me with all she had. "There's a Detective Rawls on the phone. He's calling for Mr. Clavin."

Barbara Clavin nodded and started across the room. "I'll take it. You can show Mr. Garrett the door."

Amanda turned and gave me a triumphant glare.

"Never mind," I said to her. "I've already seen it...both sides."

I left and walked down the hill to the Buick and listened to the night breezes rippling through the acacias. It was almost dark now, and the tree frogs were crooning to each other. Another time, I might have stopped to listen. But not tonight. I was too busy not being proud of myself. I felt as if

I'd just picked a blind man's pocket.

Chapter Five

Just for the hell of it, I drove back to town through Beverly Hills. I drove through neighborhoods thick with trees and watered lawns and limousines. Cold silvery lights winked through the trees as the homes peered out from behind lush foliage, proud of their fuzzy furniture and their heart-shaped bathtubs. The streets were empty. Everyone was inside counting money or counting ways to spend it.

After several minutes of not being one of the millionaires, I turned off Sunset Boulevard and then onto Rodeo Drive, and the winking lights gave way to neon. The shops were all open, and every corner café was crowded with the usual Hollywood hopefuls, dark men in flashy suits talking to eager young girls who ought to know better. Ever since Billy Wilkerson discovered Lana Turner, every sweet young thing from Bangor to Boise was hocking her trousseau to come west. You could always find them parading around Hollywood and Beverly Hills in skimpy skirts and sweaters as tight as tourniquets. They lived on hope and soda crackers, and they were easy marks for any sharpie with a fast line. Tonight, they were all on display, crowding around every drug store and soda fountain, hoping to be seen. The more designing ones sauntered artfully along the sidewalks, singing sweet songs with the movement of their hips. I drove slowly and took it all in. I was in no hurry. I would have driven faster to my own funeral. I was on my way to see Fran Brekhammer.

Fran's office was in the 600 block of Melrose Avenue, not far from La Brea. It was an older building with tall casement windows and a baroque-style cornice, and it had the well-kept look of a wealthy dowager. Except for a single light on the third floor, the building was dark.

I parked the Buick across the street, went inside, and climbed the two flights of stairs to the third floor. As I walked up the corridor, the sound of my heels on the cold, gray tile rang through the silence like a blacksmith's hammer. I could feel the hair on the back of my neck beginning to stir. There's nothing quite so empty as a deserted office building at night.

Fran had a suite of offices at the end of the corridor. The hall door was open, and a receptionist's desk just behind it tidied up for the night. Past the desk, a short inner hallway showed several more closed doors, and beyond them, a door partially open at the far end was leaking soft strands of light. I walked quietly up to the open door and tapped softly.

Fran hardly stirred as she sat behind the big desk that took up the middle of the room. A large book full of photographs was spread out in front of her, and she was leaning over studying it, her expression steeped in memories. She glanced up at me and then looked back down at the book without saying anything.

I pulled a chair around in front of the desk, sat in it, and lit a Lucky. I blew the smoke up over the desk and watched it drift around the ceiling in gentle plumes. The angry blare of the traffic in the street rose and echoed a dismal tune off the walls of the old building. I sat and chewed on the Lucky and listened, and the minutes fell like dead leaves.

Fran turned the pages of her book slowly, pausing now and then to study one of the pictures. After a long time, she leaned back in her chair and closed her eyes.

"Almost twenty-two years. I can hardly believe it." She opened her eyes slowly and looked at me, her features now heavy and pale. "Where could they have gone, Michael, all those years?"

I didn't answer.

She held up the book so I could see the cover. It said, "Glendale High School, 1927." She turned it over and pointed to a picture crammed with several dozen innocent faces.

"There we were," she said. "So young." She moved her finger around the picture, a girlish light flickering in her eyes. "There's Danny and me and

Alice Dearing. Alice and I used to trade clothes. She was the only one in class who was my size. And there's Bobby French. He and Danny were best friends. They were always together. If anybody picked on Danny, he had Bobby French to deal with."

Fran leaned back in her chair, and her eyes drifted up to the ceiling. "I remember when they both went out for the ball team. The coach didn't even want Danny around; only Bobby said he wouldn't play unless Danny was with him. Danny never got into any games, but he was so tickled just to be on the team that he went out early every day and helped rake the infield." She paused, and her mouth settled into a sad smile. "And Danny was stuck on Bobby's little sister Jeanie. It just about took the heart out of him when she left. Even Bobby couldn't understand it. But he and Danny stuck together just the same." Fran's eyes suddenly dimmed. "Until Bobby was killed at Anzio."

Fran sighed heavily. Her voice threaded out like something thin and frail. "Poor Danny. He wanted so much to go with Bobby, but the Army wouldn't take him because he had flat feet." She shook her head. "Somehow, it was that way with everything Danny tried to do. He couldn't make the police force, couldn't even last as a house detective in that crummy hotel. I tried to help. I gave him all the business I could." Her eyes fluttered down to the desk. "But he lost the jumpers more often than not. I guess that's why he finally started drinking so much."

I started to say something, but Fran's head darted up again, and she glared at me, her jaw set defiantly. "But he was a good man, Michael better than most. He never had any money, because every time he could pull together a couple of bucks, he'd give it away to some panhandler. He knew he'd never see the money again, but it didn't matter. He did everything he could for people, even the ones who didn't deserve it. And he never complained." Her voice began to falter. "He had a heart as big as a football, only it didn't do him any good."

I crushed the Lucky out on my heel, tossed the butt end into the office wastebasket, and tried to work up something brilliant to say. "I guess you've heard from Rawls."

She made a soft choking noise and nodded.

I reached into my pocket and pulled out the envelope. "I found this in Danny's desk. The cops haven't seen it yet, because I figured you should see it first." I placed it on the desk in front of her. "You'll have to give it to Rawls, of course."

Fran nodded absently and stared at the smudged envelope. She ran her finger delicately over the spot where her name was written, slowly tracing the letters. After a long moment, she picked up the envelope, slowly, carefully, as if it were a valuable relic. She opened it and took out a single folded sheet of paper. Then she sat and read as if her life depended on each word. I sat and watched her and listened to the thunder of silence in the room.

I lost track of time. Maybe it stopped; maybe it turned around. Maybe the seasons changed, and I grew old and didn't notice. I just sat there and watched a woman with a hide like shoe leather slowly turn frail. Fran finally put the paper down on the desk and tentatively pushed it over toward me. Then she rose and turned and stood with her back to me, staring out the window. Staring but not seeing, almost like Nugent.

I picked up the lightly crumpled sheet of paper and looked at it. One side was blank. On the other side, some familiar brown smudges surrounded a moronic scrawl written by someone who might have been suffering through a morning after or a night before:

Dear Fran:

I'm meeting a man tonight who might be coming to kill me. He's a rich man, and he's powerful and dangerous. Somebody with a lot of downtown grease. If things work out, I might just settle a big case and make you proud of me. If not, then you better give this note to the cops.

As I write this, I've been thinking of all the things I should have told you and didn't. Now there's so little time. I threw away a lot of years, maybe a lifetime on someone who never really existed. You always said I was a sucker, and you were right. It was just my luck. The one I thought I loved died years ago, and the one I really loved was here all the time.

Maybe I'm still a sucker. Guys like me shouldn't love anybody. I haven't done much in my life that's come out right. Maybe now I can.

Danny

I tried to swallow, but my throat was as dry as Carrie Nation's cupboard. Fran heard me drop the note on the desk, and she turned to look at me. Her eyes were suddenly full of a quiet fury.

"It was Clavin, wasn't it?" The words hissed through her teeth like a snake's tongue. "Edward told me his name was in Danny's appointment book. I hope they fry the son of a bitch."

"If they can prove he did it, they will," I said.

A satanic smile drew up the corners of her mouth and darkened her eyes. "Well, we'll just make sure they prove it, won't we?"

"What are you talking about?"

"I'm talking about evidence." She snatched the note off the desk and waved it in my face. "Like this. And anything else we need to convict that bastard. I've done business with him, bailing out the crumbs he represents. I know what kind of man he is. I want you to go out and get the goods on him. He killed Danny, and I'm not going to rest until I see him in the gas chamber."

I drew in some air and held it and thought about taking up a more promising occupation, like taxidermy.

"Maybe you ought to let Rawls handle it," I said.

Fran lowered herself slowly into her chair and placed her hands flat on the desk, fingers spread wide apart. Her voice was hushed, her features hard. She was a hundred pounds of menace.

"I'm not walking away from this one, Michael," she said. "Not with Danny murdered. I've got nothing against Edward Rawls. I believe he's a good cop. But you know as well as I do that law is where you buy it in this town. And Sterling Clavin has deep pockets."

"So do the people he runs around with."

She folded her hands deliberately and brought up a nasty smile. She spoke with deadly politeness. "Well, Mr. Garrett. If you're afraid…"

"Of course, I'm afraid," I said. "I'm afraid of death and destruction. I'm afraid of growing old and being forgotten. I'm afraid of you getting on your horse and riding after Clavin like Annie Oakley. If he's a killer, he's a cunning one, and he won't be brought down by a dame with a lust for revenge."

Fran jumped out of the chair and stood with both fists clenched over the desk. Her eyes were black fire. "You bastard!"

I crossed my legs, folded my hands, and looked at her. "Danny Nugent is dead, Fran. You can't bring him back."

She waved her fists, started to say something, then stopped. As suddenly as she had jumped up, her expression changed. The anger ran out of her face like water through a sieve. She sat down slowly, folded her hands again, breathed deeply, and looked at me from somewhere miles away. Then she nodded slowly. Whatever else Fran was, she was a pro.

"I know," she said quietly. "Do you think Edward can nail Clavin?"

"Could be," I said. "If he tries. Right now, he's stalking a hood named Joey Paris, one of Clavin's clients. If he thinks he can get Paris by taking Clavin down,…"

"Will you help him?"

"Eddie doesn't like it when I stand in his shadow."

She rubbed her hands back and forth and nodded again. "I know. And I'm sorry. I didn't mean to put you on the spot."

I shrugged. "That's what I get paid for."

Fran looked at me and nodded again. I could see moisture growing along her lower lids. I stood up.

"I'll be going," I said. "I think I've done all I can. I'll check with Eddie tomorrow."

I got as far as the door when Fran's voice stopped me. "Michael, I am sorry."

I looked back. "So am I, Fran."

I turned and went out. I shut the door behind me and stood for a minute.

There was a sound of pages turning, then the soft thump of a head laid on a desk, then a quiet sob. I walked up the hall and out of the office.

* * *

By the time I got home, the air was heavy with the smell of rain. I left the Buick on the street, went into a drug store on the corner, bought a paper, then trudged into the lobby of my apartment building. A sign on the elevator door told me the thing was out of order, so I headed for the stairs. It was only three flights to my floor, but to me, it was a long, lonely hike. I felt like a losing pitcher on his way to the showers. One guy is dead, and two women are in tears. Not much of a game, Garrett. Didn't have the good stuff today. Couldn't get the ball over the plate.

I let myself in, put the paper in a chair, and dropped my hat and coat on it. Then I loosened my tie and went into the kitchen. I opened a cupboard and found my dinner waiting in a bottle of Scotch. I pulled the cork and had a quick appetizer. It seemed passable, so I took down a glass, poured in about three ounces, added a couple of ice cubes and some seltzer, and went back into the living room.

I put on the radio and heard an announcer with a mouth full of cotton batting introduce a local viola player who was about to lead some other locals in a performance of a Mendelssohn concerto. The music started, and the guy began his assault, and in a few minutes, Mendelssohn was beaten into submission. I shut off the radio, opened the window, and sat down to read the paper.

Reading didn't get me very far. The lines kept running together, and I kept seeing the look on Fran Brekhammer's face as I left her office. I drained my Scotch, mixed another, and sat there trying to think of all the reasons a man might have for sitting alone and drinking too much Scotch. Maybe it was the company. Maybe it was the weather. Maybe if I had some more Scotch, I could figure it out. I was about to get some when the phone rang.

I reached over to the little stand next to the reading lamp, yanked up the receiver, and gave it my mannerly best. "Yeah?"

There was a kittenish voice on the other end, quiet and smooth, but with tattered edges. "Mr. Garrett, this is Barbara Clavin. I must see you."

"I'm not seeing people tonight, Mrs. Clavin. It's for their own good."

"I don't understand."

"Looks like rain," I said, as if that meant something.

A disturbed silence came over the line. I could imagine her chewing on her lip again. "Please, Mr. Garrett. It's very important."

"Hold the line."

I put down the receiver, went into the kitchen, and emptied my glass in the sink. Then I walked back into the living room and stood by the window, looking out at a night full of nothing. Silent flashes danced over the horizon and flickered away in the hills. I waited for the rumble of thunder, but none came.

I unwound a Lucky from what was left of the pack, lit it, and listened to that little voice that visits me on such occasions. It's the same voice that warns me about playing with guns or standing in front of a moving train or drawing to an inside straight. Now, it was telling me to hang up the phone. It's a voice that makes sense. I've learned to listen to it. Every word. I walked over and picked up the receiver.

"All right, Mrs. Clavin. What's so important?"

"Mr. Garrett, it's my husband. The police questioned him tonight about that man Nugent. When he came home, he was in a rage. I was honestly afraid for my life. Then he got another call and...and...Mr. Garrett, I've never seen him like this."

"Has he threatened you?"

"No. He didn't say anything. He just raced out of the house."

I took a long drag on the Lucky and studied the smoke as it swirled around the open window. Studying smoke. That would be something to do. Something worthy of a man with my means and experience. Better get off the phone and get busy.

"Look, Mrs. Clavin. If you're afraid of your husband, you'd better talk to the police or to a good divorce lawyer. Better still, talk to both. I can't help you."

"But you don't understand," she snapped. A sharp edge had crept into her voice. "I'm not afraid *of* him. I'm afraid *for* him. I think someone is threatening to kill my husband."

I felt the receiver turn wet in my hand. I held it out and looked at it. It was suddenly as heavy as an elephant's leg. I had all I could do to get the thing back to my ear.

"All right," I said. "I'll be there in an hour."

"No," she said quickly. "Not here. I'm afraid of Amanda overhearing. I'll come into town. Just tell me where to meet you."

I looked at my watch. It was just nine-thirty. "You know where Lacy's is, on Alvarado north of Wilshire?"

"I'll find it," she said. "I'll be there as soon as I can."

There was a sharp click and a long droning buzz, and she was gone. So were all my good intentions for minding my own business. I reached out slowly, cradled the receiver, and just sat there staring at it.

Chapter Six

It took me ten minutes to get to Lacy's. The crowd was thin for a Wednesday night. A few fashionably dressed couples sat in booths and a handful more busied themselves at the tables lining the dance floor. There was a trio on stage, with a tall ash blonde in a midnight-blue sequin dress caressing the microphone. She had a scarlet mouth, gray eyes full of bedroom promises, and a low, wispy voice that crawled across the room like ground fog. It reminded me of a Humphrey Bogart film I'd seen the week before.

I found an empty booth on the far side of the room where I could sit and see the door. I slid in and sat down just in time to watch a redhead with an easy smile and a tray full of empty glasses glide over to the booth. She had the nose and green eyes of Greer Garson, and she agreed to bring me a Scotch. I agreed to drink it. She smiled and headed toward the bar, and I sat admiring the way she walked. She had moves Busby Berkley hadn't thought of. Maybe I'd been seeing too many movies.

The blonde on stage finished her number, and the trio stepped up the tempo. A few couples started grappling with each other on the dance floor, and the redhead brought me my drink. I sat and nursed it and tried not to think about Fran Brekhammer and the note from Nugent. I'd have had better luck trying to ignore a boil on my backside.

The trio kept playing, and the blonde kept drawing into the microphone, and about a dozen minutes passed. I was just making friends with my second Scotch when Barbara Clavin walked in. I didn't recognize her right away. She was wearing a dark gray hat with an extra wide brim that sloped down toward her shoulders. A black veil covering the hat was pulled down over her face. And the rest of her was carefully arranged in a tailored ebony suit and a vanilla blouse with the collar pulled up and folded outside her jacket. She looked like something out of the display window at Macy's.

She looked around quickly, spotted me, and came over to the booth. "Mr. Garrett, I'm so glad you agreed to meet me."

I motioned her into the booth, and she sat down across from me. She placed a small black brocade clutch purse on the table, then peeled off a pair of chalk-white gauntleted gloves and laid them neatly next to the purse. The redhead came over, now wearing something less than a smile. Barbara Clavin ordered a gimlet, and the girl drifted back to the bar.

I looked across the table. "Do you always dress that way to meet detectives?"

"I didn't know what kind of place this would be." She made a perfunctory inspection of the room. "It's rather nice, isn't it?"

The redhead brought the gimlet, gave me a poisoned look, then stomped back toward the bar like a bugler moving to a Sousa march. Barbara Clavin lifted her veil, folded it over the brim of her hat, and sampled her drink. The bruise on her eye had been carefully covered with makeup, but it was still there.

"Umm," she murmured. "This is quite good."

After a couple of sips, she put down the glass, folded her hands, and rested them on the edge of the table. She glanced around the room again, then glanced at me, then looked down. Slowly, deliberately, she inhaled.

"Mr. Garrett," she began, "I want to apologize for this afternoon. I shouldn't have acted the way I did. I was very upset and very frightened. I couldn't talk to Sterling about it. He's just…." She shook her head. "Anyway, I'm sorry. As the wife of an attorney, I should have been more composed." She angled her head slightly and looked across the table at me, mostly out of one eye. "Will you forgive me?"

"I forgive you."

She rubbed her hands together and waited through a heavy pause. "You don't have much to say."

"I came here to listen."

Barbara Clavin looked down at the table, took a preparatory nibble on her lower lip, then started again. "I'm afraid this is rather embarrassing. I'm not used to this sort of thing."

"If you mean talking to a detective," I said, "people rarely are. Just tell it."

She reached into her purse, brought out a folded piece of paper, and pushed it across the table to me.

"I found this tonight in my husband's study under some papers," she said. "He doesn't know that I have it."

I picked up the paper and opened it. Someone had cut words out of a newspaper and pasted them together to form a message. It read: "Let Joey Paris hang or you'll hang in his place."

I folded up the paper and pushed it back across the table. "Is this why you think your husband is being threatened?"

She nodded. "Yes. Don't you think so?"

I shrugged. "It could mean anything. Blackmail, or maybe just an outraged citizen with bad handwriting."

She frowned. "Mr. Garrett, I'm quite serious."

"So am I, Mrs. Clavin. Real killers don't send notes. Chances are this is from some crackpot maybe an old rummy who picked up the paper, read about your husband, and then figured this note would put some of the old pep back into a threadbare life. It happens all the time."

She shook her head. "No. I'm certain it's the real thing and that Sterling is in danger."

I inhaled slowly and then exhaled loud enough for her to hear it. "I'd ask if your husband has any enemies, but it would just be to hear myself talk."

She gave me another frown and started to say something, but I held up my hand.

"Never mind," I said. "What do you know about Joey Paris?"

She shook her head again. "Only that he's one of my husband's clients. Beyond that, nothing. I stay out of Sterling's business affairs. Do you think this man Paris could be the one threatening him?"

"That wouldn't make much sense," I said. "But nothing else has today.

Has there been anything else other notes, threatening phone calls, strange characters at the door…besides me?"

Her face reddened, and her lips stretched tight over her teeth. "Please, Mr. Garrett. Don't make fun of me. There was only this note and the envelope it was mailed in. I didn't think that was important."

I let out another long breath. "I'm sure it all means nothing, Mrs. Clavin. But if you're serious, the police will want to examine both the note and the envelope."

Her eyes widened to the size of poker chips. "Oh, no. I can't go to the police."

"Why not?"

"Mr. Garrett, my husband is very…highly strung. And I'm afraid the police…well…"

I said, "Uh-huh."

She set her jaw and looked at me evenly. Her eyes were suddenly as clear and hard as bulletproof glass.

"Mr. Garrett, I'm no fool. I know how Sterling makes his living. I know what kind of people he defends and what the police think of him. He does something that people resent, even though the law says everyone is entitled to the best possible defense. And you said yourself people resent Sterling because he does his job very well. They just don't know how torn he is, how he suffers because of his clients because of what he knows about the things they do. But he believes in the law. He's devoted his life to it. And if you were in trouble, you'd want someone like Sterling to defend you."

She reached across the table and squeezed my forearm. Her blue eyes seemed to reach out and squeeze me at the same time.

"I can't believe that you think the police would really help him," she said.

I started not to care who her husband was. She had something you don't often find in a Bel Air housewife.

"Why did you call me?" I asked her.

She took her hand off my arm, but her eyes wouldn't let go. "You're the only detective I've ever met, except for that Mr. Nugent, of course. You seem to know your business, and somehow, I just feel I can trust you. I wanted to show you the note this afternoon, but…"

I fished out a Lucky and lit it, and kept staring into those blue eyes. "Look, Mrs. Clavin, in his line of work, your husband must get a lot of threats like this. What makes this one worth noticing?"

She stiffened. "Because I found the note. It was mailed day before yesterday, to Sterling's office." She spread her hands out on the table. Her eyes were pleading now. "Don't you see? If Sterling didn't think it was serious, he would simply have thrown the note away. But he kept it. And he put it someplace where he didn't think I'd find it."

"All right," I said. "Let's say the note does mean something. What do you want me to do?"

She started to speak, then caught herself. Her face went blank, and she sat back in the booth. "I don't know. I guess I just want you to help him. You can do that, can't you?"

I shrugged. "I don't see how."

She blinked rapidly, several times. "But I thought a private detective…."

I shook my head. "A private detective can't do what the cops can in a case like this. They have a dozen clear-eyed little men with microscopes who can examine this note and the envelope it came in, dust for prints, maybe find out where the paper was sold and who bought it. They can cover a lot of ground, ask a lot of questions. Then, if your husband really is in danger, they can put someone with him, twenty-four hours a day if it comes to that. They can wrap him up so tight that he'll start to smell like a cop. And that's usually enough to discourage the kind of character who would threaten someone this way. It's only in the scandal sheets and dime potboilers that police protection doesn't work."

I gulped down the rest of my Scotch and took a heavy drag on the Lucky. Barbara Clavin stared across the table, eyes fixed, unwavering.

"On the other hand," I said. "I'm just one guy in a very big city. And when it comes to dealing with the cops, I don't draw a lot of water. I can't call a police chemist and have him analyze this note and then canvas a few hundred stationary stores. I also can't spend every minute trying to keep tabs on your husband so some gun-happy squirrel won't take a pop at him.

A real killer would love it if I tried that. All he'd need is some punk fresh off the needle to keep me busy while he went after your husband…or you."

I took a last drag and crushed out the Lucky. It was a good speech. It was mostly true. "Take my advice, Mrs. Clavin. Go to the police."

She slumped dejectedly in the seat and let out a long, loud sigh. "I didn't realize it was like that."

"People usually don't."

"Are you sure you can't help me?" She gave me one of those demure up-from-under looks that women are so good at. "I'd pay you well."

"And with a couple more Scotches and another good look at your legs, I might be enough of a heel to let you," I said. "But you'd be wasting your money."

A quiet smile played at the corners of her mouth. "You're not much of a businessman, are you?"

"Try offering me the Brooklyn Bridge. I might just buy it."

The smile widened a couple of notches, and she angled her head again. "How did you get to be a detective?"

"By being invited to leave the police force. A certain detective captain and I disagreed over the species of his parents."

She nodded and kept on smiling. "Somehow, I can see how that might happen. If you'll forgive my saying so, I think you can be rather…blunt."

"I forgive you."

She looked down and fiddled with her glass, and the smile subsided.

"I just don't know about the police," she said. "If it were anyone but Sterling, they might…. But he'd be absolutely furious if I went behind his back. If he even found out I was here with you,…" She rubbed her hands over her upper arms and gave a quick shudder.

"Why not talk to him?" I asked her. "Get him to call the police himself."

"I'm afraid he wouldn't listen to me." She put her hands flat on the table again and leaned toward me. Her eyes were wide and innocent. "But maybe…maybe if you spoke to him…"

"He doesn't even know me."

She reached out and clutched at my arm. "But you're very logical and persuasive. I'm sure he'd listen to you." She swallowed hard. "Please, Mr. Garrett. It would mean so much to me. Please talk to him."

I got out another Lucky and took my time lighting it while I looked across the table. Her blue eyes were like mirrors. I could see my whole day in them. Two women coming at me all cranked up over a man I'd never met. One of these women would hate me if I helped him; the other might hate me if I didn't. Just another day for Garrett big city detective, mender of broken hearts. I felt like someone standing on top of a burning building, wondering whether to jump off.

"Look, Mrs. Clavin. I really don't think I can help you. But I have to see your husband on another matter. Maybe I can at least find out if he's really afraid of something."

She clasped her hands together and brought them up to her chin in a kind of praying gesture. "That would be wonderful. Do you think you can do it without letting Sterling find out that I spoke to you?"

"So what if he finds out?" I grunted. "Just keep your left up."

She flushed and looked down at the table.

"All right," I said. "Have you got any money?"

She looked up quickly. "I brought my checkbook. But I thought…"

I shook my head. "Uh-uh. Cash."

She glanced at her purse, then eyed me uncertainly. "Just a few dollars. Cab fare home and a little mad money."

"Get it out."

She reached tentatively into her purse and brought out a handful of bills, which she laid in a little pile on the table. I took a couple of singles off the pile and pushed the rest back to her. Then I held up the two dollars.

"This is a retainer," I said. "You've just hired a detective. As far as your husband is concerned, you're protected by client privilege. And there won't be a canceled check to tip him off."

She leaned back in the seat and seemed to relax all at once, as if a switch had been thrown. "Oh, Mr. Garrett, thank you. I'm so grateful."

I chewed on the Lucky and didn't say anything.

Barbara Clavin sat quietly for a minute, then let out a soft sigh. Finally, she took a healthy slug of her gimlet, put down the glass, and eyed my cigarette. "Could I have one of those?" Her lips pursed into a half smile, and her eyes filled with conspiracy. "Sterling doesn't like me to smoke."

I tossed the pack across the table to her, and she extracted one of the Luckies while I struck a match. She tenderly inserted the end of the cigarette between her lips, leaned over, and took my hand in hers, guiding the match. There was something about the way she held my hand. Her grip was strong yet delicate, firm as a blacksmith's paw and frail as the wings of a butterfly. The touch of an angel. I pulled my hand away, and she blew a tall column of smoke over the table.

"What else doesn't Sterling like to have you do?" I asked.

She put a wry tilt to her mouth, as if she had already caught my meaning. "Lots of things if they involve other men."

I grunted again. "God, I thank thee that I am not as other men are.'"

She leaned back and grinned. Her dimples sent a message across the table. "Scripture, Mr. Garrett? I'm impressed."

I shrugged. "I once had to track down a Bible salesman who skipped out on his wife."

She lifted an eyebrow and laughed quietly. "No, you didn't. That's just your way of being modest." Her eyes suddenly narrowed. "I think you're really a lot like Sterling. You're honest and uncompromising, even when that might not make you very popular. You work hard for your clients, and sometimes you get disappointed. But you keep on working for them because underneath, you're full of conviction and purpose."

"Yeah," I said. "I'm full of it, all right."

She smiled again and shook her head. "I'm sorry. I didn't mean to go on like that. It's just that people don't know Sterling the way I do."

"From the look of your eye, maybe Sterling doesn't know Sterling."

She shrugged out another sigh. "Perhaps not. He certainly isn't easy to live with."

"Has he done that to you before?"

She flushed again and looked down and spoke in the direction of her lap. "Once. About a year ago. He thought I was having an affair. He's very possessive, and I'm afraid he sometimes gets quite jealous." She looked up at me. Her eyes showed a ripple of sadness. "Even if I haven't given him a reason."

"What about this time?"

She shrugged again and looked away. "This time I think he's simply frightened. Someone's been threatening him, and it was convenient for him to take it out on me."

"That's not very convenient for you."

"No," she said. "But he *is* my husband."

She put out her cigarette, then held up her left arm and took a quick look at a thin gold watch ringed with small green stones. "Mr. Garrett, I'm afraid I must go. I'm not sure how long Sterling will be out, and it will take me a good hour to get home."

"All right," I said. "I'll call you after I've talked with him."

She held up her hand. "Oh, no. I think I'd better call you. I don't want to take any chances." She folded the veil back down over her face and began poking in her purse. "How much do you suppose the drinks are?"

I put her two dollars back down on the table. "My treat."

She gave me another look at the dimples. "Thank you, Mr. Garrett. Thank you for everything."

She slid out of the booth, went across the room, then out the door as easily as butter melting. I just sat there looking after her, not seeing anything but the way she had looked at me. I could still feel the touch of her hand. It reminded me of things I didn't want to remember. A dame with those eyes and those legs and a husband who beats her up. Try figuring that one, Garrett.

Some women like to get slapped around. There's no telling why. And there's no telling about the guys who'll do it. But there are plenty of both. Every now and then, you see a woman who could be on the arm of Carey Grant, only she's with some mug who treats her like a side of beef. She clings to him until he cracks her on the mouth. Then she just gets up, licks her wounds, and comes back for more. Maybe Barbara Clavin was like that. Maybe I should have belted her.

I sat and fretted and thought about what a nice night I was having. I wondered what else I could do to cheer myself up? I was just thinking another Scotch might help when a familiar face came through the door.

Detective Ed Rawls ambled over and slumped down at the far end of the bar. He dropped a weathered gray snap-brim fedora on the stool beside him and said something to the bartender. I picked up my hat and walked over next to him. I took his hat and dropped it on the bar, then placed mine next to it and sat on the stool.

Rawls didn't look at me. He just sat grim-faced as the bartender brought him a glass of beer. He dusted the foam off the top of the glass with a meaty index finger, took a long swallow, and then rolled the glass back and forth between his palms.

"A guy just can't come in here and have a drink in peace," he said.

I waved at the bartender and ordered another Scotch. We waited in silence until it came.

Rawls sipped on his beer and kept staring straight ahead. "So, what're you doin' for eatin' money these days?"

I sipped the Scotch. "Nothing. I'm on a liquid diet."

He snickered and drained the rest of his beer. "Me too."

He banged the empty glass down on the bar, and the bartender brought him a full one even before the sound had died. Rawls took a swig out of it and grumbled.

"They ain't as quick as they used to be in here. I told him not to let the damn glass get empty."

I nursed the Scotch and waited, hoping the storm would pass. "You talked to Fran."

"Yeah," he growled. "One of the great things about bein' a copgettin' to go out and spread bad news on the citizens. Feels real good." He prodded his chest with his index finger. "Makes the old ticker run like a top. Know what I mean?"

"I'm glad you did it," I said, "instead of somebody like Brice."

He snorted and guzzled some more of the beer. "What the hell difference does it make? Guy's just as dead either way."

"Sure," I agreed. "You get anything from Clavin?"

He finally turned and looked at me, his eyes in a tight squint. "How'd you know we button-holed him?"

I stared down into the Scotch. "I know the routine, remember?"

"Hah," he said. "As if I could forget."

He put down his glass and squeezed his hands on the edge of the bar hard enough to turn his knuckles white. He spoke as if each word tasted like sawdust.

"We traced *Mister* Clavin to The Pillers, where he was bein' entertained by *Mister* Paris. He said he didn't know anybody named Nugent and didn't know anythin' about a homicide. He said if we had any more questions of him or *Mister* Paris, we could just come back with a warrant."

He pulled his glass off the bar savagely and drained it. Before he could put it down, the bartender was there with another. Rawls looked at him and grinned. "Nice goin'. Now bring me a hooker of Crown Royal."

"I saw Fran," I said. "Nugent's death hit her pretty hard, and she's in a lather to see whoever did it put away."

He gave me a raking look and spoke out of the side of his mouth. "And she thinks I'm not?"

I shook my head. "She got the idea from you that Clavin was the killer. She might try to do something about it."

"Well, she can goddamn well wait in line. I'm startin' to want that bum almost as much as Paris." He put away another few ounces, smiled, and spoke half to himself. "Not that I'd really mind. If somebody decided to ice that bastard, I think I'd have lead in my shoes. Whoever did it might never get caught."

I took another sip of Scotch and looked away. "Why would Clavin want Nugent dead?"

"How the hell should I know?" he blurted. "And what's it to you?"

"Just asking."

He grabbed my arm and turned me toward him and shook a fist the size of a cantaloupe in my face. "Listen, smart-ass. I'm investigatin' that Clavin like he's never been investigated before. He's my lead to Joey Paris, and I'm gonna play him for all he's worth. I'll go by the book, all right. But if I have to, I'll ram the goddamn book down his throat. You get in my way, and I'll throw your license up a tree and you after it."

Sometimes words don't work. Sometimes it's better just to say nothing. That's what I said.

Rawls finished his beer and drained the Crown Royal in a single slug. We left some money on the bar, went outside, and stood in the heavy air. Across the street, a young weasel in a striped suit was leaning on the door of a lavender convertible. He was talking to a brassy blonde in a tight peach-blossom dress and heels you could stick in a dartboard.

Rawls spotted the two of them and poked me in the shoulder. "One of Paris's boys. Watch this."

Before I could say anything he stormed across the street. He grabbed the kid by the lapels and began hollering in his face. "Don't you punks know not to park here? This is a safety zone!"

The kid screwed up his face. His voice was thin and brittle. "Who sez?"

"I sez, you little crumb. What the hell you doin', followin' me?"

The kid looked uneasily at the blonde, then shook his head. "You're nuts."

"Izzat so," Rawls roared. "Well, I think you're followin' me. I think you're tryin' to obstruct justice."

He tightened his grip on the lapels, hoisted the kid off his feet, and slammed him against the side of the convertible so that his head bounced off the canvas top like a carom shot off a cushion. The blonde began shrieking, but Rawls kept holding the kid against the car with one hand and with the other flashed her his badge. She shut up like a clam, turned, and legged it down the street, her heels popping like cap pistols on the dry pavement.

Rawls reached into the kid's coat and pulled out something dark and shiny. He held it up and looked at it. From where I was standing, it looked like a .45. Rawls waved it in the kid's face and spoke to him in a voice dripping with contempt.

"This is too much gun for a little worm like you." He tucked the gun in his pocket. "I'll just hang onto it until you're big enough not to need your nose wiped. Now you go and tell *Mister* Paris that I said he should behave himself. And tell him and his fancy-pants mouthpiece if they got any ideas about tanglin' with the law, I'll come around there and crack their goddamn headlights for 'em."

Almost in a single move, Rawls spun the kid around, picked him up, and threw him head first into the front seat of the convertible. There was a scramble of arms and legs behind the wheel. Then the engine roared, the lights came on, and the car screamed off down the block and around the corner out of sight.

Rawls walked easily back across the street and stood looking at me. The smile on his face almost reached his ears. "That was fun."

He patted me on the shoulder and walked up the street, whistling. He got into his car, rolled down the window, and drove slowly away. I could hear his whistling all the way into the next block. I just stood and watched the taillights slowly fading into the night. It was time for me to go home, but somehow I couldn't move. My feet had been planted in cement. All I could think about was that burning building. I had just jumped off.

Chapter Seven

I t was a little after nine the next morning when I picked up the phone and dialed Sterling Clavin's office. After a night of too much Scotch, too many memories, and not enough sleep, I was feeling as cheerful as a giraffe with strep. I sat in my living room with the phone balanced on one knee and a cup of very strong coffee on the other. After a couple of rings, a familiar young voice full of too much morning came on the line.

"Clavin and Marcus."

"The name's Garrett. I want to see Sterling Clavin."

"Are you one of Mr. Clavin's clients?"

"Not yet," I said. "But I got a ticket for double parking. I may want him to represent me."

"I'm sorry," she purred, "but Mr. Clavin isn't taking on any new clients at the moment. Perhaps Mr. Marcus can help you."

"Not unless he knows about something untidy that was left down on Paloma Place."

There was a muffled sound, as if a hand had just been placed over the mouthpiece. I sipped the coffee and waited. After a minute, the voice came back. It was still pleasant, but now there was a hint of caution peeking out from the corners.

"Aren't you the same one who called yesterday afternoon?"

"That's right," I said.

"Are you with the police?"

"Lady, if I were with the cops, you wouldn't be talking to me on the phone. I'd be standing in front of your desk."

Her voice took on the feel of early morning frost. "I'm sorry, but Mr. Clavin has left strict instructions...."

"Look," I said. "My name is Michael Garrett. I'm a licensed private investigator. He can check that out with one phone call to City Hall. Tell him I have a private matter to discuss, and he can talk to me or read about it in the papers."

There was a quick intake of breath, and her voice modulated up an octave and a half. "Really? A detective? Oh, my. Just a moment, please."

I heard the muffled sound again and some quiet rumblings behind it. This time, she was back on the line while I still had a mouthful of coffee.

"Mr. Garrett, Mr. Clavin can see you here this afternoon at two. Will that be all right?"

"Fine."

There was a short pause, and her voice fell to something just above a whisper. "Are you really a private eye?"

"Yeah," I said. "As private as they come. I'm even housebroken."

There was a mischievous giggle. "That's wonderful. I can hardly wait."

She hung up.

I hung up and sipped my coffee. You meet all kinds in Los Angeles.

* * *

Showered, shaved, and full of coffee, I drove down to the office. I stopped at the stand in the lobby, bought a paper, and thumbed through it while I rode up in the elevator. The obituary section had just a couple of lines about Nugent, nothing more. He attracted about as much attention dead as he had alive.

I strolled up the hall and opened the door to the outer office. I always leave the outer door unlocked so the city's desperate people can come in and rest their troubles until the detective arrives. I only do it from habit. I never expect to find anyone waiting. This morning, I found someone.

She was a strawberry blonde in her early twenties, with aimless pale eyes, over-rouged cheeks, and a Cupid's bow mouth thickly coated with flame-colored lipstick. She had some kind of stole wrapped around her shoulders made from something that might have given up its life crossing the freeway. Underneath it was a scoop-necked salmon-pink dress that fitted her like a coat of paint and beneath that, a body that really did it justice. She had an imitation alligator purse looped over her left arm, and with her right hand, she was waving a cigarette holder as long as a pool cue, waving it almost in rhythm with the wad of gum she was chewing. She looked like something Al Capp might have dreamed up.

She stood up as I opened the door and walked over to me. The dress made that an effort. "Mr. Garrett?" Her voice was like barbed wire.

I nodded. "Uh-huh."

"I'm Lorna James. Maybe you've heard of me?"

"Not since yesterday."

She inhaled deeply and took another short step toward me. She made Mae West look like a toothpick. "Well, I want to hire you."

I stepped around her, unlocked the inner door, and held it open. "Come on in and see if I can talk you out of it."

She turned and strutted past me into the office as if her knees were tied together. A trail of cheap perfume followed her inside. I shut the door, went over and opened the window, then sat down behind the desk. By then, she was carefully lowering herself into the client chair as if every photographer west of Denver might have her in his sights. She sat and crossed her legs, and the hem of her dress rode up high enough to make Will Hays and his board of censors break out in a sweat. Finally, she sat back in the chair, inhaled again, and projected a triumphant smile.

"I'm in show business," she said.

I stared at her for a brief moment. "You're kidding."

She shook her head and fretted her eyebrows together. She was thinking. That seemed to cause her as much trouble as walking in the tight dress.

"Uh-uh," she said. "No kiddin'. I'm in pictures." A mild flush crept up under the layers of makeup. Her eyelids gave a slight flutter. "Leastwise, I'm gonna be. My agent says I'm gonna be a big star. Says he might just land me the lead in a new Zanuck picture."

I slit open a fresh pack of Luckies, shook one out and lit it, and tried to look suitably impressed. "A speaking part?"

"Yeah." She snapped her gum a couple of times, then paused. "Only my agent says I gotta practice. He says I ain't got good diction."

I shook my head. "The nerve of some people."

Her eyes widened, and she put the gum in neutral. "Yeah." She sat staring at me for a few seconds. Then her eyes narrowed, and the gum started again. "Say, whacha tryin' to do, gimmie the business? I know when I'm bein' kidded."

"Sorry," I said. "I left my manners in the laundry. What can I do for you, Miss James? It is *Miss* James, isn't it?"

"Yeah," she grinned. "It is for now. I got this boyfriend, and he wants to get married in the worst way, see? Only, I tell him he's gotta wait, 'cause my agent says them Hollywood big shots don't like it when a girl gets hitched. And I ain't lettin' nothin' spoil my big chance, see?" She leaned forward and put both hands on the front of the desk. "A fella oughta understand that, oughtn't he?"

"Sure he ought," I said. "Hollywood's full of boyfriends who sacrificed themselves for love."

She grinned, sat back in the chair, and worked on the gum. "Yeah. That's what I told him. So, he's coolin' his heels."

"Which is not why you came to see me, is it?"

Her eyes clouded, and she shook her head. "Uh-uh. My agent sent me."

She reached into her purse, brought out an unopened pack of cork-tipped cigarettes, opened it, and fitted one into her holder. Then she took out the wad of gum, wrapped it in a bit of tinfoil, and dropped it back in the purse.

I watched her take out a book of matches and eye the end of her cigarette. I thought it might be fun to see if her arms were long enough for her to light it. Instead, I struck a match and held it out to her. She leaned forward and puffed eagerly, the top of her dress falling open. I almost had to rearrange the desk to keep her torso from dragging in the ashtray.

She sat back in the chair and blew a pale cloud across the desk in my direction. "My agent says I should come and see you on accounta I got this little problem."

She watched me for a reaction. When I didn't give her any, she clamped the cigarette holder between her teeth and drew in on it hard. Her cheeks puffed out as if she were playing the oboe. She sat staring at me for a minute, her face slowly turning the color of uncooked fish. Then suddenly, she belched out the smoke and fell into a fit of coughing.

I put out the Lucky, then went over to the water cooler next to my filing cabinet and filled one of the paper cups. I handed it to her, and while she drank, I pulled the cigarette out of her holder and crushed it out in the ashtray. Then I sat down behind the desk again and watched as she pulled a handkerchief out of her purse and dabbed furiously at her eyes.

"You'd better lay off those things," I said. "They'll only stunt your growth."

She coughed a couple of times and shook her head. "I don't smoke. I only did it 'cause my agent said it would make me look sophisticated." She wiped the handkerchief over her face and held it up. There was enough rouge and lipstick on it to make it look as if she'd just given someone first aid. "And I don't really look like this. He said I should make myself up and dress this way so I'd look mature."

"He's just full of good advice," I said.

She twisted the handkerchief in her lap and stared down at it. Her voice had lost the sharp edge. "I guess you know I'm no actress either. I work at the Hot Foot. It's a dime-a-dance joint down on Fourteenth Street." She looked up at me, her tired eyes streaked with mascara. "But I wanna be an actress, and my agent says I got a good chance. I've even done a little modeling." She looked down again, and her voice trailed off. "That's really why I came to see you."

"How did you get my name?" I asked. "Did someone refer you, or did I just happen to be on the right page in the phone book?"

She shook her head. "No. It's like I said. My agent sent me. He says you're the best. He even gave me your card."

"Who's your agent?"

"His name's Paul Milton. He's an independent agent very exclusive. I met him at the Hot Foot just a couple of weeks ago. He liked me right away.

Said he was gonna take a personal interest in my career." She looked at me expectantly. "You've heard of him, haven't you?"

"No," I said. "But don't let that bother you. This town's full of people I never heard of."

She stared down and twisted the handkerchief again. "Oh, dear. I thought…Maybe I'd just better leave."

I sat and looked across the desk at her. Her face had the same pathetic look as all the other young faces. And her story would be the same as all the others.

"Since you're here," I said, "why not just tell me what kind of trouble you're in?"

She looked up, and her face started to brighten. "Oh, if you could help…"

She put away her handkerchief and took a deep breath that made her dress stand at attention. "It's about something that happened a while back. Ya see, I came here two summers ago, 'cause I figured if I was gonna be an actress, who'd notice me in Toledo? I went straight to Hollywood and tried to find work. Only it wasn't as easy as I expected."

I shook my head. "It never is."

She nodded. "It's really tough out here, ya know? I ran outta money in just two weeks. I mighta starved if I hadn't gotten this dance hall job. Anyway, I met this guy there who says he's a studio photographer and that he's willin' to spring for some publicity shots. Says I can't get nowhere in Hollywood if I ain't got some good shots to leave off at the agencies. So, I go to his studio and he takes all these pictures. Musta taken a coupla rolls. Then he says I can have all I want, for free. Only…only I gotta pose for some other pictures."

I said, "Uh-huh. And not the kind you'd want the people back in Toledo to see."

She clamped her jaw shut and shook her head. "I was so embarrassed. I'd never done anything like that." She looked up again with that same longing in her eyes I'd seen too many times before. "I figured I just had to go along and do what he asked. Mr. Garrett, you don't know what it means to me to get into pictures."

"Who's the photographer?"

"He said his name was Myron Weeks."

That was a name I knew. A sleazy character who kept a camera and a police band radio in his car. Whenever there was an accident call, he'd beat all the other jokers to the scene and shoot every bit of twisted wreckage and mangled flesh he could find. The more gruesome the pictures, the better. Most of them, even the tabloids, wouldn't take.

I lit up another Lucky and sat back in the chair. "So now that you've got an agent who thinks he can get you some real work, this guy Weeks pops up with a handful of photos of you in your birthday suit."

She nodded. "He called me last night."

"And he's willing to sell the pictures back to you."

"He wants $500 for the prints and the negatives."

I said, "Uh-huh. And what do you want from me?"

She inhaled deeply. "I'm supposed to meet him tonight when I get off work and give him the money. Then he says he'll give me the pictures." She inhaled again. "I was hoping you'd go along with me to his studio just to see there isn't any trouble and to make sure I get all the negatives."

I took a long drag on the Lucky. It tasted as old as her story. "Look, Miss James…"

She held up her hand and looked at me sheepishly. "Mr. Garrett, I'm afraid that's not my real name. Mr. Milton gave it to me. He said I'd never get anywhere with a moniker like Lorna Huffnagle."

I couldn't help smiling. Maybe this guy Milton had something after all.

"All right," I said. "But, look. Sugaring these people never solves anything. Even if I went with you, chances are Weeks would just make tracks. But if he did show and you did get your pictures, you still couldn't be sure of what you had. All he'd have to do is hold back a set of prints. From the positives, he could make more negatives and, from them, more prints. Then, before you know it, he'd be around again looking for another handful of C-notes."

I took another drag and watched her eyes fill with disappointment.

"Listen," I said. "Most of the agents and casting directors in this town are familiar with this kind of stunt. Some of them have even tried it themselves.

If the pictures are any good, they might help as much as not." I shrugged. "If they're not, or if your skin isn't thick enough, then maybe you and your boyfriend are better off back in Toledo."

"Oh, no," she said. "We couldn't go back there. My boyfriend's from L.A. Besides, I just couldn't face everybody. Please, Mr. Garrett. Mr. Milton says I should try to avoid any bad publicity. I trust him to do what's best for my career. Why, he's even putting up the five hundred dollars himself. And he says if you come with me, then this man Weeks won't dare try anything like this again."

She picked up her purse and rooted in it. Then she brought out several bills and laid them on the desk in front of me: three tens and a twenty. More money than I'm used to saying no to.

She looked across the desk at me uncertainly. "Mr. Milton gave me this and said I should give it to you. If it's not enough,..."

"It's more than enough," I said, "considering I probably can't do anything for you."

I sat there staring at the money and remembering Barbara Clavin's crack about my being a lousy businessman.

"How do I reach this Paul Milton?" I asked.

She hesitated. "But why do you want him?"

"If he's shelling out fifty bucks, he might have more of a reason than just some dirty pictures."

Her eyes clouded with worry, and she started to say something. I held up my hand and stopped her.

"Relax. It's just to let him know I'm taking an interest in your career too."

A sigh whistled out through her teeth, and she smiled. She took an eyebrow pencil and a scrap of paper from her purse and scribbled a number. Then she pushed it across the desk to me.

"He's unlisted," she said. "That's his number."

"Where's his office?"

Her eyebrows fretted again, and she poked at her bag self-consciously. "I don't know. He's kinda hard to reach. Guess he travels a lot. I've always met him at his house, a little place out on Lakeview Terrace."

"Uh-huh."

She put her hands on the desk and leaned forward again. "Mr. Garrett, I'm so grateful. Really. I just don't know how I'm going to be able to thank you."

I stood up and walked over by the door before my libido fell on its face. Two women were grateful, and I hadn't done anything.

"I'll check on this guy Weeks," I said. "Maybe I can get him to come clean. Where can I find you?"

She stood up, picked up the cigarette holder, and walked over next to me. "You really think you can get my pictures?"

"No promises."

She grinned. "Mr. Milton said you'd say that. I'll be workin'. Come by later, around ten-thirty." She moved into the outer office, then stopped and looked back. "You like to dance?"

I shrugged. "My feet are all thumbs."

She chuckled. "We'll see."

She turned and strolled out of the office, twirling the cigarette holder in her fingers. I listened to the sound of her heels clattering up the hall. You meet all kinds in Los Angeles.

I went back to the desk, put the money in an envelope, and wrote the name Lorna James on the front of it. Then I put the envelope in the office safe and picked up the phone. I tried the number she had given me. All it got me for my trouble was an answering service and an old hen who sounded as warm and friendly as a beat cop nursing a bunion. Yes, she'd give Mr. Milton my message when he called in. No, she hadn't heard from him today. No, she didn't know where to reach him. And I was an impertinent young man for wasting her time. She had important things to do. I told her to go and pour another one. She hung up.

I grabbed the phone book and thumbed through the yellow pages, looking at the listings for theatrical agents. No Paul Milton. Then I tried the residential listings and found no one named Milton on Lakeview Terrace. Somehow, I wasn't surprised. There was a chance he was legitimate. And there was a chance he and Weeks were playing a skin game that the folks hadn't heard of back in Toledo. Still, if it was a con, it had a new wrinkle. Lorna James wouldn't have enough money to interest a grifter. And unless Hollywood had changed since the last time I went to bed, she was as likely to star in a Zanuck picture as I was to be elected queen of the Rose Parade. But someone named Milton was willing to pay five hundred dollars of his own money to protect her career. That raised an obvious question. I had other things on my mind, but it was still early. And at a guess, I thought it might be fun looking for an answer.

Chapter Eight

I had no trouble finding Myron Weeks in the phone book. He lived on the second floor of a dingy apartment building just off Figueroa, down in the southern end of the city, the part of town you never read about in the travel folders. It was a crummy place in a crummy section, but for the kind of guy Weeks was, it seemed just right. The place had the rancid smell of something gone sour. The dusty-gray carpet covering the stairs had been partially eaten away by rats. And except for the sound of a radio blaring behind a door near the entrance, the building seemed deserted.

I found Weeks's apartment one flight up, his business card taped to the door. I stood there for almost five minutes hammering on the door until my knuckles hurt. There was no answer. Downstairs, where I'd heard the radio, the door had the word "Superintendent" stenciled on it. I knocked, and a bald, stocky man with a rumpled face answered. He wore an undershirt and had a half-burned cigarette in the side of his mouth, and he filled the corridor with the odor of stale beer.

The man had nothing to say until I offered him a picture of a president. Then he allowed as how he hadn't seen Weeks around for several days. He wasn't worried, though. The rent wasn't due until Monday. I thanked him, went outside, and figured I had come up with exactly nothing. The guy wouldn't have noticed anything that didn't need a bottle opener.

It wasn't quite eleven o'clock, so I decided to make another stop before heading uptown. It was only about eight blocks to Descanso. On the way, I stopped at a liquor store and bought a pint of gin. I figured I knew someone who'd be interested in drinking lunch. Five minutes later, I pulled up in front of the Hobart Arms.

Beatrice Almore squinted at me over the chain lock again. This time, when she saw me, her eyes lit up with a greedy twinkle, and she opened the door right away. She stood tottering and breathing heavily. Her hair was even weedier than the day before, and her face looked like a plate of worms.

"Well," she said. "Didn't take you long."

I held up the bottle. "I found a friend who could use some company."

Her fat face wound into a leer. "Come on in, dearie. Come right on in."

As I walked past her, she shut the door quickly, then grabbed the gin out of my hand. She prowled past the sofa and into a small kitchenette, where she rummaged around in a cupboard and brought out a couple of glasses. She poured about an inch and a half into each, then tipped her head back and took a long glug straight out of the bottle. Watching her almost made my teeth chatter. She tucked the bottle into the pocket of her bathrobe, gave it a comforting pat, and carried the two glasses back into the living room.

She handed one glass to me and held the other up in front of her. "Here's to good friends and no livin' relatives."

She threw the gin down her throat and then worked her way unsteadily over to the sofa and sat down. Her face twisted into something like a grimace, and she squinted at me. I guessed she was trying to be coy.

"Ain't you gonna sit down?"

"I can admire you better from here," I said.

She grinned and showed off a less-than-full set of yellow teeth. "You're a nice enough fella, bringin' me this jug and all. But you don't want poor old Bee to be drinkin' alone, do you?" She cackled half to herself. "Besides, a fella can't talk about money with his mouth all dry."

"What makes you think I want to talk about money?"

She gave me another squint. "You're here from that insurance company, ain't you? Come about Danny?"

I stared at her. A nice old woman. Easy to like. I was ready to be sick.

"Have another one," I said.

She twinkled some more and poured another dose into her glass, without quite taking the bottle out of the pocket of her robe. Then she drank half of that and pressed the bottle against her flank almost lovingly, like someone comforting a stray kitten. After a minute, her head rolled upright, and she spotted me watching her.

"Gotta keep this warm," she said. "He ain't happy if he ain't warm."

"I guess that means Danny Nugent isn't happy."

She slugged down the rest of the gin and made a burbling noise, her eyes rolling around like marbles tossed into a sink.

"I'll say he ain't happy. He's dead. Cops was here. Said somebody shot him."

She poured out some more of the gin and sampled it almost in a single motion. Then her face turned sour, and she stared into the glass.

"Why would somebody wanna do that? He was a right guy. Real polite, you know? Always called me 'Miss Bee.' Only one around here ever stopped and passed the time with me. How come somebody would wanna shoot him?"

"Maybe somebody wanted to keep him quiet," I said. "Did he ever talk about his business?"

She ran a set of gnarled fingers through her hair and frowned and thought about it. That pained her too much, and she stopped thinking and shook her head.

"You said a lawyer came to see him last week," I went on. "Did he say who he was?"

She went on shaking her head.

"Can you describe him?"

She assaulted her hair again. "I dunno. Kinda tall, dark, expensive suit."

Her eyes suddenly narrowed and took on a distant glint. She took another drink and looked at me over the glass. Her look had a hardness I hadn't seen before.

"How come you're askin' all these questions? Somethin' to do with the insurance?"

I put my glass down on the coffee table and grinned at her nastily. "You're a clever one."

She put down her glass and cackled again, this time louder. Her voice sounded like glass breaking. She brought her hands together in a clumsy tangle of fingers.

"Mister, if there's money in the room, I can smell it. Almost as much as I can smell…"

She began pawing around on the sofa as if she had just misplaced the Hope Diamond. Her hand fell on the bottle in her pocket, and she looked up and grinned sheepishly.

"Here he is. Still nice and warm." She brought the bottle out and clasped it to her with both hands. She began rocking slowly back and forth on the sofa while she looked at me. "So, what happens to the money now Danny's dead?"

I shrugged. "The insurance company might be willing to cough up if someone helps find the killer."

"Reward, huh? How much?"

"Depends on what the information is worth."

"Ahh," she snarled. "Them insurance companies don't pay out nothin' if they don't hav'ta."

She kept rocking. Her eyes were morose now, and her face was turning the color of marsh grass.

"Don't matter anyhow," she said, half to herself. "They shouldn't ought ta've done that to Danny. They shouldn't."

"Who shouldn't?"

"I dunno," she slurred. "Seems like he was always on the outs with somebody. Then this bum shows up."

"The lawyer?"

She nodded absently. She stared at me with glazed eyes. I could have been a hungry lion or a wooden Indian. It was all the same to her. She spoke in a voice as toneless as a crypt.

"Comes to the door and says he's gotta see Danny right away. Says there's gonna be trouble if he don't. Legal trouble and maybe worse. I follow him up to Danny's room, but I don't hear nothin'. Then, after a while, the guy leaves, and pretty soon, Danny comes out. I ask him what's wrong, but he just says, 'It's all right, Miss Bee. It's all right.' That's the last thing he ever says to me." She shook her head. "Only real company I had around this place."

"I'd like to have another look at his room," I said.

She sat and rocked. "Go ahead. It ain't locked. Cops took everything."

I started for the door, but her voice stopped me.

"Don't forget my reward, dearie." She let out a cackle that almost took the paint off the walls. "No, sir. Don't forget Miss Bee's reward."

I stood there for a minute and watched her. A washed-out old woman, alone and bitter clinging to memories of things she never had. She cared about what had happened to Nugent almost as much as she cared about Italian opera. I went out and shut the door behind me.

The boys from the station had done a job on Nugent's room. The bed was stripped, and the mattress rolled back. The dresser drawers were all pulled out and empty. Even the medicine chest looked naked. On the wall above the nightstand, someone had scrawled "1927" in pencil. The markings were faded and difficult to read. There was no telling how long it had been there.

I opened up the closet in the corner. Rawls's crew had left nothing in it but a wire coat hanger and a newspaper up on the ledge. I chuckled to myself and thought of all the old jokes about how cops can't read. Without even thinking about it, I took the newspaper down and glanced at it. It was the Tuesday morning edition, and it had a story about Joey Paris at the bottom of the front page. One of his runners had been picked up, and the D.A. was speculating on how long it would take him to pull the plug on Paris. There was a mention about Sterling Clavin. It said he couldn't be reached for comment.

I tossed the paper on the nightstand, but I used a little too much muscle. The paper slid off and went down to the floor, falling open to the back page. I leaned over and picked it up and felt a cold knot in my stomach. It was the kind of feeling you get when you lay down a flush and find the other guy's got a full house. Several of the back pages were in tatters, not torn but cut. Someone had carefully taken words out of several headlines and some ads. One of the ads showed a travel agency promoting tours, London, Naples, and one that was missing. It could have been Paris.

I put the paper down on the bed and went over to the window. I took out my pack of Luckies and deliberately got one out and deliberately lit it up and deliberately pushed things around in what passes for my mind: A down-at-the-heels dick is roughed up and shot in his office at about the time he's supposed to be meeting a ritzy attorney. This attorney stands up for one of the city's better-known tough boys. He also beats up his wife and otherwise makes himself scarce, which might be the result of his receiving threatening notes cut from newspapers. Now, what appears to be one of those papers turns up in the dead man's closet.

I didn't know what kind of connection Nugent had with Clavin, but it was starting to look like an ugly one. Fran had said that Nugent was a softhearted slob who liked everybody and would give his last nickel to a panhandler. I glanced over at the paper. There must have been one guy Nugent didn't like.

I leaned against the window and worked on my cigarette. I noticed that the shade was drawn all the way up to the top of the window and bunched unevenly around the roller. Something about the way it was wrapped struck me, like a roll of butcher paper with a thin strip of meat inside. I pulled the shade down slowly all the way over the sill, drawing it down as far as it would reach. On the last turn, a piece of stiff orange paper about the size of a matchbook slipped out and fluttered to the floor at my feet. I picked it up and looked at it. It was a ticket from a pawnshop in Laguna Beach.

I stood looking at the ticket and scraping my thumbnail across my front teeth. It probably didn't mean anything. It could have been there for years.

"Like hell," I said out loud.

I put the ticket in my pocket and went out of the room. Being lucky is better than being good.

* * *

The drive out to West Hollywood took better than an hour. On the way, I stopped at one of the dozens of hash houses that squatted along the strip. For six bits, I got elbowed and jostled for the right to a stool at the lunch counter, and a few minutes with a cup of coffee and a hamburger you wouldn't feed to a lizard.

It had gone that way since the War. A lot of new places had sprung up, catering to the hurry-up crowd. Run in and slap down your money, and they'll throw the food at you. But don't try to sit there and eat it. Just get the hell out of the way. Real restaurants were slowly being outnumbered. They were being replaced by diners and cheap cafes, and now even drive-ins places you could drive into and eat without getting out of your car. And California was made for them. A state that for years had thought only to take its time and enjoy the sea and sunshine had now somehow made up its mind to do it all on wheels.

After sparring with lunch and wishing I'd stopped for a drink instead, I drove the remaining few miles out to Laurel Avenue. The building where Clavin had his office was a marvel of postwar construction steel framed and square with panels of tinted glass, like an ice cube tray stood on end. It sat in the middle of the West Hollywood business district, a place where more money changes hands every day than in any other town west of Chicago. A small fleet of limousines lined the street in front of the building, with a cadre of uniformed chauffeurs idly dusting and polishing the cars and ignoring each other.

It was quarter of two when I parked the Buick across the street and got out. I walked past the limousines and up a carefully laid flagstone walk lined with well-barbered hedges and then through an over-large set of revolving doors. The lobby inside was tall and square and as warm as aspic. A floor of black marble glistened like a hockey rink under walls tiled with alternating squares of polished granite and alabaster. Two large steel doors that I took to be elevator entrances stood on either side of a building directory at the back of the lobby. One large security guard with a good piece of iron strapped to his hip stood directly behind a desk just in front of the directory. He drew a bead on me with a baleful stare as I entered. Then, as I neared the desk, he yawned and silently disapproved of my suit.

When I told him I was there to see Sterling Clavin, the guard eyed me suspiciously and picked up a phone on the desk. He mumbled something into it, waited a moment, then hung up. He pointed to a large open notebook that resembled a hotel register next to the phone and told me to sign in. I wrote my name under an entry made by Ernest Paddington of Dent and Schlimmer, Inc. When I finished, the guard looked at the book and growled at me.

"You didn't write the name of your firm."

"You couldn't pronounce it," I said and walked into one of the elevators.

The building directory had told me that Clavin's office was on the top floor, nine stories up. I was alone in the elevator. That made it a nice ride.

It had only been a hunch that had first made me want to meet Sterling Clavin. Maybe I had gotten the hunch from something Rawls had said, or Fran, or Barbara Clavin. Or maybe it was from something they hadn't said. Now it didn't seem to matter. All I could think about was an old newspaper, a pawn ticket, and Nugent at his desk.

The elevator throbbed quietly and then stopped, and the doors rolled noiselessly open. I stepped into a hallway as wide as Wilshire Boulevard, with a thick-piled gray carpet, recessed overhead lighting, and cork-lined walls. Directly across the hall from the elevator was a set of massive double doors of polished maple, with "Clavin & Marcus" printed on them in two-inch high gold letters. I waded across the carpet and tried one of the doors. It gave a little and then seemed to run into something. There was a definite thump followed by a rustling noise, and the door opened. I went inside.

It was a wide office of the modern type, with more recessed lighting, several tall potted ferns, and low furniture that was an uncomfortable-looking mix of chromium and plush brown leather. On the walls were several familiar seascape paintings, and on the back wall were two large unmarked doors. A wooden secretary's desk stood in front of the doors, holding a typewriter, a couple of telephones, and an assortment of the usual office clutter. The desk had a nameplate reading "S. Anders" on top of it, and it had a girl on the floor in front of it.

She was sitting upright with her back against the desk, legs splayed in front of her, and a dazed expression on her face. I placed her in her early twenties, but she looked like someone who could just as easily pass herself off as being older and probably had. She had raven hair and milky skin covering broad but delicate features, and her eyes were Nile green. She was wearing a crimson blouse with long sleeves and a ruffled collar and a beige skirt spotted with white powder. On the floor in front of her were more spots of powder and next to them a compact, a small makeup brush, and a magazine.

As I came through the door, she looked up at me unsteadily and began rubbing her forehead. A small red knot was beginning to form just over her left eye. I squatted down next to her and felt her pulse. She didn't move, but her pulse did, so I figured she was alive and not going into shock.

I picked up the magazine between her feet and looked at it. It was off-size and cheaply printed, the kind you get from the mail-order houses. There was a drawing of a magnifying glass and a pair of handcuffs on the front, and across the top, it said, "How To Be A Criminal Investigator," by C. D. Burnham. Inside the cover was a picture of a skinny character with glasses and a bow tie pointing to a framed certificate on a wall behind him. Under that was the familiar pitch: "Earn big money helping to enforce the law. Become a detective in twelve easy lessons."

I dropped the magazine, dabbed my fingers in the white powder, and sniffed it. It was talcum. I looked back at the door. There were traces of the powder around the doorknob. I stood up and tried not to laugh.

The girl angled her head and looked up at me, still rubbing the spot over her eye. "Where did you come from?"

"I came with the thirteenth lesson," I said. "Don't try dusting the knob with the door closed."

She looked bleakly over at the door, then down at the spots of powder in front of her. "I was only practicing." She picked up the magazine and began pointing at it insistently. "It says you can find latent fingerprints in ordinary talcum powder. Then, you can lift them off with clear plastic tape and save them as evidence. That way, you can keep them almost indefinitely, so they'll be good in court months, even years later."

"You can," I agreed, "if you happen to have talcum powder and clear plastic tape with you and if you can manage to lift the prints without getting conked. Of course, anything you get isn't likely to be worth much, because a doorknob is about the worst place to try and take a set of prints. First, because a lot of people use it. Second, because when they do, they tend to grab it with the palm more than the fingers. That leaves only a partial print and one that's likely to be smeared."

She wrinkled her forehead and kept pointing at the magazine. "But it says..."

I just grinned at her and nodded. She didn't like that.

"And just what makes you so smart?"

I shrugged. "I always read Dick Tracy."

She started to say something, then stopped. Her mouth hung open, and the wrinkles disappeared from her forehead. "You're Mr. Garrett!"

"Well," I said. "You have been practicing, haven't you?"

She scooped up the brush and compact, dropped them with the magazine on the desk just above her head, then bolted upright. She inhaled as if to speak, but before she could get anything out, her eyes began rolling, and the color trickled out of her face like water running off a tin roof. She tottered sideways for a second, then pitched forward against my chest. I caught her under the arms and held her upright against me as her head rolled over on my shoulder.

Just at that moment, the door on the left opened, and a slender, dark-haired man in a gray suit stepped through it. He started for the desk and then glanced up and saw the two of us in a clinch. A mixture of shock and embarrassment started doing handsprings all over his face, as if he'd just walked in on his grandmother while she was making time with the mailman.

"Oh! Pardon me," he blurted.

Before I could say anything, he turned and disappeared back through the door, shutting it behind him.

I took a quick look around the office. There was a low divan along the wall on the left behind a glass-top coffee table with a display of the usual outdated magazines. I dragged the girl over to it, laid her out, and began looking around for a water cooler. I didn't find any. I was about to go out and look in the hall when she began to stir.

"Unnh," she murmured. "What happened?"

"Lesson fourteen," I said. "When you've been hit on the head, don't be in a hurry to get up."

"How long was I out?"

"Not long."

"Did anyone see me?"

"A skinny character in that office over there." I nodded over my shoulder.

"That's Mr. Marcus. He won't say anything. Just so long as Mr. Clavin didn't see me."

She swung her legs over the edge of the divan and sat up. She planted her elbows on her knees, held up her hands, and rested her head on them.

"Oh, Mr. Garrett. I'm so embarrassed. I've been looking forward to meeting you all morning. I didn't even have lunch. I was so nervous."

She rubbed her hand on the back of her neck and then looked up at me. Her eyes had the look of a kid kept after school. "You see, I'm studying to be a detective. I've never had a chance to meet a real one, and I thought…That is, I was hoping that I…that you would…"

"Tell you all about it?"

She sucked her lower lip in under her teeth and nodded.

"You wouldn't like it," I said.

"Oh, but I would." She stood up, a little unsteady but not ready to pass out. "Really, I would."

I pushed my hat back on my head and looked at her. She was a funny little thing who barely came up to my chin and who stared at me with soft green eyes that said she could still believe in Peter Pan. But her expression didn't go with the rest of her. From the neck down, she had a chassis with all the right equipment. And I'd have given odds it worked in all the right ways.

"Look, Miss…Anders?"

She nodded. "Stephanie."

"All right," I said. "You work in a nice office in a nice part of town. You get to wear nice clothes and meet nice people. What I do isn't nice. It's dark and dirty and sometimes even dangerous. If you're not satisfied here, take up stamp collecting, go to the beach, or better still find yourself a man."

She flushed all the way to the temples. "But you don't understand."

"What I understand is that I've got an appointment with Sterling Clavin."

Her hands flew up against her cheeks. "Oh, my gosh. I almost forgot." She brought up her arm and glanced at a wristwatch that was about as wide as a piece of string. "It's all right. It's just two o'clock."

She darted over to the desk and punched a button on an intercom unit. "Mr. Clavin, Mr. Garrett is here for your two o'clock appointment."

There was a long pause followed by a low growl from the unit. "Tell him to wait."

She looked up at me apologetically. "He doesn't usually see people, at least people who aren't his clients. And he isn't taking on any new clients."

"How did I earn such a privilege?"

She came around the desk and stood in front of me wide-eyed. She spoke almost in a whisper, as if she were letting me in on some kind of secret.

"I told him you had something vitally important to talk to him about," she said. "That you had information that might directly relate to one of his biggest clients and that it had to do with that killing down on Paloma Place."

I folded my arms and stared at her. She was either a lot smarter than she had first seemed, or she was just brainless and lucky. Both possibilities suddenly looked very dangerous.

"Just how many lessons have you finished?" I asked.

Before she could answer, the intercom unit made a soft buzz. She went quickly around the desk and pressed the button again. "Yes, sir?"

The same growl said, "Send him in."

Chapter Nine

The office was an odd mixture of the new and the old. The same recessed fixtures overhead dropped the same pale antiseptic lighting on more of the same chromium furniture. To the right, a row of bookcases held the obligatory law volumes, and on the left, the wall was covered with framed certificates and diplomas the trademarks of a practicing attorney. On the near wall by the door, a large ornate frame held a photograph of a cabin cruiser. It didn't look like much, no larger than the Queen Mary. The name "Albacore" was painted on the side.

The picture hung above another divan and several chairs that were arranged in a semi-circle around a low driftwood table with a glass top. A tall, polished brass sextant stood in the middle of the table, attached to a wide bowl that I took to be an ashtray. The furniture faced across to the far side of the room, where an antique wooden desk the size of a small moving van sat a good six inches off the floor on a kind of dais. There was a picture window behind the desk that took up most of the far wall. And there was a man behind the desk who took up a good part of the window.

Standing on the dais, Sterling Clavin looked about eight feet tall. He stood with his back to me, his hands folded behind him. He had black hair, wore a navy-blue suit, and stood staring out over a sun-streaked vista of the Hollywood Hills like Charles Laughton on the bridge of the Bounty. He stood without moving or speaking for a full minute after I entered. Finally, a low voice with a sound like distant cannon fire rolled across the room.

"You may sit down, Mr. Garrett."

I dropped my hat on the table next to the ashtray, shoved my hands in my pockets, and just stood and waited.

"Not a bad view from up here," the voice went on, "but it's nothing like the ocean. A man needs to feel the ocean moving under him, see it stretching to the horizon. There are no boundaries on the ocean. Only freedom and power."

Suddenly, he turned away from the window and trained the full stare of his gunpowder eyes on me.

"The captain of a ship is like the ruler of a nation," he said. "His power is almost limitless; his every command obeyed without question."

I looked him over for a minute. He was on the high side of forty and carrying it well. He had a broad, even face, with a square jaw and a slightly cleft chin. His mouth seemed unusually small, with deep creases at the corners. And there were more creases around the eyes, where the skin was beginning to show that leathery look that comes from too much time in the sun. He was a big man, my height and a little more. His large frame carried a lot of weight that might have been like granite once but now could be getting soft without quite showing through an expensive suit.

He walked around and stood beside the desk, still looking down at me from the dais. "I said you could sit."

"Shouldn't I get your permission to come aboard first?"

Clavin stepped down off the dais and walked over in front of me. He stood grim-faced and close enough, so I could count the little white anchors on his powder blue tie. The tie was held in place by a gold pin with an emerald as big as a chestnut. He slowly brought up two large, meaty hands, carefully stretching his arms out of his jacket sleeves and revealing a pair of brilliant emerald cuff links. He reached inside the jacket, brought out a box of Players cigarettes, and offered one to me. I took it.

From his side pocket, Clavin produced a gold lighter with a handful of green stones set into the side forming the pattern of a star. I didn't have to guess what kind of stones they were. He lit my cigarette, then his, then held up the lighter admiringly.

"I like emeralds," he said. "They remind me of the ocean."

"They remind me of money," I said.

The corners of his mouth twitched upward slightly, and he nodded. "Perhaps that, too. Money is, after all, simply power in another form. But the power of money is limited; it has no real value until it's spent. Then, once it is spent, the value of the money is gone, and, therefore, its power. The secret is to use the limited power of money to accumulate real power, the power of the ship's captain."

"And what does the captain do with all this power?"

The dark eyes narrowed. "He claims the ocean as his. And he... commands."

He flicked an ash into the brass bowl and motioned toward the divan. Then, without looking at me, he walked over and settled into one of the chairs on the far side of the table. I sat down on the divan and watched him.

Clavin crossed his legs, blew a lungful of smoke across the table, and eyed me with the indulgent air of a night court judge.

"I know who you are," he said. "What do you want?"

"I came to offer you a trade."

"Amusing," he said without smiling. "Go on."

I took a drag on the Players and flicked the ash into the bowl. "I thought you might have some information about a detective named Nugent, who was murdered last Monday night. I want to know what he was working on. And I want to know what kind of connection he had to Joey Paris or, for that matter, to any of Paris's playmates."

Clavin shifted slightly in the chair and held his cigarette up in front of him. He eyed it with a kind of idle curiosity and spoke to it as if I were no longer in the room.

"Assuming I had this information and were to give it to you, what would you be offering me in return?"

"First," I said, "I can tell you what the police already know about the killing. Second, I can tell you what they don't know but soon will. You can add the rest up for yourself. That should buy you some time to prepare a defense. With a Grand Jury investigation of Paris going on, I figure time might be important to you."

"And what makes you think I might need a defense?"

88

I drew in a quarter inch of the Players and let the smoke casually drift over the table. "What I think doesn't matter. But murder tends to make the cops a little cranky."

"Are you insinuating…?"

"Insinuating is for people with money," I said. "I don't make enough to insinuate anything."

He took a long drag and blew the smoke in my direction. "Just what is your interest in all this?"

"Let's just say I have a client who doesn't like loose ends."

Clavin took a concluding drag on the cigarette and crushed the butt out in the bowl. Then he placed his fingers together in an arch and tapped the point of the arch against his chin. "And if I refuse your offer?"

I shrugged again. "The police will have the whole story eventually, and so will the papers. It's only a matter of time."

He sat without moving for a long moment, then slowly rose. His eyes turned shiny and hard. His large hands balled into fists. His voice came out like a clap of thunder.

"What you're suggesting could be considered extortion!"

I shrugged again. "Not enough to bruise anyone. I'm only asking for information that you'll eventually have to spill to the cops anyway. And I'm not threatening to do anything but go away and mind my own business."

The anger in his face moved away as quickly as it had come. A smirk etched itself into the corners of his mouth. "An unusual attitude for a detective."

"So I've been told."

Clavin walked slowly around and stood behind his chair, leaning on it. His face held the same intensity of expression I imagined he would use on a jury.

"Now I will tell you how things really are," he said. There was a sneer in his voice. "You are nothing but a cheap private detective who was dismissed from the police force. Apart from your military record for serving in the Pacific, there is nothing to distinguish you but a rented apartment, a run-down office in the Patterson Building, and a marginal investigative practice that consists mostly of looking for stolen property and scurrying after bail jumpers. At this moment, in fact, I imagine that you are working for that Brekhammer woman. You drive a run-down old Buick. You wear run-down old clothes. And you have no real friends of any consequence."

He straightened up and began pacing around the room. His voice heightened. "I, on the other hand, have all the things you do not: wealth, position, influence. I am a professional man and a public figure. I have many friends on the police force, in state and local government, and in the business community. In short, I have power."

He stopped pacing and glared at me. He was now bellowing with rage.

"Did you really think you could come in here and threaten me? With one phone call, I could deprive you of your license and have you thrown out on the street. What would you say to that offer?"

I took a last drag and slowly stubbed out the remains of the cigarette. "I'd probably have hysterics."

Before he could respond, a buzzer sounded on top of the desk. Clavin stepped onto the dais, pressed a button, and spoke impatiently into the intercom. "Yes?"

Stephanie's prim little voice floated into the room. "There's a call for you, Mr. Clavin. It's a Mr. Stark."

"Tell him I'll call him back," he said abruptly. Then he straightened, turned back toward me, and resumed his glare.

I stood up and picked up my hat. "Sorry I bothered you, Mr. Clavin. I came here with the goofy idea that you might need help, that maybe somebody was trying to fit you into a frame. But you don't need anybody's help. You're a professional man. You've got important people to see, like Joey Paris and Lefty Stark. You don't need anything. You've already got it all, including a possible murder rap. Only don't waste your time trying to impress me. Save it for the D.A."

I put my hat on and started for the door. I didn't quite get there.

"Mr. Garrett, wait."

I turned and looked at him. He rubbed his hands together and slowly stepped down off the dais. A hint of uneasiness tiptoed into his expression.

"Perhaps we should talk further," he said. "Please sit down."

I hesitated, then took off my hat and dropped it back on the table. I sat down on the divan again and watched him settle back into the chair.

"All right," I said. "Talk."

He folded his hands slowly, deliberately and then spoke to me the same way. "If you will give me the information for my…defense, I promise to tell you what I can, that is without violating the confidence of a client."

"How do I know you won't just give me the bum's rush?"

He waved a hand at me impatiently. "You have my word. And the word of a ship's captain is irrevocable." He eased back in the chair. A note of reluctance entered his voice. "Besides, it's possible that I may need to employ you."

"Would I have to change my suit?"

He gave another testy wave with his hand. "Just get on with it."

"All right," I said. "Let's see where it goes." I pulled out a Lucky and took my time lighting it. "To begin with, the cops have Danny Nugent,another cheap detective in his office, apparently shot to death during a fight with a very large man. The indications are that Nugent was shot sometime late Monday. In his desk, they find his appointment book with your name written in for eight that evening, and that's the last in the book. Next, the cops talk to the landlady at Nugent's apartment. From her, they hear that a man claiming to be a lawyer visited Nugent several days before he was killed. And they hear that this man was threatening trouble."

I paused and took an easy drag on the Lucky. Clavin just sat and watched me without moving so much as an eyelash.

"If they haven't already," I went on, "the cops will soon be talking to someone who spoke with Nugent the day he was killed. They'll hear that Nugent claimed he was meeting with a client that evening to wrap up a big case. Then they'll be given a note that Nugent left, saying that this man was rich and powerful with what Nugent called a lot of downtown grease and that this man could be coming to kill him."

Clavin's jaw tightened. A large dark vein stood out on the side of his neck.

"Finally," I said, "the cops will talk to the cheap private detective with the run-down Buick. From him, they'll learn that they overlooked a newspaper in Nugent's apartment, one with several words clipped out words that could have been pasted together to form a note. And it would be just the kind of note that might be used for a death threat or a kidnapping…or blackmail."

Clavin swallowed hard and rubbed his hands together. Then, abruptly, he got out of the chair, climbed up behind the desk, took out a key, and unlocked one of the drawers. From this, he took two folded pieces of paper. He stood for a minute, tapping them against his thumbnail. Then he stepped off the dais and handed them to me.

"You'd better have a look at these," he said.

I unfolded the papers and found two notes made from words cut out of newspapers. They both said the same thing: Quit the Paris case, or its curtains. I dropped the notes on the table.

"When did you get these?"

Clavin sat slowly down in the chair again. "Last week. They came about three days apart."

"Do they mean anything to you?"

He shook his head. "Only that someone doesn't want me to defend Mr. Paris."

"Any idea why not?"

He shook his head again.

"In your business, you must get these all the time," I said.

He snorted and then glowered down at the table. "Phone calls notes handwritten or typed but never in pairs and never like this. Someone went to some trouble to make sure these notes couldn't be traced."

"The police might trace them," I said. "But I gather you haven't been to see them."

He gave me a grim smirk. "And if I did? In light of what you've just told me, what do you think the police would say about all this?"

"Nothing you'd like." I took a final pull on the Lucky and crushed out the rest in the bowl. "From what I can see, you don't stand very well with the police. I think they'll have no trouble believing that Nugent had something on you and that he was using it to blackmail you. The notes would have been to conceal his identity. But somehow, you found out he was the one sending the notes, so you went to his apartment to get him to lay off. When he didn't, you arranged to meet him at the office. Maybe you just figured you'd shake the goods out of him. But there was a struggle, and in the struggle, there was a gun. After Nugent was plugged, you panicked and tried to make it look like suicide. Then you beat it out of there without stopping to look in his desk and find the appointment book. After all, Nugent was just a deadbeat who probably wouldn't be missed. And who would connect him with someone like you?" I shook my head. "I don't think the cops will have any trouble believing that story."

Clavin folded his hands and nodded slowly. A strange sort of calm settled into his face. "It's all circumstantial, of course. But I'm afraid you may be right. It's not conclusive, but it could be enough to put before a jury."

"How well did you know Nugent?"

"I didn't," he said. "I never met him. I never even heard of him until last night when I was accosted by a police detective named Rawls. And I certainly made no appointment with him."

"Where were you the night Nugent was killed?"

He hesitated. "I was having dinner with…a client."

"Uh-huh. And if that client was Joey Paris, the D.A. will have no trouble convincing a jury that Paris would say anything to protect you."

He grabbed the arms of his chair and thrust his chin forward at me. "Now, see here!"

"Skip it," I said. "What could Nugent have had on you?"

His voice grew icicles. "Mr. Garrett, I am not in the habit of giving people cause to blackmail me."

I shrugged. "It sometimes happens even without cause. What would Nugent have been to Joey Paris?"

This time he shrugged. "Nothing that I know of. Mr. Paris has never mentioned him."

"Who else might be interested in having you dump *Mr.* Paris?"

He rubbed his hands together again, and his gaze drifted up to the ceiling. He thought for a moment, then brought out his words as carefully as an out-of-work showgirl takes off her last pair of nylons.

"Considering the reputation Mr. Paris has, one could conclude that any number of people might not wish him well."

"And one could conclude that these people might include some of your clients?"

He nodded slowly. "It's possible."

"And it's possible that one of them might be Lefty Stark?"

He inhaled and let his breath out heavily. "I really can't say any more."

"All right," I said. "What can you say about wanting to hire me?"

He got up from the chair and began pacing again. Deep creases wrinkled his forehead. He was thinking. He seemed to be a man with a lot to think about. Finally, he stopped in front of the desk, turned, and looked at me with the same hint of uncertainty in his eyes.

"I believe you mentioned that someone might be trying to frame me," he said. "What makes you think that?"

I inhaled slowly and crossed my legs, as if I had a reason that was worth listening to. "Nothing specific. You have a reputation for being a smart lawyer. Whoever killed Nugent left a trail that was easy to follow. That wasn't smart."

"Don't you think the police would conclude the same thing?"

"They might," I agreed. "But I could be wrong. The police might point out that you also have a reputation for having a violent temper and that when a man gets his dander up, he stops thinking. They might say that Nugent backed you into a corner and made you mad. They might say that someone who likes to throw his weight around the way you do could easily kill a nobody like Nugent."

The ruddy color in his face deepened. He leaned back in his chair and scraped his voice off the back of his throat. "I *am* being framed, and I want you to prove it."

"And just how do I do that?"

"That is your affair," he said. "How much do you charge?"

I stood up and gave him a nasty grin. "I'm cheap, remember? Thirty bucks a day plus expenses."

He got up and returned to the desk and pulled a large leather-bound checkbook out of the top drawer. He scribbled for a minute, tore out one of the checks, then stepped down and held it out to me.

"Two hundred dollars," he said. "I have just a week until the Grand Jury convenes; after that I expect to be very busy. So that's how long you have to find out who is trying to frame me and to obtain the necessary proof. If you require more money, let me know."

"Are you expecting an indictment?" I asked.

He gave me a blank stare and pushed the check toward me again.

I put on my hat and grinned at him once more. "Put it in the mail. That'll give me time to think about whether I really want it."

His face turned the color of a cooked eggplant. He folded the check in half and stretched it tight between his fingers. Then he ground his teeth and glared at me.

"Mr. Garrett, let's understand each other. I require your services because I am pressed for time. If it were not so, you would not have so much as set foot in this office. I possess wealth and power and property, and I will protect what is mine, both professional and personal. If you are not up to the job, then I will find someone who is. Meanwhile, what I said about you still stands. I offer no apologies."

"Aye, aye," I said and gave him a mocking salute.

Then I turned, opened the door, and walked out of the office.

Chapter Ten

Stephanie was sitting behind her desk, writing something on a pad. In front of the desk was the same thin character in the gray suit. He was a slightly built man, about five-ten, with fluid green eyes set into angular features, a pencil-thin mustache, and jet-black hair slicked back in the style of Rudolph Valentino. He was standing beside a leggy blonde in a tight cameo pink dress, a luxful smile, and an anemic-looking moleskin hat that dangled an ostrich feather over her right ear. She had distant lapis lazuli eyes and too much makeup, and she had long fingers with cardinal red nails that were clutching the arm of the man next to her. She kept her lips pressed tight together, and her eyes danced around the room, moving like fireflies in the night, as if she wanted to avoid looking directly at anyone.

As I approached the desk, the man spoke to Stephanie in a reedy voice. "And I want you to make a reservation for me at The Pillars for eight-thirty this evening—for two." He reached up and gave the cardinal nails a comforting pat.

Stephanie nodded, made another note, then looked up and saw me. "Oh, Mr. Garrett." She stood up and motioned toward the front of the desk. "This is Mr. Anthony Marcus, Mr. Clavin's partner." She turned and spoke to the man with something that resembled admiration. "Mr. Garrett is a private detective."

The man extracted his arm from the fingernails, stretched out a tight, professional smile, and thrust out his hand. I shook it. He had the firm practiced handshake of an alderman running for re-election. He cleared his throat with an effort.

"How do you do," he said. "I haven't seen you around the office before. Are you working on one of Sterling's cases?"

"Could be, if there is a case to work on."

One of his eyelids drooped, and his mouth turned up quizzically. He started to say something, but the blonde grabbed his arm again. He looked at her, then reluctantly back at me. He cleared his throat once more.

"Mr. Garrett," he said. "This is Mrs. Beverly Cornish—one of our clients."

The blonde glanced furtively in the direction of my tie, nodded, and tightened her grip on Marcus's arm.

"Tony," she twittered. "Can't we just go and talk about the case?"

"By all means." Marcus nodded to me, tossed Stephanie a sideways glance, then projected his voice as if he were speaking in a union hall. "Right this way, Mrs. Cornish. We want to go over every detail of your settlement demands."

The two of them turned and strolled briskly out of the office without looking back.

Stephanie leaned forward on the desk and scowled in the direction of the door. "Who does he think he's fooling?"

"About what?"

She straightened and folded her arms and kept scowling. "They're not going to talk about any settlement. They're just going to...to...You know."

I chuckled. "How do you know they're going to 'you know'?"

She looked at me with a shade of disbelief. "Well, you saw them leave. He wasn't carrying a briefcase. Whenever Mr. Clavin or Mr. Marcus go to a business meeting, they always take a notebook or a pad, something to make notes on. Then, they bring the notes back and have me type them up for the file. And they *always* carry a briefcase."

"All right," I said. "So what if he's going off to snap her garter? She looks old enough."

Stephanie made a sputtering noise, then gave me a look that could have punctured my spleen. "Do you have to be so crude?"

"That's the kind of guy I am. What does Marcus do around here?"

She glowered and folded her arms a little tighter. "He handles divorce cases—nothing else. And all his clients are young, attractive women...with money." She snorted disdainfully. "If you ask me, he's interested in more than just business."

"Careful, darling. Your cat whiskers are showing."

She reddened all the way to the floor. "Why, I never...Why should I...?"

"Relax," I said. "If you insist on being such a good detective, there may not be enough work left for the rest of us."

The anger ran out of her face as if someone had pulled the plug. "Do you really think so?" She stood entranced for a moment, then caught herself and flushed again. "Oh, I see. You're teasing me."

I shrugged. "Not enough to drop a stitch over. How long have you been working here, Stephanie?"

"Just two weeks. Why?"

"I guess that's why you've never met a real detective."

She nodded. "You're the first one."

"And you've been here every day for two weeks?"

She nodded again.

"Did a guy named Nugent come up here about ten days ago? A sandy-haired character in shabby clothes?"

She glanced at my suit. "You mean like...?" She shook her head quickly. "No. No one like that has come into the office since I've been here." A glimmer of fascination sidled into the corners of her eyes and perched there for a while. "Is that part of the case you're working on?"

I put on my hat and started for the door. "I don't know, Stephanie. I don't even know if I am working on a case."

She bolted around the desk and stopped me. "Mr. Garrett, what about your meeting with Mr. Clavin? I mean, how was it?"

"It was a pleasure."

She grinned and wrinkled her nose like a kitten sniffing the wind. "No, silly. I mean, did you learn anything...about the killing?"

"Not much," I said. "How do you know about it?"

She kept grinning. Her green eyes flashed streaks of light. "Well, when I told Mr. Clavin what you said about Paloma Place, he suddenly became very interested in meeting you. Then, after I hung up, I noticed a newspaper over there on the coffee table. I think it was Mr. Clavin's. It was open to the obituaries, and I saw the item about that man Nugent being killed." Her voice fell into a whisper. "Do you think Mr. Clavin could have done it?"

"What do you think?"

Her eyebrows fretted together, and she wrinkled her nose again. "He's very gruff. I suppose he…" She shrugged. "I guess I just don't know."

"Might be better to keep it that way," I said and turned back toward the door.

"Wait!"

Stephanie went back to the desk, scribbled something on a piece of paper, and handed it to me. "Here. It's my address and phone number. Please call me."

"What for?"

"I want to know what you find out about the killing and how you solve the case. I really do want to be a detective."

"Is that all?"

Her face went blank. "What do you mean?"

I shrugged. "You could have been making a pass at me. It's been known to happen."

I turned and went out of the office and left her standing there with her mouth hanging open.

* * *

The sun was searing the pavement as I left the office building. The palm trees along the sidewalk hung limp in the still air, like mops put out to dry. Off in the distance, a line of tall clouds, the undersides tinted purple-black, began forming around the far end of the mountains north of the city. With any luck, they might mean rain and breathable air. I went across the street to the Buick, tossed my hat and suit jacket in the front seat, rolled down the window, and climbed in. The steering wheel blistered my hands as I pulled out and headed back downtown.

I drove into the center of the city and left the Buick across Main Street from City Hall—a palace of unrefined Art Deco in limestone. It was abutted by an annex the cops called home, where the politicians and soft-handed high rollers made their rounds by day and the drunks and good-time girls lolled uneasily by night. Upstairs in the back corner of the annex, I found the squad room mostly empty, rows of gray metal desks littered with folders and phone slips and dirty ashtrays and paper cups half full of curdling coffee. In the back of the room, a pebbled glass door carried black stenciled lettering that read, "Detective Captain B. Thornhill."

Rawls was sitting at his desk just in front of the door, staring at the contents of a Manila folder and chewing on the end of his unlit cigar as if his jowls needed a good workout. I walked up the aisle formed by the desks and sat down in a straight wooden chair beside him. He didn't look at me. He just grunted and kept on chewing.

"With concentration like that, you must be reading the funnies," I said.

He aimed a go-to-hell glance in my direction, then grunted again. He turned a page in the folder, sighed, and closed the folder on top of the desk. He took out the cigar and placed it carefully beside the folder. Finally, he put his elbows on the desk, hands flat in front of him, and gave me that empty-eyed stare that cops use when they think they have something you don't.

"Well, the suicide theory's been shot all to hell," he said. "Not even Brice believes it now. Nugent was shot with a .32, not a .38. Pierced his left lung and nicked the lower left ventricle. Coulda died in anywhere from twenty seconds to twenty minutes."

"So, he could have had time to put one in the guy who shot him?"

"Could've," he drawled. "Odds are he didn't, though. We checked every trace of blood in the office. All B-positive. Nugent's type. Nothin' else."

"Did you find the slug from the .38?"

He shook his head. "Nope. The place was clean. No slug and no prints, except Nugent's and yours."

I crossed one leg over the other and examined my fingernails. "Have you talked to Fran?"

He nodded. "She came in this morning and gave me that note you found." He squinted at me, and his voice turned crusty. "Thanks for holdin' out on me, gumshoe."

I shrugged. "The envelope was sealed, and there was no telling if it had anything to do with the killing. I was acting in the interest of a client. I told her she'd have to turn the note over to you."

Rawls leaned back in the chair, folded his arms, and snorted at me. "I could burn your ass for that. And if it was anybody besides Fran, I would." A slow smile edged up from under his shirt collar. "But that note plus Nugent's appointment book should help us tie a string on *Mister* Clavin."

"How do you know it's not a fake? Anybody could have written Clavin's name in that book. How do you know someone's not trying to build a frame?"

His smile widened. "Uh-uh. We showed the book and the note to a handwriting expert downstairs. He says they were both written by the same person. And Fran swears it's Nugent's handwriting." The smile moved into a gloat. "She says she'll testify to that in court."

I shrugged again. "So what does that prove?"

He leaned forward on the desk and growled at me. "It proves there ain't no frame-up, for one thing. Fran says Nugent was workin' on a case, wrappin' it up Monday night. So maybe he calls Clavin and sets up a meeting for eight. But then he gets cold feet, figures maybe he's in over his head. He writes this note thinkin' he's gonna use it for insurance. Only Clavin shows up and plugs him before Nugent can tell him about the note."

I went back to studying my nails. "How could Nugent use the note for insurance? It was still in his desk. All Clavin had to do was take it."

"I dunno," he snapped. "Nugent wasn't the brightest citizen around. Maybe he figures to try and bluff his way through, only Clavin doesn't buy it. Or maybe Nugent never gets around to tellin' him, like I said."

"All right," I said. "But just suppose Nugent didn't call Clavin. Suppose it was someone pretending to be Clavin who called Nugent and made the appointment."

Rawls snorted once more and looked at me with something resembling amusement. "Nugent was dumb, but not *that* dumb. Clavin's got a voice you don't forget, like a foghorn on that goddamn boat of his. Even Nugent woulda recognized a ringer."

I shook my head and said it as quietly as I could: "Not if he'd never heard Clavin's voice before."

Rawls rose slowly, placed both fists on the desk, and leaned on them. The corners of his mouth were white, his eyes as hard as stainless steel. His voice had the low, throaty sound of an alley cat defending its dinner.

"Yeah? Well, listen, wise guy. We also stopped in on Nugent's landlady, and from her, we get that a guy who says he's a lawyer and fits Clavin's description has been comin' around askin' for Nugent. We also get that a detective named Garrett has been there askin' the same thing. She even shows us your business card. So now, no thanks to you, we got two pieces of evidence—two that you been sittin on."

"I went to see her," I admitted. "I told you that Fran hired me to look for Nugent."

Rawls reached out and grabbed a handful of my shirt, and lifted me out of the chair. "Don't gimmie that crap. She didn't hire you to conceal evidence or protect Clavin. Just what in hell are you doin', comin' in here and defendin' that bastard? Are you mixed up with him?"

I used both hands and carefully pried his fingers loose. "Take it easy, Ed. I've only had this shirt for five years. I'm still breaking it in."

Rawls shoved his hands in his pockets and scowled. "Get the hell outta here, you son of a bitch."

"Relax," I said. "I'm not defending anybody. I'm just looking for holes. The D.A. will be doing the same thing."

He went on scowling. "Since when did you start doin' the D.A.'s job?"

I pushed my hat back on my head and stuck my hands in my pockets. "Maybe if you kept a tighter rain on Brice, I wouldn't have to."

His scowl eased, and his left eyebrow flicked upward. "What d'ya mean? You got somethin'?"

I took in some air and let it out heavily. "That's why I'm here. I went back to Nugent's apartment today to have another look around. Your boys missed a newspaper in the closet. There were words missing from it, as if somebody clipped them out with scissors."

Now, both eyebrows shot up. "Like for a blackmail note?"

"Could be," I agreed.

He slammed a fist into his palm. "So that's it. Nugent was tryin' to put the bite on Clavin. That's motive enough for anybody."

"Not so fast," I said. "You can't prove blackmail, at least not yet. All you've got is a bunch of circumstantial evidence and an unreliable witness."

He eyed me carefully. "Unreliable?"

I nodded. "You must have shown Clavin's picture to the Almore woman. Did she identify him?"

Rawls looked down at the desk and cursed under his breath. "Maybe yes, maybe no. With all that gin in her, she couldn't be sure."

I nodded again. "Uh-huh. And there's still the question of that slug from Nugent's .38. What happened to it?"

Rawls waved a hand impatiently. "How the hell should I know? Maybe Clavin shoots the thing out the window and then plants it on Nugent."

"That won't wash, Ed," I said. "Maybe the one that killed Nugent could have been muffled. But firing a gun through an open window tends to get people's attention. Someone would have heard the shot."

He held both hands out in front of him, almost pleading. "Aw, gimmie a break, will ya? Down there in that neighborhood, people make it a point not to hear things."

"Maybe," I agreed. "But you'll need more than that for the Grand Jury."

He put his hands back in his pockets and nodded slowly. "Yeah, you're right. We need to find that blackmail note." A sly grin began working its way up the sides of his face. "Or maybe we just need to find out what Nugent could've had to blackmail Clavin with."

A cold, tight feeling began gnawing behind my belt buckle as I remembered the pawn ticket in my pocket. I nodded. "That might do it."

Rawls sat down contentedly, picked up his cigar, and stuck it back in his mouth. He sat chewing for a minute, then looked up at me. "Anything else?"

This was my chance to tell him, to dump the whole lousy mess in his lap.

It was one of those put-up-or-shut-up moments that always seem to come when you're not ready for them. I stood there for a minute, then shook my head. "I guess not."

"Then go ahead and blow," he said. "Thornhill's on a tear, and you know you're on his list. If he finds you in here, we'll all get hung out to dry."

I turned and started up the aisle. I had passed about half a dozen desks when he called to me.

"Garrett."

I stopped and looked back.

Rawls took out the cigar, rolled it around in his fingers, and looked at as he spoke. "There's real big-time muscle in back of Clavin, some real tough boys. I figure there's gonna be some trouble when this thing finally breaks open. Try to be missing when it does."

I gave him what I hoped was a smile. It took everything I had.

Chapter Eleven

The Pacific Coast Highway is a placid strip of asphalt that begins just below the redwood country in northern California and trickles south, clinging to the shoreline like a seam on a stocking, until it reaches the border just below San Diego. After skirting L.A., the road moves quietly through Long Beach, around San Pedro Bay, and then meanders past about twenty miles of bare and unspectacular coast to Laguna Beach. It took me a good hour to drive that far from downtown. On the way, I rolled down the window and listened to the quiet droning of breaking surf and thought about cut-up newspapers and blackmail notes.

Fran Brekhammer had believed in Danny Nugent. She was convinced that he wouldn't hurt anybody. But Rawls would have disagreed with her, and I was beginning to have doubts. Barbara Clavin had said that her husband was honest and uncompromising. I could believe at least part of that. Now it was starting to look as if maybe Nugent had tried dipping into something dirty after all. And there was a good possibility that Sterling Clavin was lying about it. I knew that someone was lying. Or else I was nuts. I wouldn't have given odds either way.

The sun was falling into late afternoon, painting orange flecks on the twenty-six miles of ocean leading out to Santa Catalina. A formation of seagulls flew across the highway and fluttered down toward the breakers as I turned onto the road leading into Laguna Beach. The town sat huddled across the highway from the ocean—a dreary collection of shabby office buildings, empty parking lots, retirement hotels, and pawn shops. The ticket in my pocket directed me past three blocks and then left and up a sleepy one-way street. The hock shop was on the corner next to a greasy spoon, where the odor of stale frying fat mingled with the smell of kelp drifting up from the beach. I left the Buick in front and went inside.

Crouched on a stool behind the counter was a thin, gray man who was pushing sixty hard enough to make it fall over. He had heavy jowls, pale, stringy eyebrows, and coarsely veined folds of skin under his eyes. He had on a faded green baseball cap, with a grimy undershirt showing under a badly bruised tweed sport coat, and rimless bifocals that looked like the bottoms of milk bottles. As I approached the counter, he pulled a cigarette out of his mouth and dangled it in a set of gnarled, arthritic fingers. His mouth moved slowly, with an obvious clicking of false teeth.

"Help ya?"

I took out the ticket and laid it on the counter in front of him. "How much to redeem this?"

He gently tapped the ash off his cigarette and onto the floor, picked up the ticket, and held it about two inches in front of his nose. He adjusted the bifocals and peered at the ticket, then he adjusted them again and examined me with large, watery gray eyes.

"You ain't the one what first come in here; else you'd already know how much." He waved the ticket at me. "I give this ta someone else."

I offered him the polite smile that detectives save for special occasions. "I don't imagine a guy could get very far trying to fool you."

The man clicked his teeth and gave me back what I guessed was a grin. "Pays ta watch out fer things in this business. You'd be surprised as ta what some people try ta pull, comin' in here."

"I'll bet I would. Does it matter that I'm not the one you gave this ticket to?"

He made an uncomfortable shrug with his shoulders. Then he wagged his head and waved his cigarette over the counter. "Don't make no never mind ta me, bub. Just so long as ya got enough o' the old long green."

"How much?"

He reached around and pulled a faded blue ledger off the shelf behind him. He opened it, adjusted the bifocals again, then prodded the pages with a crooked finger. After a minute that seemed like five, he paused at one of the entries.

"Ten bucks." He sat clicking his teeth pensively without looking up. "Huh. Guy didn't gimmie no reclaim date. Guess he wasn't plannin' ta come back."

"Did he give you a name?"

"Yup. Smith."

"Do you remember what he looked like?"

The old man poked a finger in his ear and took a labored drag on his cigarette. "Lessee. Tall he was. And dark hair—black, I think. And dressed pretty good, too. Coat and pants matched." He pulled down his glasses and eyed me over the top of them. "Same as you."

I pulled a five-spot out of my pocket, laid it down next to the ten, and grinned at him. "Will that cover it?"

He glanced down and then gathered the bills in his fingers. "Yup."

The old man bent over, rummaged under the counter, and brought up a small brown envelope, which he pushed across the countertop to me. I opened it up and took out a roll of undeveloped film, the kind you could get at any drugstore.

"Is this all?"

He nodded. "That's it, bub."

I thanked him and went outside and stood in the acrid salt air. I studied the roll of film for a minute, then slipped it into my pocket and made a mental note to remember the old man in my will. A lot of men could have fit the description he had given me. But Danny Nugent wasn't one of them.

* * *

It was dark when I got back to the city. A warm breeze was stirring in the streets, and the air was larded with the smell of rain. I made a quick stop in the office, found no one waiting, and put in a call to Myron Weeks. There was no answer. I figured the sleazy photographer was out chasing an ambulance or trying to hustle some dame at one of the local strip joints. Either way, he wasn't on the other end of the phone. That meant I'd have to keep my date with Lorna James. I bought a drink from the bar in the lower drawer of the desk, then strapped on my Luger and left the office.

Outside, a black Plymouth sedan was parked partway up the street, with two characters in gray felt hats lounging inside, eyeing the entrance to the Patterson Building. As I started up the street, the car began rolling easily along behind me, keeping its distance about half a block back. When I got to the corner, I stopped at a newsstand and picked up a paper. I pretended to read and watched out of the corner of my eye as the car rolled quietly to a stop. I stood for a minute with the Luger nestling under my arm and waited. Nothing happened. Finally, I dropped the paper, turned and faced the car, and tipped my hat to the two characters inside.

The spark from a cigarette glowed above the wheel in the front seat, and the Plymouth pulled slowly away from the curb. I reached a hand inside my jacket and held it there as the car cruised past the newsstand. I got a flash of a youngish face with what might have been a scar under the right ear. Before I could see more, the engine roared, and the car hurtled into the next block and moved quickly out of sight. I started walking again and gave myself a pat on the back for not getting shot. Nice move, Garrett. It takes a lot of work to be that dumb.

A few doors up the street, I went into a drugstore and gave the roll of film to a muffin-faced man in a smock. I told him there was a rush and that I needed two sets of prints right away. He yawned and began moving about as fast as one of Pharaoh's bricklayers. I took out a fin and laid it on the counter. He took a good look at the bill and then said I could have the prints the next afternoon. Apparently, Abraham Lincoln meant more to him than I did. I went outside, got into the Buick, and headed for home.

The phone was ringing when I walked into the apartment. I dropped my hat and coat on a chair and walked over and picked up the receiver. It was Fran.

"Michael, I have a skip for you. I want you to leave tonight for Yuma on the Super Chief."

"What's in Yuma?"

"A second-story man named Wheezy Dawson. He skipped out on a thousand-dollar bond, and I need to have him back by Monday."

I stood there for a minute holding the receiver and listening to the empty sound of breath being held. "I'm busy, Fran. You'll have to get someone else."

"I want *you*, Michael," she insisted. "You'll have to leave right away."

I cradled the receiver on my shoulder and began unstrapping the Luger. "What's so important about a grand skip? You've never sent me packing for less than five."

The receiver almost jumped off my shoulder onto the floor. "Don't argue. Just get down to the Union Station as soon as you can. I'll meet you there."

I dropped the Luger on the stand next to the phone, sat down, and began reaching for a Lucky. "Sorry, Fran. No dice. Not unless you give me the straight goods."

I could hear her exhale. Her voice became muted. "Michael, I want you to drop the case."

"What case?"

"Don't be smart with me," she said tartly. "I spoke with Edward Rawls this afternoon, and he says that you're still investigating Danny's death, that you went to his apartment this morning."

"Did he tell you I found something that might help tie the killing to Clavin?"

She hesitated for a long moment. "Yes."

"I thought you wanted me to help Rawls get the goods on Clavin."

"Not anymore. I just want it left alone."

I lit the Lucky and took in a steep drag, let the smoke out slowly, and shifted the receiver to my other ear. "Look, Fran. Calling me off won't help. Rawls wants Clavin, wants him bad. He's going to keep pushing whether I'm around or not."

"Michael." Her voice had a hitch in it, almost like fabric unraveling. "Edward says Clavin represents some very bad men. I don't want anyone else...hurt."

"It's a nice thought," I said. "But that's not what's on your mind. You've never cared what kind of gunneys I might have to go up against chasing after your jumpers. Why should you care about these birds?"

There was a soft sigh. "All right. Edward told me that Danny may have been blackmailing Sterling Clavin. He says that if he handles the investigation himself, he may be able to get both Clavin and Paris and still keep Danny's name out of the papers. But if you keep poking into it, the papers are certain to sniff it out. So please just get on the train to Yuma and stay there until Edward is finished."

I took another drag and thought about how much fun Stephanie Anders would have being a detective. "Sorry, Fran. The hard boys already know I'm involved. I'd rather take them on in my own ballpark."

"God damn it, Michael," she roared. "Can't you understand? I don't want Danny's memory destroyed. Can't you at least leave me that?"

There was a choking noise followed by a sharp click, and the line went dead.

I slowly cradled the receiver, stabbed out the Lucky, and went into the kitchen. I poured out a healthy dose of Scotch from my jug under the sink and drank it down. It didn't teach me anything, so I poured another and thought about things.

I had found a murdered man who may have been dabbling in blackmail. I had met another man who might have been his victim. The second man had denied being blackmailed or even knowing the first man. But the first man had been cutting up newspapers for anonymous notes, and the second man had apparently been receiving them. If that wasn't confusing enough, the first man had hidden a pawn ticket from a hock shop that had been visited by someone whose description could have fit the second man. I had no idea what might be on the roll of film I had gotten. And I had withheld most of this information from the police.

What I had for my trouble were people barking at me. First, Clavin, then Rawls, and now Fran. But all that wasn't enough for Garrett, the big-city gumshoe. Thanks to my keen investigating, I was almost out of work. I had found Danny Nugent for Fran, and now she wanted me to call it quits. I had talked to Barbara Clavin's husband, so now she would be satisfied. And Sterling Clavin had offered me a retainer that I had all but refused. It was a good thing I hadn't seen Lorna James since morning. She might have gone running back to Toledo.

I leaned against the sink and tucked the second Scotch away with the first one. I felt as cheerful as a lost dog.

Chapter Twelve

The Hot Foot was a gaudy little hangout in the honky tonk section about two miles south of Main Street. A fiery red neon sign flashed shamelessly over the entrance, reflecting a fitful incandescence off the puddles of rain now collecting on the sidewalk. It was a little after ten when I pulled up outside. It had been raining for almost an hour. I left the Buick across the street, turned up the collar on my trench coat, dueled through the rain, and went into the entrance.

A flight of well-worn stairs led me to the second floor and into a torrent of loud music. In the doorway at the top of the stairs, a matronly old woman sat behind a table, fingering a roll of tickets and a cash box. Behind her was a burly, florid-faced man with a crew cut. Every move he made said "bouncer." The woman told me there was a dollar minimum—ten dances. I gave her the buck, stuffed the tickets in my pocket, and began peeling off my trench coat.

"I'm looking for Lorna," I said.

The woman explained that she didn't know any of the girls by name. The bouncer yawned. I hung my coat over my arm and started inside.

It was a large open room shrouded in a puree of smoke. Several rows of wooden tables and chairs ringed the dance floor, parted only by a bar at one end of the room and a bandstand at the other. What passed for a band included half a dozen withered and graying men in rumpled dinner jackets who looked like leftovers from an American Legion parade. And behind a microphone in the middle of the stage, a fat lady with a voice like broken glass was giving her all to "I've Heard That Song Before."

I walked over to the bar and laid a bill down in front of a swarthy kid who had one eye on the crowd and the other on the drinks he was watering. I ordered a Scotch with no ice and no water. He gave me a crusty stare.

"Ya wanna glass?"

I told him I did. He poured a couple of ounces out of an unfriendly-looking bottle and pushed the glass over to me. I tried it. It tasted as if it might have been a high school chemistry experiment. Reluctantly, I took the drink and walked over to an empty table in the back of the room. I dropped my hat and coat on a chair, sat down, and looked the place over.

There wasn't much of a crowd, only about a dozen couples stumbling around the floor as if following the music might be too much trouble. Several tables away, a group of girls with more mileage than years sat idly sipping soft drinks, smearing on lipstick, and trying to look interested. Not so many years ago, this place would have been filled every night with GIs and sailors on leave, getting a last taste of home before shipping overseas. Now, it was just an emporium for flesh peddling, with hard-faced young girls fawning over paunchy old men who were desperately clinging to the unkept promises from too many passing years.

I started to take another sip of the Scotch and then thought better of it. As I was looking for a potted plant or a trash can where I could empty my glass, the band stopped playing, and Lorna James came over to the table. She was wearing heels as thin as hypodermic needles and a tight cobalt-blue sequin dress that hoisted her torso up around her chin. On her left was a thin, mousy brunette in a saffron-yellow dress that left one shoulder bare and then wound around her like a sarong. With her right hand, Lorna was dragging along an elderly gent in a dark suit. He had white hair and skin like dried fruit, and he was breathing like someone running a marathon.

Before I could finish standing up, Lorna stepped over and slapped a hand on the table. "Mr. G. I seen ya come in. Say hello to Harvey Jones."

She nodded to the man next to her, and he stuck a hand across the table. I shook it. It was warm and moist and as limp as an empty balloon.

"A pleasure," he wheezed.

"Mr. Garrett's a frienda mine," Lorna said to him. "He's a private dick."

The man's eyes widened in a look of shock and despair, as if he'd just been told he'd forgotten to put on his pants. He stepped back and edged around behind Lorna like someone hiding behind a tree.

Lorna motioned to the girl on her left. "This is Francine. She's gonna entertain ya till Harvey and me finish the next dance." Lorna gave Francine a friendly poke. "Not too close, now. I seen him first."

The band started another number, and this time, Harvey dragged Lorna over to the other side of the dance floor. Francine looked demurely across the table at me.

"Wanna dance?" she asked.

"Let's just sit this one out."

She shrugged and pulled out a chair, then sat down hard and eyed me uncertainly. "If ya don't wanna dance, what brings ya in here?"

"The bartender and I are old friends," I said. "Would you like a drink?"

She shook her head. "Nah. Only thing I like's a Singapore Sling. They don't make 'em here."

"I thought they made those everywhere."

Her dark eyes narrowed, and she spoke to me cautiously out of the side of her mouth. "You really a shamus?"

I nodded. "When I'm not in the park composing fugues or studying a racing form."

She gave me a blank stare. Then her eyebrows knitted together, and she thought for a minute. That seemed to cause her some trouble. "So, what's up? How come you're pokin' around here?"

"What's it to you?"

She leaned forward and put both elbows on the table. "Nothin'," she said innocently. "Only you're the second one in here in just over a week."

I didn't say anything.

"There was this other guy," she went on. "Come around askin' about Eddie Franks. Ya know, one a' The Stick's bookies?"

My stomach muscles tightened all the way to my collar. "What did he look like, this detective?"

She shrugged. "I dunno. Light hair. Not real great clothes."

114

"What else did he want?"

She wrinkled her mouth and thought again, then shook her head. "Nothin'. Just where ta find Eddie." Her eyes narrowed once more. "Why? What's goin' on?"

I reached into my coat pocket and pulled out the dance tickets. I peeled off all but one and handed them to her. "Only that you've just done a night's work."

Francine beamed and scooped up the tickets just as the music was ending. "Say, Lorna was right. You're Okay."

Lorna came back, this time without Harvey, and Francine drifted over to the table with the other girls. I pulled out a chair and held it for Lorna as the music started again.

She put her hands on her hips, grinned, and shook her head. "Oh, no, you don't. I saw you sittin' over here with Francine. You're not pullin' that one on me. Gimmie your ticket. My shift's almost over, and I saved the last dance for you."

"If I had known, I'd have worn a better suit."

She ran her eyes down the front of my clothes, then slowly back up. "You look all right ta me."

Lorna took my hand and led me into the middle of the dance floor as the band began pummeling "I'll Never Smile Again." She slid her fingers up behind my neck. nestled her thigh against my leg, and pressed as close to me as her figure would let her. That was close enough. We cruised around the floor for a couple of minutes while Lorna's body worked me over like a steam iron. Finally, she leaned back, looked at me, and grinned.

"You're pretty good," she said. "Where'd you learn ta dance like that?"

"Bayonet practice," I said. "On the way across the Pacific."

"Come on," she laughed. "You're kidding me again."

"You're right," I said. "I'm kidding you again."

She kept smiling and tightened her grip on the back of my neck. "I sure do like you, Mr. G. Most guys don't take me serious. Some of 'em don't even talk ta me. All they want is ta hustle me outta my clothes. But you're different. You make me feel like a lady, even when you're pullin' my leg. I think you and me could really get along."

I swallowed hard. "That's a nice idea, Lorna. But you might not feel the same way after tonight."

"What d'ya mean?"

"I mean, I still don't think I can do much about your pictures."

Her eyes widened, and she pulled back. "Holy Moses. I near forgot. Mr. Milton called tonight...just before you got here. He says the plan's changed, and we ain't supposed ta go ta the studio."

"Did he say why not?"

She shook her head. "He just says we're supposed ta go somewheres else. He gimmie an address. Says Weeks'll be there with the pictures and the negatives."

A quiet storm began brewing in the pit of my stomach.

Lorna leaned forward, rested her head against my shoulder, and murmured contentedly under my chin. "I'm sure glad you're gonna be with me, Mr. G. Mr. Milton says he's gonna meet us there. And he says he's lookin' forward ta meetin' you too."

"Then we're even," I said.

* * *

The address was on Front Street in the warehouse district down below Century Boulevard. A handful of pale-yellow streetlamps barely lit the narrow, rutted roadway as it rolled for about two hundred yards past rows of trash cans and loading docks and dead-ended at a chain link fence. Lorna directed me to number 1142, the last building on the street.

It was mostly brick, two stories, with wide, slotted windows pleading to be washed and a single door next to the loading entrance. The entrance was closed, and there were no lights on. Taking a wild guess, I figured there was nobody home.

I looked over at Lorna. She was sitting next to me in the front seat of the Buick, clutching the front of a thin raincoat and looking grimly out at the rain.

116

"Are you sure this is the right address?" I asked.

She nodded slowly. "1142 Front Street is what Mr. Milton said. I got a good memory for stuff like that."

I sat and looked at the rain, then looked at the warehouse, then looked at the rain again. Finally, I turned back to Lorna. "I'm going over to have a look."

She reached out and grabbed the sleeve of my trench coat. "Please, Mr. G. Stay here with me."

"We could be early," I said. "And I want to look the place over, just in case Weeks decides to bring some muscle of his own."

She blinked rapidly several times. Her eyes were as wide as pie plates. "Let's just wait in the car. Mr. Milton'll be here soon. And…" She looked down toward the seat. "And I'm kinda scared."

I patted her hand gently. "Me too. But I want to earn that fifty bucks. Just wait here and don't worry."

I got out of the car, turned up my collar, and pulled my hat down tight. Sheets of rain were coming down, flooding the street and making it hard to see. I stepped up onto the sidewalk opposite the warehouse and began walking back up the street. I walked slowly, moving directly under every streetlight, making sure I could be seen by anyone inside the warehouse.

When I had gone far enough to be out of sight, I went quickly across the street and up an alley between the buildings. Another row of warehouses in back formed a corridor that extended the entire length of the block. I tiptoed around more trash cans and stacked up packing crates, heading back toward the end of the street. At the last building, I stopped, hugged the wall, held my breath, and just listened. The only sound was the steady slapping of rain in the back alley.

After what seemed like a three-hour minute, I edged out into the alley and took a look at the back of the building. There was a solid-looking door and a line of windows at about the second-story level. The one just to the left of the door was broken. I eased over to the door and gently placed my hand on the knob. I held my breath again and listened. Still no sound but the rain. Gradually, I twisted the knob, making slow, agonizing movements.

117

It was nice work. It made as much noise as bread crumbling. The door was locked.

Across the alley, I saw a couple of discarded packing crates. I moved as stealthily as I could in the rain and stacked the crates under the broken window. Then, like a dime-novel sleuth, I climbed up on top of the crates. I did that well, too. I tore my pants on a nail and scraped my hand on the edge of a crate.

Standing on tiptoe, I was just able to reach through the broken pane and turn the latch above the sash. I used my fingers and carefully eased the window open about a foot and looked inside. I saw only darkness. No shapes, no sound, no movement. By now, I figured anyone waiting would know I was there. And it could be a mistake to go any further. But that didn't bother me. If you want a mistake made, just call Garrett. He's an experienced man when it comes to doing the wrong thing.

I threw an arm over the ledge and hoisted myself up enough to get my head through the window. I was just dragging my knee up to the ledge when I heard the sound—a door opening. I froze. There was a long pause and then footsteps—short mincing strides making sharp reports, like spike heels hitting a wood floor. They were a woman's footsteps. I thought about reaching for my Luger. Then I heard the voice.

"Hey, Mr. G. You in here?"

I started to yell, but nothing came out. In fact, nothing happened at all. Everything just stopped, as if the world had been frozen in mid-stride like statues in a park. Somewhere behind my eyes, there was a brilliant flash of light. Then, a scream. Then, a tableau of darkness.

Chapter Thirteen

The sound came up slowly around me, rising gently like the tide moving up on the beach. I imagined myself lying on the sand with a towel over my face. The towel was warm and moist, and someone was rubbing it over me the way a shoeshine boy buffs a pair of brogues. As I lay there, the sound of the breakers rose into a high-pitched crescendo—a shrill, abrading noise, like rain pounding on pavement. The towel moved roughly over my face, and I kept my eyes shut tight under it. I thought about moving my arms and legs, but somehow, I hadn't brought them with me. All I could move was my head. I moved it and wished I hadn't. A heavy throbbing hammered into the back of my head and rippled down through my neck and into my shoulder blades. Off in the distance, I heard the moaning voice of someone who wasn't feeling well. The voice was familiar. It could have been mine.

The towel rubbed my face again, and I decided there was nothing to do but open my eyes. I blinked them open, and the towel moved away. Suddenly, it wasn't a towel anymore. It was a tongue, and it was hanging out between the jaws of the largest, ugliest basset hound I had ever seen. The dog stepped aside, and I looked up at the back of the warehouse. The window was still open. The rain was still falling. And I was occupying a position that my business had made a little too familiar. I was flat on my back in an alley.

There was a tugging on my trench coat, and I painfully propped myself up on my elbows. An old wino was pulling at my coat, trying to get it open so he could rifle my pockets. I lay there for a minute, watching him with a sort of detached curiosity, the way an entomologist examines a dead spider.

After a few more tugs, the old man looked up and saw that I had come to. He made a quiet yelping noise, turned, and started running down the alley. The dog bounded after him, and before I could move, the two of them were lost in the shadows.

I slowly lay back down and shut my eyes. The rain washed over me, and I wondered how long I could just lie there. I wouldn't be in anyone's way. They could put a building on top of me. I wouldn't mind. Just let me lie there without any fuss. It seemed like a good idea. Maybe that's why I didn't do it. Instead, I took a deep breath and gritted my teeth. I rolled over and came up on my knees, and slowly stood up. It felt like the most work I'd done in a week.

Out of blind habit, I reached down, picked up my hat, and tried putting it on. My head objected with another long, loud throb, and I staggered against the building and swore to myself. Someone had used the back of my head for batting practice, and now it weighed about three hundred pounds.

After a few minutes of feeling sorry for myself, I began looking around the alley. It seemed the same as before; only the crates I had stacked up under the window were now strewn around like fallen soldiers. I thought about stacking them up again, but just for the hell of it, I decided to try the back door first. It was open.

The warehouse was as dark as the inside of a safe deposit box. I used my pocket flash and groped along the right-hand wall until I reached a flight of stairs that ran up toward the back of the building. I shined the flash up the stairs and saw that they led to an empty loft that stretched from one side of the warehouse to the other. Whoever had conked me would have been waiting up there by the window when I tried to climb in. By now, he seemed as far away from me as L.A. is from Mars.

A pale yellowish glow from the street was coming through the windows in the front of the warehouse, poking into the unfriendly shadows and outlining a door. For no reason at all, I thought about the Buick out in the street. I took a couple of steps toward the door, then stumbled against something soft and unmoving. Sometimes, your instincts figure things out before the message even gets to your head. My instincts told me to keep going and not look down. Just get the hell out of there and forget the whole thing. I shined the flash down toward my feet. What I saw told me that my instincts had been right again. Lorna James would never be starring in any Zanuck picture.

She was sprawled at the foot of the stairs, her raincoat partly open and her purse on the floor beside her. Her head was turned partway to the right, her empty eyes bulging in their sockets. A hole a little bigger than a dime had been blown into her left temple, the skin around it scorched and torn and tattooed with particles of gunpowder. That meant the shot had come from very close range.

There wasn't much bleeding on the side of her face. There seldom is with entry wounds. I prodded her chin and gently turned her head just enough. The cavitation caused by the slug and the resulting pulping of her brain had left an exit wound on the right side of her forehead bigger than my fist. Her life had instantly gushed out of that wound in a gelatinous glow that was now spread out on the floor under her. That meant someone had put a cannon to her head.

I stood up and looked away. After deliberately taking a few deep breaths, I reached down and picked up her purse. Using the flash again, I poked through the purse and found the usual female arsenal of combs, lipsticks, face powder, mascara, perfume, and tissues. Underneath the clutter, I found a wallet that seemed undisturbed and a set of keys. Then, further underneath all that, I found a slip of paper with a bit of feminine scrawl: "Be at 1142 Front Street. Will meet Mr. G. with money."

I reassembled the purse, placed it down next to the body, and then walked over by the front door of the warehouse. I lit a cigarette and looked out into the street. I watched the rain, somehow seeing it and not seeing it. As I stood there, I thought about going over and having a last look at Lorna, just in case I might be missing something. The rain kept falling, and I kept looking at it without moving.

I decided not to go back. I decided I didn't need a clearer picture. You never could tell: Someday, I might run into someone from Toledo, someone who had known Lorna Huffnagle. Whoever it was would remember her smiling on her way to California so she could be in the movies. It was a good way to remember her. Why spoil it? Why tell the folks back home about how she looked when she died? I'd carry that picture with me from now on, but they didn't have to. Through a lot of dismal nights and bottles of Scotch, I'd be seeing the girl who came to me for help, who danced with me, and who felt safe with me. And I'd be seeing the torn and lifeless face lying in a pool of blood on the floor. It would be my memory. But it didn't have to belong to anyone else.

* * *

They put me in one of the interrogation coops up the hall from the squad room. It was small and untidy, with no windows, no ventilation, and walls painted the color of someone getting seasick. A wooden table with nothing on it but an overcrowded ashtray sat in the middle of the room, ringed by several plain wooden chairs. I sat in one of the chairs, fed myself a Lucky, and stared across the table at Sergeant Earl Donlevy. The uniformed officer sat staring back at me—arms folded, feet together, his face showing as much expression as the side of the building.

After leaving the warehouse, I had phoned Rawls at his home. He wasn't thrilled to hear from me at that hour. He was even less excited over the reason. The prowl-car boys and the coroner's man had then made it to the warehouse in just over thirty-five minutes—under the circumstances, not bad for a killing. I had tried explaining things to a Lieutenant Gregory, who seemed to want to be in charge. He had made a quick call over the squad car radio, and I had then been relieved of my Luger and my investigator's I.D. and given a ride to the station. From there, I was escorted into the back room by Sergeant Donlevy and two other officers. They had been polite. They hadn't shoved me around hard enough to break anything. They had even invited me to sit in a chair and shut up and not move for an hour. I sat in the chair, shut up, and didn't move. After a while, the hour seemed like a month.

Just as I was starting to go numb from the waist down, the law walked in—

grim and deadly. Captain Bradley Thornhill sauntered over next to Sergeant Donlevy and waved his thumb in the direction of the corner. The Sergeant grabbed one of the loose chairs, retreated to a distant part of the room, and watched his Detective Captain sit down behind the table. Thornhill brought a hand the size of a pineapple up from under the table and dropped Lorna James's purse next to the ashtray. Then he folded his hands, drew a pair of heavily foliated charcoal-colored eyebrows together, and glared at me with an expression as soft and yielding as a sidewalk.

Thornhill was a big man, with a broad, sardonic face, salt-and-pepper hair cut close to his head, skin mottled like the surface of a medicine ball, and sullen hazel eyes that never seemed to close or even blink. He had been running Homicide for a long time, and some would say successfully. For those who kept score, the number of people being murdered in L.A. every year didn't seem any higher than the number in Chicago or New York or Philadelphia. And when Thornhill brought in a suspect, as often as not the guy seemed eager to confess.

In the past there had been fingers pointed at Thornhill, with talk that he had taken bribes. But then, at one time or another, there had been fingers pointed at almost everyone in the building. No one ever hung anything on him, and Thornhill had outlasted all his accusers. There was no middle ground with him. As he saw it, you were on his side, or you weren't. If you weren't, you could do yourself a favor by considering a different line of work. A lot of people had done themselves that favor, including a guy named Garrett.

Thornhill sat eyeing me as I took out a Lucky and lit up for the nine-hundredth time in the hour. As I dropped the match in the ashtray, he leaned forward and growled at me like a hungry bear just before dinner. "Put it out."

I took a long, slow drag and eased back in the chair, and just let the smoke drift out into the room.

Thornhill sat watching, and his features slowly twisted into a malignant grin. He rose from his chair, keeping the grin in place, and walked over in front of me. He took a deep breath and exhaled in my face. He had the breath of a crocodile. "I said put it out."

I saw it coming, but I wasn't quick enough to get out of the way. His right hand shot out and slapped across my lower jaw, knocking the cigarette over into the corner in front of Sergeant Donlevy. The Sergeant picked up the butt and casually crushed it out in the ashtray, while Thornhill folded his arms and leaned back on his heels and gloated.

"I remember you," he said. "It's more than a dozen years, but I remember you like I remember a blister—something festering and sore and filling up with pus until you can't wait to put a spike through it. I don't give a good goddamn who tries to put in a word for you. In my book, you're nothin' but a smart-assed smart-mouthed son of a bitch. You're a cheap punk in a cheap racket. And you're stupid. You've always been stupid. You say the wrong goddamn things, and you say 'em at the wrong goddamn times."

"I think I'm starting to get it," I said. "I must be stupid."

Thornhill's face twisted with the same grin again, and he hooked a massive shoe on the leg of my chair. Before I could move, he jerked his foot sharply to the left, and the chair collapsed under me. I sprawled out face first in the corner of the room in front of Sergeant Donlevy and dusted off the floor with my nose. Mostly from instinct, I glanced up at the officer in the corner. He hadn't moved, and his expression hadn't changed, but from where I was parked, he looked about a hundred feet tall.

I started to get up when a foot that felt like an anvil came down in the middle of my back. I lay there with my chest pinned to the floor and listened to the deadpan growl somewhere up over my head.

"Maybe you think you can just come waltzing in here to headquarters anytime you like, and we'll just roll out the red carpet. Maybe you think we like having to play footsie with you while we're investigating a homicide." He leaned over and breathed close to my ear. His voice was cold menace. "And maybe you think a guy can't get worked over without having it leave marks."

With what seemed like reluctance, Thornhill took his foot out of my back, then walked around and sat down behind the table again. Donlevy set the chair upright again. And I thought about getting off the floor again. I worked myself back into the chair and managed to focus my eyes on the other side of the table. Thornhill was sitting with his hands folded, working his lower jaw in and out like a bullfrog.

"I'm going to say this just once," he said. "I want a statement—complete, factual, nothing phony, nothing left out. You give me that right now, and maybe we can do business. You give me a stall, and mine'll be the last face you ever see without bars in front of it."

I swallowed hard. My mouth felt like the underside of a football shoe. "Am I accused of something?"

Thornhill gave me the slow-cold smile of an undertaker. His fingers idly tightened around the ashtray. This time, I was quick enough. The ashtray pounded into the wall just behind me, then showered the floor with ashen remnants. Thornhill stood and leaned forward on the table, glowered, and thrust his chin out at me.

"You don't ask questions, goddammit. I ask the questions. Right now, I've got a homicide with you at the scene, and I want a statement. I can hang you up for the D.A. like a ham in a smokehouse, but I'm giving you a chance to come clean. It's more than you deserve, and it won't last long enough for you to draw too many more breaths."

I inhaled deeply and sat there. As a rule, a bluff comes at you wrapped in a lot of noise. But there are those times when standing up to a loudmouth only wins you a fist in the teeth or a knee in the groin. I thought this could be one of those times. That's what makes a bluff work.

I shrugged. "Okay, I'll spill it. It was me, John Dillinger, Baby Face Nelson, and Pretty Boy Floyd."

Thornhill's eyes narrowed to slits. "Listen, wise guy. In case you don't know it, we've got enough on you now to lock you up on suspicion."

He lifted Lorna's purse and dumped the contents out on the table in front of him. Then he pawed through her things, passing over the cosmetics and settling on her wallet. From this, he pulled a card and a small slip of paper. He held the card up to the light and read from it:

"Full privileges granted to Lorna Huffnagle, Public Library, Toledo, Ohio." Next, he unfolded the paper and read: "Stills and negatives, five hundred dollars or else."

Gloating like a peacock, Thornhill poked through the debris on the table. He picked up another card and read again: "Fifty dollars to meet and get pictures." He flipped the card over and held it up in the light so I could see it. It was smeared and water-streaked, but it was legible. It was my card.

"It took a beating in the rain," he said. "But it's still enough to hang you—that is, when the D.A. matches it up with this." He waved another piece of paper from the pile on the table. I didn't have to look to know what it said. He opened it, leaned across the table, and leered at me. It says here, 'Mr. G.' Now, who do you suppose that is?"

I didn't say anything.

Thornhill stepped back from the table. He began pacing back and forth, rubbing his hands together and gloating to himself.

"Now, here's the way we lay it out for the D.A.," he said. "This innocent little frail from the Midwest comes out here with eyes full of stars. She doesn't connect in pictures, so she goes to work in this dime-a-dance joint down on the south side. This place is also frequented by a certain broken-down private dick, one who—according to the bouncer—was seen there tonight and could have been there at least a dozen times in the last few weeks."

He stopped pacing and gave me a nasty grin, then went on. "The dick sees the frail and decides she might be worth a small-time skin game. So, he pours a little sympathy into her ear, waltzes her off to a studio where he's got some cheap shutterbug in the know, and before the sun comes up, she's been photographed from every angle this side of high school geometry."

He sat down and crossed his legs. He folded his hands, looked off somewhere over my head, and grinned contentedly. "Later on, with the frail upset and worried in case someone from back home finds out, the dick explains that the photographer didn't understand, that he got carried away. But the dick thinks he can buy the guy off for five-hundred clams. So, they agree to meet at this warehouse down on Front Street to pay off the photographer and get the pictures. Only there's no photographer and no pictures. Then, the frail gets suspicious and threatens to call for some law. That's about enough to panic the dick, so he ices her, and then, trying to make himself look clean, he phones it into Homicide."

Thornhill folded his hands and looked at me. He was wearing a smile that made the Cheshire Cat seem like a piker.

"From what's in her purse," he said, "we've got motive. From having you at the scene, we've got opportunity. Right now, your gun's being tested. That'll give us means." He waved a finger in the direction of the door. "Any minute now, that door's going to open, and I'll get a report with enough in it so I can just sit back and watch you step off. If you think I'm bluffing, just keep your lip buttoned. But if you like breathing, you've got until that door opens to make your statement."

It wasn't a bad line. Except for my part in it, he'd put the pieces together pretty well. I pulled out another Lucky, slowly, carefully, and took my time lighting it. I took in the smoke and thoughtfully blew a cloud down over the floor. Finally, I crossed my legs and looked back across the table.

"All right," I said. "She was my client. She hired me to try and recover some pictures taken by one Myron Weeks. You can look him up in your book of nice names. The meeting at the warehouse was arranged by her manager, a man named Paul Milton. You won't find him in any book anywhere that I know of. I went with her to protect her and to keep the game honest—only I bungled the job. I'm not clever. I'm not smart. I may be all the contemptible things you said. But I didn't kill her, and you can't prove I did."

Thornhill's eyes hardened, but he didn't say anything.

"Forgetting about the crack on my head," I said. "Those notes in the girl's purse could be taken to mean a lot of things. Any rookie detective could tell you that. And finding one of my cards doesn't mean anything; I leave them around everywhere. As for my being at the Hot Foot—even if I had been there more than just tonight, it would still be my word against the bouncer's." I shrugged. "Stand the two of us up in front of a jury in the daylight, and I'll take my chances."

Thornhill jumped to his feet. The color in his face rose up like high tide in the morning. He grabbed Lorna's purse and waved it across the table at me.

"By God, that's just what I'm going to do. I'm going to stick your ass in front of a jury and watch you squirm. I'll spill it all for the D.A., and I'll show everybody this purse and what's in it. And you know what they'll say?" He leaned far enough forward to put his hands on the outer edge of the table. "Well, do you, you smart-aleck son of a bitch?"

I looked at the purse and shrugged. "They'll say it's just the right color for you."

He tramped around from behind the table and took hold of my shirt in his left hand. With his right hand, he reached out and grabbed a fistful of air, his fingers tensing, the muscles in his arm tightening all the way to his collar. The room became still. Everyone in it knew he was about to hit me. Only one of us was worried about it. There was a rap on the door. The door opened.

Rawls stepped in, not looking at anybody in particular. He carried a Manila folder and waved it in the direction of Thornhill. The Captain of Detectives let go of my shirt, took the folder, and sat down behind the table, while Rawls just stood and worked the dirt around under his fingernails.

Thornhill opened the folder and read the contents, then closed the folder again, and glared at me with a face full of crimson rage. Without taking his eyes off me, he threw a few clipped syllables out of the corner of his mouth at Sergeant Donlevy. "Leave the room."

The uniformed man in the corner rose and went noiselessly out before the words had even fallen out of the air. Thornhill glanced impatiently at Rawls, then spoke to him while he turned and aimed his stare at me again. "You too."

When Rawls didn't move, Thornhill finally turned and gave him a grudging scowl. "Didn't you hear me? I said get out."

Rawls shook his head. "Uh-uh. I don't figure it's worth a career just to beat up this bum, Captain. Not yours for stayin' in here and not mine for leavin'. Even with the door shut, you got a squad room with a full shift out there and a couple dozen reporters with their tongues hangin' out. They heard there's been a shooting. All they need now is a little sniff of somethin' like a rubber hose, and they'll start sharpenin' their pencils." He made a shrugging motion in my direction. "Just take a good look at this creep. He's not worth it. Our careers are more important."

Thornhill glared at Rawls through the loudest silence I had ever heard. Finally, with infinite slowness, he brought his eyes back around to me. There was still the rage, but now a hint of resignation went with it.

"Right now," he said, "I have to do something that every cop hates. I have to put a bum back on the street. The coroner's report says that the girl was shot with a large caliber gun, probably a .45. And the report says that the Luger in question probably couldn't have inflicted the wound and hasn't been fired recently enough to be considered the murder weapon." His face slowly molded into the deadly calm of a hangman. "So, after you dictate and sign your statement, you're free to go. You can pick up your gun and your license at the property window."

He stood slowly and wrung his hands together like a washerwoman strangling the laundry. "But you just remember this. If you ever come within sight or sound or even smell of this office again, you'll wish you'd been born a snail at the bottom of the goddamn ocean."

Thornhill went out and slammed the door behind him with a report that would have shaken fillings in Denver. I stood slowly and began rubbing a pair of tired, aching arms.

"Thanks, Eddie."

Rawls turned and looked at me with dark, hollow eyes. He didn't speak. His face was as unmoving as a block of marble. I was nothing to him. I wasn't there. He turned and quietly went out the door.

* * *

I dictated and signed the same statement I had given Thornhill. Then I collected my Luger and elbowed my way through about a dozen bawling reporters and went out of the squad room, out of the building, and got into the Buick. It was a little after one. The night was clear now, and the air in the streets had that hint of freshness that always follows a good rain. It would last until just before sunrise when the traffic would start, and the smog would come up, and the whole cluttered, aimless parade would start again.

I drove home and climbed the stairs to my apartment, feeling as if someone had strapped a pair of barbells to my legs. I went in and looked at the usual bare walls and tired furniture. Nothing had changed. Maybe nothing ever changes.

I tossed my coat and hat on a chair, went into the kitchen, and grabbed the Scotch and a glass. I walked back into the living room and, on the way, filled the glass about a third full and then drained it. The living room didn't look any better to me, so I went over to the window and opened it, and looked out.

The night was full of a bland sort of darkness, the same as every other night in L.A. Dark enough to hide in, but not too dark to be seen. A faint glow spread over the buildings, rising from the endless blocks of neon that rolled through the city. Night after night, every want, every need, every lust was courted and comforted by the glittering promises held in the lights—promises made and seldom kept. This was a town of unkept promises. And it didn't matter if the promises were made to foppish Hollywood dandies or star-struck girls from the Midwest. Chances were always better than even that the promises would never be kept. They all knew it, and still, they went along. It never seemed to change.

I turned away from the window and looked at my living room and thought about how my life was trudging by with all the promises quietly forgotten. I thought about a drab and dusty office, about a worn-out car in need of a brake job, about a closet where a moth could starve to death. I thought about how nothing ever changes. But one thing had changed. Lorna James was dead.

I picked up the Scotch and drank from the bottle.

Chapter Fourteen

The sound of the phone cut into the morning like a knife opening a melon. I pulled the pillow over my head, waved a wooden hand in the direction of the nightstand, and heard the phone clatter on the floor. Somewhere in the distance, the voice coming through the receiver made an insistent buzzing noise, like the sound of a bee trapped in a well. I reached out slowly, picked up the receiver, and held it against my ear without speaking.

"Mr. Garrett? Are you there? This is Stephanie Anders. Are you alright?"

"Depends on what you call all right," I mumbled, my mouth half-buried in the pillow. "What time is it?"

She hesitated. "It's eight-fifteen…in the morning."

That was enough to get my eyes open. I held the receiver up in front of me and snarled at it.

"What the hell are you doing calling at this hour, recruiting for the Breakfast Club? Get off the phone and let me sleep."

"P-p-please, Mr. Garrett," she stammered. "Don't be angry. I was afraid you might need help."

"Help?" I rolled over on my back and tried to bring the ceiling into focus. It fought me all the way. "What are you talking about?"

"Haven't you seen the paper?"

I lay the receiver down on my chest and gave myself the luxury of a long, loud yawn. Then I rubbed my eyes and picked up the receiver again.

"Stephanie, the last thing I remember seeing is an angry cop and then a Scotch bottle. Both of them seemed to have it in for me. Right now, I don't

131

plan to read anything beyond the labels in the medicine chest."

An impatient tone rose in her voice. "But you're on the front page."

That got my eyes open again. The ceiling was in focus now, and the rest of my apartment and the whole grim episode from the night before. I remembered coming home and trying to lock the entire mess outside. I might as well have tried to stop the wind from blowing.

"All right," I said. "What am I doing on the front page?"

"Well, the story is all about that girl who was murdered last night down on Front Street. It says that she was your client and that you discovered the body. Is that really what happened?"

"Something like that. What else?"

She paused and seemed to catch her breath. "It says that the police brought you in and were considering holding you—as a material witness. There's a picture of you and a Detective Captain Thornhill. It shows you walking out of the police station, and it shows him standing behind you, pointing and looking very upset."

I grunted. "Keep going."

She hesitated again. "Well, there's more. I'm afraid you're not going to like it. But I'll read it to you."

There was a brittle rustling noise, and she began to read:

"Detective Bradley Thornhill told reporters that the killing of the James girl was the second brutal murder in the city's south side in less than a week. In another incident two days ago, Daniel Nugent of Los Angeles was found shot to death in an office building on Paloma Place. Both victims were discovered by a local private investigator named Michael Garrett, who could not be reached for comment. Asked if the two killings were linked, Thornhill replied, 'We've had two shootings down there this week, and this guy Garrett was at the scene both times. You figure it out.'"

I exhaled heavily. "Is that it?"

"Pretty much," she said. "The rest is just background on the girl, where she was from, where she worked. Mr. Garrett, do you think the police are right? Is there a connection between the two murders?"

"There may be," I said. "But if there is, Thornhill isn't looking in the right place for it."

"What do you mean?"

I yawned again. "Don't ask me what I mean. It's too early in the day for me to be figuring things out."

"What are you going to do?"

I raised myself up on one elbow, rubbed my eyes again, and took a good look in the morning. "Maybe I'll have a drink."

Her breath caught again, and she made a little squeaking noise. "But it isn't even eight-thirty in the morning."

I chuckled. "Somewhere in the world, it's five o'clock."

The impatient tone rose in her voice once more. "Can't you be serious? Two people are dead."

"Look," I said. "If being serious would help them, I'd be as serious as Moses. I'd get up and tear my clothes and cry all over the floor. I'd walk the streets singing dirges, and I'd give away my entire fortune. I'd go somewhere and write melancholy poetry and compose sad songs. I'd be damn serious. But it won't help. So instead, I'll get up, and I'll try to do the nasty work of being a detective—something you won't read about in your book. I'll go out, and I'll turn over rocks, and I'll peek around corners, and if I'm lucky, I'll run into some characters who make a living being tough and mean, and I'll try to be a little tougher and meaner than they are. And then maybe, just maybe, I'll be able to do something. Not something big, and not something daring or heroic. But something. I know it isn't much, but it's all I've got. And being serious won't make anything more out of it."

I threw my legs over the edge of the bed and sat there and listened to the echoes of my own foolishness. After a long silence, Stephanie's voice trickled over the line.

"I'm sorry. You must think I'm a fool."

"No, I don't," I said. "And it wouldn't matter if I did. Being a fool is easy. You have lots of company."

"Mr. Garrett," she said bravely, "I want to help. I know I've only read about being a detective, but I really have learned a lot. And for years people have been telling me how smart I am. Maybe if I could study the evidence with you, I could help you work out some theories."

"That's nice," I said. "But Nugent and Lorna James weren't killed by a theory."

"I know. But I'm sure I can help."

"I'll keep it in mind. Goodbye, Stephanie." I hung up.

With more than a little effort, I hoisted myself up off the bed and climbed into my bathrobe. Then I began trudging toward the kitchen with nothing on my mind but coffee. I was about halfway across the living room when a fist like a bowling ball began bruising the door. I stepped over, jerked the door open, and got a quick look at a lanky character in a dark suit and a hat that might have been run over by a train. I remember that he had a weather-beaten face with a generous amount of five o'clock shadow. But that was all I saw. Another man stepped quickly out from behind him, and the flash went off in my face.

I stared at a blue spot, and a voice said, "Stanley Walsh, Daily Examiner. We're covering the two south-side killings. Thornhill says you found two bodies. That right?"

I didn't say anything. The blue spot was swelling and pulsing, and I stared into it like a pilot lost in a fog bank.

The voice came at me again. "I figure maybe you're down here on a case. So, who's your client?"

I gave him more of nothing.

"C'mon. Spill it," he said. "A little publicity might be good for your business." The voice became cagey. "Just want to give you a chance to tell your side of the story. Thornhill figures the killings are connected and that you know about them. Sounds like you might even be the prime suspect. Any comment?"

"Yeah," I said. "Get fried."

I slammed the door and continued my trek to the kitchen. So much for the Fourth Estate.

After going two out of three falls with the coffee pot, I managed to pour myself a cup of something hot and strong enough to dissolve paint. I sipped it, carried the cup into the living room, and sat down just in time for the phone to go off next to me. I winced and grabbed the receiver, and bellowed into the mouthpiece.

"What the hell is it now?"

There was an embarrassed pause, then a silky voice. "Mr. Garrett, this is Barbara Clavin. Are you alright?"

I sighed heavily and took another sip of coffee. "I've been better. What can I do for you, Mrs. Clavin?"

"I'm sorry," she said. "You must be very busy. Perhaps I should call at another time."

"Why should I be busy? It's just another killing—not enough to slow down for. After all, it's a new day. The birds are singing, the town is awake, and Garrett's drinking his coffee."

Another pause. "Killing? Birds? I'm afraid I don't understand."

"Never mind," I said. "I seldom do myself."

"Has something happened?"

"In this town, something always happens. How can I help you?"

"Well, I...I need to see you."

"What for?"

She hesitated. "It's difficult to say at the moment."

I sighed again and put the coffee down by the phone. "That would mean that Amanda has her ears out, and you want to talk about your husband."

I could almost hear her swallowing. "Yes."

"I don't think that's a good idea, Mrs. Clavin. I might be working for him, you know."

"That's why I want to see you." Her voice became muffled, as if she had cupped her hand over the mouthpiece. "Please, Mr. Garrett. It's very important. Will you be in your office around noon?"

Something in her voice moved me gently yet firmly, like an offshore breeze filling a sail. I stood up and looked at my watch. It was a little before nine.

"I'll be there," I said and hung up.

* * *

135

The morning sun was just drying up the last patches of rain on the sidewalk as I drove down Figueroa into the lower part of the city. A shower and shave and another jolt of coffee had gotten me moving, and now I was out in the sunshine. I was out in the almost clean air, where the peddlers and shopkeepers were going through their ritual of sweeping the sidewalks and dusting off their storefronts. For them, it was just another day for business. For me, it was a day to go and see a wormy little photographer.

The sunshine didn't do much for the apartment building where Myron Weeks had his studio. The place had the same rundown look and the same rancid smell I remembered from the day before. I climbed the same flight of stairs and found the same business card taped to the door. When I got within knocking distance, I heard voices from inside—high-pitched voices, shrill and taut, sounding like a chorus at a hen party. I stood there for a minute, and another voice tore the air into shreds.

"I don't give a damn about your good side. The man wants your gams, not your puss!"

I put a fist to the door and waited.

Silence. Cautious footsteps. The door opened just enough to let in a forefinger. An eye stared through the opening. It was a nervous eye, small and brooding and of that uncertain color that is neither green nor blue. A voice followed the stare into the hall. "Yeah?"

"Myron Weeks?"

"Who's askin'?"

I shoved the door hard, catching him just above the bridge of the nose and knocking him back into the middle of the room. As the door opened, I stepped inside.

It was a cramped little apartment, with almost no furnishings and a curtain on the right drawn back in front of an alcove with a fold-away bed. The bed was pulled down and rumpled, one of the sheets torn off. The sheet had been hung on the wall on the far side of the room, forming a mottled backdrop behind a scrawny davenport. A camera on a tripod and a pair of photo flood lamps sat in front of the davenport, and a pair of young lovelies in swimming suits sat on top of it. They sat unmoving, like porcelain statues, staring at me with questioning eyes. One had ebony hair and pale skin, and her robins-egg blue suit fitted her like the skin on a sausage. The other was deeply tanned, with chestnut-brown hair and a flaming carmine mouth, and she was wearing two pieces of jet-black fabric that I could have used to lace my shoes.

The man in the center of the room was short and reedy and built like a pipe cleaner. He wore flannel trousers and a shirt that he might have slept in, and he had thinning hair the color of wet sand. His pinched-up face was mostly nose, and he held his hands over the nose and blinked a wounded look in my direction over the top of them.

"I think ya broke it," he whined. "Now I'll have to go and get it fixed."

"Live with it awhile," I said. "It'll give you character."

"What the hell do you want?"

"I want to talk about Lorna James."

The pain in his expression deepened. "Not again." He reached slowly into his back pocket and brought out a well-traveled handkerchief. He dabbed it over his nose, looked at it, and then sniffed.

"I just went through all that with the cops, not more'n an hour ago," he said.

"Then it ought to be fresh in your mind."

Weeks went on dabbing and inspecting the handkerchief without looking at me. "Just who the hell are you?"

"The name's Garrett," I said. "I was hired to get back some pictures you took of Lorna."

"Aw Christ," he wailed. "You're the one what was with her down at the warehouse." He pulled his nose out from behind the handkerchief and looked at me through a mixture of fear and impatience. "Well, there ain't no goddamn pictures."

"Then what were you trying to sell?"

He started to answer, but his breath caught. Then his shoulders shook, his head jerked forward, and he sneezed into the handkerchief. He fell into a paroxysm of sniffling and more dabbing, then finally straightened himself and put the handkerchief away. He raised his head slowly, like a battered fighter pulling himself off the canvas. A murky sadness clouded his eyes.

"Look," he said. "It's like I told the cops. I been up in Frisco for the last three days—at my brother's funeral. Just got in last night. I hadda stand out in the rain at the burial for damn near half a day, and I come down with this lousy cold. I oughta be in bed takin' care of myself, only I gotta get these leg shots for a guy what wants ta do a magazine ad." He made a quick motion toward the two girls. "That's the truth. If ya want, I can give ya the names and addresses of a dozen people in Frisco who'll back me up."

"You just happen to have them handy?"

"Damn right, I do." He sniffed again. "Like I told ya. I just give the whole works ta the cops."

I stepped close to him and leaned forward so I could get a good look at his eyes. "Tell me about Paul Milton."

He edged back toward the davenport. "I don't know nobody named Milton. I told the cops that, too."

"Who's your friend, Myron?"

It was the one with the chestnut hair. She raised herself off the davenport like a cat waking from a nap. Then she sauntered over and leaned against Weeks, resting an arm on his shoulder. She looked at me with hungry eyes showing pupils as big as hockey pucks—not what you would expect from someone sitting under bright lights.

"Don't we get an introduction?" she purred.

Weeks pushed her away. Then, before he could say anything, he sneezed again, this time down the front of his shirt. He pulled the handkerchief out of his pocket again and waved it at the girl.

"Not now, Doreen. You girls take a break, will ya?" He motioned toward the alcove. "Go on."

The two eased across the room and slowly drew the curtain. The dark-haired girl disappeared, but Doreen paused in the doorway and threw me a look that reached all thee way to my back pocket.

"Drexel three-three-three-one-eight," she cooed. "Think you can remember that?"

"It would be a crime to forget," I said. "But I don't have a bathing suit."

She batted her eyelashes and played out a sulky smile. "Yes, you do." Then she stepped through the curtain.

Weeks went through his ritual with the handkerchief, then made a pleading gesture with his hands. "Look. I told the cops everything I know. I ain't got no pictures of that James kid, and I was outta town when she was bumped off. So, what d'ya want from me?"

"I want a straight story."

I told ya the truth," he whined. "I can't tall ya no more than I told the cops."

"Like hell," I said. "Someone in your racket never spills the whole story to the law. If you did, then half the people you do business with would be around here trying to trample you."

I took a couple of steps in his direction and, without even touching him, I backed him into the davenport. He sat down hard, and I leaned over until I was no more than a foot from his face. I lowered my voice and spoke quietly.

"Somebody set me up, Myron. I was supposed to get the long dark chill the same as Lorna James. And I can't let people get away with that. In my racket, it's bad advertising. So, I want to know all about the pictures and about Paul Milton. And if I don't get the straight goods, then I'll just have to talk to the cops about Doreen. Right now, she's juiced up like a waltzing monkey. But when she comes down, she'll sell you out just to get another fix. And I don't have to tell you what the cops will do if they think you're dealing in white goods."

Dread seeped into his eyes. His mouth barely moved. "Aw, Jeez. Gimmie a break, will ya?"

"I'm giving you one," I said. "Me or the cops?"

The little man licked his lips and rubbed his hands together. "All right. All right."

He started to get up, but I pushed him back down onto the davenport. Then I spun him around on it sideways, putting his back to the curtain, and stepped over in front of him so I could see the curtain over his shoulder.

"Stay there and keep looking at me," I said. "I don't want you giving a high sign for one of your girls to bop me with a shoe."

"He made a soft moaning sound and licked his lips again. His voice came out muted and flat. "Okay, okay. But keep it down, will ya? That Doreen's got ears a yard long."

He cleared his throat nervously. "I did take some pictures of the James kid about a year and a half ago. Whenever I run inta one o' them young babes, I try ta get some prime shots, ya know? Then I keep 'em around in case the doll gets herself known. Sometimes the studios offer ta buy, and so for a business fee, I give 'em the prints and the negatives. I mean, I don't never hold nothin' back on accounta that wouldn't be right, ya know?"

He started shifting around on the davenport, but I grabbed his shoulder and kept him facing me.

"Go on."

"Well, anyway, I took these pictures, see? Only after a while I get ta thinkin'. This dame ain't goin' no place. I mean, she was strictly no talent, ya know? She was workin' in that dance joint, and I just figure she's gonna be there forever. So, I burned the pictures, negatives and all."

"Didn't you tell her that?"

His eyes widened. "I never saw her again, I swear. I mean, what was I gonna do, go inta that joint just ta tell her I ain't got her pictures no more? It wouldn'ta made no difference. Them babes is all a dime a dozen. Believe me, mister. She was goin' no place."

"Somebody thought she was," I said. "Somebody was trying to sell her those pictures."

Weeks wrinkled up his face and shook his head. "Nah. No such thing. I figure she gets some fast talk from some slick hustler what says he can put her name on a billboard. Happens all the time."

I straightened up and folded my arms. "Maybe. What about Paul Milton?"

"Like I said, I don't know the guy." Before I could respond, he held up his hand. "Only, I heard about this guy who's been hangin' around the Hot Foot lately, claimin' ta be an agent. That ain't nothin' ta take notice of, ya understand. I mean, a lotta guys drift in there tryin' ta work that angle so's they can hustle the girls. Only this guy just shows up in the last coupla weeks. And he ain't interested in nobody but Lorna. With all the other babes in that joint what might have some talent, all this guy can see is her."

"Anything else?"

His eyes narrowed, and a quizzical smirk tugged at the corners of his mouth. "Yeah, maybe. They say this guy's got plenty o' the folding—wears hundred-dollar suits, drives a fancy car. Doesn't sound like the kinda guy ta be goin' inta the Hot Foot."

"What *does* he sound like?"

He shook his head. "Dunno."

I had no reason to ask, so I asked anyway. "You ever hear of a man named Nugent?"

He seemed genuinely surprised. "Nope." He reflected for a minute, then swallowed hard. "Look, mister. That's all I know. Honest. I mean, I'm sorry the kid's dead, but I didn't have nothin' ta do with it. You can even check with the cops if ya want. They'll tell ya that, too. Only, please. Don't say nothin' about Doreen."

I stepped back into the middle of the room and turned and looked at him—a shifty little character who would take pictures of his mother on her deathbed if he thought there might be some money in it. You hear a lot of lies in my line of work. I wasn't sure why, but this time, I didn't think I was hearing one.

"Just remember, I've got Doreen's number," I said.

He winced and dragged himself off the davenport. "I'm tellin' ya the truth. I swear." He made the sign of the Cross, then sneezed and began fumbling with the handkerchief again. "On my dead brother's grave, it's the truth."

I took a lingering look around the shabby apartment. "Somebody was ready to shell out five C-notes for Lorna's pictures. Down my street, that's a lot of money."

Weeks blew his nose hard and came up sniffling and shaking his head. "Her pictures weren't even worth a fin. Anybody what knew her would know that. And besides, if I was goin' in for blackmail, I'd be askin' for a lot more than five hundred bucks. I mean, what kinda chiseler do ya think I am?"

I turned and left.

Chapter Fifteen

After stopping to buy cigarettes, I made it to the office a little after ten. Two more of the rag boys were waiting in the lobby. They said they were after the real lowdown on the killings. I said I was too. Then they told me that Thornhill was threatening to lift my license and have me locked up. I told them I could use the vacation and left them chewing on their pencils.

I went upstairs and opened up the office. The air inside had the stale closed-in smell of an old deserted house. I opened a window and then returned the Luger to its usual residence in a desk drawer. Despite what people like Stephanie Anders might think, detectives don't usually carry guns. They're heavy, they spoil the cut of your suit, and, as a rule, they're bad advertising. Most clients don't want somebody who might be too quick with a gat.

The mailman had slid his usual tidings under the door, so I sat down and sorted through the bills and the rest of the junk. Most of it I wadded up and pitched into the wastebasket by the side of the desk—a fast ball on the outside corner.

At the bottom of the stack, I found an envelope with embossed lettering in the corner reading "Clavin and Marcus." Inside was Sterling Clavin's check for $200. I held it up for a minute and looked at it, then slipped it into the middle drawer of the desk. I wasn't fond of the idea of working for Clavin, but work is where you find it.

I was just reaching for the telephone when the thing went off like a fire alarm. I waited for a second ring, then picked it up. Rawls was on the other end.

"Heard you went to see Myron Weeks," he said.

"You knew I would."

He grunted. "Get anything?"

"No more than you did. He said he was at his brother's funeral, and he sneezed at me to prove it."

Rawls grunted again. "Well, we called the boys up in Frisco. His story checks out."

"It would have to," I said. "Why else would he be using you for a character witness? You find out anything about the girl's agent, Paul Milton?"

"Nothin'." There was a pause. "I understand you been hangin' around the Hot Foot."

"Why not? Don't you want me to have any fun at all?"

"I also hear you been talkin' to people there about Nugent." Another pause. "You think the girl's killing might be tied to him?"

"Why don't you ask Thornhill?"

"Listen, flatfoot," he growled. "You better not be playin' a lone hand. There's a lot at stake in this thing, with the heat bein' put on Joey Paris. Right now, Thornhill figures you might just be his ticket to nail that bum, and so he's out after your ass. And I'm not so sure I've even got a mind to stand in his way."

"Well," I said. "I've always had an urge to see Paris."

"Aw, go to hell." He hung up.

I cradled the receiver, then went over by the window, lit a Lucky, and watched the smoke curl out into the street. Maybe Thornhill was right. Maybe someone like Paris was pulling some strings. Nugent had been in the Hot Foot looking for Eddie Franks not long before he died. But there was no telling what that might mean. Nugent could have had any number of reasons for trying to find one of Paris's bookies, none of them involving Lorna James. Just the same, I let my mind kick it around.

Maybe Lorna had seen Nugent at the club. Maybe she had talked to him. Maybe she had seen him there with someone else. And maybe she had made up her story just to string me along for reasons that I couldn't begin to guess.

I chewed on it for a while, then spit it out. Lorna wasn't smart enough to tell a good lie, or to recognize one. That's what killed her. There was still nothing I could see that tied Nugent and Lorna together. Nothing except that I had found them both dead. I tossed the Lucky out the window and went back to the desk. I felt like an empty bucket.

Mostly for something to do, I dug out the number Lorna had given me and tried Paul Milton's answering service again. The same old hen gave me the same old greeting. Yes, she had given Mr. Milton my message, and it wasn't her fault that he hadn't called. I asked her again to have him call me. I told her it was an urgent matter involving some money. She took my name and number and hung up. She sounded as interested as a cow chewing grass.

I sat and stewed through a good part of the morning, thinking about Joey Paris and his bookie and about Myron Weeks fiddling with his handkerchief. All it got me was a new lease on my headache. The morning was just beginning to wind down when I heard the reports of a pair of spike heels stabbing the tile floor in the hall.

Barbara Clavin came through the outer door and strolled easily into the office. She was wearing a white flannel suit with a lime-colored blouse, and her hair was tucked up under a creamy white, feathered hat that looked as if it had been kicked out of the nest too soon. Two brilliant emeralds hung at the ends of a pair of pendant earrings that dangled on either side of her face. Somehow, they made her skin seem more tanned and her eyes bluer than I had remembered.

She walked over, stood in front of the desk, and looked at me impatiently. "Mr. Garrett, are you busy?"

I glanced at the empty desk top, then looked back at her. "Do I look busy?"

She hesitated. "Well, I…I"

"Have a seat, Mrs. Clavin."

She settled into the client chair and began kneading a small black purse. The sun coming through the window glinted off a ring on her right hand. In the center of it, a circle of minute diamonds surrounded an emerald the size of a headlight.

"Emeralds must run in your family," I said.

She glanced down at the ring, then gave me an embarrassed smile. "Oh, this. Sterling gave it to me…and the earrings. He's very fond of emeralds. He gives them away as gifts to friends and important clients." The corners of her mouth fell slightly. "In fact, you could almost say he's obsessed with emeralds, just as he is with the ocean and his cabin cruiser."

I nodded. "The Albacore. I saw the picture in his office."

"It really is quite magnificent."

"Uh-huh. I'll think of it every time I eat a tuna sandwich."

She smiled faintly. "Sterling spends all his spare time on it. Sometimes, I hardly see him for days. She bit her lip and stared in the direction of the window. When she looked back, a trace of sadness lay in her eyes. "What is it with the ocean, Mr. Garrett? Why are men drawn to it?"

"Not all of them are," I said. "For some, it's a place to look for life. For others, it's a place to hide from it."

"Do you think Sterling is hiding from me?"

"What I think doesn't matter."

"I know. It's just…" She looked down and went on kneading the purse. "I hope I've done the right thing. Last night, I told Sterling that I had come to see you, that I thought you could help." She looked up again. "You will help him, Mr. Garrett, won't you?"

"Maybe," I said, "if he really wants my help. Is that why you came to see me?"

She let out a heavy sigh. "No. No, it isn't."

She stood up, walked over to the window, and spoke without looking at me. "Sterling has always been a jealous and possessive man, Mr. Garrett. But lately, he's gotten much worse, and I'm…I'm afraid. Last night, when I told him I'd been to see you, he simply exploded. He accused me of…of having an affair. Then he hit me and left the house. I haven't seen him since."

Finally, she turned and looked at me. A single tear traced a line down her cheek. "Mr. Garrett, I'm so frightened. Something is happening to Sterling. Something terrible."

I stood up and went over to her. Before I could say anything, she clutched the lapels of my jacket and buried her face in my shirt. Almost by themselves, my arms went around her. She was trembling like a kitten left out in the rain. I held her and breathed in the scent from her hair. She smelled like a vacation. After a minute, she stepped back and looked up at me. The sunlight rippled in her blue eyes the way it plays over the breakers in early morning. I could almost see her walking along the beach barefoot, her hair blowing in the wind.

"I'm sorry," she said. "You must think I'm just awful. But he is my husband. Mr. Garrett, I'm afraid Sterling is hiding something, and I'm terribly worried."

I led her back to the client chair. Then I got a cup of water from the cooler and handed it to her. She sipped it while I sat down.

"Have you been to the police, Mrs. Clavin?"

She shook her head grimly.

"If he's beating you up..."

"What makes you so sure he's hiding something?"

"Just...just a feeling."

I let my breath out heavily. "Look, Mrs. Clavin. If you won't go to the police, there's nothing I can do. I can't keep you from being worried, and I can't keep Sterling from having a temper."

"I know. That's not why I'm here." She leaned forward and placed both hands on the edge of the desk. "I want you to come to the house this evening. Sterling is giving one of his cocktail parties. Every month, he entertains a number of important people at our home. He says it's good for his business. Sometimes, he even takes some of them out on his boat afterwards. I want you to come and...keep an eye on things."

"Wouldn't you be better off with a good caterer?"

She tried to smile, then looked away. "Mr. Garrett, there's something I haven't told you about Sterling. He sometimes drinks...quite heavily. When he does, even the slightest thing can set him off. I want you to make sure nothing happens to him." She stared down at her purse again. Her voice fell almost to a whisper. "Or to me."

I leaned back in my chair, scratched my chin, and thought about turning the whole mess over to Rawls. "Being a bodyguard isn't exactly my line of work, Mrs. Clavin."

She looked up quickly and grabbed the desk again. "Mr. Garrett, maybe if Sterling sees you there with the other guests, he'll see that you're just doing your job. Maybe he'll understand that there's nothing between you and me."

I sat and looked at her, and she read the doubt in my face.

"Please, Mr. Garrett."

I looked at her for a long time. I looked into those deep blue eyes for some sign of trouble. I didn't see any. Maybe I didn't want to.

"All right," I said.

She sank back in the chair, and a real smile grew on her face for the first time. "Oh, Mr. Garrett. Thank you. I'm so relieved. You don't know how much this means to me."

I looked at my watch. By now, it was a little past noon. "Then you can tell me over lunch."

"I...I shouldn't."

"Just tell Sterling you were entertaining some important people. Tell him it's good for business."

She grinned, fumbled with her purse, then took a long breath and slowly let it out. "All right."

We went to a little cafe around the corner, where about a dozen hungry citizens sat at a lunch counter munching and drinking beer. Around to the left, a half-empty row of wooden booths ran along the wall and into a plain but respectable dining area in the back. Barbara Clavin walked in front of me and settled into the last booth. I took off my hat and sat down just as a waitress came up behind me.

The woman wore a plain but respectable dress, and she had a plain but respectable face with a sweep of grayish-white hair knotted in a bun on top of her head. I ordered a plain but respectable Scotch, and she pulled a pencil out of the bun and wrote on a pad. Mrs. Clavin ordered a gimlet, and the woman wrote on the pad again, then dropped a pair of menus on the table and headed off. She returned in only a minute with the drinks, and I told her to come back after we'd had a chance to get hungry.

When we were alone, Barbara Clavin reached across the table and took hold of my hand in both of hers. "We won't be seen here, will we? I mean, Sterling mustn't know."

"Take a good look around," I said. "Except for the rocks you're wearing, you won't see an emerald in the place. "

"I feel positively devilish." She grinned. "I feel like a schoolgirl playing hooky."

"Didn't you play hooky when you were in school?"

She took a big swig of the gimlet and sighed. "Oh, no. I wanted to a few times, but I never did."

"What about later?"

"Later, I was just too busy."

I eased down some of the Scotch. "With what?"

She traced a finger around the top of the glass. "With…dreams."

" What kind of dreams?"

She took another long drink, then put the glass down, angled her head, and lifted an eyebrow. "Now, wait a minute. I should be asking the questions. After all, I'm relying on you for a great deal." A coy smile edged into the corners of her mouth. "Besides, you've had me in tears twice in three days, and I hardly know a thing about you. I think you owe a girl that much."

This time I took a big drink. "There isn't much to know."

"Well, I know that you were a policeman and that now you're a detective. But there must be more than that. Where were you born? Where did you grow up? What made you choose police work? And what do you do when you're not working?"

I drained the Scotch, then took out a Lucky, lit it, and dropped the pack on the table. Barbara Clavin sipped her drink and eyed me from behind it.

"All right," I said. "I was born in L.A. I haven't any family, and there probably isn't anyone who would call me a friend. I grew up looking for a job and became a cop because it was better than being on a breadline. When I couldn't be a cop anymore, I became a detective because the pay is bad and the hours are worse. I drink, I smoke, I swear, and I sometimes read the sports page. I do that even when I'm not working. "

She giggled and reached for a cigarette. I struck a match and held it out over the table. She held my hand in hers and puffed slowly without taking her eyes off me.

"You're not an easy man to know," she said. "But I can't help being curious. Hasn't there been someone in your life?"

"There's always someone in my life, Mrs. Clavin. That's what makes me a detective."

She giggled again. "Please. Call me Barbara." She leaned forward and put both elbows on the table. A slow flush crept up the sides of her neck. "And what shall I call you?"

I leaned forward and looked into her eyes. "Call me when you're not married."

She leaned back and laughed. "Well, it said 'Michael' on your office door. I guess that's good enough." She folded her arms and gave me a mocking smile. "Poor Michael. Just like Don Quixote, all alone with his windmills."

"Not quite," I said. "Windmills don't shoot."

The waitress came over, and I ordered another round and a sandwich. Barbara ordered a salad, and the woman disappeared and came back in another minute with the drinks. I sipped the Scotch and watched as Barbara dived into the second gimlet.

"Tell me about your dreams," I said.

She put down the glass and sighed. "Well, all right, since I'm not going to get anything out of you."

She took a deep drag on the cigarette, blew out the smoke, and looked wistfully at it. "I used to dream about being in the theater. I always loved the stage and acting. I even acted a little in high school." Her mouth fell into a sardonic curl. "But my parents couldn't understand my wanting to be an actress. They thought it was just a silly little girl's dream. They wanted me to live the kind of life they did—be a cheerleader, go to the prom, marry a football player, and then settle down here and have six children. I tried, but that life just wasn't for me."

By now, the story was becoming all too familiar. I crushed out the Lucky and took another pull on the Scotch. A picture of Lorna James flashed in my head.

"So, you decided to leave home and become an actress."

She took some more of her drink and nodded. "I tried getting on with some of the studios out here, but you know how that is. And what I really wanted was to be on the stage. So, I went to Chicago, then Philadelphia and New York, and finally, I wound up in Boston." She shook her head, and a smile of recollection moved up her face.

"It was very hard, but I was very young…and determined. I worked as a waitress during the day so I could pay for acting school in the evenings. And finally, after two years, I was asked to join a small theater group. I was absolutely thrilled, that is, until…"

She finished her drink,took a last drag on the cigarette, and looked down at the table.

"Just before I was to start with the group, I received word that my brother Robert had been killed during the invasion of Italy and that my mother had had a stroke. I came home and nursed her for eight months until she died. After that, I went back to Boston, but naturally, the opening with the group had been filled. I still had no real experience, and so I couldn't get an acting job anywhere. By then, I was alone,broke, and very discouraged. That's when I met Sterling."

Barbara folded her hands on the table and looked up at me with a bittersweet expression. "Life certainly doesn't turn out the way you expect it to."

"That's what comes from having expectations," I said.

She smiled. "I'm sorry. I'm afraid I'm bending your ear." She leaned forward and put her hand on my arm again. "It's just that you're very easy to talk to."

I sat there being easy to talk to until lunch came. We chewed at it for a while. Afterwards, I lit another Lucky and spoke to her again.

"So, you married Sterling in Boston?"

She nodded. "He was just out of law school, and he was very dashing and very idealistic. He used to talk about how justice can't work unless everyone, even the people we don't like, get the best possible defense. He was very persuasive, and…and when you really get to know Sterling, you can't help but care for him."

I took an easy drag and watched the memories swimming in her eyes. I tried to picture someone besides Sterling caring for Sterling. "How did you wind up here?"

"Sterling's home was in Los Angeles, so we moved here, and he set up his practice. At first, it was wonderful. Sterling did very well financially, and he was a devoted husband." The same quiet sadness filled her face again. "But over the years, as Sterling became more powerful, he also became more possessive. One by one, my friends stopped coming around. Now, I hardly ever see anyone or even go out. I don't know what Sterling would do if he saw me in here with you."

I took another drag and let the smoke slowly drift up over the table. Part of me wanted to ask the obvious question. Part of me didn't. "Why do you stay with him?"

She leaned back and sighed heavily. "I suppose it's partly loyalty. I really loved Sterling when I married him, and I think I still love the man I remember." She sighed again. "But I'm afraid it isn't just that. Before we were married, Sterling had me sign a legal document agreeing to forfeit any claim against him if we were ever divorced. His will even stipulates that after his death, his money goes into a trust and that I am to get an allowance only as long as I don't remarry."

Barbara leaned forward on the table, her eyes locked on mine. "You see, Michael. If I left Sterling, I'd have nothing. I suppose it's vain and selfish of me to think that way, but I'm not young anymore. And I'm afraid that starting over would be very difficult." Her eyes suddenly brightened, and she smiled. "Besides, Sterling is really an honest and decent man. Somehow, he's just gotten off the track. I'm sure that after you help straighten out whatever is bothering him, everything will be all right again."

I crushed out the rest of the Lucky. "Maybe."

"I'm sure it will." She reached out and took my hand. "Somehow, you give me confidence. You remind me of Sterling, back when we first met. If this were another time and another place…" She paused, and her voice lowered.

"Michael, has there really been no one…no one special?"

I didn't answer.

She reddened and looked away. "I'm sorry. I didn't mean to pry."

Before I could say anything, she glanced at her watch. "Oh, my. Look at the time. It's nearly two. I have to go home and start getting ready for the party. Can you be there around eight?"

"Will it take you that long to get ready?"

She grinned. "You want me to look my best, don't you?" There was no answer for that one either.

I paid the waitress and gave her a little something extra for leaving us alone. Then I helped Barbara out of the booth, and we started up the aisle toward the front of the cafe. When we were about halfway to the door, a chunky man in a vaguely familiar gray felt hat stood up at the far end of the lunch counter. He threw down a handful of change without bothering to count it, then turned quickly and went outside. By the time Barbara and I reached the street, he was gone.

We stood for a minute in front of the cafe. Barbara stepped close to me and put her hand on my arm and looked up at me. Her blue eyes were moist and deep.

"Thank you, Michael."

"Don't thank me yet. I haven't done anything."

She looked at me for a long moment. Then she reached a hand up behind my neck, drew me down to her, and kissed me softly on the cheek. "Yes, you have."

She turned quickly, crossed the street, and climbed into a cream-colored convertible. In a moment, the engine roared, and the car pulled out and sped off up the street. I strolled back up the block and around the corner to the office and thought about the check I had left up in my desk. Suddenly, I was glad I hadn't gone out and cashed it. Even if I could help Sterling Clavin, I wasn't sure I wanted to.

As I stepped into the lobby of the Patterson Building, I spotted a familiar gray felt hat hovering in front of the elevator. Standing under it was the chunky character from the cafe. He was a somber-looking man with a florid face that had taken some punishment, a wide, flattened nose, and a left ear like raw hamburger. He was wearing a dark suit, with a double-breasted jacket showing a bulge under his left arm that I didn't like. As I walked over to the elevator, he stepped in front of me.

"Feel like takin' a ride?"

"I like walking better."

He slid his right hand inside his jacket and held it there the way they always do. "Someone wants ta see ya."

"Well," I said. "Since you're being so polite."

I turned and walked back toward the door, and he followed—a step behind and to my right. I figured from that position he wouldn't need more than a second to put a slug through my kidneys.

We went outside, and he ushered me over to the curb. We waited less than a minute. A black Plymouth sedan with another felt hat behind the wheel purred around the corner, then eased up and sat idling directly in front of me. The rear door swung open, and a raspy voice drifted out.

"Let's go. The Boss is waitin'."

Chapter Sixteen

We drove over to the east side, past Lincoln Park, and up into Alhambra. The Plymouth moved easily along Valley Boulevard, then turned onto Freemont and, after a couple of blocks, headed up Mission Road. I sat in back on the driver's side behind a swarthy character with a neck as thin as a pipe stem and overlarge ears that stuck out from his head like stirrups. Next to me, the chunky one sat with his arms folded and his eyes trained straight ahead. Neither man spoke. I asked where we were going, but all I got for my trouble was a grunt and a poke in the ribs with something that wasn't a finger.

We cruised past several miles of markets, gas stations, and office buildings as plain as unbuttered bread. Traces of thickening haze were settling over the streets. But a line of tall clouds with gray edges flirted with the afternoon sun, hinting that we could get more rain. The people moving along the street didn't seem to care. They darted quickly from block to block, not looking at the traffic or at each other. Some of them would just be looking for a place to escape the gathering smog. Others would be intent on business that was best done out of sight.

After another mile, the Plymouth rolled into one of those neon neighborhoods that make L.A. what it is. There were pool halls and hock shops and cheap theaters where no one would go to see the latest Betty Grable film. We drove past several dark side streets and finally pulled up to the curb behind a modest row of Cadillacs, Packards, and Chryslers. The man next to me opened the door, stepped onto the curb, and then yanked me out by the arm. I stood there, brushed off my suit, and took a good look at the building in the middle of the block.

Two stories high with a recessed entry, it had a narrow stone porch and four cement columns extending up to the second floor. A polished wooden sign with black etched lettering jutted out from between the two central columns. The sign read, "Pillars." It was a place I had visited a time or two before.

During the last couple of years, it had become popular for the Hollywood crowd to come here after hours. Downstairs in the restaurant, they could have a late supper. Then afterward, they could go up to the bar and drink expensive champagne while they rubbed elbows with some of the city's better-known tough boys. People in the ritzy set went to The Pillars so they could be seen and then talk about it later over cocktails at the country club. I seldom went there unless I had a gun in my ribs.

The chunky man took me by the arm and led me to the door, his partner following a couple of steps behind. We went in and up a dark flight of wooden stairs and stopped on a landing in front of a pair of double doors with large brass handles. The man held me there while he ducked his head in past the doors and spoke to someone. There was a pause, then he let go of my arm, opened the doors, and motioned me inside.

It was dimly lit and smoky, a large room without windows—the kind of place where it would always be night. Several sections of raised flooring accented by wooden floor-to-ceiling columns surrounded a dance floor and a small stage. In the back, a bar with three men in shirtsleeves busy behind it extended halfway across the room and stopped at a pair of swinging doors that I guessed would lead to a kitchen. A set of wrought-iron railings bordered the raised sections, and around the walls, a series of midnight-blue velvet drapes with flaming red tassels gave the place a look that Zane Grey would have liked.

Even in mid-afternoon, The Pillars was almost jammed with the usual mixed clientele, the noise from the crowd droning like a piece of machinery. Mingling with all the locals were about a dozen up-towners in business suits and a handful of the Hollywood gentry. Most of them were huddled around tables, drinking and smoking cigars and talking to each other as if every word meant a fortune. On stage, a sandy-haired piano player in a white dinner jacket was quietly stroking the keys of a concert grand. He had long, slender fingers that moved like the legs of a grasshopper, and he was playing "Someone To Watch Over Me." From where I stood, it seemed like a good selection.

Just inside the door on the left, an oily-looking man in another white dinner jacket stood behind a kind of lectern, eyeing me the way a shark sizes up a floundering swimmer. He had thick brown hair, a sunken chin, and he smelled of Wildroot. As I entered, he stepped around and spoke in a waxy voice as slippery as a bar of soap.

"Mr. Garrett, we've been expecting you." He held out his hand and motioned toward the center of the room. "This way, please."

I followed him through the crowd, then up a couple of steps to a tiered section with about a half dozen empty tables covered in white linen. He moved over to a table toward the back and held out a chair, and I sat down facing out toward the dance floor. The two men who had been my escorts settled at a table just behind me.

The oily man snapped his fingers, and a tall honey-blonde with dewy brown eyes and a tray came out of nowhere and stood next to the table.

"Lorraine," the man said to her, "Check Mr. Garrett's hat and get him anything he wants." He leaned over and spoke confidently to me. "It's on the house."

Before I could say anything, the man marched back through the tables and took up his position by the door.

I handed my hat to the blonde and watched as she balanced it on the tray. She had long, willowy legs, and she was wearing a tight-fitting apricot cocktail dress that was cut low enough in front to make breathing look dangerous. She held the tray to the side, put her hand on the table, and leaned forward.

"What would you like?"

"Keep leaning over like that, and I might tell you."

She chuckled and licked her lips slowly. "I mean to drink, Silly."

I ordered a Scotch, and she sauntered off out of sight. When she was gone,

I lit up a Lucky and looked around the room. Except for the section I was in, most of the tables were occupied. At one of the larger tables near the dance floor, a fat gent with a head as bald as a doorknob was entertaining a platinum starlet from one of the studios. There was a bottle of champagne on the table, and he kept pouring from it while she kept drinking. As I watched, he leaned over and whispered something to her, and she let out a tinny giggle. He would be telling her how he was going to help with her career—in the morning.

Along the bar to my right, several dark men in dark suits were perched on stools, nuzzling drinks. One of them turned and gave me a shifty eye, then quickly looked away. I glanced around at the two characters behind me. They were sitting at the table, hands folded, staring back at me. The chunky one still had the bulge under his jacket.

Lorraine brought my Scotch and then stood in a statuesque pose next to the table. "Will there be anything else?"

"What time do you get through?"

She cocked an eyebrow and cooed at me. "Sorry. He doesn't like us to take up with customers."

"He?"

Her eyes widened a couple of notches. "Don't you know? The owner." She turned and motioned across the room. "Over there."

I looked over to the far corner, where a single table sat on a raised platform just to the right of the stage. Three more men of the type that lined the bar were sitting at the table. They were all watching a fourth man who sat with his back to the wall. He was lean and swarthy, with chocolate-brown hair parted in the middle and a thin dark mustache that he might have borrowed from Errol Flynn. The girls would love it, and he would let them. He wore an expensive-looking ivory-brown suit and vest, with a powder blue shirt and maroon tie, and he sat pointing a long, deliberate finger across the table as he talked to the three men. Leaning against the wall next to him was an ebony walking stick the size of a baseball bat with a polished silver knob on the end. Joey "The Stick" Paris was holding court.

Lorraine drifted away, and I finished the Lucky and nursed the Scotch. It

157

was about good enough to keep me interested. I was just emptying my glass when the three men at Paris's table stood up and began ducking through the crowd. One of them signaled to the table behind me, and in less than the blink of an eye, the two men were standing on either side of my chair. My chunky friend leaned over and spoke with the insistent purr of a small dynamo.

"Time ta meet the Boss."

"Nuts," I said. I lit another cigarette and blew the smoke all over his suit. "I like it right here."

I spotted Lorraine by the end of the bar and motioned her over to the table. She came reluctantly and stood several steps away, a mixture of fear and excitement dancing in her eyes.

"I'll have another," I told her. "And stick around. I might be having company."

A steely hand with fingers like barbed wire came down on my left shoulder. I took my time and pulled in a long drag on the Lucky. Then I reached up toward the hand and jammed the business end of my cigarette into the second knuckle of the forefinger. There was a yelp, and the man stepped back. I looked up at the other one.

"Go ahead and plug me if you want," I said. "Even in this joint, the cops can scare up enough witnesses to get you cooked—that is if your boss lets you live long enough. If he wants to see me, go tell him where I am."

He stood for a minute, tugging at his ear and looking at me through a thin, pale hatred. Then he glanced non-commitally back over my head and strode off in the direction of Paris's table. The man with the burnt finger settled back down at the table behind me and went about sucking on his knuckle. Lorraine finally eased over next to me and made a clucking noise in the side of her mouth.

"Boy, mister," she said. "You sure got a lotta sand. I hope you know what you're doin."

I took a last drag on the fractured Lucky. "Why should today be different?"

I watched the table in the far corner of the room. Paris sat stone-faced, staring at me while his henchman spoke to him. Then he slowly rose, picked up the walking stick and started in my direction. As he moved across the room, the crowd parted in front of him as if a swarm of hornets had been let loose. When he reached my table, he stood glaring down from the top of a wiry frame that had to be six and a half feet high.

"So we got a tough guy here. A goddamn Lone Ranger." His voice had the sound of gravel poured into a well. "Where's your horse and your Injun, tough guy?"

"Horses come high this year," I said. I motioned toward Lorraine. "Pick your poison. It's on the house."

Paris grunted and pointed the end of his walking stick at Lorraine. My usual doll. And make it snappy." He looked back at me with something just this side of a leer. "This won't take long."

Lorraine trotted back to the bar, and Paris just stood for a minute, eyeing me with an air of distaste, as if he'd just discovered a spot on the rug. From up close, he didn't look as good as he had from across the room. His face was thin and pock-marked, his jaw a little too heavy, and the corners of his mustache were showing uneven sprigs of white. But his eyes held the dull hardness of cast iron, just the way they would with someone whose business included taking lives.

Abruptly, he pulled out the chair next to me. He turned it backwards and then sat straddling it while he balanced the stick in front of him, his hands folded on top of it. He flexed his fingers deliberately, and I couldn't help noticing a large gold ring with a cluster of emeralds. He saw me eyeing it.

"You like this?" he asked. "Maybe you'd like one for yourself?"

"Lugging that much weight around might spoil my pitching arm," I said. "Besides, everybody's wearing emeralds these days."

The corners of his mouth twitched. "Yeah. I understand we got a mutual acquaintance who goes for these little green rocks."

"Do we?"

He banged the stick on the floor and snarled through his teeth. "Don't play cagey with me, Garrett. I know who you are and what you're doin'. You're nothin' but a crummy gumshoe that I wouldn't take time ta wipe my feet on. Only it just so happens that you been hired by a frienda mine—a guy I'm dependin' on ta be my mouthpiece. That means I gotta pay some attention ta you and make sure you don't go crooked on my friend."

I gave him one of my best grins. "Imagine you telling me not to go crooked."

A dark frown filled his face. "Keep up the smart cracks, and you could get yourself disliked."

"That'll keep me awake nights."

He snarled and started to get up, but Lorraine chose that moment to come back with the drinks. She gave me another Scotch, and she put a shot glass full of bourbon in front of Paris. Then she darted off as if someone had just promised her a free pair of nylons. Paris drained the bourbon in one gulp, then peered across the table with an uneasy smile.

"Listen, Garrett. You got a reputation for bein' on the up and up, so I'm gonna level with ya. I need Clavin, and I can't afford ta have him tangled up in some phony murder rap while I'm wrestlin' with the D.A. and the Grand Jury. That's why I wanna make sure you get him off the hook. You do that, and I'll make it worth your while."

"Tempting," I said. "'But what makes you so sure the rap's a phony?"

He twisted his face and sneered at me. "Don't be simple. What reason would Clavin have for squibbin' some broken-down sham us?"

I shrugged. "The boys at the station have a theory that Nugent was blackmailing Clavin. That ought to be reason enough for anybody. But just in case it isn't, a young girl got her brains blown out last night. And she just happened to be working at a club where Nugent was seen asking after one of your bookies. A sharp guesser might decide that she and Nugent were putting a squeeze on Clavin and that he wiped them both off."

He scowled. "The cops think that?"

I shrugged again. "They haven't said so."

"Look," he said, "I know about the notes and about Nugent's appointment book. I don't know about that frail at the Hot Foot, but I'm tellin' ya, the whole thing's a goddamn frame-up."

""Who would want to put Clavin in a frame?'"

Paris sneered and banged his stick again. "Are you really as dumb as you look? It's that goddamn Lefty Stark. Who else? He's had it in for me ever since that trial two years ago,"

I picked up my glass, took a good swig of courage, and then let him have both barrels. "Is that why Stark has been calling Clavin's office?"

His eyes blazed and then narrowed to the width of a knife edge. "Clavin ain't doin' business with Stark, and you'd better not be either. Not if you wanna stay healthy."

I leaned back and took another sip of the Scotch. "All right—for the sake of everybody's health. What about one of your own people?"

His expression turned quizzical. "What d'ya mean?"

"I mean that just before he died, Nugent was looking for Eddie Franks. If he had gotten on the hook to Franks for some serious money, that would have made him easy meat. Stark could have gotten to your man, and the two of them could have been using Nugent for a cat's paw. Maybe the James girl found out about it and got blasted before she could say anything."

He rubbed his chin and thought about it. "So, you think Stark had Franks set up Nugent as a blackmailer and then bump him off so the cops would think it was Clavin?" he snorted. "Sounds like somethin' that son of a bitch Stark would dream up."

"People have been killed for less."

He rubbed his chin some more and then suddenly stopped. "Only one thing wrong with that. Clavin ain't no dumbbell. He's smart. Sure, he's got a temper, and the cops don't like him, but he ain't gonna be givin' nobody a reason ta blackmail him." He shook his head. "Naw. It won't hold up."

"That's why I need to talk to Eddie Franks," I said. "Maybe I can prove that Clavin didn't have a motive for killing Nugent but that Franks or someone he was working for did. That would be enough to put your mouthpiece in the clear."

Paris nodded slowly. A thin smile played across his lips. "Eddie Franks, huh? All right. I'll get him for you. Meantime, I'm gonna give you a little friendly advice. I been keepin' an eye on you ever since you went ta Clavin's office, and I know you been meetin' with his wife. Now, I don't mind if you wanna go chasin' after some skirt. I figure that's your business. But Clavin don't like it when guys get too close ta his Mrs. It upsets him. And that upsets me. So, I'm tellin' you ta lay off. Just do your Job and leave the broad alone."

I drank the last of the Scotch and then folded my arms and looked at him. "And if I don't?"

He turned and waved his stick in the direction of the bar. "Hey, Butch."

A large, doughy-faced man with pale eyes and a familiar scar on his right cheek got off a stool, glided over to the table, and sat down across from me. Paris leaned over and spoke to him quietly.

"Take a good look at this guy, Butch. I want you ta remember him."

Butch sat without moving and stared at me with as much expression as a glass of water. Paris chuckled at him and then reached into his pocket and brought out a wad of bills that looked to me like a year's wages. He peeled off two handfuls of C-notes and stacked them on the table in front of him.

"I wanna make sure you get the picture," he said. "This is yours if you play ball. Just get Clavin outta this jam, and I'll give you the ten yards as a bonus on toppa what he's payn' you."

While I was looking at the money, Paris turned back to Butch and held out his hand. The man reached inside his jacket and pulled out a .45 the size of a howitzer. Paris took it and casually brought it up and aimed it at the bridge of my nose.

"'But don't cross me up,'" he said. "If anythin' happens so that Clavin can't represent me, then all you'll see is a one-eyed stare."

Chapter Seventeen

I t was about three o'clock when Paris's monkeys drove me back to the office. Paris had said he would locate Eddie Franks and then get in touch with me. Meanwhile, I was to dig up everything I could that would convince the cops not to lock up Clavin. I'd have had more fun chasing a bail jumper in Topeka. I wasn't sure Paris believed my story about Stark rigging the murders to frame Clavin. I wasn't sure I did. But Paris was right about one thing. The whole setup would fall flat if the cops couldn't prove that Nugent had something on Clavin.

Instead of going upstairs to the office, I walked up the street to the drugstore where I had left the roll of film I had gotten from the hock shop in Laguna Beach. The man behind the counter remembered me, or at least he remembered Abraham Lincoln. He said there had only been a half dozen exposures to develop, and since the film hadn't all been used, he offered me a refund. I told him to keep the money and put his kids through college.

I took the pictures up to the office. When I got inside, I locked the door, took the phone off the hook, and spread the prints out on the desk. For what seemed an endless minute, I just sat and stared at them. Finally, I pulled out the deep drawer, took a slug from the office bottle, and then lit a cigarette.

Sterling Clavin was in every picture. He was with a young girl, and they were obviously alone together. There was a shot of them on the street, one in a restaurant, two of them huddled together in a car, and two more of them nuzzling in what looked like the doorway of an apartment building. I stood up slowly and took a deep drag on the cigarette. I held it in as long as I could and tried not to scream or bite off the end of the desk. The girl in the pictures with Clavin was Stephanie Anders.

I walked over to the window and stared out into the dismal afternoon haze. Distant years and unwanted memories crowded into my mind. Nothing lives in your mind like the memory of a mistake. Nice going, Garrett, I said to myself. As if you didn't have enough mistakes to remember. You've gotten yourself on the wrong side of the law again. You failed to tell Rawls about the pawn ticket in Nugent's apartment. Now you're withholding evidence in one murder, maybe two. And when it all blows up, Joey Paris will have no reason not to measure you for a spot on a slab. I stood there and shook my head. I still didn't have all the pieces, but I was in a jam, and I knew it.

I walked back over to the desk and took another look at the pictures, half hoping they wouldn't be there. No luck. As I studied them, I thought about Barbara Clavin and her stoic devotion to her husband. I thought about Fran Brekhammer clinging to her untarnished memory of Danny Nugent. And I thought about Joey Paris telling me how smart Clavin was. A chill threaded its way down my spine like a zipper opening. If Rawls got a look at these pictures, there would be no convincing him that Nugent wasn't a blackmailer or that Clavin didn't have a perfect motive for murder.

After finishing the Lucky, I picked up the phone, then thought better of it and put it down. I took one set of the prints and locked them in the office. Then I put the other set in my pocket, put on my hat, and headed for the door. It was time to talk to someone about being a detective.

* * *

Clavin's reception room had the same expensively tidy look as the day before. The room was empty, and the door to Clavin's office was open. I went over and stepped inside. Even empty, the office held a certain presence, retaining Clavin's shape almost like an old pair of shoes. I walked over to the desk and looked back at the picture of the Albacore, hung so that Clavin could gaze at it. I could almost see him sitting there, studying the picture and thinking of himself as a captain in some world that only he could imagine. I shrugged and started for the door.

I hadn't quite gotten there when the door to Anthony Marcus's office opened. A shapely woman with dark red hair spilling over her shoulders stepped into the doorway, turned, and looked back at someone inside the office. With just a glance, I could see that she lived in a tax bracket that most people only read about. She was well made up, and she was wearing a scarlet silk blouse and a charcoal gray gabardine suit that would have been custom-fitted. Around her neck and on her fingers was an assortment of jewelry that must have cost as much as my car.

She leaned into the doorway and murmured in a smokey voice, "You'll come by later, won't you?"

A muted, reedy voice spoke back to her. "Not tonight, Grace. I'm due at Sterling's party. Business, you know. Besides we really should wait until your divorce is final."

The woman leaned in a little farther and made a petulant whimpering noise. "But Tony. You know how much I hate waiting. Can't I persuade you?"

There was a pause followed by a heavy sigh. "Grace, it's just too risky."

There was a longer pause and a faint rustling of clothes. She was persuading him. In a moment, the woman turned and walked toward the door, followed by Anthony Marcus. At the door, she turned and grabbed him again and jammed her mouth into his. I leaned against the door frame and watched them paw each other like a pair of eager sculptors molding pottery. I could be seen from where I was, but only by someone who was inclined to look. Finally, they separated, and the woman gave Marcus another whimper.

"Come over after the Party. I don't care how late it is."

Marcus hesitated. He was a tough boy to convince. She leaned against him and took a quick nibble on his ear. "All right," he said. "Now, run along."

The woman let out a victorious giggle and darted through the door. Marcus inhaled deeply, smiled, and looked pleased with himself. Once again, he had lost the battle of the sexes.

"There's nothing like playing hard to get," I said.

Marcus jumped like a startled burglar. Something that might have been recognition flickered in his eyes. Then the color fell out of his face, and his mouth moved up and down without sound, like the gills of a fish. He swallowed hard and coughed and tried to pull together the remnants of his dignity.

"What are you doing here?" His voice was a peevish twang.

"I'm desperate and forlorn. My wife doesn't understand me, and my girlfriend thinks I'm a beast because I haven't bought her any diamonds this week. I'm starved for love, and I thought I ought to sue somebody."

He drew his features into a brittle scowl. "You should have made some noise."

"Yeah," I said. "It's a bad habit of mine. I just can't resist an open door."

"What do you want?"

"I'm looking for Stephanie. She wanted to talk to me about her career."

He stretched himself up as tall as he could, brushed off his suit, and this time seemed to recognize me for real.

"Oh, yes. You're the detective. Let's see. The name was Garrett, wasn't it?"

"It still is."

He swallowed again and then glued on the kind of smile that lawyers learn from used-car salesmen. Then he stepped forward and gave me an exaggerated handshake. It was as good as ever.

"I'm sorry," he said. "But you really gave me quite a turn. I hope I wasn't too abrupt."

I told him he wasn't too abrupt. Then I asked again about Stephanie.

"She's with Sterling. He had an appointment at the courthouse, and she went with him. I'm afraid she'll be there the rest of the day." He hesitated and held his smile motionless, as if he didn't want to wrinkle it. "Is there something I can do to help?"

I shrugged and pulled out a Lucky and idly lit it, as if I might have been more interested in picking wild flowers.

"Do Stephanie and Sterling spend a lot of time together?"

He hesitated again. "Well, naturally, in the course of business, they do. Quite a lot I should say."

"Naturally," I nodded. "In the course of business."

"Well...yes."

166

"Nothing else?"

His smile started to fade, and a hint of wariness seeped into his eyes. "What are you suggesting?"

"Well," I said. "She's a very pretty girl. I'd hate to think someone was beating my time."

He scratched his ear awkwardly and kept his smile on with an effort. "Well, I shouldn't think…that is,…well, I simply don't know. I mean, they have been spending a great deal of time together lately. But I never imagined it could be anything but business."

I took a slow drag and watched him. "Probably isn't. I expect I'm just getting my dander up over nothing. You know how it is."

"Yes, quite." His smile had a few dents in it now, but the glue was still holding. "Still, I wouldn't want anything to threaten the welfare of the firm."

"Of course not."

He stood looking at me, his expression narrowing a couple of notches. "But aren't you working for Sterling?"

"We've talked about it," I said. "But I guess I'm not the only one he's talked to."

Now, he seemed genuinely curious. "What do you mean?"

"Well, I understand Sterling contacted a man named Nugent—another private detective. Ever heard of him?"

The muscles along his jaw began twitching, and he shook his head. "No. Never."

I took another careful drag. "Well, you must have seen him. Didn't he come to visit Sterling recently?"

Marcus swallowed hard and scratched his ear again. His smile was fighting for its life.

"Well, there was someone just over a week ago," he said. "He came in without an appointment."

"What did he look like?"

He shrugged unconvincingly. "Oh, medium height, medium build." He shrugged again. "Medium complexion."

"I see. He was a medium kind of guy. Any idea what they talked about?"

167

He shook his head. "No. I just assumed he wanted Sterling to represent him." He folded his arms and chewed on his lower lip. "Come to think of it, though. Sterling has seemed unusually agitated and irritable ever since that man was here. Do you know anything about it?"

I let that one pass and decided to try another tack. "Suppose I were working for Sterling. What would you think I could do for him?"

The corners of his mouth fell slightly. "I'm sure I don't know."

"Do you think he's in trouble, like with the police?"

He rubbed his hands together hard enough to chafe the skin. "I certainly hope not."

"What do you know about his clients?"

"Nothing. Sterling and I never discuss our cases."

I pushed my hat back on my head and watched him. "So, if I were working for Sterling, you really couldn't help me."

"Really, Mr. Garrett," he said, "I'm very busy with my own practice and with matters of the firm. I haven't time to be keeping track of Sterling."

"An unusual sort of partnership," I said. "Just what is your role in the firm, Mr. Marcus? Do you and Sterling share any of the cases?"

With the old smile dead on its feet, Marcus brought out a new one. "My gracious, no. I handle only divorce cases. You see, that provides a kind of balance for Sterling's criminal law practice."

"And since you don't take on any criminal cases, you don't get your name in the papers. I'll bet that's reassuring for your clients."

He nodded. "Precisely. They aren't anxious for publicity. Sterling is the one for the notoriety. But more importantly, I provide the firm with a steady source of income." A hint of conspiracy crept into his voice. "You see, in this part of town, the divorce business is really quite lucrative."

"From the looks of your clientele, I'd have guessed that," I said. "And you must be very good at your work."

He angled his head a few degrees. "What do you mean?"

I took a last drag and tossed the cigarette into a waste basket by the side of Stephanie's desk. "I mean, it must be very hard on you. It can't be easy having to spend each day soothing broken hearts and hurt feelings."

He puffed himself up with more than a little pride. "Well, one does what one has to. It's a matter of maintaining a professional attitude."

"Uh-huh. And what was your attitude when that redhead was chewing on your face?"

His smile did a full jackknife and dove to the floor. "Now, see here. Your manner is insulting."

"Yeah," I said. "It's always been like that. I even write notes about it in my diary, but it just keeps getting worse. Maybe my manner would improve if, once in a while, I got a straight story."

The twitching in his jaw heightened, but he didn't say anything.

"It's not much of a job, being a detective," I went on. "But you learn to notice things, like the way your foot itches when it rains or when people lie to you. When I asked about Stephanie, you were only too glad to let me stay suspicious. Sure, you were worried about the firm. But you weren't in any hurry to defend Clavin. And when I mentioned Nugent, you gave me a description of the most forgettable man in the world. Not one person in a thousand would remember the kind of guy you described. But you did. And when I asked you about Clavin, you couldn't be bothered. So what's your angle, Marcus? Are you after Stephanie for yourself? Or is it something bigger, like pushing Clavin out of the firm and taking over his business?"

Marcus squeezed his fists against his sides and clamped his jaw hard enough to crack a boulder. A purple flush rose in his throat. "Get out," he screamed. "Just get out."

"I'll go," I said. "I'll leave you to your midnight law practice and your late visits and to all the broken-hearted rich women. To them, you must be hot stuff, but to me, you're just a handful of pigeon leavings."

I tipped my hat, headed through the door, and left him staring after me. Now I had something more to think about, and so did he. All the way down in the elevator, I grinned to myself. I really hadn't accomplished much. But I felt better.

169

Chapter Eighteen

The drive back into town took longer than it should have. Traffic was light, but my mind wasn't on making time. That little voice was prodding me again—the one that comes from back in the shadows, then flits around and darts off before you can catch it. It can be as elusive as the lost chord and as clear as a lunch whistle. As often as not, it has something to say that you don't want to hear, and catching it isn't easy. But you damn well better try.

I entertained the notion that some of what Marcus had told me was true and some of it wasn't. The latter was easy. I could imagine Marcus getting wind of Clavin's carrying on with Stephanie and trying to put the bite on him. With Clavin out of the way, Marcus could take over all the firm's business and have a clear field with the girl. But there was no reason to doubt what Marcus had said about not handling criminal cases. And if that was true, he'd have nothing to gain from Clavin's practice but a lot of publicity and enemies. It wasn't hard to believe what he had said about making a killing in the divorce business, either. Lawyers in Beverly Hills were making more than the lovelorn clients they represented. Finally, with all the skirts Marcus had parading in and out of his office, I couldn't picture him being jealous of any intentions Clavin might have had toward Stephanie Anders. None of it played out to give Marcus a motive for murder.

That brought me back to Nugent and the pawn ticket. Nugent had never actually told Fran that Clavin was his client. If he'd been hired by someone else to check up on Clavin, he could have found out about the office affair and then decided to play both ends. But the notes to Clavin hadn't mentioned a

170

payoff. They only told him to stop representing Joey Paris. And it hadn't been Nugent who took the roll of film to the pawn shop in Laguna Beach. From that, it followed that Nugent had a partner or that whoever hired him was dealing from a stacked deck. Either way, Nugent probably got cold feet and was rubbed out before he could queer the deal. The thought struck me that Paris could be right about Lefty Stark. And it crossed my mind that Fran Brekhammer might know more than she was telling about Nugent. None of this got me anything but a long, dreary ride downtown.

I left the Buick on Temple Avenue near Main and walked around the corner to the courthouse. The afternoon sun was poking through the haze and scalding the pavement, and the air hung without moving—leaden and sulky. I climbed the steps slowly, feeling every inch of my legs and realizing how old they were getting. At the top, I went through the revolving doors, through the foyer, and past the elevators, then down what seemed a quarter mile of rose-tinted, marble-tiled corridor.

At the end, I rounded a corner to the right and started up the hall that led to the courtrooms. I only got about halfway. More than a dozen reporters and photographers were clustered in the middle of the hall, snapping pictures, shouting questions, and scribbling notes. Sterling Clavin was standing in the middle of the crowd with a smug look on his face, as if he were hating it and loved hating it.

I gave the crowd a quick once-over and didn't see Stephanie, but right away, I spotted the reporter who had pounded on my door that morning. Since I was about as eager for publicity as Anthony Marcus, I ducked through an open door into an empty courtroom. But not before I caught Clavin's eye. I stood in the doorway out of sight and listened.

The reporters kept firing questions about the murders, wanting to know if Joey Paris was involved. Clavin found a dozen ways to tell them that was ridiculous. Someone asked him if he thought the murders were related. Clavin said that was a matter for the police. A familiar voice asked him if he knew a private detective named Garrett. Clavin asked who that was. Finally, one of them suggested that the murder investigation might have an effect on the Grand Jury session. Clavin replied, "No comment," with the eloquence of Churchill.

After a while, the game of hide and seek was ended, and a clattering of shoes sounded in the hall. I waited until I couldn't hear anything but the endless busy silence of a public building. Then I stepped toward the door and stepped back again just as it swept open and missed swiping me in the jaw by the width of a kitten's whisker.

Sterling Clavin stormed into the room and stood in front of me. He slammed a briefcase down onto the floor beside him, dug his fists into his hips, and leaned toward my face. "Just what the hell have you been doing?"

I shrugged. "Trying to stay off the front page."

"Well, you've been doing a damn lousy job of that," he bellowed. "But that isn't what I meant. I want to know what the hell you're after."

"I'm after Stephanie. I heard she was here with you."

That seemed to slow him down, but just for a moment. He straightened up and raised an eyebrow, and gave me a cold scowl. "What do you want with her?"

I shrugged again. "I'm interested in her views on early Renaissance sketching."

I could see his hair bristling all the way down to his shirt collar. "God-dammit, Garrett," he yelled. "Never mind the wisecracks. You've been meeting with my wife, and I want it stopped, do you hear? Stopped!"

"Check," I said. "You want it stopped."

Somehow, that didn't satisfy him. "I hired you to investigate an extortion attempt and to prove that I wasn't involved in a murder. Now I find that you've gotten involved in a second murder and that you've been meeting secretly with my wife. I hired you to work for me and to keep me out of trouble, not to get me more bad publicity, and not to make time with Barbara. If I treated my clients the way you treat yours, I'd be out of business in less than a day."

I folded my arms and leaned against the door. "With clients like Joey Paris and Lefty Stark, you'll be in business a long time. And you haven't hired me yet. Not until I cash that check."

He thrust out his jaw and scowled again. "Don't try to be funny. I gave you two hundred dollars."

"You can have it back," I said. "It isn't damaged."

His face slowly turned medium rare. He started to say something, but I held up my hand and stopped him.

"You want me to find out who killed Nugent or at least find out enough to prove that you didn't do it. And you want me to do in a few days what the police sometimes take weeks or even months trying to do and maybe never get done. For that, I might have to dirty the carpet a little. It means I have to find out what Nugent was doing and where and with whom. It means that I have to cozy up to some nasty people where bad things happen—like a young girl getting murdered. Maybe there was a connection between her and Nugent. And maybe she died just because she was young and innocent and living in a world that is neither of those things. Either way, you don't know what I have to deal with trying to do your job for you. It isn't like practicing law. It isn't clean, it isn't neat, and it can't always be done out of sight. You knew that, or you wouldn't have tried to hire me in the first place."

Clavin stood fuming in front of me, but he didn't say anything.

"As for your wife," I said. "She came to see me because she's worried about you. A lot of guys would think that was worth something."

He raised a heavy eyebrow and glared under it. "Just what are you implying?"

I took in some air and slowly let it out. "I'm not implying anything. It's too hot, and I'm too tired."

He folded his arms and went on glaring. "Just remember, Garrett. You can be fired just as easily as you were hired. And I can fix it so that no one will ever hire you again. So, don't think you're getting away with anything. I look after what's mine!"

"And just what is yours?"

"You know damn well what's mine," he snapped. "You stay the hell away from my wife. You got it? Or I'll break your goddamn neck."

"Oh, stop it. You're terrifying me."

The color in his face deepened, and he began sputtering, but no words came out. I put a hand against his chest and pushed him back a couple of steps.

"Save your tantrums for the courtroom," I said. I looked around at where we were and snickered, but Clavin didn't get the joke.

"You think this is funny," he said in a half snarl.

"Clavin, I don't think anything you do is funny. And I don't see anybody around you laughing—not at your home, not in your office, and especially not in here. Somehow, you've sold people on the idea that helping weasels like Stark and Paris get away with murder is doing a noble service for mankind and that you're entitled to make a fortune at it. If that's the way you want to make your living, fine. But don't think it's given you anything I might want. What little money I make comes to me fairly clean. And even in my trade, there are rules about wives of clients or almost-clients. That's more than I can say for some in your profession."

He scowled again. "What do you mean?"

I shrugged and decided not to get into it. "What am I, a genius? How the hell do I know what I mean? All I want is to find Stephanie."

His eyes stabbed at me for a long moment. "She went home."

"Fine," I said. "Do I have your permission to talk to her?"

He waved his hands in a futile gesture. "Why the hell should I care?"

"Fine."

I turned and walked out. All the way up the long corridor, through the foyer, and down the front steps, I could feel Clavin's eyes in the middle of my back.

* * *

There was a note stuck under the windshield wiper of the Buick. It was a single sheet of paper about the size of a postcard, with nothing on it but a phone number carefully written in pencil. I put the note in my pocket, walked down the block to the corner, and went into a drugstore.

The place was mostly empty, just a couple of teenagers sipping sodas at the counter and another one at the magazine rack. He was a pimply-faced kid in dungarees, and he was making an elaborate show of turning the pages of *Popular Mechanics*, while behind it he was busy peeking at the girls in *Esquire*. I walked past him down the aisle to the back of the store, slid into a phone booth, and dropped in my nickel.

There was a distant buzz followed by a sharp click and then a muffled silence, as if a hand had been placed over the receiver. Then, almost reluctantly, sounds came over the line. Glasses clinking. Laughter. Even music. Finally, a voice like a sledgehammer. "Yeah?"

"This is Garrett."

There was a disdainful grunt. "Hold the line."

I waited for almost a full minute. The noise from the crowd played quietly in my ear. Finally, a familiar voice full of gravel clawed through the receiver.

"You keepin' your nose clean, tough guy?"

"As clean as the rest of me," I said. "What do you want?"

"We talked to Eddie Franks. I mean...*talked* to him, if you get my drift."

"What took you so long?"

He snickered. "Nobody's outta my reach, Garrett. Nobody. Understand?"

I said I understood. "It must have been quite a conversation."

"Yeah." He snickered again. "It was the kind of conversation where everything gets laid on the line, where it's lights out if somebody ain't levelin' with me. And I'll tell you somethin'. The man is clean."

"What do you mean?"

"I mean, he never talked to Nugent, didn't know him, never went within a mile of him."

"You're sure of that?"

There was a pause and another snicker. "Listen, tough guy. Maybe you'd like us to have the same kinda conversation with you—just so you can see how good we are at gettin' the straight dope. You're headin' up a blind alley. The guy had nothin' to do with Nugent."

"All right," I said. "Thanks."

"Don't mention it." His voice turned syrupy. "Only I ain't through. I got somethin' for you, and for this, you owe me."

"I'm all goose flesh."

175

"Just shut up and listen," he snapped. "We went through Eddie's whole book, got the goods on every one of his customers. Your boy Nugent didn't owe him any money. But Clavin's partner Tony Marcus does. He's into us for a bundle, and he's late on payin' off. For that, we're gonna talk to Eddie again."

I squeezed the receiver hard enough to turn it to pulp. "How much?"

"Enough. More than he can make in six months of hustlin' them rich babes with his divorce racket."

I felt a cold knot growing in my stomach. "All right. Thanks again. Maybe I do owe you one at that."

"You can settle up by doin' the job Clavin's payin' you for. No more blind alleys and no more drinkin' tea with his frail. Just get my mouthpiece off the hook and do it quick." A quiet menace settled his voice. "And Garrett, don't mess this one up. Or else we'll be talkin' again."

There was a sharp click and a long empty buzz.

I left the drugstore, got into the Buick, and, for a long while, just sat there. I thought about Marcus and Nugent scheming to blackmail Sterling Clavin. And I thought about Clavin giving them something to do it with. Somehow, Marcus still didn't seem like the blackmailing type. But owing that much money to someone like Joey Paris would make anybody desperate, and Marcus did seem like a boy who could be easily rattled. It was a long shot, but maybe he figured that by keeping Clavin on the hook, he could stay out of Paris's reach long enough to make the payoff.

I rolled it over in my mind a dozen times. I took the pieces apart and put them back together a dozen different ways. But I kept coming up with the same answer. Beatrice Almore had said that a dark-haired man claiming to be a lawyer had gone to visit Nugent. And the description I had gotten from the old man at Laguna Beach could have fit Marcus. The picture I was getting wasn't quite clear, but what I could see of it, I didn't like. And what I liked even less was having to spill it all to Fran.

The sun was slipping toward the coastline, and an uneasy breeze was starting to break up the lingering haze. Now more than ever, I wanted to talk to Stephanie about the pictures in my coat pocket. But since I was downtown, I decided to make another stop first. I pulled out and headed south for a handful of blocks, then turned east and wound down into the dingy section below the market district. It was close to five when I turned onto Paloma Place.

Chapter Nineteen

The Hurley Building was as dry and dusty as an old maid's hope chest. The same old man sat in the elevator, leaning against the wall and breathing through his mouth with heavy, rattling sighs. I took out a dollar bill, stuffed it in the pocket of his work shirt, and described Anthony Marcus to him. I asked if he might have given such a man a ride in his elevator recently. He looked at me for a long moment, thin, veiny lids drooping over glazed eyes. Then he shook his head and slowly rolled the gate closed behind me.

The elevator squealed up to the third floor, then back down to the lobby, and I stood in the same dark hall. Just to the right of the elevator, a sickly-looking potted fern sat living out its life next to an empty beer bottle. Next to that were a couple of cigar butts and above them in the corner a wide, intricate web that an entire platoon of spiders must have worked on for a long time.

For most of a minute, I stood in the still, musky air and looked up the hall at the dark offices. The transoms were all closed, and there were no lights on. I walked up the hall and stood in front of number 316. I waited, and I listened. There was no movement, no sound. I tried the door. It was open.

I stepped into Nugent's office, shut the door behind me, and flipped on the light. The place looked much the same as before, except for the usual traces of dusting powder the cops always leave behind. I walked into the middle of the room and stood there for a minute, looking around. I wasn't sure what I was looking for, and that gave me a good chance of not finding it.

The cops had given the place the usual going-over. They had gathered up the usual scraps of paper and blood scrapings and bits of cigarette ash, and they had dusted everything but the ceiling for prints. They were looking for a killer, and the name in Nugent's appointment book had given Rawls the scent. That was enough for them. They had seen Nugent as a victim, not as a blackmailer who might be connected to another fancy uptown lawyer. People see what they expect to see.

I looked through the filing cabinet, found nothing, then tried the desk. I pulled out every drawer, checked the undersides, and even looked into the empty slots. Still nothing. Rawls had even taken the bottle of Old Forester. I went over to the window, sat on the sill, and lit a Lucky. Then I chewed on it for a while and laughed at myself for thinking I might be smarter than the cops.

For no reason at all, I glanced at the potted fern next to Nugent's desk. Something about it interested me, so I moved over and sat on the desk and looked at it. The leaves were thin and brittle. They still had the brown spots where Nugent had bled on them, and there were more spots along the upper edge of the pot. The soil in the pot hadn't been disturbed. There were still the finger holes in it where someone had tested for water. Still, for no reason, I reached down and picked up some of the soil. It was like powder in my hand. I reached up and felt the leaves. They broke and crumbled and fell in dry fragments to the floor. The plant had been watered about as often as the Washington Senators had been winning pennants.

I leaned against the desk, worked on the Lucky, and stared down at the finger holes in the soil. There was nothing special about them. Just four holes in a ragged pattern made from the fingers of an outstretched hand. I stared at them until they seemed to be staring back, like the empty eyes of a corpse. Somewhere in the shadows of my mind, a thought was working its way out into the light: If someone were going to test the soil, it would be with one finger, not four.

I was just finishing the cigarette when I noticed that one of the holes was larger than the other three and seemed to set off by itself. I tried to picture the way someone would have to hold his hand to make that kind

179

of pattern. It would have taken a concert pianist. I leaned over for a closer look, then straightened up and shook my head. It was a million-to-one shot. The closest thing to impossible. I reached into my pocket and laughed loud enough for anyone in the hall to hear. While Sherlock Holmes and Philip Marlowe were solving cases with flawless logic and brilliant deductions, here was Garrett digging in the dirt.

I squatted down next to the pot and used my pocket knife to probe into the large hole. I loosened the soil and made a narrow crater, the dust from the hole rising in little puffs as the knife worked its way down. For a fleeting moment, I wondered what I would say if someone walked in and saw me. Then I stopped wondering. It was there, about eight inches down in the soil. A spent slug that looked like about a 38 caliber. And I'd have given better than even-money odds that it had come from a snub-nosed Colt revolver.

I smoothed out the soil, dropped the slug into my pocket, and went back out into the hall. Then, I walked up to the elevator and carefully inspected the empty corner on the right. The light was bad and getting worse, so I bent down and struck a match. In the corner directly across the hall from the other fern was a faint circle in the dust, broken at one point as if something had been dragged away. Just next to it was another brown spot.

I stood up and grinned and pushed the buzzer for the elevator. The same squealing noise rose up from below, and the old man rolled open the gate. I stepped in and rode down as he studied me with his tired, mirthless eyes. When we reached the lobby, I took out another dollar bill and stuffed it in his pocket. He looked at me with the gleeful expression of a park bench. I grinned at him and left.

* * *

The address Stephanie had given me was over on the west side—not the best part of town, but far from the worst. I thought about calling first, then decided against it. I drove up Hoover Street to Pico and then headed west all the way to Sepulveda. I turned north on Sepulveda and then went west again on La Grange. After about ten blocks of parked cars and palm trees, I found the building on a quiet corner facing south in the direction of Santa Monica. It was a peaceful section, mostly apartments and older houses, with a cemetery spread across the next block. The buildings were plain but well-tended, as if the neighborhood hadn't been disturbed in a while and meant to keep it that way.

I parked the Buick on the south side behind a late model Mercury sedan and walked across the street to Stephanie's apartment building. It was six stories of tan stucco, with tall dormer windows and carpeted steps leading up to a canopied entrance that looked familiar. At the bottom of the steps, I stopped and had another look at the pictures in my pocket. Two of them showed Clavin and Stephanie together in that same entrance. I tucked the pictures in my pocket and climbed the steps.

The entry was recessed, and the door at the back of it was locked. Along the wall on the left were two rows of mailboxes, with nameplates set into little slots. Above each mailbox was a bottom that would activate an intercom and let the tenants brush off a salesman without even opening the door. In the middle of the second row, I found a plate marked "S. Anders 4-B." I pushed the button above it.

A wall speaker crackled, and a shrill, impatient voice came out. "Yes?"

"It's Garrett. You still want to be a detective?"

There was a pause and a rustling noise. "Come right up."

The speaker died, and the door began to buzz. I pulled it open and stepped into a small lobby with a couple of stuffed chairs sitting on either side of a low table that held a lavishly flowering hibiscus plant in a slender oriental vase. Straight ahead was a flight of stairs, and to the right, one of those new elevators that you drive yourself. I decided to take the elevator.

I rode up to the fourth floor and walked up the hall on a stretch of plush carpet that was as thick as an old Scottish brogue. Number 4-B was the second door on the left, another button on the wall beside it. I stood in front of the door and put my hand on the pocket where the pictures were. Just at that moment, it occurred to me that Nugent and Marcus might have had another partner.

I pushed the button, and a pair of chimes jangled inside. I waited. Nothing happened. I pushed the button again. This time, quiet footsteps padded to the door, and the door opened just enough for a dark eye to peer around it.

"Mr. Garrett," she said. "I certainly wasn't expecting you. Please come in."

She pulled back the door, and I stepped inside and tried not to stare at her. She was wearing a white terry-cloth robe that reached almost to the floor but not quite far enough to cover a pair of dainty bare feet. A large white bath towel was wrapped around her head like a turban, and as I watched, a single drop of water worked its way out from under it, rolled deliberately down her forehead, and trickled to the end of her nose. It hung there for a moment, as if waiting to be announced, then plummeted gracefully down into the opening of her robe. From the way the drop disappeared, I guessed that the robe was all she had on.

She noticed me noticing her. "I just stepped out of the tub." When I didn't answer, she cocked her head and eyed me suspiciously. "Is there something wrong? I mean, with taking a bath?"

I shrugged. "Why should there be? I took one once."

She grinned and shut the door. "Stop teasing. I wasn't expecting you, but I'm glad you're here. Would you like a drink?"

"Yeah," I said. "I prefer being wet on the inside."

She flushed a little and kept grinning. "The liquor's in the cabinet over the sink." She motioned to an open doorway on the left past a small dining area. "And there's ice in the frig. Help yourself while I go and get dry." She turned and walked quickly to another doorway at the back of the room. When she got there, she paused and looked back. "Make me a whiskey and soda."

The robe slipped out of sight, and muffled bathroom noises started coming from the other room. I crossed to the kitchen and opened the cabinet. I found a bottle of Canadian Club, a dispenser of seltzer, and several glasses. I took one, poured out a sample, and tossed it down. It seemed to work, so I got a couple of cubes from the ice chest, dropped them into a glass, and covered them with whiskey. After another sample, I mixed Stephanie's whiskey and soda and walked back into the living room.

It was a neat room, done mostly in blue, with several watercolor prints on the walls and an odd-shaped potted palm hunched over in the corner like Lon Chaney. To the left of the palm, a wide coffee table with an ashtray the size of a fruit bowl stood between a loveseat and a couple of chairs, all thickly padded and covered in a corded blue fabric that looked new. They sat more or less facing a fireplace that was built into the wall opposite the entrance. It was one of those imitation fireplaces where the logs never burn. People seldom need fires in southern California.

On the far wall from the kitchen, an old floor-to-ceiling bookcase sat crammed with books and magazines, enough to outfit a small library. I put the drinks on the coffee table, then walked over to the bookcase and made a quick inspection. She had everything Arthur Conan Doyle and Erle Stanley Gardner had ever written and squeezed in over the books were several years' worth of *Crime Stories* and *True Detective* magazines. On the top shelf, I spotted a book of stories by Edgar Allen Poe. I pulled it down and began idly thumbing through it. Whatever else Stephanie might be, she wasn't squeamish.

I was still holding the book when she returned from the bedroom. She had taken off the towel and brushed out her hair, the long, dark strands giving off an inviting luster. She hadn't taken off the robe, and she had put on a pair of slippers. Nowadays, girls consider that dressed.

She took one of the glasses from the coffee table, walked over next to me, and eyed the book in my hand. "Do you read Poe?"

"Nevermore," I said.

She laughed and took part of her drink. "He wrote the very first detective story. Did you know that?"

"Too bad it wasn't the last."

She let out a girlish giggle, then took a step closer to me. She had put on just a hint of lipstick, and she had that fresh smell of an afternoon in the country. "Why did you want to see me?"

"You said you'd help me work out some theories…on the killings."

"Is that all?"

"What else is there?"

She flushed again and looked down. "Well, I've been thinking about what you said in the office yesterday." She looked up again. Her brown eyes were as big as poker chips. "Did you really think I was making a pass at you?"

"Could be," I said. "Any young thing dumb enough to want to be a detective might just be dumb enough for that, too."

Her eyebrows fretted together, and she squeezed her glass in both hands. "I'm not *that* young. And I do find older men attractive. They're…they're…"

"Older men are just older men—even if they do happen to be lawyers."

She angled her head and eyed me curiously around a wave of raven hair. "What do you mean?"

"I wish people would quit asking me that."

I returned the book to the shelf, then went over to the coffee table and emptied my share of the Canadian Club. I took the drugstore envelope from my pocket, opened it, and spread the pictures out on the table. The girl walked over and stood looking down at my display. I lit up a Lucky and watched her.

I wasn't sure what I was looking for, but whatever it was, I didn't see it Stephanie put down her glass, settled slowly into the loveseat, anchored her elbows on her knees, and rested her chin in her hands. After a while, she began pawing over the pictures, a look of fascination on her face. Suddenly, she clapped her hands together and grinned.

"Of course," she said, waving a hand in my direction. "Look. I'm wearing the same clothes in every picture. That means they were all taken on the same day. And everyone in the restaurant is dark. But in that one, you can see a large meal on the table. So, the pictures must all have been taken in the evening—within the space of a few hours."

She stood up and began pacing around the coffee table. By now, she was wearing the intense look of a college debater. She rubbed her hands together and licked her lips.

"Now, suppose someone wanted to photograph Mr. Clavin in what would appear to be a compromising position," she went on. "It would be easy to get his picture with some good-looking woman. All anyone would have to do is wait and snap him with one of Mr. Marcus's clients on her way in or out of the office." She paused and looked at me. "Were there any other pictures on the roll?"

I just shook my head and took a drag on the Lucky.

Stephanie turned one of the pictures over and looked at the developer's markings on the back. "These are only snapshots, probably taken with 128 film. There could be eight or maybe twelve exposures on a roll, but there are only six pictures here."

She straightened and folded her arms and gazed at me fixedly, her eyes full of dark brown triumph. "Since only six shots were taken and all on the same evening, we have to conclude that someone specifically wanted to get pictures of Mr. Clavin and me together. It had to be someone who knew that we'd be working late, and I contacted no one. So, it was either someone in the office or..." She leaned forward and grinned at me suspiciously. "Someone Mr. Clavin contacted late that day."

I crushed out the Lucky and didn't say anything.

Stephanie waited for a moment, almost like a child holding her breath. "Well, how did I do?"

I still didn't answer.

"I remember the evening," she said, apprehension edging into her voice. "It was a night last week when I stayed late while Mr. Clavin finished a brief. He was so grateful, he took me out to dinner afterwards."

"Is that all? Just dinner?"

She shrugged. "Of course. What else? We just had dinner, and he took me home and..." She caught herself. "Well, he *did* kiss me good night. But it wasn't much of a kiss, really." She giggled. "I think he was even a little embarrassed about it."

I picked up the photograph of Clavin and Stephanie in the entrance to the building, studied it for a minute, then dropped it back on the coffee table. "Uh-huh."

The girl's eyebrows knitted together again. "Why? What's wrong?"

"Don't you even care how I got these pictures?"

Her face went blank. "What do you mean? Didn't you take them?"

"Don't be silly," I said. "And stop asking what I mean. I only met Clavin yesterday, so he couldn't have called me last week. And he wouldn't have called anybody, not unless he wanted to set himself up for blackmail."

Her jaw dropped almost to the floor. "You mean someone is really…"

"Yeah," I growled at her. "Someone is really. Maybe someone found out that you've been doing more than just typing Clavin's briefs."

The color drained out of her face. Instinctively, she clutched the front of the robe and held it against her. Her voice was as tight as piano wire.

"Mr. Garrett, you can't think that. Honestly, there's nothing between Mr. Clavin and me. I only work for him." She gnawed on her lower lip and hesitated. "I could never go for someone like him. I'd be more interested in…"

She flushed again and looked down at the floor. After a long while, she stepped toward me and put a hand on my arm. She looked up at me in that guileless way women have. Her eyes were dark saucers.

"Please," she said. "Tell me you don't really think that."

I stood looking into her brown eyes. I looked into them for a long time, waiting for a sign—that little flicker that tells you someone is lying. I didn't see it.

I stepped away, leaned against a chair, and let my breath out heavily. "No, I don't think that. I was just trying it on for size. Anyone smart enough to set up this caper wouldn't be dumb enough to let herself be photographed by someone who could just as easily blackmail her. Besides, that would have involved you with two other people. And blackmail is almost never a three-handed game. Even two is a crowd."

She let out a long sigh, as if she had just survived a crisis. I could see her muscles relaxing all the way to her ankles. She emptied her glass and put it on the coffee table.

"Where did you get these pictures?"

"I got them in a pawn shop," I said, "with a ticket I found in Danny Nugent's apartment—the dick who got bumped off Monday."

"Do you think he was blackmailing Mr. Clavin?"

"He may have meant to try, but he wasn't the only one involved. Someone wants to make sure Clavin doesn't show up in court representing a toughie named Joey Paris. That would please a lot of people, including the cops and another tough bird named Stark. Nugent may have been set up as a front man so someone else could put a squeeze on your boss. But it looks as if Nugent turned the tables and decided to go into business for himself. My guess is that he found out something about Clavin and got iced before he could do anything with it."

Stephanie swallowed hard and rubbed her hands together. She glanced down at the coffee table, then snatched up the empty glasses and headed for the kitchen. "I can use another drink."

I followed her and watched as she poured some more of the Canadian Club into each glass, this time with no ice and no soda. She handed one of the glasses to me and emptied hers. As I took a swig from mine, she fretted her eyebrows again and gave me a quizzical look.

"You said I'd have to be involved with two other people. Was the other one that man Stark?"

I shook my head. "Not directly, at least. None of the strong-arm boys got to where they are by taking their own risks. Stark would have had someone do his dirty work for him. And whoever that was met with Nugent in his apartment, probably to get the film so he could take it to the pawn shop. Then he returned and gave the ticket to Nugent, so it would be found after Nugent had gotten the big freeze."

Stephanie leaned against the sink and let the curiosity show in her face. "But why would they want *my* picture with Mr. Clavin?"

I shrugged. "You may have been right about any good-looking dame filling the bill. Maybe they picked you out just because you were there and because it would make a good story. He *is* your boss, and you do spend a lot of time with him."

"But I told you there's nothing between Mr. Clavin and me except business."

"Do you think he sees it that way?"

She didn't even hesitate. "I certainly do. Mr. Clavin must be deeply in love with his wife, because he's terribly possessive about her. Why, one day, just after I'd started working there, Mrs. Clavin came into the office, and I heard him yelling at her. I don't know what started it, but he told her that if any man ever came within arm's length of her, he'd break the man in two."

She rubbed her hands over her upper arms as if she had a chill. "He's a big man, and very strong. I think he could do it."

I just nodded. I thought so, too.

"So, you see," she concluded, "those pictures really don't mean anything."

"They don't in here," I said, "but in court, it would be different. Any cheap shyster could use those pictures to make a jury start doubting. And with Clavin's temper, those pictures would be just enough to make them believe he had a motive for killing Nugent."

Her mouth fell open. "My God. What are you going to do?"

"Find the other party before the cops close in on your boss with a net."

"Do you know who it is?"

I didn't answer. I walked back into the living room, lit another Lucky, and sat on the loveseat. Stephanie followed me and nestled into one of the stuffed chairs on the other side of the coffee table. A playful smile tempted the corners of her mouth.

"You want me to work it out for myself, don't you?"

I still didn't answer.

"Well, let's see." She crossed her legs and thought, while I studied the trim lines of her exposed calves and ankles.

"Assuming someone wanted to take the pictures in the evening, so they'd look suspicious, it would still have to be someone who knew when Mr. Clavin and I would be working late. None of the clients knew that, and you didn't. That means it had to be someone else in the office."

Her head jerked up, and she grabbed the arms of the chair. Her eyes were wider than ever. "Do you think it was Mr. Marcus?"

I took a long drag and blew smoke at the fireplace. "What can you tell me about him?"

She shook her head. "Nothing I haven't told you already. He only handles divorce cases, mostly young, attractive women. He's obviously a ladies' man, and I don't think Mr. Clavin likes him very much."

"What else does he do besides provide expensive crying towels?"

She shrugged. "He keeps to himself mostly. I guess he can't afford to be seen in public with his clients." She grinned sourly. "At least not until the ink is dry on the divorce papers. Mostly, he entertains them at his home. He's got a place out on Lakeview Terrace."

The little voice started in me again. Only this time it was screaming.

I stood up and put out the Lucky. Then I gathered up the pictures, put on my hat, and started for the door. "Well, thanks, Stephanie. I'll be running along."

She bolted out of the chair. "Wait a minute. If you're going to see Mr. Marcus. I want to go, too." She caught herself and smiled sheepishly. "If I'm going to be a detective, I ought to see how one works."

"Detective work can be dangerous," I said, "and you'd just get in the way. Besides, you've already got a date."

She angled her head and gave me the same quizzical look. "How do you know that?"

I shrugged. "A girl who likes men at any age doesn't run home from work on a Friday night, take a bath, and wash her hair just so she can curl up with a good book—even if it is Poe."

With that same instinct, she clutched at the front of her robe. She shook out her hair and thought for a moment, then set her jaw and looked at me gravely.

"I think you must be quite a good detective. And I guess you're probably right about the danger. But I can break my date, and honestly, I won't be in the way. So, please take me with you. I don't care how dangerous it is."

I stood there and looked at her, a bright young girl who had no more idea of what it took to be a detective than I had about raising elephants. She should have been waiting for some young kid with a crew cut to take her to the movies and then to the malt shop and then try and coax her up to Mulholland Drive for a little necking. Good, clean, American fun, just the way things were supposed to be after the War. Only she wanted to tag along with me. It didn't make good sense, but not much else did either. And for me, being smart just wasn't in season.

I leaned against the door and pushed my hat back on my head. "All right, get dressed. We're going to a party."

Chapter Twenty

Lights were on all over the Clavin house, as if a new department store had just opened. Despite the growing breeze, most of the windows were raised. They always are at such events. After only a couple of drinks, the air inside gets as stale as the conversation. A fleet of freshly polished cars surrounded the entrance and took up most of the drive, enough expensive iron to make Detroit declare a holiday. I parked at the bottom of the hill, thinking it wasn't worth testing the Buick's brakes again.

Stephanie walked beside me as I headed for the house. She had put on a pair of high heels and a dress so tight that she had to take two steps for every one of mine. Halfway up the driveway, she stopped for a breather and grabbed my arm.

"Do you think Mr. Marcus will be here?"

I nodded. "I heard him tell one of his better-built clients that he would be."

She snorted. "I'll bet."

We made it up the rest of the driveway with Stephanie hanging on to me. At the entrance, I let her stop for another breath while I checked my watch. Just eight o'clock.

Barbara Clavin was standing in the doorway greeting several guests. She had on a clinging, gossamer blue dress that sloped just off her shoulders and didn't hurt her appearance at all. Her hair was done up on top of her head, revealing the same dangling emerald earrings and the long, graceful lines of her bare neck. As I watched, she smiled and bowed and went through the usual welcoming ritual like someone with a lot of practice.

A parade of the usual well-dressed well-fed people filed by into the house until finally Barbara was alone on the porch with a somber-looking couple. One was a slender man with graying hair and dour features, wearing the kind of dark suit most men get buried in. He was with a plumpish woman in a white fox stole. She had hair like cast iron, a heavy jaw, and a face as hard and sharp as a meat ax. Barbara smiled sweetly and held out her hand.

"Doctor Washburn and Estelle, how nice to see you."

The man bowed curtly and returned a perfunctory handshake, and the woman clutched her stole and twisted her mouth into something she might have thought was a smile. After several tortured seconds of silence, Barbara motioned toward the house.

"Please, come inside and be comfortable. Amanda will take your things. The other guests are out by the pool."

As the two went inside, Stephanie and I stepped up onto the porch. Barbara turned, glanced at me, and then smiled at the girl.

"Why, Stephanie. What a pleasant surprise. I wasn't expecting you."

Stephanie swallowed and cleared her throat. "Hello, Mrs. Clavin. I'm here with Mr. Garrett. I hope it's all right."

"Well, of course, dear. But please, call me Barbara."

Stephanie flushed a little. "Thank you, Mrs. Clavin...I mean, Barbara."

Barbara smiled warmly and guided the girl toward the door. "Why don't you go inside and join the other guests. I want to speak with Mr. Garrett for just a moment."

Stephanie looked back at me uncertainly, then went into the house.

When we were alone, Barbara turned and gave me a playful smile. "I didn't know you knew Stephanie."

I shrugged. "Every now and then I am allowed out of the monastery."

She chuckled and lifted an eyebrow. "Well, naturally. It's just that I wasn't expecting you to bring a date."

I shrugged again. "I figured it would make me look less like a floorwalker."

She nodded in recognition. "Of course. I see. That's a very good idea."

Barbara took me by the arm and led me over to the side of the porch, away from the door and out of earshot. "Michael, I'm terribly worried. Sterling still hasn't come home, and he hasn't called. I'm afraid something may have happened to him."

"Have you tried his office?"

"Yes. There was no answer." She wrung her hands together. "This just isn't like Sterling."

"What about his partner Marcus? Is he here?"

She frowned slightly. "I'm not sure. He's supposed to be, but I haven't seen him." Suddenly, I felt her fingers digging into my arm. "Michael, I'm afraid for Sterling. Do you suppose he's all right?"

I slowly pried her fingers loose. "I wouldn't worry. I saw him this afternoon. He seemed all right at the time."

She looked vaguely surprised. "You saw him? Where?"

"At the courthouse. We exchanged pleasantries over my professional ethics and his desire to rearrange my face."

Anguished lines creased her forehead. "Oh, dear. I hope nothing's wrong."

"With his charm and good manners, what could be wrong?"

She caught her breath, then seemed to relax all at once. A look of relief trickled into her face followed by a tired smile. "I suppose you're right. I guess he's just cross with me about last night." She took my arm again and guided me back to the door. "Go ahead in and enjoy yourself. I'm sure everything will be fine."

In the doorway, Barbara stopped and looked at me with a mocking grin. "After all, I'm sure Stephanie is a charming girl."

I dodged the bullet and went inside.

Amanda was waiting in the front hall. She gave me a sneer, took my hat, and threw it in the armoire. Then she put her hands on her hips and scowled at me.

"Don't know why you gotta be here."

I grinned at her. "Who else would you have to talk to?"

She grunted and motioned over her shoulder. "Party's out back. And no funny stuff. Just remember, I got my eye on you."

I walked through the doorway at the back of the hall, past a dining room

192

and a kitchen, then out through a small breezeway and down a flight of stone steps to a wide cement terrace. A ring of urns holding tall sculptured evergreens lined the terrace like a horseshoe and stretched all of sixty feet to a kidney-shaped pool on the far side. Strings of paper lanterns ran from tree to tree and swung gently in the evening breeze, casting soft waves of light on the terrace. Beyond the pool, nothing but a knee-high hedge separated Clavin's estate from two hundred feet of canyon wall and the luxurious expanse of the Hollywood Hills beyond. Despite the gathering darkness, it was a setting that would make even the most jaded director go scurrying after a cameraman.

More than a dozen circular tables were set out around the terrace. Some of them were occupied, but most of the people stood in little groups drinking and chattering the usual meaningless party drawl. A cadre of white-jacketed waiters with trays full of glasses flitted from group to group like bees spreading pollen. As I stepped onto the terrace, one of them bobbed up in front of me and stood there as if he wanted to keep his nose up above the smog. He glanced disdainfully at my suit, then walked away after handing me a martini that tasted like gin and brass knuckles. At the first chance, I poured it into a potted plant and hoped the thing wouldn't grow up to hate me in another life.

Stephanie got up from one of the tables and trotted over to me, holding a glass of something with bubbles. "Look," she said. "Imported champagne. I've never had anything like it."

"It's just ginger ale with a reputation."

She looked at me with a face full of wonder. "This is a magnificent place. Aren't you impressed?"

"Yeah," I said. "I'm impressed. Have you seen Marcus?"

She shook her head. "He isn't here. But you won't believe who is."

She turned and stared off over the tables to the edge of the swimming pool, where a knot of people, mostly women, stood crowded around someone as if he were handing out C-notes. In the middle of the crowd, I saw a familiar face with smooth black hair, a pencil-thin mustache, and ears like the handles of a loving cup. He was smiling and making the usual Hollywood small talk, and the women were clinging to every word.

Stephanie turned back and looked up at me eagerly. "Don't you recognize him?"

"Frankly, my dear," I said. "I don't give a damn."

She took a quick drink and glanced back toward the crowd. "Well, I think he's dreamy."

"Don't start dreaming so much that you don't remember why we're here."

She caught herself and flushed again. "I'm sorry. I know I promised. Besides, he isn't my type either."

"What type is that?"

She looked up and started to say something, but I held up my hand. "Never mind," I said. "I'm afraid you might tell me. Just keep looking for Marcus."

"What are you going to do?"

I glanced over to the left. A small bar had been set up between two of the overgrown. A short, stocky man in a white shirt and bow tie was standing behind it with his arms folded, looking as if he would pay a fortune for someone to talk to him in words shorter than four syllables. I looked back at Stephanie.

"I'm going to visit a man who might speak my language."

She gave me an odd sort of smile, then reached out and touched my arm. "Mr. Garrett, thank you for bringing me."

I left her and walked over to the bar. The man behind it studied my approach, moving nothing but his eyes. I leaned on the bar and studied him back. "Buy you a drink?"

He half snorted. "I've heard better ones than that at the bus station, Mac."

"So have I. How about a Scotch?"

He reached under the bar and brought up a bottle of Ballentine's, poured a generous helping into a glass, added some ice, and was about to threaten it with a bottle of seltzer when I waved him off.

"Don't bruise it," I said. "It looks frail."

He gave me the other half of the snort and then narrowed his eyes and studied me again. "You ain't one of the regulars."

"From the sound of it, neither are you."

"Hah," he said. "I'm just fillin' in for my wife's brother. Lousy bum. Lines up this job, then goes out ta the track and gets juiced. Comes home with a snootful and says I gotta cover for him. Only gimmie twenty minutes ta get dressed and get up here."

I held the glass up in front of him and took a drink. "Glad you could make it."

He leaned forward, put both elbows on the bar, and spoke in the confidential tones of a tout. "So, what's yer racket? You ain't one o' this crowd."

"Just a hired hand," I said. "I'm the new marshal, here to keep the peace."

He let out a raspy guffaw. "Hell, there ain't nothin' ta that. Ain't no noise up here. Leastwise, not unless ya figure on a crowd o' fancy-dressed numbers spreadin' out a lotta expensive grease."

"Then maybe I'll just have another drink and go paint my little toenails."

He leaned over a little farther and lowered his voice a little more. "Course there's prob'ly nothin' to it, ya understand. But if I was you, I'd pay a little mind ta that charmer over there with them two frails."

I followed his gaze over to the far side of the terrace. I saw Stephanie standing with another girl, a tall redhead with more curves than a canyon road. They were talking with a dark man, late twenties, with coal-black eyes that moved deliberately around the room

"What about him?" I asked.

"I ain't sure, but I think I seen him at the track. Could be a collector. Know what I mean?"

"Uh-huh."

I was about to ask what the man might be doing in Bel Air, when a platinum haired woman in a gold lame dress cut to her sternum wobbled over and slapped a hand on the bar. "Gimmie another Bacardi, Jerry."

She leaned over and spread a lot of herself on the bar, and Jerry looked at her as if she had four elbows. He took a glass, put in some ice and soda and then tipped over the bottle. He grabbed a napkin and mopped furiously, then managed to get a little of the rum into her glass. She took it, held it up, and made a kind of gurgling noise. Then she pushed herself upright, rolled her eyes, and stood weaving around like a loose channel marker. Being the brilliant detective, I deduced that she was sauced to the eyelids.

She drank some of the rum, then turned and looked at me. She had a pale, almost gaunt face, with a wide, unfriendly mouth and about a dozen coats of lipstick. She kept staring. I turned and let her stare at my profile.

"Hey," she said. "I know you. You're..."

I turned back and gave her my best grin. "Rex Ransom."

She smiled wide enough to crack her lipstick. "Yeah. I seen your last picture. You were terrific—the way you rescued that girl from them Indians. What was her name?"

"Tess Truehart."

"Yeah," she slurred, then turned back to the bar. "Hey, Jerry. You shoulda seen this guy. Rides inta this Indian camp with about a hundred of 'em gettin' ready ta burn this girl Tess at the stake. But ol' Rex just rides up ta the chief and says he loves the girl and that he's gonna take her place. The chief is so touched, he turns her loose, and she jumps on his horse. Then she and Rex ride off inta the sunset—real romantic like."

She emptied her glass, reeled around a little, and then looked at me a little too wistfully.

"Real romantic," she said again.

She wobbled over to me and prodded my chest with a forefinger. A wolfish grin arose on her face. "Just what did the two of you do after the sun went down? Tell me that, big boy."

"We fed the horse," I said.

She let out a shriek that must have brought a stare from both sides of the canyon. "The hell you say."

She leaned against me, threw her arms loosely around my neck, and burbled in the direction of my face. "Show me whatcha did. Come on, cowboy. Ride away with me."

Instinctively, I grabbed her to keep her from falling, then looked over at the bartender. He was busy looking in every direction but mine. I was thinking of lugging her over and dropping her in the pool, when a dumpy guy in a herringbone sport coat and shirt open at the collar stepped out of the crowd and stood just behind her.

He was a paunchy character, with reddish hair and a face that would make a toad look handsome. He gave me a quick sorrowful glance, then leaned over and spoke to the woman.

"Come on, Gladys," he said. "No trouble, huh? It's time to go home."

The woman wrestled herself loose, turned, and sprawled over the guy. "Whatever you say, Harry."

Harry glanced back at the bartender, then at me, and then gave us both a long-suffering look. Then he slipped an arm around the woman's shoulders and guided her unsteadily toward the breezeway, while she waved her arms around like a Navy signalman.

"Come on, Harry," I heard her say. "Ride away with me, ya big lug. Tear my clothes off and mail 'em ta Butte."

She and Harry disappeared into the house, and I moved back to the bar. Without being asked, Jerry poured out some more of the Ballentine's. I drank it, then looked around at a dozen or so wondering faces.

After a minute, the faces stopped wondering, and the noise started again, and Jerry leaned on the bar and spoke to me. "Them Hollywood people. What can ya say?"

"Nothing that helps," I said.

Dr. Washburn came out of the crowd, moved over to the bar, and ordered a plain seltzer with ice. He eyed me narrowly through a veil of distaste, then turned his back and drained half of his drink. I sipped the Scotch, lit a Lucky, and thought about the Hollywood heritage—all the spent lives, where dreams came in bottles.

I looked around the crowd and didn't see the man Jerry had pointed out as a collector. But before I could ask, Stephanie came up and took hold of my arm again.

"My God," she said. "What was that all about?"

"Just somebody looking for an autograph," I said. "What about the guy you were just talking to?"

She stepped close to me, eyes intense, and breathed the words in a heated whisper. "He told me his name was Desmond or something and that he was in real estate. He said he was meeting someone here and was going to take him to see a house. I didn't think anything of it until he asked me if I knew the man—Anthony Marcus."

"Did you tell him?"

She shook her head. "I didn't like his looks. There was something about him I didn't trust."

"Good girl," I said. "Where is he now?"

"He's gone. I saw him go out the front door." She looked at me eagerly. "What do we do now?"

I took a drag on the Lucky. "We rely on an infallible investigative technique."

"What's that?"

"We wait."

* * *

The party lumbered on, and the noise grew with each round of drinks. Shortly before nine, a trio came down the breezeway—bass, drums, and horn. They set up on the far side of the terrace from the bar and began playing some passable numbers that most of the crowd ignored.

Barbara Clavin moved from table to table, smiling and chatting and being the perfect hostess. After she had visited every table and spoken to the people by the pool, she looked over at me and then stopped one of the waiters. She whispered something to him, and he went off and began rearranging the tables in front of the trio, while Barbara walked over to me.

"Michael, come and dance with me."

I looked over at the waiter, clearing space in front of the band. Then I took a swig from my latest Scotch. "Let's just drink this one out."

She laughed. "Don't be so shy. Besides, it will be a good example for the guests."

I emptied my glass, and she took my hand and led me across the terrace. The trio saw us coming and began playing "That Old Feeling." Then, before I knew it, Barbara was stuck to me like flypaper.

198

We danced around for several minutes, with most of the crowd giving us only polite notice. Barbara didn't seem to care. She rested her head on my shoulder and hummed with the music while I held onto her. She fitted in my arms like fingers in a glove. I had all I could do to remember where I was.

Finally, the music stopped, and Barbara stepped back and looked up at me. "My goodness, what a good dancer you are. You quite literally swept me away."

I started to say something, but a picture of Lorna James darted through my head, and I shut my mouth.

The trio began again, and Barbara leaned against me and smiled. "It's not such a bad assignment, is it? Dancing with me?"

"As assignments go," I said, "I've had worse."

She laughed and worked her way back into my arms, and we began dancing again. Barbara sighed contentedly and murmured in my ear. "You're an unusual man, Mr. Garrett."

"Your husband's unusual. I'm just out of place."

She tensed suddenly, stopped, and stared up at me with a quiet look of fear. "Oh, My God. I forgot. He still isn't home."

I motioned toward the crowd and then coaxed her into dancing again. "For these people, the night's barely started, and he's only fashionably late."

She clutched at my neck and pressed her face against my chest. "You're right. I'm sorry to be such a worrier. I must be a terrible bother to you."

I held her and thought about what a bother she was. I was about to tell her, when I noticed Stephanie standing by the edge of the crowd, watching us with a strained expression on her face. It occurred to me that maybe I ought to give her some kind of signal, but I didn't know what, and I sure as hell didn't know why.

Of course, it didn't matter. Barbara suddenly stepped back and stood rigid, staring past my shoulder at the breezeway. Her eyes were wide, and her mouth gaped in horror.

I turned and saw Sterling Clavin standing at the foot of the steps, only ten feet away. His suit was rumpled, and his tie was undone, and he was breathing heavily through tightly clenched teeth. His large hands were rolled into fists as dark and hard as sewer pipe, and his eyes held the red glassiness of a three-day binge. He took a couple of steps toward me, and then stopped and made a sharp hissing noise.

"I told you to keep your goddamn hands off my wife!"

His voice rang through the canyon like a rifle shot. While it was still ringing, he reached out, grabbed one of my lapels, and began shaking.

"I told you nobody takes what's mine," he roared. "And I'll get rid of anyone who tries. Now get your ass off my property before I cripple you. You're fired."

Barbara stepped in front of him and pushed desperately against his chest. "Sterling, please," she pleaded. "It's not what you think."

Clavin looked at her and growled. Then he stepped forward, swung his right arm, and backhanded her across the face. Barbara reeled in the direction of the trio. The musicians scattered, and she fell over the bass and sprawled on the grass beyond the terrace. Clavin lumbered toward her, raving like a madman.

"I told you, didn't I? I told you to stay away from this bum and that other little weasel. Well, tonight, I'm taking care of both of them."

He started to reach for her, but I got to him first. I yanked his arm and spun him around. He tottered a little, then became steady and focused on me with a dark red rage.

"Why not take a poke at someone who's standing up," I said. "If I'm fired, I ought to have something for the road."

He was big, and he was powerful, but he was still full of too much liquor. He dropped his shoulder and lunged and swung at me with a right that I could have seen coming from Cleveland. I ducked under it easily and came up with my own right and caught him squarely on the point of the chin. It wasn't just a punch; it was a perfect punch. It was the kind that gives you that instant recognition, that certainty of outcome—the same feeling you get when Ted Williams lays a bat against a ball.

Clavin went down like a sack of cement. He fell on his side, then his weight carried him over onto his back, and he lay face up and didn't move. I bent down and loosened his shirt and checked his breathing while Barbara struggled over and knelt beside her husband.

"Oh, My God," she wailed. "Oh, My God."

I looked toward the gathered crowd and spotted Stephanie. I motioned to her, and the girl came over and helped Barbara up and into a chair. Then, before I knew it, Dr. Washburn appeared and began ministering to the fallen host. He raised the eyelids, checked the pulse, then looked at me with something like a twinkle.

"Pretty good punch," he said. "I'd like to see you do it when he's sober."

"So would I," I said.

Dr. Washburn and I carted Clavin into the house, and Amanda directed us upstairs to the master bedroom. We dumped Clavin on the bed, and I went out into the hall and waited while the doctor tended to his patient. In a few minutes, Barbara appeared at the foot of the stairs. She hesitated for a moment, then charged up the stairs and tore into the bedroom without even looking at me.

After another ten minutes, Dr. Washburn emerged. He walked with me to the head of the stairs, then stopped and looked at me with the satisfaction of someone who had just heard Caruso sing an aria.

"He'll be all right. He's got quite a constitution. Although this time, he's apt to have more than just a hangover." He grinned, then reached out and shook my hand warmly. "Nice to have met you, Mr. Garrett."

He bowed graciously and went down the stairs whistling.

I leaned against the railing at the top of the stairs and waited. Pretty soon, Barbara came out of the bedroom. She walked over to me like a zombie, deep lines of worry creasing her face. She stopped in front of me brought her hands up to her mouth, and stared down at the floor.

"The doctor says he'll be all right," she said.

"That's what he told me."

"Sterling will be in a rage when he wakes up. And he'll be furious with you. He might..."

"I'll take my chances."

She raised her head slowly and looked at me, her eyes filled with liquid pain. "I'm sorry for the way it all worked out. I didn't mean for this to happen."

"You couldn't help it," I said. "If it didn't happen here with me, it would have happened somewhere with someone like me."

Barbara drew her hands together into a large fist and pressed them against her mouth. A tear came silently down her cheek. I could see her trembling.

"Michael, what am I to do? How can I go on like this?"

"Leave him."

"But I can't," she said. "You know I can't."

"You can do whatever you want. The only hold he's got on you is money. And it looks like you're paying a damned high price for that."

She nodded reluctantly. "I know. But he's my husband. And he's…"

"Sure," I said. "He's your husband and you ought to love him, and you think he's really a great guy. Only from where I'm standing, he's just another drunk in a suit."

She dropped her hands, swallowed hard, and put a resolute set to her jaw. "Perhaps you're right. But I just can't leave."

"Well, I can," I said. "And you can have this to remember me."

I grabbed her by the arms, held her against me, and kissed her, quickly and firmly. She didn't struggle, but she didn't respond. She just hung limp in my grasp, as if all hope had run out. I let her go, and she stepped back and looked at me with a trace of sadness but without surprise.

"You shouldn't have done that," she said."

"I know," I said. "But I've been so well behaved all day, it was time for me to break some dishes."

She bit her lip and shook her head. "And I thought you were such a nice…"

"Yeah," I snarled. "You thought I was such a nice guy. Garrett, the great lover of humanity. The guy who goes out every day and gets sapped down and run in by the cops and threatened by hired guns and fired by rich wife-beaters. And why does he do it? Just so he can collect his thirty bucks a day and expenses. Well, I'm all that and a lot worse. So, don't tell me what a nice guy I am. I'd rather be a bastard."

Her mouth fell open. The expression slid off her face. "But why?"

I glanced toward the bedroom, then started down the stairs. "You figure it out."

Stephanie was waiting at the bottom of the stairs. I stalked by her, dug my hat out of the armoire, and headed out the front door. She trailed after me with mincing steps and finally called to me at the top of the driveway.

"Hey, wait a minute. Where are you going?"

I stopped and let her catch up to me. "Did you see Marcus?"

She breathed through her mouth several times and shook her head.

"Then I'm taking you home."

The girl dug her fists into her hips and leaned forward, and glowered up at me. "Like hell you are! I've come this far with you, and I'm sticking for the rest of the trip. You're going to find Mr. Marcus, and I'm going with you. I know his address, and when you question him, I'll know if he's lying."

I glared down at her. I'd had enough of women for one night. I didn't want to hear them. I didn't want to be with them. I didn't want to know they existed."

"To hell with it," I said. "This is a one-man job."

"I don't care," she blurted back. "Besides, driving me into town and then coming all the way back out here will take you half the night."

I went on glaring at her. She had me, and I knew it.

"All right," I growled. "Come on."

* * *

I pulled the Buick to a stop in front of 1313 Lakeview Terrace. It was an unpretentious little bungalow set back behind some trees on one of the distant asphalt strips that coil through the hills near Laurel Canyon. The nearest neighbor was almost a gunshot away.

I barely had the car stopped when Stephanie climbed out and bolted up the driveway. I called to her, but she didn't stop. By the time I got to the front porch, she was ringing the bell and tapping her foot on a thick brush pad that said, "Welcome."

"I don't think he's home," she snapped at me.

"So what? It's not my fault."

She glowered at me and kept tapping her foot. "What was going on with you and Mrs. Clavin?"

"Just settling accounts," I grumbled. "Try the door."

She tried it and got nowhere and glowered at me again. "It's locked. So, now what?"

"More detective work," I said. "Follow me."

She followed me around past the garage and through a thicket of pine trees and mimosa bushes into a small, dark back yard. A single door with a narrow window beside it looked out over a small spread of cleared land leading to more trees and rocks and canyon wall. By now, there was a smell of rain in the air, and the wind was rippling through the trees, letting craggy streaks of moonlight fall on the back of the house. One of them draped over some lawn furniture that had probably been sitting there rusting since the announcement of Repeal.

I tried the door, found it locked, pried one of the lawn chairs off its rusted moorings and placed it under the window. I climbed up on it, used my pocket knife, and pried the window open. With this done, I turned and looked back at Stephanie.

"Lesson twenty-one on page sixty-seven: Breaking and entering."

She stood and idly scratched her arm and stared at me. "Are you serious?"

"Look," I said. "Either we're both going in there, or one of us is staying out in the woods with the owls and the varmints."

She glanced around quickly, then hoisted the hem of her dress and climbed up on the lawn chair next to me. "Not on your life."

I boosted her up until her head and part of her upper body had disappeared through the window. Then I carefully placed my hand on part of a truly delightful rump and ushered her all the way in. There was a metallic rustling noise, followed by a crash and then an indignant female voice. "Damn."

In a moment, a light came on, and I peered over a sink at Stephanie. She stood there pulling her dress back in place and glaring at me as cross as a cat caught in a shower. I hoisted myself over the ledge and settled into the kitchen.

"The idea is not to make noise," I said.

She bristled and tugged at her dress. "*You* try being a burglar in high heels and this thing."

I couldn't help grinning at her.

"Oh, shut up," she said. "What the hell are we doing here?"

"Who knows?" I said. "Maybe we'll be here when a certain real estate agent shows up."

Her face turned the color of a boiled egg. "You mean Desmond? You think he's coming here?"

I just waved a hand at her and started out of the kitchen.

A swing door let me into a neatly arranged dining room and, from there, into the front hall. There was enough moonlight leaking through a narrow window at the entrance to make a living room visible. It looked well-tended and undisturbed, like a display room in a museum. Stephanie came up behind me and peered around from in back of my shoulder.

"Doesn't look as if it's been lived in very much," she said.

I said, "Uh-huh." She had a better eye than I'd given her credit for.

I turned to the left and went down a short hall with a closet on the left and a lavatory at the far end. To the right was a closed door. It would lead to the bedroom, of course. The place where Marcus would spend most of his time—when he was home.

Out of some grim instinct, I stood beside the frame and gently eased the door open. I waited. Nothing happened. I stepped tentatively into the doorway and looked inside. It was as black as the cargo hold of the Titanic. I slowly lifted my hand and groped along the wall for a light switch, then stopped. Stephanie moved over beside me and clutched at my arm.

"What is it?" she asked in a strained voice.

I didn't answer. Even without light, there was no mistaking the feeling. There was someone in the room—someone who wasn't breathing.

Chapter Twenty-One

I moved my hand around on the inside wall, found a switch, and flipped it on. A muted overhead light dropped a pale glow into a small, neat bedroom furnished with an intimate air of corruption. To the right in the corner, a plush chair and matching footstool covered in a velveteen fabric the color of fresh blood crouched between a low walnut bureau and a chest of drawers. They all sat on a vanilla-shag carpet and stared rakishly across the room at a closet in the corner by the door and a floor-to-ceiling mirror that took up the rest of the wall. On the other walls, a series of Japanese sketches and prints showed an assortment of oriental couples in an assortment of poses; all engaged in that oldest form of exercise.

In the center of the room, against the far wall, a massive double bed stood on extra-long legs that held it at least three feet off the floor. It was covered by a thick cream-colored quilt and accented by plum-colored pillows. One corner of the quilt had been folded down over a luxurious set of gold satin sheets. Next to the bed on a metal tripod, a sterling silver ice bucket held an open bottle of champagne.

I stepped into the room and stood at the end of the bed. Stephanie came gingerly up behind me, then sucked her breath in hard and jammed a fist partway into her mouth. This was just the kind of bed in just the kind of room where a smooth attorney with an eye for the ladies would hold his late-night conferences. But there had been one conference too many. Early or late, Anthony Marcus would never entertain anyone again.

He was sprawled on his back, one leg draped over the side of the bed. From what I could see, he was wearing nothing but a bathrobe. There was a puzzled, almost bemused expression on his face. His mouth was partly open, and his eyes stared straight up at the ceiling in that dull, empty gaze I'd seen too many times before. A small neat hole had been blown into the middle of his forehead, traces of scorching showing around the wound. He hadn't bled much; he hadn't needed to. A single reddish-brown trickle had run down past his left temple and fallen into a dark crimson stain the size of a pancake on the sheets.

I reached down and poked at the stain and the smear on his forehead. It was cold and sticky, with a crust starting to form around the edges. I checked the pockets of the robe and found nothing. He was wearing a watch on his left wrist, no other jewelry. I lifted his arm enough to get a look at the watch without touching. The crystal was smashed, and the watch was stopped. The time on it read eight-thirty.

Stephanie stood wide-eyed and finally pried her fist from her mouth. "Is...is he dead?"

"What do you think?"

She stood with her hands squeezed together and her mouth open and didn't move. I stepped over in front of her, grabbed her by the upper arms, and gave her a good shake.

"Are you all right?"

She swallowed hard and nodded.

"All right then," I said. "Go out and find a phone. Call the police station and ask for Detective Rawls. If he isn't there, tell them to wake him up. When you get him, tell him what's happened. Give him the address and tell him to bring his crew. You got that?"

She nodded slowly without taking her eyes off the bed.

"Then do it," I snapped at her. "Go now. Get out of here."

Stephanie turned woodenly and started for the door. She moved out into the hall without looking back. After a long pause, a light went on in the front of the house, and I heard a phone being dialed.

I reasoned that a call downtown would buy me some time. When the city hall boys got the report, they would naturally figure to put in a call to the Beverly Hills substation and send a couple of the local uniforms. But not if

207

someone told them to contact Rawls. And once he got wind that Clavin's partner had been shot, it would take a troop of Marines to keep him from coming to the scene.

While I was standing next to the bed, I checked the ice bucket. The ice in it had melted, but the water was still cold. I used my fountain pen and tipped the bottle back enough to see that it was still about half full. Someone had decided to end the celebration with another kind of slug.

Next, I made a careful inspection of the closet and found the usual lawyer's suits and a good supply of sport clothes, tasteful and expensive. After that, I used my pen again and went through the bureau. There were several sets of monogrammed underwear, socks, and silk pajamas. And in the top drawer in the center, I found a variety of ladies' undergarments—probably left by someone who figured to be in residence for a while. Maybe Marcus had decided to entertain a young lovely who hadn't brought a change of clothes. Whoever it was might have found what was in the top drawer and decided to serve Marcus up on a plate. People have been killed for less. I looked through the dainty finery, hoping for some clue as to the owner. All I learned was that she was well-built.

In the corner next to the bureau, a half-empty suitcase had been left open on the floor. Since it was in an odd place, I took it that someone hadn't wanted it noticed. And since it was half empty and Marcus hadn't been on a trip recently, that suggested that someone had interrupted him while he was packing.

I went over to the chest of drawers. Marcus's wallet and change lay on top of it undisturbed. I went through the drawers and, at first, only found more clothes. But in the bottom drawer, I found an address book sitting on top of a necklace—a thin gold chain with an emerald pendant. And next to it was a small camera, just the kind that would have taken the pictures of Clavin and Stephanie. I pushed the necklace aside, picked up the address book, and began thumbing through it.

I handled the book by the edges so as not to smear any prints. Even with that slowing me down, it didn't take long to see that Marcus hadn't just been keeping the book for business. Most of the entries listed women, with notations indicating that they were divorced, separated, or married and not liking it. Occasionally, there were numbers beside the names that I took to mean money. Almost halfway through, I turned a page and came to an entry that froze me. Beside it in the margin was a note that read, "Young, willing, will go for anything." And the name was Lorna James.

I closed the book, put it back in the drawer, went over to the bed, and stared down at the dead man. Somehow, he looked different now. He wasn't just a slippery shyster. He wasn't just a heel who took advantage of lonely and desperate women. He was a con man, a gambler, a blackmailer, and maybe worse. It had taken a while, but I had finally found Paul Milton.

As I turned away, my foot came down on something hard just under the edge of the bed. I knelt down, pushed Marcus's leg aside, and lifted the quilt. On the floor under the bed was a nickel-plated Browning automatic, small and neat and deadly. I guessed it to be a .32 caliber. I slipped my pen through the trigger guard, lifted the gun, and sniffed the muzzle. The tart smell of cordite hit me right away. The thing had been fired recently, probably within the last two hours.

I stood up and started to look around some more when a sharp intake of breath caught my attention. Stephanie was standing in the doorway, her eyes riveted on the automatic.

"Is that…is that what did it?"

"I think so."

I tapped the gun on my palm and released the clip. It was full. I slid it back and looked at the girl.

"Nothing used from the clip," I said. "But there could have been a slug in the breech. From the look of things, whoever used it only needed one shot."

She took a step forward and rubbed her hands together nervously. "Should you be handling it like that? I mean, aren't you supposed to put a pencil or something in the barrel to pick it up?"

"Not if you want to stay friends with the ballistics boys. Ramming something into the muzzle could make it impossible for them to match the markings on the bullet. Despite what your book says, it would only be destroying evidence."

"Oh," she said. She kept rubbing her hands together idly and stared at the bed. Finally, she looked at me and cleared her throat with some effort. "I spoke with Detective Rawls. He's on his way."

I dropped the gun on the bed, then went over and stood in front of Stephanie.

"Look," I said. "There's no point waiting in here. Let's go see if Marcus has something to drink. I think we can both use it."

She bit her lip, looked down at the floor, and nodded. After a moment, she looked up at me. Her face was calm, almost placid. But she wasn't happy.

"I never expected this," she said.

I tried to think of something clever to say, then tossed it aside. "Neither did I."

* * *

Rawls sat behind the table in the interrogation room, chewing on the same unlighted cigar and prodding a stack of loose papers. After getting Stephanie's call, he had come to Marcus's house with the usual cadre of men in cheap suits and squeaky shoes. They had dusted, measured, and photographed Marcus from every angle. Each of them, in turn, had made Stephanie and me repeat our story.

At first, Stephanie was fascinated, but after the fourth time, her patience wore out, and she started getting as jumpy as a flea on a griddle. I had found a bottle of pretty good rye in Marcus's kitchen, so I just milked it slowly and took everything in. Once the crew was finished, Rawls had told me to bring the girl and meet him at headquarters. And he had said to make no detours.

Stephanie sat in the chair beside me, across the table from Rawls. It was late, and Thornhill had long since gone home. That left Rawls in charge. He made a show of pushing the papers around on the table, then folded his hands, clamped down on the cigar, and stared at us intently.

"All right," he said. "Let's have it. From the beginning."

Stephanie edged around in her seat and looked sideways at me. "Not again."

"Relax, sweetheart," Rawls said to her. "I know about the yarn you gave the boys at the house. And I'm not much interested in what you've got to say. It's your boyfriend's line I wanna hear."

"He's not my boyfriend," she snapped at him. "He's..."

She flushed and looked down while Rawls leered at her. "Too bad," he said.

"What line is that?" I asked.

He worked on the cigar some more and squinted at me. "Well, like, for instance, how come you took it to go and pay a visit to this Anthony Marcus?"

I shrugged. "He was due at a party and didn't show. Some of the guests were getting worried."

He leered at me this time. "Uh-huh. And how come you're out there at this fancy-pants party to begin with? Were you workin' or are you just travelin' in some new kinda social circles?"

"A little of both," I said.

"And just to make it a nice all-around day," he sneered, "tell me you're not workin' for Sterling Clavin."

I let my breath out heavily. "He tried to hire me. He even sent me a check. But I haven't cashed it. After tonight, I don't plan to."

"So, you ain't gotta protect a client." Rawls stood up slowly. He walked easily around the table, leaned against it, and folded his arms. "Just for the record, we got witnesses who saw you at Clavin's house. They saw you playin' cozy with his wife, and they saw him arrive and threaten to knock your block off."

"Were they looking the other way when he slugged her?"

He shook his head. "Nope. Nor you, either. They said you clipped him real good." He snickered. "Kinda wish I'd seen that."

"Then let's go wake him up," I said. "I'll do it again."

Rawls gave me a nasty grin. "If it was just me, I might arrange that. But we got a goddamn can of worms here. Three killings in a week, and one way or another, all of 'em connected to a guy that figures in a Grand Jury investigation. It ain't just Paris we're after now, brother; it's Clavin. And the D.A.'s tongue's hangin' all the way down to his belt. Now, with all of this, just imagine how much rope he and Thornhill are willin' to give some cheap gumshoe that happens to get in the way."

I crossed my legs, lit a cigarette, and looked at him. "Just enough for a hanging."

"Yeah," he nodded. "Yours. Right now, you're standin' out in the cold. One word, one move, or even one look that the D.A. don't like, and they lift your license and send you to the lockup. And, brother, I'm here to tell you, you won't be gettin' out this side of the hereafter. Now, I know that Fran was payin' you to look for Nugent. And I know you've been sniffin' around Clavin and his wife and…"

He nodded toward Stephanie. She just stared at him and didn't move.

"What I'm sayin'," he went on, "is that I know you ain't been puttin' everythin' on the table, that you been holdin' somethin' out. You've played it pretty cute so far and managed to slip by. Only now, you're at the end of the string, and it's about to get cut off. I don't much care, you understand What happens to you doesn't matter to me any which way. But I get to tell you officially. You've got one chance, and this is it: Cooperate."

I sat there and wondered for just an instant if I really did have anyone to protect except myself or if any of this was really worth letting Thornhill have his licks again. Fran wanted me off the case, Clavin had fired me, and I had said goodbye to Barbara. That only left Lorna James, and she was past caring.

"All right," I said. "Clavin has been receiving threatening notes cut from newspapers telling him to lay off the Paris case. He's afraid someone's trying to frame him for Nugent's murder, and he tried to hire me to prove he didn't do it."

Rawls snorted. "I thought it might be something like that. So whatcha got?"

I took a long drag on the Lucky and studied Rawls's face. He studied me back, working on the cigar with the plodding motions of a cow chewing grass.

"I found a cut-up newspaper in Nugent's room," I said, "on the shelf in the closet. You'd better start giving Brice some lessons."

212

CHAPTER TWENTY-ONE

He snorted again. "Keep goin'."

"I also found a pawn ticket that I redeemed for a roll of film. It had half a dozen pictures of Stephanie and Clavin together during a night on the town."

Rawls scowled and started to say something, but Stephanie interrupted him.

"It had to be Mr. Marcus who took them," she said. "He was the only one who knew that Mr. Clavin and I would be working together that night. And Mr. Garrett found a camera in his room."

Rawls gave her a kind of pained expression. "What're you, his mouthpiece?"

"No," she said, mustering a handful of courage. "I'm helping him with the case. You see, I'm planning to become a detective."

Rawls almost swallowed the cigar. He stared at Stephanie for a long time without moving. Then he slowly took the cigar out of his mouth, shook his head, turned, and gazed at me with the bemused look of a man who had just been told California was now a dry state. "Is she kiddin'?"

I just waved him off. "There's more. The old codger I spoke to in the hock shop described a man who sounded like Marcus as the one who brought in the film."

Rawls stood up, then moved around behind the table and sat down. I watched as he rubbed his hands together and mulled things over. He wasn't one of the new breed of cops—the flashy boys with the crisp suits and polished shoes. He was a pre-war item, like a lot of the rest of us. He could be easygoing one minute and as tough as scrap iron the next. He didn't much care for the new ways of doing police work, and sometimes he came up short. But it was always a mistake to underestimate him.

"So, Marcus takes some pictures and stashes them in a hock shop, then passes the ticket to Nugent. Then you waltz into Nugent's place after he's been wiped off, dig up the ticket, and go claim the pictures. Tell me you haven't been concealing evidence."

I shrugged. "I didn't know the ticket was evidence at the time. And I might have had a client to look after. It's happened before."

He snorted once more and chewed on the cigar. "Where're the pictures now?"

I reached into my pocket and laid the pictures out on the table. Rawls studied them for a minute, glanced admiringly at Stephanie, then leaned back in his chair.

"So, Marcus and Nugent were puttin' a squeeze on Clavin," he said, "maybe threatenin' to spill to his wife or even the papers. Only he found out about it and sloughed 'em both."

"Maybe." I crushed out the Lucky in the precinct ashtray. "But there's got to be more to it. I found out tonight that Marcus was pretending to be Paul Milton, the theatrical agent who sent the James girl to see me. And even if she was tied in with Marcus and Nugent, her killing doesn't make sense. They wouldn't have let her in on the scam. She was simple enough to be used, but too simple to be trusted. So, there was no reason for anyone to bump her off." I pointed to the table. "What's more, Clavin never received those pictures, so it's possible he didn't even know about the blackmail."

I reached into my other pocket, took out the .38 slug, and placed it on the table in front of Rawls. He picked it up and studied it.

"What's this?

"Something I found buried in a potted plant in Nugent's office this afternoon," I said. "It was buried deep between a set of finger holes, as if someone had poked the gun into the soil and fired. My guess is that ballistics will say it came from Nugent's gun."

Rawls looked at the slug again, then back at me. "So Clavin shot Nugent's gun into the plant, then stuck it in his mitt to try and fake a suicide. So what?"

"So, something isn't right. Anybody who wanted it to look like suicide wouldn't have put a slug in the plant. He'd have taken the gun and shot Nugent with it. And if you believe that Clavin used the plant to muffle the sound of the shot, then you have to ask why someone that clever would just leave the slug to be found. And while you're at it, you have to ask why he'd go to Marcus's house, plug him, and then just drop another gun on the floor and leave." I shook my head. "Either Clavin is a lot dumber than we both think he is, or someone else is a lot smarter. Someone who doesn't want to see Clavin representing Joey Paris."

"Yeah? Like who?"

"Like someone who has it in for Paris as much as you do. Someone Paris double-crossed by tipping off the D.A., and someone who could hire all the pros he wanted to frame Paris's lawyer."

It was a long shot, but it was all I had.

Rawls chomped down on the cigar and banged his fist on the table.

"Goddammit, don't gimmie that. Sure, Clavin's smart. But when it comes to killing, he's just an amateur like so many others. Yeah, a real pro woulda dug out the slug if he'd shot it there on purpose. But you're only guessin' that it wasn't Clavin when all the evidence points the other way."

He stood up, shoved his hands in his pockets, and began pacing behind the table. "The way I see it, Clavin killed Nugent and Marcus and maybe even that James girl."

He kept pacing, talking to himself as much as to Stephanie and me. Stephanie squeezed her hands together in her lap and looked nervously in my direction.

"It starts with Clavin receivin' these threatening notes," Rawls went on. "And you say the paper they coulda come from is in Nugent's closet. We know from the Almore woman that a man who coulda been Marcus went to visit Nugent. So maybe Clavin gets suspicious of his partner, trails him, and then puts the bee on Nugent. From the appointment book and the note Nugent left for Fran, we know Clavin was goin' to the office that night and that Nugent was afraid of bein' killed. And Clavin's a big guy with a mean temper. He coulda thrown Nugent around the office like a dishrag. That would account for all the blood we found. And maybe Nugent's gun just went off into the plant in the struggle."

Rawls stopped and sat down behind the table again and folded his hands. He gave me a sly grin.

"Since Marcus was in the same office," he said. "He coulda known Clavin was lookin' to hire you. So maybe he sets up the James kid as a ringer to draw you away while he finishes his business with Clavin. Only Clavin gets wise. In fact, he not only gets wise, he gets mad—so mad he ain't thinkin' straight no more. He figures maybe you ain't playin' square with him. So, he trails you down to the warehouse and bumps off the girl. Maybe he figures to hit you too, only your comin' to scares him off."

There was no point in interrupting. Rawls was on a roll. I lit another Lucky and watched him. He broke into a nasty grin.

"By now," he continued, "Clavin has had enough of Marcus. Not only has he pegged the guy as a blackmailer, he figures maybe the crumb has been playin' footsie with his old lady. We talked to at least three people at the party tonight who heard Clavin accuse his wife of messin' around with a coupla guys. And they all heard him say he was takin' care of both of them tonight. So maybe Marcus was the first. His watch was busted at eight-thirty, and you said yourself that Clavin didn't show at the party until after nine. That woulda given him plenty of time."

He leaned back in his chair and went on punishing his cigar and looked satisfied. "Maybe it isn't all filled in yet. But just ask me, brother, and I'll say we've got the makings of a pretty good case."

"Yeah," I said. "Good enough to drive a truck through."

Rawls glowered at me and spat his words out around the cigar. "What the hell are you talkin' about?"

I took a long, slow drag on the Lucky and let the smoke curl up toward the ceiling. Rawls watched me through it impatiently.

"To begin with," I told him, "if a guy with Clavin's temper followed Marcus to Nugent's apartment, wouldn't he just bust into the place and kill them both? Why single out Nugent? Why go to the trouble of making an appointment with him? And why kill Nugent at all? He was small potatoes. Next, if Clavin did follow Lorna and me to the warehouse, he would have seen that we were waiting for somebody. So why would he jump us before finding out who that somebody was? On top of that, the girl and I were both attacked by someone who was already in the warehouse. That means Clavin would have had to get there ahead of us and to do that he'd have had to know where we were going. The girl didn't know until that night, and she didn't tell me until just before we left."

I reached over, crushed out the cigarette, and blew the last puff across the table. "If all that isn't enough, think about this. Clavin is smart enough to figure out that the brains behind a setup like this could only be Marcus. So, why would he kill Nugent, then spend four days palling around the office with Marcus, and finally kill him tonight?" I shook my head. "You haven't got enough evidence to convict Clavin of anything except being a bad host. But you could tie his hands while the Grand Jury's convening—just what he and Joey Paris have been afraid of all along."

Rawls just sat and gave me a frozen stare. He started to say something, but a rap on the door behind us stopped him. A uniformed officer came in, placed a manila folder on the table, and made a curt exit.

Rawls picked up the folder and idly browsed through it. After turning a couple of pages, he stopped and stared. He read slowly to himself, a smile coming up on his face like the morning sun rising. Finally, he closed the folder, brought his hands together, and gave me his nicest go-to-hell smirk.

"The ballistics report," he said. "We checked the gun you found at Marcus's place. It's a Browning .32, registered to one Sterling Clavin of Bel Air. It's the gun that killed Marcus, and it also happens to be the same gun that killed Danny Nugent."

Rawls stood up. He rubbed his hands together and gave me a look that was half grin, half snarl.

"I don't give a damn what you think about my case." He tapped a finger on the folder. With this, I've got enough to go and get Clavin and haul his ass in here on suspicion."

* * *

Stephanie sat brooding next to me in the front seat of the Buick as I drove back to her apartment. As I pulled onto her street, she let out a long, heavy sigh and shook her head.

"I just can't believe it. I can't believe that Mr. Clavin really killed those people. He just never seemed the type."

"Killers seldom do," I said. "That's why so many of them get off, because people can't believe it."

"Do you think he did it?"

I pulled up against the curb in front of her apartment, cut the engine, and lit a cigarette. "A lot of evidence says he did. He had means, motive, and opportunity."

"But what about what you told Detective Rawls?"

I took a long drag and watched the smoke curl slowly over the dashboard. "Rawls was right. I was only guessing. And in court, my guesses wouldn't stand up against what he's got. The only way would be to find the real killer."

She turned and looked at me suspiciously. "Do you know who that is?"

I took another drag and decided to let that one pass. "When I was in Clavin's office the other day, he got a call from someone named Stark. You remember that?"

She thought for a minute, then nodded slowly.

"Did he say what he wanted?"

She shook her head. "No. He just said, 'This is Stark. Let me speak to your boss.'" She reached up and slowly rubbed a finger over her chin. "He was very hard to understand. He had a high-pitched voice, and I remember thinking that he must have his hand over the mouthpiece. I was about to ask him to speak up, but Mr. Marcus came out and asked me who it was. I said it was someone named Stark, and then he asked me who was with Mr. Clavin. I told him it was you, and he went back into his office. Then I buzzed Mr. Clavin, but by the time I got back to the phone, the caller had hung up."

All at once, her mouth fell open, and she reached over and took hold of my arm. "Is Stark the one you were talking about with Detective Rawls? Is he trying to frame Mr. Clavin?"

I took a last drag on the cigarette and tossed it out the window. "I'll let you know."

Stephanie took her hand away and looked down. "Thank you for letting me come with you tonight. I know you really didn't have to."

I didn't say anything.

"Will you walk me to the door?"

Before I could say no, she was out of the car. I followed her up the walk and onto the porch. The night was quiet now, and the soft glow from the light above the door fell over us like strands of cobwebs. Stephanie stopped at the door and just stood hesitating. She seemed to have something in mind. As I came up behind her on the porch, she turned toward me. She stepped close, stretched up, and stared intently into my face.

"They're brown."

"What?"

"Your eyes," she said. "They're brown, with little gold flecks in them."

I shrugged. "I just polished them this morning."

She placed her hands against my chest and looked up at me mockingly. "Michael, what am I to do? How can I go on like this?"

I just looked at her and waited. Somehow, I knew what was coming.

In a moment, she stuck out her lower lip and threw up a pert frown. "Well, dammit. Aren't you going to kiss me too?"

Chapter Twenty-Two

It was just before midnight when I pulled up in front of The Pillars. The front door had been propped open, and a flood of music and crowd noise rushed down the stairs and into the street. I left the Buick and started toward the entrance to the club. A harsh breeze was stirring the dust along the curb, and the air was larded with the smell of rain. I pulled my hat on tight and started up the stairs. On the way back into town, I had thought about stopping at the office to pick up my Luger. I had thought about it and then decided against it. There were already enough guns in this place.

At the top of the stairs, I stopped and looked through the double doors into the main room. Midnight was game time at The Pillars. Thick knots of people crowded the bar and the tables, and on stage, a jazz combo was belting out a heavy blues number over a dance floor tangled with couples milling around like troops on an assault craft. There was the usual clattering of glasses broken by occasional shrieks of laughter and loud talking. And the air over the crowd was thick enough to write on.

I walked inside and began looking around for Joey Paris. I hadn't gone three steps when a pair of dark suits, bulging in every direction, flanked me and moved in close. A swarthy character with ravenous dark eyes and a heavy covering of five o'clock shadow leaned against me. And the doughy-faced man named Butch pressed something hard against my ribs and purred like an idling cement truck.

"Nice of ya ta save us the trip. Let's go see the boss."

The other one took my arm, and the two of them easily cleared a path through the crowd to a door on the far side of the room. We went up about thirty feet of hallway, through another door, and into a windowless office with the closed-in smell of a mausoleum. A series of ornate light fixtures along the near and far walls dropped an unfriendly glow into the middle of the room. The stained panel walls were crowded with pictures, mostly photographs of dark men with leering faces, the kind you would expect to see in the police mug books. Against the wall on the right, a long leather-covered couch sat behind a pair of straight wooden chairs and faced a mahogany desk that was big enough to live in. The top of the desk was clear, except for a lamp, a phone, and a large ashtray. And the ashtray looked as clean and clear as a photographer's lens.

Butch ushered me into one of the chairs in front of the desk. Then he went over and picked up the phone. He dialed a single number, waited, and then intoned quietly.

"He's in the office."

He hung up and then folded his arms and leaned against the desk, eyeing me thoughtfully while the other man settled into the couch directly behind me. I stood up slowly, took the ashtray off the desk, sat down again, and balanced the ashtray on my lap. Then I lit a Lucky and blew the smoke at Butch. He didn't move. He didn't even blink. He just kept eyeing me with the unwavering intensity of a panther stalking an antelope.

I sat there and smoked and listened to the muted sounds of the crowd trickling in from the hall. I was just finishing the Lucky when Joey Paris came in swinging his walking stick. He moved around behind the desk and lowered himself deliberately into a high-backed chair. He studied me for a moment and then reached out and tapped his stick on the desk. Immediately, Butch moved away and walked past me in the direction of the couch. Paris wrapped his fingers around the stick, held it against his chest, and kept looking at me. Finally, he shook his head and let out a sigh.

"I thought I told ya ta stick ta business," he said. "But you had ta go and get mixed up with Clavin's old lady. Then ya hadda put the slug on him in fronta all them nice people. And ya hadda go and put the finger on him for the johns, so pretty soon I gotta go and bail him out." He leaned forward and put his elbows on the desk. "You disappoint me, Garrett."

"And I'll bet you could just cry."

He gave me a rueful grin. "I'll say this for ya. You got a lotta brass comin' in here like this."

I lit another Lucky and let the smoke slowly trail out toward the edge of the desk. "Clavin's partner died tonight. He took a single shot head-on from Clavin's gun."

"I know," he said. "As soon as I heard, I told Butch and Lenny, here ta go after you. And they'da rounded you up, except you were stuck ta that young broad from Clavin's office." He leaned forward and sent a leer across the desk. "You sure like ta play all the angles, don't ya, Garrett?"

"Sure," I said. "I'm a regular Lothario."

Paris sat back in his chair and frowned. "What's that?"

I waved my hand and blew smoke at him. "Just somebody from another mob. How did you know about Marcus? Was it Desmond, or do you have somebody downtown?"

He twisted his mouth disdainfully. "I got eyes and ears all over this town. If I wanna keep tabs on a guy, he don't blow his nose or pick his teeth without I know about it."

"Then you must know that Danny Nugent was also killed with Clavin's gun and that the police are ready to bring Clavin in."

Paris sat motionless for just a moment. Then he slammed his stick on the top of the desk, jumped out of the chair, and roared across the desk at me.

"Yeah, goddammit. I know about it. And as soon as them rubber-heel boys haul him in; I'll have someone there ta spring him—no thanks ta you."

He stalked around the desk and stood in front of me. I could hear Butch pull himself off the couch. Paris reached out with his stick and flicked my hat off onto the floor. Then he placed the end of the stick against my chest and pinned me to the chair with it.

"I've had enough of you and your goddamn interfering. I told you just what would happen if ya didn't stick to business. You've caused me some trouble, and I'm gonna give ya some back."

Just as Paris raised his stick to swing, a pair of steel hands grabbed my upper arms. They were tough, but they were holding me too high up. I flung the ashtray back over my shoulder and jammed it into Butch's face. I heard the sickening crack of breaking cartilage followed by an anguished yell. I didn't look around. Instead, I lowered my head and dove forward into Paris's midsection. We crashed against the desk, and the air whooshed out of him, and he fell across my shoulder like a bag of old clothes. In an instant, I spun Paris around and held him up in front of me as I looked at Lenny and a very large automatic.

"Go ahead and shoot," I said. "That looks like a .45. It's enough gun to keep me from walking out." I reached around and tore Paris's shirt open and stuck my thumb just below his rib cage. "Put one right here. There'll be nothing to stop it but his liver, so you'll get me real good. Then, put the second one through the base of his throat. I'll have a slug in me by then, so I won't be moving much. That one ought to get me right between the eyes."

Lenny looked at me uncertainly and licked his lips. He glanced over at Butch. The man was crumpled on the couch, holding his hands over his face. A torrent of blood was rushing through his fingers, streaking his suit and falling in large drops on the carpet.

"He broke my goddamn nose," he wailed. "He broke my goddam nose."

Paris wheezed heavily and waved his hand at Lenny. "Put it away." He pointed an unsteady finger at Butch. "Take him outta here and get him patched up."

Lenny's eyes narrowed, and he slipped the gun back into his coat. Then he took Butch by the arm, hoisted him off the couch, and led him out the door.

I let Paris go, then I went behind the desk and started through the drawers. In the upper right, I found a .38 revolver resting comfortably beside a bottle of bonded whiskey. I picked up the gun and held it on Paris. Then, I sat down in the tall chair and set the bottle on the desk.

"Have some," I said. "Looks like you've had a hard day at the office."

Paris took the bottle and drank from it greedily. Then he put the bottle down, coughed, and glared at me with cold hatred. "What the hell do you want?"

I helped myself to the whiskey and then leaned back in the chair. "This

223

may sound funny to you, Paris. But I want the same thing you do. I want to know who's putting the frame on Clavin."

Paris straightened and began tucking in his shirt while he eyed me suspiciously. "Yeah? Well, I know who, and it ain't so damn funny. Stark hired you ta do them killings and pin 'em on Clavin."

"Tsk, tsk." I shook my head. "Just like every other hood. All lip and clothes and no brains."

He stopped tucking and frowned. The suspicion grew deeper in his eyes. "All I know is you come up with three stiffs in a week and go runnin' around with Clavin's wife and secretary. Then all of a sudden, my lawyer's on his way ta the clink."

I took another drink and propped my feet up on the desk. "Listen, Joey. You're right about Clavin. He's probably being run in right now. So, if Stark hired me, my job would be done. In that case, why would I be here talking to you? Why wouldn't I just go and collect my dough and head for the tropics?"

Paris grabbed the bottle and took another long swig. Then he moved back and sat in one of the wooden chairs and shook his head grudgingly.

"I dunno."

"What do you know about Clavin's partner?"

He snorted. "That creep. A skirt-chasin' little welcher. He's better off dead."

I nodded. "Well, just for the sake of argument, let's say that you killed him."

He snarled and started to get up from the chair, but I waved the gun at him.

"But that wouldn't make any sense, would it?" I said. "After all, he still owed you money. Did you know that he was hanging around the Hot Foot pretending to be a theatrical agent?"

Paris snorted again. "He pretended ta be a lotta things. Anything ta cozy up ta them babes of his. The ones he didn't drag out ta his house in Bel Air he used ta bring ta this room he rented at the Burcey Hotel—around the corner from Lacey's." He clamped his teeth and hissed through them. "I'll tell ya again. The goddamn weasel got what he deserved, but Clavin didn't kill him."

"How do you know?"

He looked at me defiantly. "Because he was here with me. He came in around six and started gettin' himself sauced. He was real upset about people makin' time with his wife. He said he was gonna get ridda you, and he was gonna kick Marcus outta his firm."

"What time did he leave?"

Paris rubbed his chin and thought for a minute. "Around eight."

I shook my head. "You'd better not tell that story to the cops. Clavin didn't arrive home until an hour after he left here, and the cops have Marcus's death placed around eight-thirty. If Clavin was all steamed up when he left here, and he can't account for that hour, he's as good as cooked."

Paris got up slowly. He moved over and leaned both hands on the desk. His voice was little more than a whisper. "That goddamn dumb bastard. Are you telling me that he really did it?"

"Maybe," I said. "How long did Marcus owe you that money?"

He frowned. "Coupla months. Why?"

"Did you ever try to collect?"

He stood up and shrugged. "We nudged him a little. But we rode him easy on accounta he was Clavin's partner."

"Uh-huh. And you said he owed you more than he could make from his divorce cases."

Paris frowned and traced his finger across the top of the desk. "Yeah. He was inta me for a lotta dough. So what?"

"So, he needed a way to pay off," I said. "A way that would bring him a bundle in a hurry and not make it appear that he was doing anything unusual. From the look of things, he may have hired Nugent to set Clavin up for blackmail. Only he never got to spring it. He just couldn't keep away from the ladies, being the lover that he was, so he got mixed up with that James girl. But she saw Nugent hanging around and somehow put two and two together. So, Marcus panicked. He shot Nugent and made it look as if Clavin did the killing. Then the girl figured she was next, so she came to me. She didn't want to spill the beans on the guy she thought was a big Hollywood agent. She probably figured if she had something on him, she could parlay that into the career she wanted. I was just supposed to look like hired muscle and scare Marcus into behaving himself. Only she miscalculated and wound up dead. From there, Marcus figured he was home free. He never counted on Clavin's jealousy or his temper."

Paris folded his arms and scowled. He didn't say anything.

I stood up and shook my head. "No. I don't like it much either. But the cops will."

"But you said Marcus did them killings."

I shrugged. "He could have killed Nugent and the James girl. But that's just guessing. And it doesn't explain tonight. He sure as hell didn't put a bullet in his own forehead." I shook my head again. "Your man Clavin's tied tight to this one. And it's going to take a lot to get him off."

Paris angled his head and raised an eyebrow. "How much?"

I grinned at him. "Are you planning to buy off the D.A. and the Grand Jury? Even you don't have that much grease."

He bared his teeth and snarled at me. "Just you watch what I'm gonna do. I'm gonna take care of things. And if you try ta get in my way, I'll blow your ass ta kingdom come."

"Maybe." I waved the .38 in his face. "But not with this."

He scowled and folded his arms. His voice fell almost two octaves. "I don't get it. What's your game? Just what are you after?"

"I'm a romantic," I said. "All I want is peace in the world. I just can't rest until everyone is happy and all the howling hearts of hate are quiet again. I can't wait to go out and rescue a miserable wife-beating attorney, so he can spring into action defending a pile of frog filth like you."

Paris scratched his chin and looked at me uncertainly. "Who's paying you?"

"Lana Turner. I bumped into her at a soda fountain." I went over and picked up my hat, and started for the door. "Right now, she's waiting for me with a chocolate malt."

He glared at me and edged his hand across the top of the desk. "Don't think you're gonna get very far, even with my gat."

I put my hand on the doorknob and looked back at him. "Paris, I don't much care if you trust me or not. But before you start pushing buttons or sending out more of your dim-witted muscle, stop and think. If Clavin is innocent, then as long as I'm walking around, somebody's going to be nervous. And nervous people make mistakes. Give me some room, and maybe I can get your boy off the hook."

"I don't like it," he snarled.

I grinned at him once more. "What choice have you got?" I held up the .38 and then tucked it into my belt. "Just in case things get crowded between here and the street."

Paris folded his arms and leaned against the desk. His thin lips were stretched tight over his teeth. "You better watch your back, Garrett. 'Cause if you don't come across damn quick, then you're cold meat."

"Fine," I said. "Then we both have just one thing to worry about."

"What's that?"

"That Clavin might be guilty."

* * *

I stepped through the door and went up the hall. Then, I eased my way through the crowd, down the stairs, and into the street. Nobody said anything. Nobody shot at me.

I crossed the street, got into the Buick, and started for home. A light rain was falling now, mixing with the road dust and the remnants of smog and smelling like the inside of a mortician's parlor. I turned on the wipers, but all they did was leave a dull brown smear caked on the windshield.

I drove through the dismal streets and stared out at the apparitions that loomed out of my own consciousness. I saw Fran sitting in my office, smoking and gazing at me with her quiet, care-worn eyes. I saw Lorna James in my arms at the Hot Foot and lying on the floor of the warehouse. I saw Barbara Clavin at the head of the stairs, looking anxiously in the direction of her husband. I saw the silky luster of her hair and smelled the soft fragrance of her skin. And I saw Stephanie in her bathrobe, looking young and innocent, and I saw her standing on her front porch, looking all grown up and dangerous. I'd had tough cases before. And I'd run into my share of women. But not all together.

I got to my apartment, parked the Buick on the corner, and went inside. The elevator was still out of order, so I dragged myself up the same three flights and up the same dusty hallway and stopped at the same tired door. I yawned and let myself into the same tired apartment, then I stopped. Right away, I sensed that something was different. A familiar smell hung in the air.

I shut the door and waited before turning on the light. Slowly I brought my hand up to my belt and held it on the butt of the .38. A quiet rustling noise came from the far corner of the living room.

"Michael, thank God it's you."

Chapter Twenty-Three

I took my hand off the .38 and flipped on the light. Barbara Clavin stepped out of the corner and stood wide eyed in the middle of the room. A damp kerchief covered her hair, and tiny drops of water dripped from it and ran down the front of a trench coat with an extra wide belt. She rubbed her hands together nervously, then reached up and pushed the kerchief back off her head. An angry red welt stood out on her left cheek.

"Michael, I just can't take it anymore. I just can't."

I tossed my hat on a chair, put the .38 on the stand beside it, and walked over next to her. "What happened?"

"Sterling is completely unstable," she said. "About an hour after you left, he woke up and began raving like a madman. I tried to explain, but he wouldn't listen. He…He…" She brought her hand up and touched the tips of her fingers to her bruised cheek. If the police hadn't come,…Michael, I'm terrified. They said Tony Marcus was murdered, and they think Sterling did it."

Barbara's eyes became full. Suddenly, she reached out, threw her arms around me, and pressed her face against my chest. I held her and waited. For a long time, there was only the sound of breathing.

Finally, she loosened her grip, and I stepped back and looked at her. "How did you get in?"

"I found the building superintendent downstairs," she said. "I told him it was an emergency, and I gave him some money. He came up and opened the door." She bit her lip and looked down. "I…I'm afraid your building isn't very safe."

"What is these days?" I grunted. "Does Sterling know you're here?"

She shook her head and turned away. "When the police came, they said they wanted to take him in for questioning. Sterling made a terrible scene, and they practically had to carry him out. Before they did, he said he was going to take care of the men I'd been seeing. And then he said,..." Her voice began to break. "He said he was coming after me."

She turned and faced me again. A pair of tears made wet tracks down both sides of her nose. Slowly, she unbelted her coat, slipped it off, and dropped it on the couch behind her. She was wearing a plain skirt and the same sand-colored blouse I had seen on her the first time I went to the house. She eased the blouse up out of the skirt, undid the bottom two buttons, and then lifted the pale fabric up over her left side. The skin of her stomach was creamy, smooth, and supple—something to make older men go running for their heart medicine. But along her rib cage were several dark bruises and a nasty scratch.

"That was from falling over the instruments this evening," she said. Then she turned, reached up, unfastened the top button, and slid the blouse down off her right shoulder, revealing the strap of her brassiere and another series of welts on her shoulder and back. "And that was from last night."

After letting out a soft sigh, Barbara began buttoning her blouse. She carefully tucked it back into her skirt, pausing once or twice to wipe a tear off her face. Finally, she finished and looked at me squarely, her eyes sad but firm.

"I just can't take any more of this, Michael. You were right. I can't stay with him. I left a note at the house, telling Sterling that I'm leaving and that I'm not coming back. Even if it means that I wind up without a cent, I can't stay with him any longer."

"What are you going to do?"

"I don't know. I threw a few things in an overnight bag. It's in the car." She tossed a listless arm in the direction of the window. "I thought I'd just check into a hotel for tonight. Then, in the morning, I'll start back east."

"Why did you come here?"

She flushed and looked down again. "I wanted to see you before I left—to thank you for trying to help."

I shrugged. "There's nothing to thank me for. Would you like a drink?"

Before she could answer, I picked her coat up off the couch and hung it on the rack by the door. Then I took the .38 and headed for the kitchen. Barbara followed. I stopped at the sink, reached down into the cabinet, and laid the gun down behind a Scotch bottle. When I straightened up, Barbara was looking at me with a mixture of fear and curiosity.

"Just in case we get some unexpected guests," I said.

"Do you think we will?" She reached out and clutched my arm. "Oh, Michael. Maybe I should just leave. I couldn't stand it if something happened to you, too. As soon as Sterling gets out of jail,…"

I took her hand and squeezed it. "He won't get out before morning. Rawls will see to that."

She stepped back, rubbed her hands over her upper arms, and nodded uncertainly.

I hauled out the jug of Scotch and poured some in a pair of tall glasses with some ice and seltzer. I handed one to Barbara and took a long drink from the other. She sipped hers, and we walked back into the living room. I guided her over to the couch, and she settled into it and let out a long, heavy sigh. The unmistakable signs of strain and fatigue showed in her eyes and at the corners of her mouth. I sat down next to her.

"How long has Sterling been roughing you up like that?"

"It started shortly after we were married," she said. "He'd have occasional fits of temper, and he'd throw things. He struck me once or twice, but nothing really serious, and after a while, it subsided. Then, just recently, something seemed to come over him. I couldn't get near him. Every time I tried,…"

"Have some more of the Scotch," I said and then nodded. "You said Sterling threatened to take care of the men you were seeing?"

She took a long drink, squeezed her glass in both hands and nodded.

"All right," I said. "Assuming that I'm one, I'm guessing that another was Marcus."

231

Barbara exhaled sharply, put her glass on the floor, and squeezed her hands together. Again, she nodded.

"Tony came to see me several months ago. He had seen one of Sterling's outbursts one night after a party at the house when I thought everyone had gone home. He was kind, and he seemed very sympathetic. We became friends—not close, but I would stop and talk with him whenever I visited the office. Then, one night, just over a month ago, he called and told me he had been doing some legal research. He said he had found a loophole that would break the agreement I had signed and let me divorce Sterling without forfeiting my right to a community property settlement. He told me to meet him at his home, and he would explain it all to me."

"So, you went."

She rubbed her hands together and swallowed hard. "I agreed to go. Looking back now, I'm not sure why I did. When I got to his house, he gave me a drink—a very strong one—and tried to seduce me. I fought him off, and then he admitted he had lied about the divorce. He told me that if I ever said anything to Sterling, he would say that I had approached him. So, I just kept quiet about it."

"Judging from his address book and the look of his house," I said, "he probably tried that stunt with a lot of women. Only they didn't all fight him off."

She shook her head and smiled grimly. "It's terribly ironic. Sterling figured out for himself what a heel Tony was. He was actually planning to dismiss him from the firm. He even had papers drawn up. He was going to do it tomorrow."

"The police figure it differently," I said. "They're saying he just got tanked up and went gunning for Marcus tonight."

"I know." Suddenly, Barbara clutched my arm again. Her lips were pale and taught. "Michael, what frightens me the most is that I think Sterling really could have killed Tony. In his present state, I think he might be capable of anything."

I stood up, walked across the room, and picked up the ashtray I had parked next to the phone. I brought it back, set it on the arm of the couch, and lit a

CHAPTER TWENTY-THREE

Lucky.

"If Sterling was planning to tie a can on Marcus tomorrow, what set him off? Why would he draw up papers and then suddenly go after Marcus tonight?"

She looked up at me, her expression suddenly blank. "I don't know, unless Tony let something slip in the office."

"Could be," I agreed. "But then why would Sterling go to The Pillars first? Why wouldn't he just go right out to Marcus's house?"

She shook her head. "I don't know."

"Did your husband say anything recently about a man named Stark?"

She lifted her hands in exasperation and then dropped them at her sides. "Michael, lately, Sterling has hardly said anything to me at all."

"That's not something to complain about," I said.

I emptied my glass and strolled out into the kitchen. Barbara slowly raised herself off the couch and followed me, moving with listless resignation. She finished her drink and put the glass on the counter. Then she leaned against the refrigerator and stared off into the space above my head, while I poured out two more doses of Scotch.

"Look what it's all come to," she said. "All those years of performing, of playing a part." She laughed quietly, without humor. "It's so terribly funny. I thought I was giving up an acting career when I married Sterling. Instead, I wound up playing the biggest part of my life, being the wife of a famous attorney." She sighed. "All that pretending, for his clients, for his friends, even for..."

"You were pretending to be in love with him?"

She folded her arms and traced a pattern on the tiled floor with the point of her shoe. "Not at first. I was deeply in love with Sterling, and I thought he was in love with me. Then, somehow, he just seemed to grow distant. It was as if he was in love with someone who wasn't there."

"Why did you stay with him for so long?"

She picked up her drink, took a sip, and shrugged. "I don't know. Why do you keep doing anything? I guess it just became a habit."

"Habits can be broken," I said.

She nodded. "I know. But it isn't easy." Suddenly, she stopped tracing the tile and looked at me earnestly. "Michael, what's going to happen?"

"About what?"

"About Sterling. What's going to happen to him?"

I took a fresh dose of the Scotch and set the glass down next to the sink. "The cops will hold him for a while for questioning, and then if Rawls has his way, they'll book him on suspicion of murder. He'll be arraigned and bound over for trial. Since it's a murder case, the judge will set bail fairly high, but with Sterling's record and connections, it won't be so high that he can't get it posted. All that should take until the middle of the morning on Monday." I shrugged. "Say, around ten. Maybe ten-thirty."

"What about the trial? When will that be?"

"Hard to tell," I said.

"Do you think he'll be convicted?"

I took another swig of the Scotch and thought about it for a minute. "That depends on the jury and how good the prosecutor is. From what I can see, the cops haven't come up with anything that isn't just circumstantial evidence. But even so, plenty of men have been hung based on that." I glanced at my watch; it read twelve-thirty. "Of course, they'll be trying to break down his story for most of the night. Sterling's pretty tough, but not many men can stand up to an all-night police grilling. If he cracks, they'll fry him for sure."

I glanced over at Barbara. She had put her glass down and was rubbing her arms again and shivering, as if a blast of Yukon air had just come through the kitchen window. I emptied my glass and put it on the sink.

"Oh hell," I said. "What do I know? I'm no expert."

"I think you are," she said quietly. "Michael, I can't stay with Sterling anymore. I know that. But I'm afraid for him just the same. Even if he...if he did do something wrong, I don't want anything to happen to him. Can you understand? Do you think I'm crazy?"

I exhaled heavily. "One of us is."

Barbara looked at me for a long moment, her eyes beginning to cloud over. Then quickly, she stepped forward, put her arms around me, and pressed her face against my chest again.

"Hold me," she said. "Just hold me. Please."

I held her. We stood locked together, surrounded by our own thoughts and the quiet hum of the refrigerator. After a while, she stirred and began murmuring softly into my shirt.

"I'm sorry," she said. "About the way I behaved tonight."

"What do you mean?"

"You know. When you kissed me. I guess I shouldn't have gotten so upset over it. It really wasn't anything."

"Thanks a lot."

She giggled softly and wriggled her nose on my chest. "That isn't what I mean. I mean I understand you were just trying to get me to be honest about Sterling. You really weren't making a pass at me." She hesitated. "Were you?"

I didn't answer.

"Michael," she said again. "What you said about not wanting to be a nice guy. You shouldn't think that." She turned her head, leaned back, and gazed up at me, her eyes a deep twilight blue. "You really shouldn't."

Nice guy or not, it didn't matter. I kissed her anyway. Her lips parted under mine, and she made those soft sounds women make—the kind you feel more than hear. I held her, and we drifted away into one of those moments when time stops and memories fade. Finally, we separated, and she held onto me and sighed softly.

"How does it happen? How do we wind up this way, living lives we despise yet afraid to do anything else?"

"What difference does it make? One way or another, we all get where we're going."

I could feel her shudder in my arms. She cleared her throat and looked up at me gravely. "Have you always lived alone?"

"Not always," I said. "Once, I lived on an island with a few dozen starving GIs and a couple hundred angry Japs."

She made a slow, rueful smile and shook her head. "That's not what I mean."

"I know."

I picked up my glass and walked back into the living room. I went over and lifted the shade, and looked out into the street. A hard, steady rain was falling now, large drops hopping off the pavement and sparkling under the streetlamps. As I watched, a black Plymouth sedan cruised silently up the street, paused in front of the building, and then slowly drifted off around the corner.

I turned and looked back at Barbara. She was across the room, studying the contents of my bookshelf. After a quick inspection, she straightened and gave the room the once-over. Then she frowned and looked at me.

"I don't see any pictures," she said. "Don't you have a family?"

I shrugged. "No one who would own up."

"But everyone has a past. And we all hang onto things that remind us of it." She motioned toward the bottom shelf. "You have some very old books. And this chess set. Are they keepsakes?"

I dodged the question. "What about you? What kinds of memories are you taking in your overnight bag?"

She strolled over next to me, angled her head, and looked up with mild curiosity. "Every time I ask about you, you change the subject."

"I'm not much of a subject."

"You are to me. Why haven't you ever been married?"

I took a long drink, then put the glass down on the windowsill. "The few women I thought enough of to marry were too smart to get mixed up with a private eye. The others you don't need to marry. Sleeping with them a few times is enough."

"You sound bitter."

I shook my head. "Just old and tired."

She eyed me with a kittenish grin. "Not so old or so tired that you couldn't go out with an attractive young lady tonight. I think Stephanie's quite fond of you."

"She doesn't know what she's fond of," I said. "And I have ties that are older than she is. So, what about your memories?"

Barbara turned and looked dejectedly out the window. "The only good ones are from very long ago. All I have to show from those years with Sterling are bruises and a handful of precious emeralds." She shook her head and sighed. "Somehow, I think I was like his emeralds—something to be shown off. He even seemed to resent any life I might have had before I met him. The few things I had from then, he threw out. A cheerleader's outfit, my prom dress, pictures of my family, even a baseball that I got from a friend of my brother's. It was just sentimental—something a sweet boy gave to a girl in high school. But Sterling wouldn't tolerate it. He got rid of everything. And he insisted that I not see anyone but his friends and associates. If any of my friends came to the house, he was rude and made them leave. After a while, they just stopped coming." She turned and put her hand on my arm. "Now, except for Amanda, the only one I have to say goodbye to is you."

I took her in my arms and kissed her again. It was getting to be a habit and she didn't seem to mind. After a minute, we uncoupled, and I held her against me and breathed in the summer fragrance of her hair.

"Never mind saying goodbye," I said. "Not for a while. You can stay here tonight." I motioned toward the bedroom. "There's a bed in there that won't treat you any worse than a slab at the morgue. And I've slept on the couch before."

She frowned and hesitated and dragged out the words one at a time. "I'm not sure…"

I didn't let her finish. I sensed a dark movement out in the street, and instinct became the stage manager. I pulled Barbara away from the window and quickly snapped out the light. Then I eased back over next to the window and peered out of the darkness in time to see the same Plymouth sedan roll quietly to a stop in front of the building. There was an uncertain movement in the front seat, and the beam from a flashlight stabbed through the night and played on my Buick. In a few moments, the beam disappeared, and the Plymouth eased around the corner again.

Barbara made a strained motion to my left, and I realized that I was still squeezing her arm. I let go of the arm and she began rubbing it and speaking to me in a hoarse whisper.

"What is it?"

"I don't know," I said. "Maybe nothing."

I went over and reached into the pocket of my jacket and fished out the paper with the number of the Pillars. I picked up the phone and dialed the number while Barbara watched. Even in the darkness of the apartment, I could see that her eyes were as big as half-dollars.

There was a quiet buzz on the other end of the line, followed by the usual crowd noise and the usual friendly greeting. "Yeah?"

"Let me talk to Paris."

"Who wants him?"

"Tell him it's Garrett," I hollered into the phone. "And snap it up."

There was a pause and the muted sound of a hand being held over the mouthpiece, then the voice came back as smooth and slippery as a bar of soap."

"He ain't here. Him and Lenny took Butch to get patched up. But he left word he wants ta see ya. Said he wants ta do a little business."

I could feel icicles forming in the pit of my stomach. "Tell him to behave himself or I'll do my business with Lefty Stark."

The voice wrenched out a coarse laugh. "Not likely, brother. Stark's dead. Got sloughed tonight by one of his own gang. Now ain't that somethin'?"

I didn't answer. I hung up the phone and turned to Barbara. "I have to go out. You stay here and leave the lights out. Don't answer the phone, and don't open the door."

"What is it? What's wrong?"

"One of your husband's clients has a score to settle. I'm going to talk him out of it."

She rubbed her hands together nervously. "But…but my bag. It's down in the car."

"All right. After I leave, wait ten minutes and then go down and get it. Then come right back up here and lock the door."

I thought about the gun I'd put in the kitchen, then decided I didn't want to frighten Barbara by going to get it. Instead, I went quickly into the bedroom and collected the .22 automatic I keep in the nightstand. I slipped it into my pocket, then returned to the living room and put on my jacket and trench coat. Barbara was waiting at the door with my hat.

"Michael, I'm afraid," she blurted.

I went over to her and put my arms around her. "Relax. It's probably just a false alarm. Nothing to worry about."

She squeezed me around the middle and breathed heavily against my chest. "I wish you didn't have to go."

"So do I."

"Will it be dangerous?"

I stepped back and gave her an exaggerated shrug, as if all I had in mind was going out to water the lawn. "Don't worry. It's just routine."

It was a good act, but she wasn't having any. She reached up and wrapped her arms around my neck. I could feel the warmth of her breath against my cheek.

"Michael, I'm so frightened. Please be careful."

I kissed her lightly on the cheek, then quickly went out into the hall and shut the door behind me. In a few seconds, I heard the lock click, and I started down the stairs, stepping softly on the balls of my feet. Even on the carpeted steps, every footfall brought creaking sounds that echoed through the halls like a steam drill breaking pavement. I reached the lobby with the .22 in my hand, half expecting someone to be waiting for me. No one was.

I went outside and stood at the entrance, looking through the yellow-gray luminescence of the rain under the streetlamps. The street lay empty. There was no movement and no sound except for the rain. A dark, shapeless thought with no substance I could name began crawling out of the recesses of my mind. Just a chilling impulse, almost like death whispering. It nagged at me with a cold insistence. It seemed to be telling me that I was about to make another mistake.

I turned up my collar, pulled my hat down tight, and ducked through the rain to the Buick. I climbed in under the wheel, adjusted the mirror, and then just sat. Nothing happened. I opened the window a crack and listened. There was only the monotonous droning of the rain. Maybe it was a false alarm. Maybe I was being skittish over nothing.

I was almost convinced when a pair of headlights lit up the street behind me. A familiar dark shape eased partway up the block and stopped across from the entrance to my building. Doors opened on either side, and two men got out. There was no recognizing them in the soaking dimness, but each man moved with that certain stealth of someone bringing business. When they reached the middle of the street, I started the Buick.

I pulled out sharply and tore up into the next block. In the mirror, I could see a wet scramble as the two figures plunged back toward the Plymouth. In barely a minute, I covered another six blocks, then braked sharply and made a slow, deliberate turn onto Wilshire, heading in the direction of my office. The street was almost empty at this hour, and I cruised easily downtown, moving fast enough to stay ahead but not too fast to be followed. For several blocks, there was no movement behind me, and I began to feel as if I'd been caught looking at a third strike. Then, the headlights loomed in the mirror.

Chapter Twenty-Four

The rain pummeled the car and splashed in the street and made the two miles to the office seem like a hundred. On the way, I let the whole scene play out in my head. With Clavin getting hauled in on suspicion of murder, Joey Paris would have been jittery enough. But now, with his rival Stark out of the way, he would be swinging for the fences. It wouldn't take much for him to figure that I had become excess baggage. He still had the idea that I might be working for Stark, and I had been clever enough to let him go on thinking that. Now, with Stark gone, chances were that no one would object if I got squibbed off. It was a plausible idea, but I didn't like it too well. It hadn't exactly been a promise, but somehow, I had the feeling that Paris had meant to give me a little more time.

But of course, it could all be going another way. Paris could be convinced that Clavin was really guilty and wouldn't be getting out to defend him. He'd have to take his chances with the D.A., but he could still get some shyster to delay things long enough so Paris could start filling the right pockets and get himself out of trouble. Only now, he had to worry about what might be going on in Stark's organization. Whoever was taking over could decide the time was right to try and take back the territory Paris had picked up two years before. Paris couldn't be sure where my allegiances were, and if I had been working for Stark, I could just as easily become a soldier for the new gang leader. The smart thing for Paris to do would be to bump me off just to avoid the risk. I didn't much care for that idea either, but it made sense.

I chewed on these cheerful notions for a while and eased the Buick steadily down Wilshire. In the rear-view mirror, I could see a familiar pair of headlights holding steady about a block back. There was no telling if Paris was in the car, but it was enough for me Just to get whoever it was away from the apartment and from Barbara. I thought about flagging down a cop or even driving down to the station. But that would only scare my two playmates off. And besides, my office was closer.

I reached the Patterson Building in just under five minutes of nimble driving. I parked directly in front of the entrance, ducked inside, and watched as the Plymouth cruised slowly past and around the corner, like a hungry shark circling a floundering swimmer.

I knew the routine, of course. They would drive around the block once, maybe even twice, to make sure there were no cops and no witnesses. And they would look carefully for anything that might suggest a setup. A car facing out of an alley. A movement in a doorway. Anything out of place. Once they were satisfied, they would park out of sight of the entrance but close enough so they could get back to the car in a hurry as soon as their business was done. Then, they would walk quickly up to the entrance, staying together but ready to move in opposite directions if any shooting started.

At the entrance, they would stop, and one would case the lobby while the other checked the street again. Then, they would head up to the office. Since the elevator was closed at night, they would have to take the stairs. One would stay about a flight back, ready to plug anybody who came out of the door at the wrong time.

Once they got to the office, there would be no knock, no how-do-you-do, no message from the mob. That stuff only happened in the movies. They would try the door softly. If it was locked, they'd shoot the knob off. Then they'd go in fast and low, shooting at everything that might be breathing. One would aim for the middle of the room and swing around to the left; the other would fan to the right. It would be nice teamwork. Nothing left alive. In and out in less than two minutes. You have to admire professionals.

I ran up the stairs and through the dark corridor to my office, fumbled with my keys until the door opened, then tumbled inside and locked it behind me. Paris had never been to my office, and as far as I knew, neither had any of his boys. That meant they wouldn't know the layout and that I did my thinking in an inner office past another door.

I went in and took the coat rack from next to the water cooler, brought it over, and stuck it in the middle of the inner doorway. There was a wire hanger on it, and I twisted that almost into a full nelson. I draped my trench coat over the hanger, wedged it over the top of the rack, then carefully placed my hat on top of that. Once this was done, I turned the whole thing around and faced it at the outer door.

Without even stopping to admire my handiwork, I beat it over to the desk, went straight for the bottom drawer to the left, and pulled out my Luger—oiled and ready. Then I reached into the middle drawer and found the clip. Working from instinct, I rammed the clip into place in the butt and hefted the thing in my hand. It had that extra ten ounces of authority, that feeling of certainty that flows up your arm and into your brain and says you're ready to deal out some death.

I couldn't see my watch in the dark, but I guessed that all of this took about a minute. That gave me time to raise the shade behind the desk and let the damp glow from the street heighten the shadows around the grotesque shape in the inner doorway. With that done, I gathered up the Luger and went over and crouched down along the left wall behind the office safe.

Just for comfort, I took the .22 out of my pocket, shifted it to my left hand, and filled my right hand with the Luger again. If ever a man was ready, I was. In the dark of the office, I could almost see myself. Don't worry, ma'am. The ranch is safe. The rustlers'll never get the herd. Two-gun Garrett is on the job. Any other time, I might have laughed at myself. I took a deep breath and waited for the faint sound of footsteps in the corridor. I waited. And the phone rang.

In a single breath, I reached out, yanked the noisy contraption off the desk, and muffled the receiver against my chest. "What is it?"

"Well, dearie. It's about time. I been tryin' ta getcha most of the night."

"Who is it?" I whispered.

"Whadya mean 'Who is it?' ya big, good-lookin' palooka? It's your ol' friend Miss Bee. I thought you an' me might get together with some more o' your hooch and talk about spendin' that reward money."

"Call me tomorrow," I snapped and started to hang up.

"Now listen, dearie," she slurred. "I'm jus' a lonely ol' woman here all alone. The least ya can do is gimmie a lil' company. I been callin' all night." She paused, cackled, and then belched. "The card you left's got a lil' gin on it now, but I can still…" She belched again. "…still read the number. So whyn't ya c'mon over?"

"Tomorrow," I said and hung up.

I crouched there in the dark with the phone in my hand, feeling as if I'd just been hit in the face with a snow shovel. After a moment, my hands moved by themselves, and I began dialing a number. I was almost finished when a faint but unmistakable rattling came at the outer door.

The rattling lasted only an instant. It was followed by a roar and a shattering noise as the door was blown open. Streaks of flame came through the darkness, tearing into the shadowed figure in the doorway and hammering against the front of the desk. I stayed huddled behind the safe, listening to the roar and counting the flashes, as wood chips flew around me and the coat rack was hurled to the floor. I counted enough shots to kill my trench coat a dozen times.

For several long seconds after the shooting stopped, the sound of gunfire still rang in the office. Then a single figure stepped through the inner doorway, paused, and began groping along the wall, as if looking for a light switch. That was all I needed.

I said, "All through?"

The figure wheeled and threw another shot into the darkness. He was surprised and off balance, and the shot went into the wall a good four feet above me. Before he could get off another one, the Luger burped hard, and the figure seemed to jump back through the doorway into the outer office. A shadow moved in the direction of the floor, and there was that solid, bumbling sound of someone falling and not getting up.

Then there were footsteps in the hall, someone running. That would be part of the routine, too. If someone starts shooting back, assume the worst and get the hell out fast. Don't stop and wait for your partner. Just get out. It isn't a question of courage or loyalty. It's simply a matter of the odds. If someone's waiting, then you've lost the advantage of surprise. Without that advantage, you're left short-handed in a high-stakes game. And a professional always goes with the odds. In a game with guns, only amateurs and fools play against the house.

I waited for several minutes after the footsteps faded at the end of the hall. Then, I inched my way along the baseboard to the door and into the outer office. There was no sound but my own breathing and damn little of that. I crept over to the smashed outer door and stood next to the frame, listening. There was always a chance that three men had come up the stairs and not two and that the one running away was really a decoy. I waited and heard nothing. Finally, I readied the Luger and flipped on the light switch. Still nothing. I poked the Luger through the door and peered around it into the hall. It was empty.

I turned and looked back into the office. A man was lying on the floor, face down, a large automatic clutched in his right hand. I held the Luger on him just in case, and with my left hand, I rolled him over on his back. One look told me I could put the Luger away. The front of his shirt was now soaked with red. His jaw hung slack. And his eyes stared off into nowhere with an expression as empty as the hallway. It was Lenny, the gunsel I had put the bluff on at The Pillars.

I walked slowly through the inner office and around behind the desk. Without thinking, I flicked on the desk lamp and looked at the Luger, still warm in my hand. Suddenly it weighed a hundred pounds. I laid it down and slowly, carefully went through the motions of lighting a Lucky. I took a deep drag and felt the reassuring chafing against the back of my throat. For a long time, I just stood behind the desk and slowly sucked in the poison. The cigarette was burned almost to the nub when I picked up the phone and dialed the number.

The usual cold voice came on the other end, and I asked for Detective Rawls. There was a jarring noise as the receiver was laid down, then a long silence. Finally, the familiar drone.

"Yeah?"

"Eddie, it's Garrett. I just made a mess in the office. Better send some of your boys to clean it up.

A short pause. "Anybody I might be interested in?"

"Not now. He used to be a button man for Joey Paris."

"Well, well," he chuckled. "Ain't that a shame. So, Paris is after you now. Serves you right, shamus. You oughtn'ta been holdin' out and playin' footsie with those bastards."

I took a long hard look at the body out in my front office. "Yeah. You're right."

"Goddamn right I am," he said. "You okay?"

"No holes. But thanks for asking."

"Go to hell," he grunted triumphantly. "Just stay put, and I'll send somebody." He paused, and his voice took on a sour tone. "You know, I oughta run your ass in, you closed-mouthed bastard. What made you ask for me anyway? You know I usually work the day shift."

"I also know you brought Sterling Clavin in for questioning tonight," I said. "I figure that so long as he's down there, you will be too."

"Nice guess," he said tartly. "But your goddamn client ain't here. Some shyster named McDermott came in and sprung him on a writ not more than fifteen minutes ago. I'll lay odds that Paris sent the son of a bitch in here. You're movin' in some pretty nasty circles, brother."

I squeezed the receiver hard enough to crack it. "Where is Clavin now?"

Rawls grunted again. "Are you kiddin? He's on his way to your place. His secretary phoned about the time that shyster was here. Left a message for Clavin to meet you at your apartment and gave him your address."

"And you let him go?"

"Well, what the hell do ya think I did?" he roared. "Of course, I let him go. I know the law as well as you do, you goddamn flatfoot."

I barely breathed the word. "Damn."

Rawls began ranting on the other end. "Well, of all the goddamn ...
If you think..."

"Eddie," I interrupted him. "Just get over there. Get over to my place fast."

He stopped ranting and spoke softly, almost without tone. "What for?"

I almost screamed into the mouthpiece. "To try and stop a killing."

Chapter Twenty-Five

The Buick tore through the night, the spattering of rain making a drumbeat on the hood and windshield. The streets were empty now, and the darkness hovered, muffling the streetlights and masking the thousand corruptions that thrive in L.A. at this hour. I drove through it all without noticing. It was something apart from me—something distant that barely moved as I flow past.

I pulled up in front of my building just as a Yellow Cab was nosing away from the curb. Without hesitating, it rolled slowly into the middle of the street and ambled off through the rain. I got out and sprinted into the building, through the lobby, and up the three flights of stairs without even thinking of what a good target I was making of myself. I ran up the hall past several curious faces peering out from several dark doorways. From instinct, I reached into my pocket and began fumbling for my keys as I approached the door to my apartment. But there was no need. The door was open.

From the darkness of the corridor, I stepped in and squinted toward the glaring interior of my living room. It wasn't the same place I had left only thirty minutes before. The rug in front of my sofa was crumpled and twisted. The end table with the phone was overturned. And the small lamp next to it was on its side, the naked bulb radiating up into the middle of the room.

I took another step, and my foot came down on something hard. I glanced down and saw the remains of the doorknob and latch mechanism, broken into pieces as if someone had hammered the door open. The door was swinging free on its hinges, the hole where the knob used to be staring up at me as empty and vacant as the open eye socket of a decaying skull.

The rasping sound of shallow, irregular breathing came from across the room. I looked up and saw Barbara leaning against the far wall, her face tear-streaked and a spot of blood at the corner of her mouth. She was wearing a pale blue bathrobe, torn at the shoulder, and her arms hung limp at her sides. Her right hand was clutching something dark and heavy.

She was staring down at the floor at something lying just beyond the wooden chairs and table I keep set up to make people think I have regular meals. I stepped around the table and looked down at a man sprawled face down on the floor. He was a large man, well-dressed, with black hair. He wasn't moving.

Without stopping, I went over to Barbara and took the gun from her hand. The butt end was scratched and gouged as if someone had used it for a can opener. I slipped the gun into my coat pocket and then took hold of Barbara. She stared at me, and her mouth moved idly, without sound. I was afraid she might faint, but her eyes were clear, the pupils were not dilated.

I said. "Are you all right?"

She moved her mouth again, then cleared her throat. "I...I don't know. He just came at me. It all happened so fast."

I led her to the couch and propped her against one of the cushions. Then I went over to the man on the floor and pressed my fingers into the main artery in the side of his neck. It felt as lifeless as a piece of string. I carefully lifted his shoulder, so I could have a look without changing his position. Under him was a fresh pool of blood that had run out of his chest and was slowly trickling across the floor. As I held him, he seemed to stare at me with a vague look of disbelief, as if being dead was only a minor inconvenience, and any minute now, he would just order himself back to life. I laid him down again and shook my head. Not even Sterling Clavin was that good.

I went over to the couch and sat down next to Barbara. She seemed to be coming around. She was sitting upright with her hands clamped tightly on her knees, and she looked at me with a grim uncertainty. I took out my handkerchief and dabbed the blood off her mouth.

"Is he...Is he dead?

"As dead as they come," I said. "What happened?"

"He…He just burst in and attacked me. I was terrified. I…"

She was stopped by the noise outside the apartment. Heavy footsteps pounded on the stairs, then up the hall, and Ed Rawls loomed in the doorway waving a police .38 special in front of him. He was followed by Brice and another man in the usual cheap suit.

Rawls went straight for the body while the others canvassed the apartment. After deciding Clavin was dead, Rawls put away the .38 and instructed Brice to phone for the coroner. Then he said something half under his breath, and the third man took up a position just outside the door. Finally, Rawls turned in our direction. He took a quick look at Barbara and then turned a marksman's stare on me.

"All right. What's the story?"

I stood and ushered him into the corner of the room, a discreet distance from the couch. "He was dead when I got here," I took the .38 from my pocket and handed it to him. "She did it with this."

Rawls hefted the gun in his hand and looked uncertainly at Barbara, then back at me. "She iced her old man?"

"He attacked her," I said. "She was defending herself."

"She all right?"

"I think so."

He gazed at her sympathetically and, without taking his eyes off her, waved the .38 in my face. "This yours?"

I shook my head. "It's a door prize I picked up at The Pillars earlier tonight."

He grunted. "The stiff in your office just came to get it back, huh?"

"Something like that."

He picked up the broken latch and gave it a quick look. "Between this and your office," he said wryly, "it's been a tough night on doors."

I ran my hand over the front of my trench coat, where you could now stick your fingers through a couple of bullet holes. "And on other things."

Brice hung up the phone, then stepped over to Rawls and spoke quietly. "Coroner's crew's on the way, chief. They say they're gettin' short-handed.

This is the second call in an hour."

Rawls looked at him evenly and held out the .38. "No use dustin' this. Just get it to ballistics."

The little man hesitated and looked at the gun. "Jeez. Looks like somebody chewed on it."

Rawls leaned over, breathed in his face and made a sound like four tigers having lunch. "Somebody'll be chewing on you if you don't get movin'. And don't call me chief."

Without a word, Brice darted out of the room. Rawls glowered after him, then turned toward me and gave me a mocking grin. "I got a lotta boys out cleanin' up after you tonight. Are you finished?"

I peeled off my trench coat and reached for a Lucky, and didn't answer.

Barbara was still sitting on the couch, clutching her knees and staring at the lifeless heap in the middle of the floor. She seemed to have no interest in anything else in the room. Rawls went over and sat down next to her and softly patted her hand.

"Mrs. Clavin, I'm Detective Rawls of the Los Angeles Police Department. Do you remember me?"

She nodded without looking at him. "You came to arrest my husband."

"That's right," he said without a ripple. "Can you tell me what happened here?"

She brought her hands together, cleared her throat, and nodded again. "I was here alone. I had come to see Mic...Mr. Garrett, but he had to leave. He said it was to see one of my husband's clients. I guessed it was that man Paris. I was terribly worried. I just sat here alone in the dark and waited. Then after a while, there was a knock on the door."

Barbara turned and looked up at me, traces of fear still in her eyes. "I thought it was you, that you'd come back. I went over and asked who it was, and someone began pounding on the door—a fearful pounding, as if to wake the dead. Then, before I could even move, the door burst open, and I saw Sterling standing there. He had this dreadful, wild look on his face, and he said he was going to kill me. I...I was terrified. I didn't know what to do."

Her breath caught, and she drew her hands up to her mouth.

Rawls reached over and patted her arm, and spoke to her in a voice as soft and smooth as butter. "It's all right, Mrs. Clavin. There's no rush. Just take your time."

Barbara breathed deeply several times and looked at him demurely. "Thank you."

She brought her hands down and took another breath. She blinked rapidly, then looked up and went on talking to me.

"All at once, I remembered that gun you had put in the kitchen. I ran out to get it, but Sterling came after me. He caught me just as I was reaching under the sink. He yanked the gun out of my hand and threw it over his shoulder into the living room."

She paused and looked away, as if fascinated by some grim recollection. Then she pointed over into the corner.

"I remember hearing it hit the radiator over there. I…I guess that's how it got scratched."

Rawls prodded her gently. "Then what happened?"

Barbara's teeth came together, and she squinted. Small tears began rolling down the sides of her face.

"Then he hit me," she said. "He hit me several times and knocked me down. Then, as I was lying on the floor, he came in here and picked up that chair." She pointed to one of the wooden chairs lying on its side next to the table. "I screamed at him to go away and leave me alone. But he just laughed—a horrible, evil laugh. He said he was going to break me into pieces, one bone at a time. He said I'd beg him to kill me and that even if I lived, no man would ever look at me again."

She bowed her head and let out a long, wrenching sob. Then she caught her breath and clenched her fists, the nails digging into her palms. Finally, she looked up again. Her eyes were wide, and the tears ran freely. When she spoke, pain throbbed in her voice.

"All those times before when Sterling hit me, I was afraid, but somehow, it wasn't the same. I always believed he didn't really mean to hurt me. But this time, I knew. He meant it. He was going to kill me." She swallowed hard. "All I could think about then was getting out. The door was open, so I ran for it. But Sterling slammed the door shut and lunged at me with the chair. He missed and threw himself off balance and fell over that small table. I tried to get by him, but he lunged at me again and blocked the door, so I ran over here by the radiator. I saw the gun on the floor, so I picked it up. I pointed it at Sterling and yelled at him to stop. But he just laughed again and kept coming toward me with the chair." She sobbed again. "I begged him, I pleaded with him to stop. But he wouldn't." Finally, her voice broke. "So, I shot him."

Barbara doubled over on the couch, covered her face with her hands, and sobbed. Rawls sat patiently and gave her shoulder a reassuring pat.

"Just take it easy," he said. "I know how hard this must be for you. I only have a few more questions."

She kept sobbing for almost a minute, then slowly held her head up and sniffled. Rawls began reaching for a handkerchief, but I got to mine first. I handed it to Barbara, and she wiped her face and blew into it.

Finally, Rawls patted her shoulder again and asked. "Better now?" When she nodded, he went on.

"What were you doing here in Garr..." He caught himself, turned, and gave me a strained look, then tried again. "I mean in Mr. Garrett's apartment?"

"I came here to thank him," she sniffled. "I had left my husband and was about to leave town and go east. Mr. Garrett has been so kind and considerate to me. I wanted to see him before I left."

"I see," he said. "Do you think that's why your husband came here to kill you? Because he thought you were going off with...Mr. Garrett?"

She nodded. "That must be the reason. Sterling always said that if I tried to leave him, he'd kill me and anyone I tried to leave with. He was always insanely jealous. I'm afraid he thought that Mr. Garrett and I..."

Rawls nodded and cleared his throat uneasily. "Mrs. Clavin, I'm sorry to be indelicate, but did your husband have a reason to be jealous?"

She turned and looked at him, all expression falling out of her face. "What do you mean?"

"Well, ma'am," he said. "I'm sure you see how it looks. You're here in another man's apartment, in a bathrobe."

"Sergeant," she said acidly. "I had no intention of staying, but Mr. Garrett invited me because it was such a bad night to travel. I was to use the bedroom, while he slept on the couch." She balled her hands into fists again. "And I don't like what you're insinuating, Sergeant. Mr. Garrett is much too honorable a man for that."

I felt as if I'd just been hit with the snow shovel again.

"It's Detective, ma'am," Rawls corrected. "And I didn't mean to upset you. It was just a routine question."

She uncurled her fingers. "I understand, Detective. I'm sorry to be rude." She rubbed a heavy hand across her forehead. "But this has been a terrible ordeal, and suddenly I just feel exhausted."

Rawls started to say something to her, then stopped, as the coroner's crew came marching up the hall and into the apartment. There were three of them in trench coats and white hospital pants. One spoke quickly to Rawls, and then they laid out their equipment and began examining the body.

Rawls stood up, took me by the arm, and walked me over into a corner. "It'd be better if she didn't have to watch this. Why don't you just take her home?"

I nodded. "All right."

He exhaled contentedly and licked his lips. "Guess this wraps it up. With Clavin gone, I can close the book on a coupla killings and save myself a lotta paperwork."

"What about Paris?"

"Oh yeah," he mused. "He's kind of got it in for you, now, hasn't he?" He angled his head and gave me a foxy look. "You hear about Lefty Stark getting bumped off tonight?"

I nodded again.

"That means Paris is gonna be runnin' scared. He's even apt to figure that you engineered the Stark killing and set up his mouthpiece for the big one so you could work your way in with the new boss and bring home a lotta the folding. Brother, I wouldn't like ta be in your shoes."

"Thanks," I said dryly.

"Point is, Paris could be on a tear, gunnin' for some lonesome private dick.

He ain't gonna have his mind on me. That makes him my meat." He started to turn away, then stopped and winked at me. "Honorable, huh?"

I shrugged. "Nobody's perfect."

He grinned, and then his eyes narrowed. "Drive her home and then come on down to the station. I'm not finished with you."

Rawls explained to Barbara that I would take her home and that she could come down to the station the next afternoon to make a formal statement. He assured her it was just routine. Without saying so, he suggested that the world was better off without Sterling Clavin in it.

Barbara went into the bedroom and dressed, and we went down and climbed into the Buick. The rain had eased into something just this side of a heavy mist. I cruised easily down Wilshire and headed in the direction of Bel Air. Barbara nestled quietly in the seat beside me and rested her head on my shoulder, her purse tucked snugly under her arm. After several minutes, she sat up and exhaled deeply.

"Is it over, Michael? Is it really over?"

"Almost," I said. "Only a few loose ends left."

Curiosity tinged her voice. "Loose ends?"

"Yeah. Like a few unsolved murders and an angry gangster left without a mouthpiece."

She gasped. "My God. I forgot. What happened tonight? When you went out, I mean?"

"What happened is that a couple of Paris's boys tailed me to my office and tried to make sure I stayed in it—for keeps."

I could feel her shudder on the seat next to me. "What a horrible nightmare. Will you be all right? Will they come after you again?"

"They might," I said. "That depends on how good a detective I am and whether I can turn up a killer that will satisfy both Paris and the cops."

I reached up and adjusted the mirror. A pair of headlights stared back at me from only half a block behind. There was probably nothing to it. It was probably just some citizen on his way home after working the late shift. After the night I'd had, I was probably just being jumpy. Only nobody who works the late shift lives in Bel Air.

Barbara said, "Michael, I don't understand. What do you mean 'turn up a killer?'"

I turned off Wilshire and headed up the main drag in the direction of the hills. The dark street yawned in front of the car as empty and still as a dead man's gaze. In the mirror, I saw the headlights turn after me. They closed steadily until they were only a few yards back.

"I mean, someone has arranged this whole thing," I said. "The killing of Marcus and Nugent, even a young dance hall girl you never heard of. It's all part of a plan."

"Michael, do you mean Sterling really did all those things the police said he did?"

I shook my head. "Not Sterling."

"Then who?"

I adjusted the mirror again, and the car in back began flashing its lights. "I think we're about to settle that."

I stepped on the gas and moved up the street toward the last major intersection between downtown and the suburbs. The Buick sped up, but not enough to make anyone upset. As I approached the corner, I thought about what I might do to shake the tail. I thought about it. But that was as far as I got.

The teamwork was something to see. The car behind flashed its lights again, and while they were still flashing, another car wheeled out of the intersection, did a pinwheel turn in the street and stopped crosswise in the lane directly in front of me. From instinct, I slammed on the brakes, and the Buick squealed to a stop, just a coat of paint away from a dark Oldsmobile sedan.

Barbara was thrown against the dashboard. She rebounded heavily against me, then came up gasping and desperately clutching her purse.

"Michael, what is it? What's going on?"

I had barely taken a breath when the door was thrown open next to me, and a large piece of artillery was thrust into my face. Behind it, a voice growled out of the glaring headlights.

"All right, shamus. Sit still."

A hand the size of a large melon pushed hard against my chest and then wrenched the Luger out of my shoulder harness. I squinted into the glare and tried to see who it was, when the rear door of the Buick opened, and a dark figure climbed in behind me. Barbara turned and gasped. Her eyes were wide, and she held her purse clamped tightly to her breast, as if it might offer some protection.

The door closed next to me, and from the back seat, I heard the chilling metallic sound of a hammer being cocked. Then something began making a steady tapping on the back of the seat just to my right. Slowly, with infinite care, I turned and looked at it. It was a long, ebony walking stick with a polished silver knob. Then, from back in the darkness, a voice full of gravel.

"Okay, tough guy. Drive."

Chapter Twenty-Six

I sat watching as the Oldsmobile did a quick turn and headed off up the street. The car in back flashed its lights again, and something as cold as death pressed against the back of my neck. I tried to swallow, but my throat was full of sandpaper. The voice from the back seat intoned almost lovingly just behind my right ear.

"Remember I told ya about the one eyed stare? Well, it's lookin' right down your neck. Now drive. Follow the Olds."

I put the Buick in gear and started after the Oldsmobile. It moved along for about three blocks and then turned and nosed up toward one of the canyons north of Bel Air. The smell of pine and eucalyptus drifted into the car as we crawled past a line of expensive homes, all dark and uncaring. Barbara sat coiled next to me, clutching her purse, her eyes riveted on the back seat.

I slowly reached up and adjusted the mirror, so I could see the man behind me. Even in the dark, there was no mistaking Joey Paris.

"What took you so long?" I asked him. "I expected you sooner."

"Just knock off the smart stuff," he growled. "It's time ta settle up."

"I imagine it is," I said. "What are you going to do now that your lawyer is dead, the Grand Jury's about to indict you, and some young punk from the south side is barking at your heels?"

He didn't even flinch. "I can get another mouthpiece. I already got my soldiers out ta take care o' Stark's boys. And I'm about ta finish with a two-timin' shamus that just got a little too greedy for his own good."

"So, you heard that Clavin got it tonight?"

"I heard. I know where and I know how, and I know who did it and who set him up. I met him outside the station when he got sprung. And I tried ta warn the stupid son of a bitch not ta go near your place, but there was no holdin' him back." He made a clucking sound. "Ya know, I might just be better off without him, considerin' how messed up he was over you tanglin' with his old lady."

Barbara edged a little closer to me in the seat.

"Too bad," I said. "He might have kept you out of trouble if he'd had his eyes open and not been blinded by all the things he wanted to own. He might have seen what was going on and that both of you were being set up."

Impatience riddled Paris's voice. "What the hell're you talkin' about?"

"Clavin was messed up, all right. He was supposed to be. Only not by me. He could have defended a thousand creeps like you, and I never would have bothered him. But someone had it in for him. Someone who even called his office and pretended to be Lefty Stark. Someone who knew I'd be there and who knew a call from Stark would stir up trouble."

Paris leaned forward in the seat, and the same cold thing poked me just above the shirt collar. "You talk like you know somethin'."

"I know who did the killings and why. And I know the real reason Clavin had for being jealous."

Barbara stared at me with a look of disbelief. "Michael, how can you say that?"

"It's very simple, darling," I said. "You set Sterling up to make it look as if he was a murderer. That is, you and Anthony Marcus."

For the first time, I heard a sneer in her voice. "You can't be serious."

"No? I'll let the Stick decide how serious I am. When I found Marcus dead after the party, I also found an emerald pendant in his dresser drawer. It was exactly like the one I saw you wearing when I first went to your house. There couldn't be too many pendants like that. And you weren't wearing it at the party. You had on a pair of emerald earrings, but nothing on your neck. That would be because the necklace that went with those earrings was in Marcus's bedroom—where you had left it."

In that instant, she froze, and her face seemed to turn to lead. Instinctively, she clutched her bare throat. There was a long silence, broken only by the sound of the tires swishing over the wet pavement. Finally, Paris poked me again, the same impatience clawing at his voice.

"Listen, Garrett. I ain't buyin' some crazy story that you dreamed up just ta get yourself off the hook."

"Sure, it's crazy," I said. "And I'm crazy for getting stuck with it. And you'd be crazy to listen to it. But it's a lonely, wet night. What have you got to lose?"

Barbara moved to the other end of the seat. "Michael, of all the..."

"Shut up," Paris barked at her. He tapped his stick on the back of the seat again, then spoke to me. "Okay, tough guy. Spill it."

"You'll appreciate it," I said to him. "It's full of lies and greed, and it's about someone who doesn't care how many people have to be killed."

I glanced sideways at Barbara and spoke to her. "When Marcus made that pass at you, you didn't dodge it the way you told me. You probably encouraged him to do it. Once you had him on the string, you convinced him to help you frame Sterling for murder. You see, if Sterling was convicted of a felony, the premarital agreement would become void, and you could claim all his money. Marcus would represent you, and the court would be sympathetic to the long-suffering wife whose husband had finally gone off the deep end. And with Sterling's temper, he was made for the frame. You probably even egged him into slapping you around, especially in public, by playing up to people like me."

The Oldsmobile cruised on ahead up the slowly ascending grade. The rain was all but gone, and the sound of tree frogs loomed in the night. I nudged the Buick along and checked the mirror. The other car had fallen back and was trailing us now by about fifty yards.

"I figure it was Marcus who first contacted Nugent," I went on. "He was the perfect mark. A stumblebum private eye that nobody would miss. But Nugent turned out to be more of a detective than you thought he was. He found out that Marcus was on the hook to a bookie named Eddie Franks, and when he started asking questions, he discovered that Marcus was also playing around with the wife of a rich and powerful attorney." I looked over at Barbara. "He must have come to the house to see you and not Sterling. He probably figured Marcus had something on you, and he would have offered to help."

Barbara sat without moving, staring out into the damp gloom. Her profile seemed gaunt now, her features strained.

"You gave Nugent enough of a line to keep him interested," I said, "but you started to suspect that you had underestimated him. By then, Marcus had taken the pictures of your husband and Stephanie, but he hadn't had time to plant them. And with Nugent getting wise, you decided you couldn't wait. You and Marcus had to get rid of him right away. Either one of you could have done it, but since Nugent was shot with Sterling's gun, I'm guessing that you did the actual killing.

Paris grumbled in the back seat. "You're right, Garrett. This is crazy. There was a fight in that office. Then somebody made it look like that bum knocked himself off."

"That's right," I agreed. "It was supposed to look like a phony suicide set up by an amateur. Someone with a temper like Clavin's. Someone who killed Nugent and then got scared and made a clumsy attempt to cover his tracks. Afterwards, the cops were supposed to find a newspaper in Nugent's room, suggesting that he had sent the threatening notes to Clavin and somehow connecting them to you. And they would also find the pawn ticket leading them to the blackmail pictures. All of this would have given Clavin a motive for murder. Then, at some convenient time later, the gun would have shown up, clinching the frame. The trouble with all that was that the cops didn't care enough about Nugent to search his room thoroughly and find the newspaper or the ticket. But I did. Only the paper in the closet was the Tuesday morning edition, when Nugent had been killed on Monday night."

I spoke to Barbara again. "That was your first mistake, darling. I couldn't be sure that Nugent wasn't trying to blackmail Sterling. But that paper told me that if he was, he wasn't doing it alone."

Barbara clamped her jaw tight and didn't say anything.

"My showing up was a real surprise," I said. "It never occurred to you that somebody might really miss Nugent and miss him enough to hire another detective to find out what happened to him. When I started asking questions, you and Marcus got worried. I wasn't some starry-eyed character you could control just by giving an occasional glimpse of your legs. So, the two of you devised a plan to get me out of the way, but only after further incriminating your husband."

Up ahead, I could see the Oldsmobile winding into a series of sharp curves that snaked upward into the side of the canyon. I gave the Buick a little gas and felt it strain up the grade as we moved past a scattering of lifeless houses and bungalows.

"You arranged to meet me at Lacy's," I continued. "Then you showed me the note and got me to agree to go and see Sterling. You knew that if Sterling went to the police with the note, they would simply conclude that it gave him a motive for killing Nugent. And if he didn't, you and Marcus could find another way to have the note surface—probably on my dead body. That way, it would look as if Nugent and I had been working together and that Sterling had done that killing, too. I knew that something was going on when you walked into Lacy's less than half an hour after I did that night. You said you were calling from home, and that's more than an hour's drive away. But it would only have been a few minutes from Marcus's little hideaway at the Burcey Hotel."

I felt another prodding in the back of my neck. "Slow down a minute."

I braked the Buick and pulled over to the side of the road. Up ahead, the Olds did the same. Paris turned and looked through the rear window at the second car. He waved his stick back and forth so it could be seen in the lights. The car moved up to within several lengths of us and slowed, and then Paris turned back to me. "All right, go ahead."

I stepped on the gas again and went on with my story.

"The idea was to distract me with a bit of fluff and set me up for a knockoff. For some time, Anthony Marcus had been pretending to be a theatrical agent named Paul Milton. It was a little grift he ran on the side, so he could line up young girls to play bedroom games with. Then, after he'd had his fun, he'd chisel enough money from them to cover his gambling debts. He sent a girl named Lorna James to see me. She must have confided in him that a little weasel named Myron Weeks had taken some nude photos of her. So, he called her, and pretended to be Weeks, and threatened her with the pictures. The girl was supposed to decoy me to that warehouse where someone was waiting to take care of me. And it might have happened that way, except that Lorna walked in and surprised the killer before I had gotten inside. All I got was conked on the head. But Lorna got her brains blown out. I might still have wound up dead, but an old wino and his dog showed up in the alley. And that delayed the killer long enough for me to come to."

I spoke to Barbara again. "Lorna was shot with a large caliber gun, not the same as Sterling's. And since she was shot from such close range, I figure it had to be someone she knew. I'll give you odds that when the police search Marcus's house, they'll find the gun that killed her."

She hissed at me through her teeth. "This is all ridiculous. You can't connect that killing to me."

I nodded. "For a long time, I couldn't, and that bothered me. I knew that Nugent had gotten tied up with someone who was trying to frame Sterling, and finally, I figured out it was Marcus. But Marcus had nothing to gain from railroading your husband, at least not directly. That meant there had to be someone else involved. I had my suspicions, but I just couldn't tie you to Lorna. That just didn't make sense—until last night."

We rounded a sharp curve and left the few remaining houses behind. The darkness moved in like the tide, leaving only the glinting red taillights of the Olds darting ahead. The Buick bucked once but kept moving steadily up the grade.

"While I was in my office waiting for Paris's two gunmen, I got a call from the landlady at Nugent's apartment. She reminded me that I had given her one of my cards, and she apologized for spilling gin on it. That's what finally put me wise. The night Lorna James was killed, a police detective-captain named Thornhill found a similar card among her things. It was streaked and smeared, and Thornhill thought it was from the rain that night. Only the card had been inside her wallet inside her purse. Lorna had told me that she got the card from her agent. But at that point, I had never even met Marcus or your husband. So, there was no way Marcus could have gotten my card except from you—not streaked with rain, but with tears. It was the same card I had given you the night before at the house, when you went into your phony hysterics." I chuckled. "You know, darling, I'll bet you really were one hell of an actress."

Paris moved forward and leaned on the seat to my right. He let out a long, heavy sigh.

I said, "How do you like it so far?"

He threw a cold stare at Barbara and then turned it on me. "I'm startin' ta get convinced. What's the rest of it?"

"The rest is even more cold-blooded," I said. "With me still alive and Lorna's murder on the front page, Marcus began to get jittery. Clavin was set free, I was getting closer to the truth, and now Joey 'the Stick' Paris was asking questions about Marcus's bookie. So, Marcus decided it was time to take a powder. He had been packing a suitcase when I found him, but he never got to finish. He didn't because Barbara saw a chance to complete the frame and grab the whole bundle for herself. She told her husband that she was seeing me, knowing that would make him furious. Then, sometime before the party, she went to Marcus's house, shot him, and left Clavin's gun to be found under the bed. She made it look as if Marcus had died at eight-thirty. But he didn't die then. It would have taken more than just a fall on the bed to break his watch, and there were no other signs of a struggle. Barbara set his watch ahead and then smashed it, so she could go home and be in a house full of witnesses at the time it appeared Marcus had been killed."

"It was a clever touch," I said to her. "But you should have taken the extra five minutes to tear up the room. With the lather he was in, Sterling wouldn't have left the place so neat."

Barbara turned and threw daggers at me with her eyes.

Paris nudged me once more. "Is that all of it?"

"Not quite," I said. "After the scene at the party, when her husband attacked her, Barbara actually became frightened. She thought she might have overplayed her hand with him. But then, when the police came, she had a stroke of inspiration. Suddenly, she saw a way to get rid of her husband

and make it look as if he tried to kill her. That way, the courts would be only too glad to give her every bit of his estate. So, she went to my place, figuring she could work me into inviting her to spend the night. Being the gracious host, I decided to play along."

Paris grumbled. "Yeah. I'll just bet you did."

"All work and no play," I shrugged. Then I went on. "So, she brought an overnight bag, but she left it in the car. Her next move would have been to send me down for it. While I was gone, she would have called the station, found out when her husband was being released, and left word that she was at my place. But as it happened, I spotted your boys prowling around and decided to let them follow me away from the apartment. I didn't figure they would be in any mood to talk, but I knew that sooner or later you would be."

"Well, ya got your wish," he snapped. "So, keep talkin.'"

I looked at Barbara once more. "It was quite an idea—luring Sterling over to my place so you could kill him and make it look as if you were just defending yourself. You even let him slap you around once or twice so that you'd look the part. I guess that's what they call method acting. But you made a few small mistakes. First, you told Rawls that you were Sterling's secretary. That was careless. Stephanie wouldn't have known where you were or that you had left Sterling. The second mistake came after you shot him. You took the gun and used it to break off the door knob so it would look as if the door had been forced. I guess you haven't seen many doors busted open. If Sterling had kicked it in, the jamb would have splintered around the lock, but the knob wouldn't have been broken off."

"Still," I said, "even with those little slipups, you were pretty much in the clear. I was the only one left who could get in your way. And that makes me your last mistake. You should have killed me, too." I shook my head. "In a way, I could almost feel sorry for you, married to that creep for all those years. Who knows? Maybe you really did love him once. Now, I guess it doesn't matter."

Barbara turned and looked at me for a long moment. Slowly, her lips formed the word. "Fool. And I thought that you..."

"Yeah," I said. "You thought I was such a nice guy."

"You can't prove any of it," she snapped.

"I don't have to. If I know Rawls, he's already suspicious. He just doesn't care a whole lot that you kissed off your husband. He's got bigger fish to fry. And I still don't think the courts would do much to you. That's why I didn't turn you over to him."

Her mouth fell open in astonishment. "Then why...?"

"Because I wanted to tell the story to someone who wouldn't just turn into mush when you flashed him your legs and a smile." I spoke in the direction of the back seat. "How does it sound to you, Stick?"

Paris let out a low, humorless chuckle. "Can't say I like it much. But I will say this. You're a pretty smart son of a bitch, Garrett. Smarter than I figured. And I could almost tell ya ta drop me off with the little lady here and then just beat it, so we could call things square. Only, I can't do it. There's still the matter of my boy gettin' iced in your office tonight. I can't let that one go by. Nothin' personal, ya understand. It's a matter of business. I mean, ya can see how it would look."

"Sure," I said. "It just wouldn't be professional, leaving a loose end like me lying around."

"Exactly." He turned in the seat and waved his gun at Barbara, and for the first time, I got a good look at it. It was a long-barreled Colt .44.

"But this little lady," he said. "That's somethin' else again. I was feelin' kinda bad about havin' ta put you away, Sweet Cakes. But now, it's gonna be a pleasure."

Barbara sat clutching her purse and staring at him, her face a mask of terror.

Finally, Paris reached over and patted me on the shoulder. "And outta respect, I'll tell ya what. I'm just gonna do the job myself, so ya won't get dusted off by some hired hand."

"I feel better already," I said.

Paris let out a throaty cackle and pointed toward the front of the car. "Just keep followin' that Olds."

I guided the Buick up the incline, and with my left elbow, I gently nudged downward to my left. I felt the reassuring weight of the .22 in my coat pocket. It wasn't much in the way of artillery, but it might get his attention.

By now, the road was pitching sharply upward into the tree-lined canyon wall. The last house was almost three hundred yards back. The headlights in the mirror were still keeping pace, but now the Olds was slowing. Paris reached up and grabbed my shoulder again.

"Flash your lights."

I flashed the lights, and the Olds pulled over to the side of the road and stopped. As we came up alongside, I felt another nudge.

"Okay. Hold it."

I braked to a stop, and Paris instructed Barbara to roll down the window. The door of the Olds opened, and a dark figure got out. The man gave a signal to the car following us and then leaned on the door and looked in.

"You guys wait here," Paris said. "I'm doin' this one myself."

The man looked uncertainly at me, then back at Paris. "You sure, boss?"

"Yeah," I'm sure." He poked me hard with the muzzle of his .44. "Go ahead."

I put the Buick in gear and started the climb up the slick canyon road. After about seventy-five yards, the road turned to gravel, and in another twenty, it disappeared altogether. I cut the motor and left the nose of the Buick angled sharply up into the trees covering the high end of the canyon.

Paris said, "This is good. Now, just sit still."

With a quick move, he opened the door, got out, and stood holding his gun on the two of us in the front seat.

"Now, climb out nice and slow." He waved the gun over at Barbara. "You too, sister. Just slide over here and get out on this side."

I climbed out, with Barbara following, and walked down toward the back end of the Buick. Paris backed part way down the hill, holding the gun on us and grinning.

"So, who wants it first?" he leered.

I felt Barbara tensing next to me, still clutching the purse against her breast. I moved my hand slowly in the direction of my coat pocket. I took a deep breath and thought about how time changes when you're staring down the barrel of a gun. Somehow, it slows to a crawl, and the smallest, most intricate details come into focus just as clear as a mountain lake. I measured the distance down the hill, the angle for the shot. I estimated the seconds it would take for me to pull out the .22 and fire. I thought of which way I'd have to jump and where I would fall. With the edge that Paris had on me, the chances were that I'd have to take a slug. That made it a matter of which part of my body I could let him shoot at so that I could still bring him down. I decided it would have to be in the legs. I'd have to fall and spin to the right, giving him a low angle. Then, even after getting hit, I could come up firing. That would still leave me to deal with the other gun-pokes down the hill, and probably with a bad wheel. But all that was a lifetime away. The main thing was to get Paris.

All this took only seconds. I stood there and licked my lips. They were as dry and rough as wood shavings.

"You don't really have to do this, Joey," I said.

I moved my left hand slowly until it was level with my hip. I coiled my weight onto my left leg and got ready to spring.

"C'mon, Garrett. Don't go soft on me. Like I said, it's just business."

He leveled the .44 on me and pulled back the hammer. I dove down the hill to the right, and Paris's gun made a quick barking sound. I rolled over and made a frantic grab for my coat pocket. As I looked up, there was a quick movement to my left, and Barbara's purse seemed to explode.

Paris was thrown backwards into the grade. He rolled over once and then lay on his back, a dark oozing cavern torn in the front of his coat. I scrambled over to him and held the .22 under his nose. But he just lay there, staring off beyond the darkness with a look of surprise that would never go away.

I came up on one knee and looked back up the hill at Barbara. She had fallen against the back of the Buick from the force of the recoil. She struggled up, stumbled forward a couple of steps, and pulled a smoking .45 out of the shredded remains of her purse. She dropped the purse, held the gun in both hands, and pointed it at me.

"You were wrong about one thing." Her voice hissed harshly through her teeth. "They'll never find Tony's gun."

I yanked Paris's body up and flattened myself behind it as the .45 boomed through the canyon. In the next instant, I had the .22 up and aimed at Barbara. As I started to squeeze off a round, I heard a familiar deep sigh.

The Buick's brakes finally gave way, and the car began rolling down behind Barbara. She was busy trying to cock the .45 when the rear bumper caught her. She turned and tried to get out of the way, but her heel stuck in the gravel, and she pitched forward on all fours. I lunged up the hill and tried to grab her, but I was too late. There was a muffled scream mixed with a sickening thudding sound, as the Buick rolled over her and then drifted down off the road and into the trees.

For a minute, I just lay there, surrounded by a crushing silence. Then, slowly, I got to my feet, brushed myself off, and looked around. The Buick was wedged backwards in a tangle of trees just off the side of the road. In the numbed recesses of my brain, it struck me that I ought to buy Lester Mack a drink.

I went over and knelt beside Barbara. I felt for a pulse, but there was none to find. The curtain had come down on her last act. I stood up and looked at her—at the mangled remains of greed and futility. With mechanical hands, I slowly pulled out a Lucky and lit it. I took in the smoke and the cold, dampness of the night. Suddenly, I felt very old and alone.

Lights flashed from down the hill, followed by several sharp reports. There was yelling and the sound of engines revving. Then, silence again. I waited without moving. A handful of lazy minutes passed. Finally, the sound of footsteps came plodding up the gravel. Then, the familiar throaty roar of Detective Ed Rawls.

"Hey, Garrett. You up there?"

Chapter Twenty-Seven

Fran Brekhamer sat across the table from me at Lacy's and fiddled with the stem of an over-sized martini glass. It was early, and the crowd was light. Outside, it was raining again. The past week had seen more rain than southern California usually gets in a whole season. Somehow, I had barely noticed. I nursed a Scotch and let my mind drift back over the last eighteen hours.

I remembered being taken to the station. I saw myself telling the story to Rawls, then to Thornhill, then to Rawls and Thornhill together. I saw the man from the D.A.'s office come in, and I saw myself dictating and then signing my statement. Everyone seemed satisfied. I saw them smiling—if you could call what came across Thornhill's face a smile. I remembered hearing the usual warning about staying out of police business, and then I remembered going home and falling into my bed as if it were an empty grave. That had been a little after four a.m. The next thing I remembered was waking up in the afternoon and feeling like a slab of spoiled meat. It was around five when I had called Fran and asked her to meet me at Lacy's.

Fran fiddled with her glass some more, then yanked it up and gulped down half of the martini. She lingered over the rim of the glass and eyed me evenly.

"Edward Rawls called me this afternoon," she said. "He told me what happened up there in the canyon. I'm glad you're all right."

I nodded to her. "That makes two of us."

She put down her glass and took a cigarillo from her jacket pocket. Before I could reach for a match, she pulled a solid gold Ronson from a side pocket.

She flicked it, held a tall flame up in front of the cigarillo, and puffed on it evenly until a heavy gray cloud covered the table. Then she put the lighter away and looked across the table without expression. But her eyes were hard, almost bitter.

"I owe you a day's wages," she said.

I shrugged. "It didn't take me a day to find him."

She reached into her breast pocket again and hauled out a long billfold. From this, she took out three sawbucks and laid them on the table in front of me. I looked at the money and didn't say anything.

She scowled. "Don't patronize me, Michael. You don't earn enough for that."

I shrugged again, picked up the three bills, and shoved them in my pocket. "You drive a hard bargain."

She scowled at me for a moment longer, until the scowl melted into a soft smile. "I ought to be angry with you. I told you to keep your nose out of it."

"Did you? Maybe you just thought you did."

She almost grinned. She took another pull on the cigarillo, then rested it in an ashtray and folded her arms. The smile faded, and her features drifted into a mixture of fatigue and sadness.

"Edward told me about how Clavin's wife used Danny to frame her husband," she said. "He said he didn't think Danny was really involved in the blackmail and that the department would issue a statement saying that it appears the woman and Marcus were in it alone." She wrung her hands together and sighed heavily. "I just hope the papers won't be too hard on Danny."

"They won't."

She gritted her teeth and glared at me. Flecks of anger hung in her voice.

"But Michael, he obviously contacted Clavin. The appointment book in his office showed that. Even if Danny wasn't really involved, the papers will make it appear that he was. They'll suggest that he was working with Marcus to blackmail Clavin. And they'll play up the idea that he was involved with that woman, because it's hot stuff, and it sells papers." She stared down into her glass. "At the very least, they'll simply laugh at him for being such a bumbling fool." She shook her head. "And everyone will remember him that way."

"No, they won't."

Fran's head darted up, and her eyes almost pierced me through the smoke. "What do you mean?"

"I mean, they won't remember him that way, because that's not the way he was."

I took a long drink of Scotch and then lit a Lucky. Fran held her eyes on me. Her features were as still and hard as granite.

"You see," I said, "it wasn't just coincidence that involved Danny with Marcus and Barbara Clavin. Barbara had known Danny for a long time, and she arranged for Marcus to contact him. She remembered Danny as a pushover who would be easy to fool, just as she had always fooled him in the past."

I took another drink and gave the words a minute to sink in.

"I found a yearbook in Danny's apartment, with a young cheerleader's picture in it. There was a note on the picture, written in 1927. It must have meant something to Danny, because he wrote that year on his wall—probably casually, thinking back over the years. He was thinking about someone he had known and loved, even after she left him and went east. That's where Barbara Clavin said she was headed when she came to my place last night. She also mentioned being a cheerleader and that she'd been given a baseball by a friend of her brother's. An unusual gift. Something sentimental from a sweet young boy in high school."

Fran swallowed hard. "What are you saying?"

"She remembered Danny. And, of course, he remembered her, not as Barbara Clavin but as Jeanie French."

Fran's jaw almost hit the table. "Are you serious? How can you be sure?"

"I can't be sure," I said. "But it's the only notion that makes any sense. Barbara mentioned a brother Robert, who died during the invasion of Italy. That squares with the story you told me about Danny and his girlfriend and about his being on the ball team with her brother Bobby—the one who was killed at Anzio. Danny had been stuck on her back then, and she was betting that he would be now. Only Danny wasn't the guy she remembered. Maybe he didn't know that Clavin was knocking his wife around, but he was smart enough to see that Marcus was bad company. And, when he found out who Barbara really was, he probably tried to get her to dump Marcus and maybe even patch things up with her husband. She shot him for his trouble."

Fran stared at me glassy-eyed and, without even looking at it, swallowed the rest of her drink. A waitress strolled over, and I ordered another Scotch. Fran ordered another martini—a double. She sat in silence until it came and then took a healthy swig. She put down her glass and poked at the cigarillo, now dead in the ashtray. Finally, she wrung her hands again and squinted at me. I could see questions racing behind her eyes.

"But, Michael. She couldn't have shot him. Edward told me that only a big man could have wrestled Danny around the office that way. Only someone like Clavin could have done that."

"Rawls is right," I said. "It would have taken a big man. And that's what made the frame so good. It would have taken someone like Clavin to throw Danny around the office. And someone like Clavin might have rigged the phony suicide, if he'd noticed the plant and thought of hiding a slug in it. The trouble with that is that the plant wasn't in Danny's office. It had been dragged in from out in the hall. I found marks on the floor where it had been sitting by the elevator. What's more, the plant hadn't been in the office for very long. It was as dry as a toothpick. And Danny Nugent wasn't the kind of guy to put a plant next to his desk and not water it just so he could watch it die."

I crushed out what was left of my Lucky and tasted my drink. Fran sat stonily, as if she were afraid even to move. I put down the Scotch and went on.

"It couldn't have been an amateur who shot Danny, no matter how big he was. Only an experienced killer would have thought of bringing the plant into the office. But a real pro would have taken the .38 slug out of the plant before he left. So, whoever staged the suicide had to know what a paid killer would do and how to make it look as if an amateur had bungled the job. Then, with Clavin's size and temper, he would be the obvious suspect. It was a clever stunt, very clever. Yet it wasn't enough to hang Clavin, because there was no evidence actually putting him at the scene. And that was the point. Clavin had to be put under suspicion but not actually found guilty."

I lit another Lucky, blew the smoke toward the ceiling, and looked Fran squarely in the eyes.

"After Danny was shot, he didn't die right away. He was left there alone and bleeding with his fading memories. Maybe he still felt he owed Jeanie something, or maybe he was just cleaning the slate with her. Whatever the reason, he set up the phony suicide himself. He dragged the plant into his office, then locked the door, opened the transom, and left his keys under it. That's why there was blood everywhere. He fired his gun into the plant, muffling the shot and leaving finger holes so the slug would be found. Then he put the gun on the desk and wrote Clavin's name in his appointment book."

Fran rocked back in her seat. Her face was ashen. "I can't believe it."

"It fits," I said. "Danny knew the police would see through the suicide setup and lick their chops over a chance to run Clavin in. He also knew that Clavin couldn't be convicted, not even with the note he left for you. The note had blood on it, meaning that Danny had already been shot when he wrote it. He didn't actually name Clavin as the one coming to kill him, which he would have done if Clavin had really been coming or had actually done the shooting. The appointment book and the note were enough to cast suspicion, but not enough for a conviction."

Fran picked up her glass in both hands and drained it. A vague look of wonder drifted over her face. "But why?"

"Danny didn't really want Clavin convicted. The man may have been a crumb, but he hadn't broken any laws. Danny figured the publicity from an arrest and trial would rattle Clavin's business and maybe even tip over Joey Paris. But most of all, it would give Jeanie time to shake Marcus and get away from the whole business. That's what Danny really wanted—to square accounts. It wasn't that he loved her. He might have once, but that love was long dead. He finally realized that when she came back into his life. My guess is that at the end, he simply didn't want to die with the thought of one of his fondest memories going to the gas chamber."

Fran started to say something, but I stopped her.

"There's more," I said. "Some men just have a sense of honor—even detectives. There's no sense to it really, no explaining it. It's just part of them. And sometimes, they stake that honor on people who don't deserve it. For Danny, it meant sacrificing himself so he could preserve the memory of someone he used to care about. But that wasn't all. He also wanted to be remembered—not as a down-at-the-heels private dick, but as someone with honor, someone you could respect. You see, you're the one he really loved all along. He just couldn't bring himself to tell you until the end. Writing that note was Danny's way of evening the score with Jeanie and of saying goodbye to you. And it was the last thing he did before he died."

Fran stared across the table. A single tear crept from the corner of her eye and slowly threaded its way down the side of her face. She breathed heavily but didn't speak.

"You don't have to worry about the papers," I said. "Rawls has a friend at the *Chronicle* who will print the facts. He'll tell about the kind of guy Danny Nugent really was. And he'll say that Danny died the way you always said he lived—giving someone a helping hand."

Fran moved her mouth, but nothing came out. She slowly reached across the table and laid her hand on top of mine. She held it there for a long moment and looked at me, her eyes full. Then, abruptly, she reached inside her jacket and brought out a handkerchief. She wiped her eyes,blew her nose, and scowled.

"Is that all of it?"

I nodded.

"I suppose you think you've done a good thing, telling this story about Danny and me to the police and the newspapers."

I shrugged. "Rawls would have come up with it eventually. And I figured you'd rather have the papers tell the story the right way."

She bit her lip and looked down at the table. Her words were barely audible. "Maybe you're right."

Fran slipped out of the booth and stood, eyeing me. There was no anger, just that stern big-sister expression I'd come to know.

"But you can just quit being smug with me, Michael. You're nothing but a romantic. You think what Danny did was noble. Well, I think he was a damn fool!"

She turned on her heel, stalked off, and left me tending my Scotch.

I checked out of Lacy's, and on the way home, I stopped by the office. I went through the usual routine with the mail and then opened the safe and took out the $200 check I'd gotten from Clavin. I endorsed it, wrote a short note, and then slipped both into an envelope. This I addressed to Mr. and Mrs. Everett Huffnagle at a Toledo address I'd gotten from Rawls. I sealed the envelope, put a stamp on it, and on the way out of the office, I dropped it into the mail slot in the lobby. Fran's words dogged me as I went outside and climbed into the Buick.

I drove through the rain to my apartment, feeling nothing but the lonely accumulation of years and mileage. I got home, trudged up the stairs, and got the door open just as the phone was ringing. It was Stephanie Anders. She had heard about Clavin and about Barbara and about me. She said she had decided on a new career. The life of a detective wasn't what she thought it was. I said it wasn't what I thought it was, either. She hung up.

I threw my hat and coat on a chair and got a jolt of Scotch from the kitchen. It didn't help. I turned on the radio opened the window and let Harry James float out into the night. The lingering sounds of the trumpet in the street filled the night with memories. I turned off the light and sat there and thought about Danny Nugent with his memories, and about the kinds of memories, Fran would be having. And I thought about Lorna and about Barbara Clavin. Sometimes, remembering isn't everything it's cracked up to be. So, I lit a cigarette and watched the rain.

Acknowledgements

David and to Jennifer and Jon

About the Author

Richard Blaine first wrote about Michael Garrett in the 1980s. As a part-time author, he also consulted with various companies and helped them produce documentation to enable staff members to understand how to use their computer systems effectively. Subsequently, Blaine went to graduate school and then became a mental health counselor, specializing in trauma and anxiety-based disorders. He had a very busy practice, lasting for twenty-five years, from which he then retired and returned to his earlier love of writing historical detective novels.

Also by Richard Blaine

The Silver Setup - Michael Garrett Mystery #1

The Tainted Jade - Michael Garrett Mystery #2